SINISTER LEGACY

AN EROTIC HORROR NOVEL

HARLEIGH BECK

Editing: Green Proofreads
Proofreading: Spooks Proofs
Cover: HC Graphics
Formatting: Quirky Circe

AUTHOR'S NOTE

It always blows my mind that out of all the books you could've chosen, you're here, holding mine in your hands. Thank you! That being said, there are a few things I'd like to point out before I shove you down the rabbit hole.

You won't find likable characters within these pages, and definitely no Prince Charming. These characters are selfish, manipulative, destructive, and volatile. They lie and cheat. If that's not your thing, I advise against reading any further.

It was also very important for me to allow Keira to have a voice. As such, this book navigates the sensitive subject of the death penalty from her perspective as the daughter of a serial killer, and the emotional upheaval she goes through. Please remember, it's a *fictional* story with imperfect, *fictional* characters. It's *not* intended as a political statement, nor is it to be interpreted as a representation of the author's views.

TRIGGER WARNINGS

Sinister Legacy is an erotic **horror** novel. Make no mistake, it's *very* dark and contains scenes of a graphic nature that can be incredibly disturbing to some readers.
I trust that you know your triggers.
Please read responsibly.

Follow the link for a full list of trigger and content warnings:
https://sinisterlegacy.carrd.co/

For all of us who love a lil' horror with our smut.

ASSOCIATIONS

KEIRA

CASSIE · MADISON · LIAM · CHRIS

MILES · MARCUS · JESSICA · SIENNA

HAZEL · AMANDA

KING

HAYLEY · AVA · KIT

JASPER · KARA

KEIRA

The rain sounds on the window while I dig out the shoebox hidden in my wardrobe. It's there, right at the back, beneath my jacket that lies neatly folded on top. I shift everything aside and pull the box out. The small black X on the left-hand corner of the lid marks it, but I know which box it is since all the others are white or brown. This one is red.

I sit back on my haunches and carefully peel the lid back. Inside is a letter, a single photograph, and a CD. The latter is scratched now. I doubt it even plays. Leaving the letter, I pick up the photograph. It has yellowed with time, and it's creased from too much usage. I would stare at it nightly at one point, trying to understand why my father killed all those women. Why did he live a double life, and how did he get away with it for so long? What drove him to become a monster?

I was seven when my world was blown apart. The police broke into our house on a Friday evening to arrest my dad for the murder of sixteen women. That night ruined my life and destroyed my mom, leaving her a shadow of her former self.

I never spoke to my dad again. He wrote a letter shortly after receiving his death sentence, and now it's hidden in my wardrobe. But I never replied. Life moves on, I guess. I have a best friend and a boyfriend, and I do relatively well at school. I'm popular by default. It's what happens when you're the daughter of a serial killer. People don't like to be associated with death, but they like to be associated with notoriety. Even the darkest kind. Besides, it's all a facade to hide how fucking broken I am inside. I don't trust anyone, I struggle to connect with people, and self-destruction is my nickname.

When I hear my mom's footsteps on the stairs, I hurry to place the photograph back inside the box. The execution date for my father is coming up in a few months. As a cosmic joke, it falls on the anniversary of his first murder. I guess I'm on edge. There's no other reasonable explanation for why I'm digging out his photograph.

My dad ruined this family, so he can rot in hell for all I care. But even as I think it, I know I'm lying to myself. There's a void in my life now. A void I can't fill, no matter how hard I try. I miss my dad, as much as I hate to admit it. I miss him even more now that his execution date is racing toward me like a sprinting wild horse.

Mom knocks on my door before peeking her head inside. "Are you ready? Cassie is downstairs."

I place the folded leather jacket back on top of the box and peer at her over my shoulder. "I'll be down in a minute."

One last look at my windows confirms that it's still raining outside. It hasn't stopped for the last two days. Halloween is around the corner. The temperatures have dropped in the last week, and the dark settles earlier in the evenings. I like this time of the year. The leaves are beginning to yellow, and the hot summer evenings are a thing of the past.

Throwing on my denim jacket, I quickly tie my hair up in a messy bun before bending at the waist to pick up my bag by the door. As I straighten up, my eyes snag on the gun on my dresser. It's for protection, my mom once said. But then they installed the metal detectors at school, so now I leave it at home.

On my way past the kitchen, I throw a wave over my shoulder at my mom and stepdad. "See you later."

"Have a good day."

Cassie waits for me in her hatchback. It stinks of dog from the previous owner, and the car freshener dangling from the rearview mirror does little to mask it. Now her car stinks of dog and pine. It could be worse.

"I like your hair," she says when I pull the door shut.

Flicking down the mirror, I tighten the ponytail. "I channeled Pamela Anderson's messy bun from the nineties."

The rain is coming down hard now, the wipers moving quickly over the windshield. We pull away from the curb and rejoin the traffic.

"You're dressed in all denim today," Cassie points out, motioning to my denim jacket and ripped jeans.

My white T-shirt has a rip near the collar. "Autumn won't get the best of me yet. Give it a few more weeks, and I'll drag out my winter coat."

Cassie sobers, worrying her bottom lip. I know what's coming even before she asks, "Are you sure you're okay? There's only what? Two months until the exe..." she drifts off, looking at me briefly before focusing back on the traffic.

I scan her profile. Dressed in a black leather skirt and a red top, Cassie is classically beautiful with her straight red hair, defined lips, and a beauty spot near her mouth. If I didn't know it was real, I'd think she was channeling Marilyn Monroe.

"I'm fine," I reply, tasting the lie on my tongue. Those two words never come out any easier.

Cassie flicks her emerald gaze to me again, looking unconvinced, but decides to drop it. Her freckled nose scrunches up. "Liam messaged me last night asking why you weren't answering your phone."

Liam, the star quarterback, is my boyfriend. Much to my amusement, Cassie dislikes him with a passion.

I didn't pick up because I was ignoring him, but I don't tell her that. Instead, I say, "My phone was on silent."

"When are you gonna dump him?"

I laugh, staring out the window at the rain bouncing off the pavement. It's loud on the roof, too. "You really don't like him, do you?"

"Of course I don't. He's good for nothing."

"He's good for *something*." My lips twitch.

Cassie rolls her eyes, but she can't hide her own amusement. "You're only with him because he's safe."

"Let Shrink Cassie back in the closet."

"No, I think Shrink Cassie needs to stay out of the closet. You're only with him because it's easy. And safe. He's the popular quarterback with two brain cells. Let's face it, Liam is good for your image, but he's not what you want."

"And what do I want?"

She lifts one shoulder and lets it fall. "You're intelligent, Keira. Liam is... not."

Laughter bubbles up from my chest. "Don't you think you're being a bit judgy now? Besides, so what if I think he's safe?"

Safety is what I need now. Liam is predictable and boring. There are no hidden surprises to be unearthed. All he cares about is parties, sex, and football. The police won't storm the school one day to arrest him. I like it. It's boring, but it's what I need.

"Fine," Cassie replies, pulling up to the school parking lot. "He must be a beast in bed for you to put up with him."

I try not to laugh, while she cuts the engine. "I sense there's more you want to say?"

Shifting in her seat and turning her body in my direction, she says, "I know you're not a jersey chaser like all the other girls here, which is why I don't get it."

"You don't get what? Why I'm with him? Or why he's with someone like me?"

Cassie pales, so I wave her off, reaching for the door handle. "It's fine. I'm Jimmy Hill's daughter. My reputation precedes me. I'm not stupid. I know Liam likes the notoriety of fucking the daughter of a serial killer. My father's legacy will follow me like a shadow until I'm old enough to escape this forsaken town. And even then, it'll still be with me. It always will."

"I didn't mean it like that," Cassie says, holding her jacket over her head to protect her from the rain when we step out of the car.

"It doesn't matter, though. It's still the truth."

I step in a puddle, and rainwater soaks my Chucks as we cross the parking lot. By the time we reach the entrance, my wet hair sticks to my cheeks, the shoulders of my denim jacket are damp, and my jeans are soaked through at the thighs.

"I can't believe how bad the rain is coming down," Cassie says, lowering her jacket from her head.

"What is it now? Day three of constant rain?"

"Something like that."

Liam's loud holler announces his arrival. He runs up behind me, picks me up, and spins us in a circle. "How's my favorite girl?"

My feet meet the floor again, and I turn in his arms. Liam, dressed in jeans and a letterman jacket, is attractive, with sandy hair, gray eyes, and a Prince Charming smile. He's so good-looking, it borders on annoying sometimes.

Before I can answer, he slings his arm around my shoulder and steers me down the next hallway, where my locker is located. "I tried to phone you last night. We had drinks at Jessica's place."

"Jessica hates me," I point out.

"She doesn't hate you."

I stop short of pointing out that they all do. I'm not a cheerleader, and it rubs the girls the wrong way that their quarterback is dating outside of their clique.

Liam stops us to do some weird handshake with one of his football friends. Before long, they're tussling. I ignore the amused sparkle in Cassie's eyes and set off walking.

"Safe," she whispers, making my lips twitch.

"Safe is good," I reply.

The words die a swift death as I turn the corner, walking straight into a very big, very hard chest. Warm hands, so warm that

I can feel them through the denim, clamp down on my arms to steady me. "Watch it."

My eyes lock on King, the hot-headed resident bad boy with a nice hush-hush criminal history to go with the family name. The only reason he's not in prison or juvie is because of his stupidly rich family. They have the ability to bail him out of any situation, apparently. Money and power speak louder than the justice system. King Knight is anything but a knight. He's the boy to seek out if you want your heart ripped out of your chest. He's a deadly weapon with his black hair, brown eyes, and killer jawline. And he knows how to wield it to get his own way.

I wrench free from his grip on me and mumble an apology. He's already on the move, turning the corner. That's the thing about King—in his world, you're no one until you're someone. And I would rather stay hidden in the shadows than have his spotlight directed at me.

Madison is waiting for me at my locker, phone in hand. She doesn't look up until I'm right in front of her, and then she slides to the side, pocketing her phone. "Did Liam tell you about the party at Jessica's last night?"

"Let me guess, she was all over him."

Madison is one of those rare unicorns who slots into all social groups. It's effortless for her.

"Of course."

After inputting my combination, I open my locker and grab the books I need. Beside me, Cassie swaps hers out.

"You should keep an eye on her."

I snort a laugh, shutting my locker. What Madison and everyone else here fail to understand is that I don't care enough to worry about Jessica moving in on Liam.

With her hands in her jacket pockets, Madison pops her gum before pushing off the locker. "Your first class is geography, right?"

I nod, shouldering my bag. "Science, right?"

Madison smirks. "You stalking me?"

I eye her pink puffer jacket and black ripped jeans. Her shoulder-length, wavy, raven hair has been dyed to cover up her natural blonde color. "Maybe."

Her tinkling laughter rings out. That's the one thing I like the most about Madison. She's dark and brooding but has the brightest laugh, which she reserves for a select few.

"If he cheats on Keira, I'll personally string him up by his balls," Cassie growls beside us as we set off walking.

I roll my eyes, but Madison nods.

"I'll help you out. The guy is a sleaze."

"A *safe* sleaze," Cassie says, nudging me with her shoulder.

"What are we doing for Halloween?" Jasper asks, dipping his fry in a dollop of mayo on his plate.

We're at our usual hangout spot, a burger joint down by Blackwoods Bay. It used to be a seedy bar before it was renovated and rebranded. But no amount of fresh paint can remove the lingering stench of stale beer.

"We're partying, of course," Kit says, his arm wrapped around his girlfriend, Kara.

"Did you know," Ava, seated to my left, starts, "that people with names that begin with the same letter as their significant other are statistically more likely to stay in a long-term relationship?"

I chuckle around my mouthful of fries. It's too funny not to when Kit scrunches up his face in confusion.

"Could you be any more random? We're talking about Halloween, and you bring up statistics?"

Ava shrugs, her musky perfume tickling my nose. "It's interesting."

Kara, dressed in Kit's gray, oversized hoodie, tucks a lock of her brown hair behind her ear. "We'll make sure to invite you to the wedding."

Kit chokes on his coke.

On my other side, Hayley inspects her blood-red nails. "This year, I think we should spice things up."

"What do you have in mind?" Jasper asks, chewing loudly.

"Can you not chew with your mouth open?" Hayley pulls an unimpressed face.

Jasper chews even louder.

Drinking the last of my coke, I place it down on the table, letting my eyes scan the crowded room. It's peak hour, and most, if not all, tables are occupied.

"Tell us then," Kara says, leaning into Kit.

Hayley shrugs, but there's nothing casual about it. She's like me—bored and restless with life.

"We should make bets."

"Bets?" I frown.

Dragging a finger through the salt on her plate, she brings it to her lips. "Well, *dares.*" With deliberate slowness, she makes a show of placing her finger on her tongue and closing her lips around it.

"What kind of dares?" Jasper asks.

Hayley looks away from me and repeats the process of collecting salt on the tip of her finger. "Anything you want. But it's Halloween, so it has to create mayhem."

Ava shifts uneasily to my left, while I pick up my phone and snap a picture of her.

"Fine by me," Kit replies as he tosses his crumpled tissue on the table. "How do we do this? Dole out a dare each?"

Kara shakes her head. "This is stupid."

"It could be fun."

"Okay, I'll start." Hayley turns her attention to me. I stiffen, leaning back and placing my phone down on the sticky table. "I dare you to fuck Keira Hill."

Jasper chokes on a salty fry, and Kit bursts out laughing.

"Jimmy Hill's daughter?" Ava turns pale.

Hayley keeps her sparkling eyes on me. "The one and only."

"Believe it or not," I start. "I don't have any interest in fucking a serial killer's daughter for sport."

"Oh, don't be like that." Hayley leans in conspiratorially. "It's just for fun."

Scoffing, I reach for a fry.

"Are you scared?" Kit asks, chuckling when Kara elbows him.

"Why the fuck would I be scared? It's just a stupid dare."

Hayley watches me closely. Too closely. "You don't think you can do it, do you?"

Now I snort. "Of course I can."

"Then what's the problem? And don't give me some shitty excuse about how it's beneath you to fuck a girl for entertainment."

"Okay, sure. How about the fact that she has a boyfriend?"

Kara levels me with a look while her boyfriend laughs behind his closed fist. "When has that ever stopped you before?"

"It's Liam," Ava breathes out.

"So?" Kara sounds incredulous. "What the fuck has that got to do with anything?"

"He's the star quarterback."

Hayley leans forward, peering at Ava on my other side. "You don't think King can fuck Liam's girlfriend?"

"I think he'll get beat up if he tries."

Everyone laughs except for Ava.

Wiping tears from my eyes, I wrap my arm around Ava's tiny shoulders and pull her into me. "He can always try."

"Look, Liam is a guy who thinks the sun shines out of his ass. It would be fun to pull the rug from beneath his feet." Hayley picks up her milkshake. "Mess with the popular kids."

She slurps the drink while I look out the window, at the rain that's racing in rivulets toward the bottom of the glass. What have I got to lose? It's just a bit of fun, right? "I'll do it."

The slurping stops. Hayley's smile grows impossibly big. "We need video evidence."

"And it has to be on Halloween night," Kit says with an excited glint in his eyes as he clicks his fingers.

"Why Halloween?" I ask, frowning.

"It's the season to cause mayhem and chaos."

"Not only that," Kara says, as though she's had a brainwave. "There's the town fair on Halloween night. The football team will be there."

Jasper nods eagerly. "You can fuck her right under Liam's nose."

Kit, who'd taken a sip of his drink, starts to cough. He places the drink back down and beats his chest with his fist. "Hell, yes."

I wet my lips as I pick up my orange lighter from the table. When I strike the flint, a small flame flickers to life. "Let's do it. Let's cause some chaos."

LIAM

"You shouldn't be here." Cassie pulls the curtains shut as though she expects Keira to be waiting outside her bedroom.

"You worry too much." Flopping down onto her bed, I put my arm behind my head. Her room smells of Cassie—vanilla, fruity shower gel, and something uniquely her.

"Why are you here? You know we need to meet somewhere else."

"Like where?"

"Well, not here," she whisper-hisses, worried her parents will hear us.

I smile at her as she walks closer to the bed. "Why not here? It's warm. You have a nice bed."

She points an accusing finger in the direction of the door. "Your car is on my fucking drive. Anyone could see it."

"So what? I've been here before. Look," I push up onto my

elbows, "no one cares, alright? People just aren't that perceptive. If my car is here, they'll assume Keira is, too."

"What if Keira comes here?" She crosses her arms and cocks her hip. "What if she decides to pop in unannounced?"

"We'll think of something." I pull her close when she gets within reaching distance, and she falls on top of me with a shriek. I roll us over, clamping my hand over her mouth. "Don't pretend you don't want me here."

Whimpering softly, her legs fall open as I roll my hips. I first fucked Cassie over spring break. Keira was away with her mom at the time, and I'd offered to give Cassie a lift home after a party at my friend Nate's. We talked and then she climbed onto my lap and rode me. Since then, we've been a regular thing. Call me a douche, but I like the sneaking around. Cassie does too, even if she would never admit it.

I yank her leather skirt up, hooking my fingers in her white, silk panties and moving them aside. Her back arches off the mattress as I tease her soft curls. While Keira waxes, Cassie prefers a landing strip. I like both. Pussy is pussy. As long as I can finger it, lick it, and fuck it, I'm happy.

"Feels good, huh?"

She nods beneath my palm, her eyes wide and glassy with lust.

"Spread your legs, baby."

She spreads them wide like a good slut and pleads with her eyes. *Fuck me, Liam.*

Unbuttoning my jeans one-handed, I shove the front down and palm my throbbing cock. I'm aching with need as I rub the crown down the length of her soaking slit.

Just then, her phone lights up. Keira is phoning her. Cassie's emerald eyes widen at the same time I ram my cock inside her.

"You're a terrible fucking friend, aren't you? Letting your best friend's boyfriend fuck you raw."

Cassie moans. It always gets her hot when I point out what a dirty slut she is. The bed creaks as I pound her into the mattress. I came here to get off, nothing more. Keira expects me later. We have plans to go to the movies, which was her idea for once. Usually, it's me who has to come up with a plan and ask her to hang out.

Sometimes I think that's why I'm here, fucking her best friend. Keira just doesn't fucking care. She wouldn't be bothered if I failed to phone her for a week. And that smarts. My ego doesn't like it one bit. But Cassie, Keira's best friend, sure likes my cock. She's writhing beneath me, her pussy pulsing. I don't have to chase Cassie. She sends me nudes, messages me at all hours, and records videos of herself finger-fucking her pussy. It's a little desperate, to be honest, but I guess I like the chase *and* being chased.

She's delusional if she thinks I'll leave my girlfriend. In some weird, fucked-up way, I like Keira. She's also good for my social status. Who else can claim they fuck the daughter of a notorious serial killer?

Cassie comes, and her tight cunt strangles my dick, her loud, muffled moans vibrating against my palm. I fuck her harder, chasing my own orgasm. The phone lights up again, but it's my own this time, tucked in my jeans pocket. And the ringtone is Keira's. I come so fucking hard that I see stars while stuffing Cassie full of cum.

KEIRA

"Such a tight cunt," my stepdad, Allen, groans on a final hard thrust before every muscle in his body stiffens, and he applies more pressure to my head. He likes to fuck me like this, with my ass in the air, a pillow over the back of my head, and my cheek pressed against the mattress.

The first time my stepdad climbed into my bed was on a Friday night. One of the few rare nights I had opted to stay in instead of going out. Cassie tried to drag me to a pool party at Sam's place—his parents were out of town—but I was too tired and too fed up with being Jimmy Hill's daughter.

"There's a good girl," my stepdad whispers, shattering my thoughts as he slowly slides his dick out, leaving me empty and lonely. I want his thick cock back inside me already. I want him to never stop fucking me. It's the only time I feel *something*.

His hand slips below the pillow to grip my neck as he drags his fingers over my sensitive cunt, collecting his cum. Then he finger-fucks it back inside me, his touch rough and dirty.

I wonder sometimes if he treats my mom like this too, or if he reserves it for those nights when he sneaks into my room to fuck me hard with a pillow covering my face. I wish he would let me see him in those moments—the man who likes to read the newspaper at the breakfast table. I want to see what he looks like when he's balls deep in my pussy, fucking me like I'm worthless. Because that's what he does. He comes in here, orders me not to look at him, throws me down on my front, grabs a pillow, and covers my face. And I love every minute of it. The more humiliating it gets, the more I soak his dick. There's something wrong with me. I know there is. But as he continues to ram his thick fingers inside me while my legs quiver and shake, I don't care.

I don't care about anything but the orgasm I'm chasing. I've already come on his dick twice, but he's never satisfied until I come on his fingers, too.

"Sshh, if your mom hears you and comes in here, playtime stops. You don't want that, do you?"

My head shakes beneath the pillow as my cunt makes a mess of his hand.

"Good girl. Now show me how much you like it when I come in here and show my little whore a good time."

I make a strangled noise, my pussy pulsing around his fingers. He doesn't stop pumping my cunt. If anything, his touch becomes even rougher.

"Did you miss me?" he asks, as I continue coming all over his hand, my body squirming on the bed. My scattered thoughts slowly return, and I whisper, "Yes," the sound muffled beneath the pillow.

"Yeah?" The bed shifts. He moves back, and I listen to the sound of his zipper when he pulls it back up. "Then show me by spreading your ass cheeks apart. Let me see that ruined cunt."

The pillow is damp from my labored breaths, and my T-shirt sticks to the sweat on my back. I reach behind me, my knees aching, and curl my fingers around each ass cheek. The cool air licks at my soaked, swollen folds, and the handprints from his earlier slaps sting my tender globes.

"Do you have any idea how you ruin men like me?" His fingers drag through a trail of cum on the back of my thigh all the way to my pussy. "Tell me you're my whore and only mine. Not that boyfriend of yours." There's a hint of desperation in his gravelly voice that I haven't heard before—a yearning.

"I'm your whore." I wish I could remove the pillow and look at him. But I know he won't like that, so I stay on my knees with my ass in the air and my cheek burrowed in the mattress.

"Your boyfriend doesn't get to see this pretty little cunt exposed like this, understood? This is for my eyes only."

I wet my already moist lips, fighting back panic now that I'm coming down from my high. The pillow feels like it's suffocating me. "No one else gets to see me like this."

Satisfied, he stands up, and the bed shifts. He leaves me like that—a used whore. I wait obediently until the door has clicked shut before removing the pillow and shifting onto my back. It's at this moment, when I'm alone with my stepfather's cum leaking out of me, that the tears fall. I want to die.

As ugly as the truth is to admit, I'm jealous of my dad. Two months from now, it'll all be over for him. But I'll have to live with his legacy. I'll have to live with this darkness inside me that slowly feeds on my soul. The only time I get to purge is when my stepdad comes in here and treats me like his own little fuck toy. And even that is not enough. I want more pain, more degradation, more ruin. I want a true monster to find me.

JESSICA

The moaning in the background is getting on my last nerve. It's fucking typical of Marcus to play porn on the big TV as though it's the nine o'clock news or a soap opera.

"Where's Liam tonight?" Chris asks, his arm slung around Amanda on the couch behind me.

I'm seated on the floor, mindlessly watching a busty redhead ride a man cowgirl on a luxury yacht.

"He had plans with the killer girl."

My mouth tastes sour. I've tried to get his fucking attention for years. Then Keira's father gets sentenced to death, and suddenly Liam is all over her? It's not my fault that my family is so normal. Besides, I'm better looking than her. At least my tits are bigger. Keira lives in loose T-shirts or wool sweaters and jeans, and she rarely wears makeup. I don't even get why he's so obsessed with Keira. It's not like he's in love with her. Or maybe he is, in his own way. I don't fucking know anymore.

"What's with the long face?" Chris asks, leaning down to tickle my chin.

Batting him off, I climb to my feet. "I'm bored."

"How can you be bored? It's Tiffany, for crying out loud," laughs Marcus, pointing the remote control at the TV screen. "Look at her, for fuck's sake. I'd sell a nut to get to fuck her."

My smile is saccharine. "If you have a sledgehammer, I'd be happy to help you out."

"I said sell it, not crush it."

"Semantics." I look at Amanda and Hazel. "Are you coming?"

Amanda snuggles closer to Chris, while Hazel scrolls on her phone.

I turn to Sienna on Miles's lap. "How about you?"

"I'll stay."

"Fine. I'm going." I don't wait for a reply as I grab my phone from the coffee table and make my way through the hallway. After putting my heels back on, I step out into the cold night. I didn't bring a coat, and I regret it now. My breaths puff out in front of me as I walk down the drive. I only live around the corner from Marcus, so I left my car at home.

Rubbing my arms with my hands, I shiver. The thin cardigan is not thick enough to ward off the cold for long. By the time I reach my driveway, my teeth are chattering. The house is dark. My parents are away at a business conference for a few days. They do that a lot. Not that I mind. I'm used to being alone.

I take a quick shower before getting dressed and making my way to the kitchen to make a sandwich. All that's left is ham. I root through the cupboards for a small plate and a glass. Then I proceed to make my sandwich and pour the orange juice.

It's not like me to be home this early, but I have zero interest in watching *Tiffany* bounce on a man's dick, while Marcus drinks his beer with his feet on the coffee table. Besides, I'm tired.

Tired of putting up a facade like everyone else in this forsaken town.

Jessica, the bitch.

Jessica, the girl with the perfect grades.

Jessica, who cares about nothing but makeup and heels.

I collect my plate and glass and leave the kitchen. The living room is dark, so I try to flick the switch with the hand holding the orange juice. Nothing happens. I try to flick it again, then mutter, "Well, isn't that typical?"

With the plate in one hand and the glass in the other, I walk deeper into the dark room. The coffee table is in front of me. I know it is. Only a few more steps. My thighs meet the hard edge. I carefully place the plate down, then the glass, before straightening back up. There's a chill in the air as I round the couch, careful not to trip on the rug on my way to the window. The silvery moonlight casts a long strip of light on the floor. I switch on the lamp on the window ledge, and the ambient glow floods the room.

My arms are lined with goosebumps from the chill in the air. I should have worn something warmer than a tank top and sleep shorts, but it's too late now unless I want to go back upstairs to my room to find my robe. Instead, I take a seat on the couch and pull the soft blanket over my lap to keep warm. I channel-hop for far too long, my thoughts elsewhere. I pause with the sandwich held in front of my lips. The scene on the screen is grotesque: a woman getting her arm chopped off while she's still alive. It looks nothing like a normal movie. This looks strangely like a... like a home video.

I'm reminded of Cloverfield and the Paranormal Activity movies. It's how they make them these days.

I take a small bite of the sandwich but spit it back out. My stomach churns at the sight in front of me of a woman, flat on her back, staring up at the ceiling with dead eyes and her arms and legs chopped off. My hand shakes as I carefully place the plate down on the table and pick the remote control back up. But before I can switch the TV off, I pause. There, on the screen, staring into the camera, is Jimmy Hill. I'm sure of it. I would know that face anywhere. His cold, dead eyes stare straight at me, his face covered in blood.

I hurry to switch off the TV, dropping the remote with a yelp. What the fuck did I just watch? That was no actor. It was Jimmy.

Jimmy...

The doorbell sounds behind me, and I release a startled scream, torn from my fragmented thoughts. It rings out again, causing my heart to jump to my throat. Slowly rising to my feet, I walk with hesitant steps toward the front door. The air puffs out in front of me. How is that even possible when I'm indoors? Is the heat broken, too?

The marble flooring is cold beneath my bare feet, and ice runs through my veins when I see the tall shadow of a man on the other side of the door. I call out, "Hello?"

Ding dong.

I jump, my heart ricocheting in my chest.

"Who's there?" I ask shakily.

No answer.

Hesitating, I hold my breath. The shadowed man is still there, looming like something out of a horror flick. My heart hammers hard in my chest, and my trembling hands have grown clammy with fear. The doorbell sounds again. This time, I press a sweaty palm over my mouth to stop myself from screaming.

Just when I think the nightmare will never end, the shadow slinks away from the door. Lowering my hand, tears beading on my lashes, I stare unblinkingly straight ahead, expecting him to come back. He doesn't. My heart slows, thudding inside my chest. Now I feel stupid. It was probably Marcus or Miles.

I turn to head back to the living room when the sound of the screen door to the kitchen being opened cuts through the silence. Icy panic slithers through my veins. I wait for another noise. Maybe I imagined it all? But no, the sound of heavy, dragging footsteps has my heart tripping in my chest. I take off, running down the hallway toward the front door. Tears stream from my eyes while I grapple desperately with the lock. It clicks, and I throw open the door. The cold doesn't register as I stumble out on the porch and spin around. There's no one there. The dark, gaping entryway stares back at me.

In my panic, I fail to realize I'm at the edge of the porch, and when I take another step back, I meet air. I fall backward down the front steps with a rippling scream, my back colliding with the hard gravel. The wind gets knocked out of me. Fighting desperately to inhale a full breath, I roll over onto my side. Then I hear it: crunching footsteps. A man in a hooded, black robe, with a metallic, blood-red devil's mask steps around the corner carrying an axe, his leather-gloved fingers curled around the handle.

I scramble back, too fucking frightened to do anything but sob desperately. "Please, no..." Climbing to my feet, I set off running. My ankle throbs with pain from the fall. The masked man is faster. I barely make it down the gravel path before he's on me. He fists my hair and pulls me back toward the house, causing me to fall. My scalp burns with pain. I release a guttural scream, but no one steps outside their house to check. No one hears me. The cold and unforgiving front steps scrape my bare skin as he hauls me up onto the porch and into the hallway. Then he shuts the door, as if he has all the time in the world. The cold marble flooring stings my wounds. I have never known pain like this before. My hair has been torn from the roots, bruises litter my body from the fall, and the open wounds on my arms and legs have pieces of gravel stuck to them.

When he walks up to me with the axe dangling from his hand, I lash out and land a kick to his shin. I'm up on my feet, running down the hallway toward the kitchen, hoping to get to the door.

The man speaks in a distorted and strange voice. "There's nowhere to run, Jessica."

I release another sob, collapsing against the doorframe to the kitchen before throwing myself inside, my palms connecting with the edge of the island. Scanning the room for anything to use to defend myself, my eyes catch on the wooden block of knives. I hobble over as he enters the kitchen. With a violently trembling hand, I pull a knife from the block and hold it out in front of me, surprised I don't drop it with how much my body shakes.

"Poor little Jessica. Always second best. Never first."

"Fuck you!" I hiss, inching further away.

"Did you enjoy the home video?" He points the axe at me. "Soon you'll look just as pretty as Jimmy Hill's first victim."

I sob uncontrollably, the panic threatening to immobilize me. "Why are you doing this?"

The masked man cocks his head. "It's Halloween. Besides..." He pretends to pounce, making me cry out in fear. The knife nearly falls from my fingers. "The execution is close."

"So what? You're a copycat killer?" I spit the words with venom. The door is at my back. If I can only distract him long enough to make a run for it.

"This is so much bigger than that. And you get to be a part of it. You get to be the catalyst."

Cold dread trickles down my spine. "You're sick."

My bare feet pound the kitchen floor as I take off running for the door. Fiery pain sears through my back, and I cry out, collapsing to the floor with a hard thud. My chin bounces off the hard surface, and my teeth sink into my tongue. The tangy taste of copper explodes in my mouth. I groan pitifully, blood spluttering from my lips.

With a sharp yank, the axe is pulled from my back, and he grabs my ankle. Streaks of blood decorate the floor as he hauls me out of the kitchen, through the hallway, and into the living room. I grab the doorframe, sobbing uncontrollably, begging and pleading for my life. But it falls on deaf ears.

My fingers slip off, and then we're on the move again. He rolls me over onto my back, putting his heavy boot on my chest and swinging his axe at his side. With his other hand, he pulls out a phone from his pocket. "I hope you don't mind if we make a little video. You want to be the star, right? Isn't that what you've always wanted, Jessica? To be the center of attention?"

"Please," I weep. "Please, I don't want to die."

"No one wants to die, but we all have to sooner or later." He steps off me, setting the camera down on the coffee table. "At least you get to die for something bigger."

I try to crawl away, but I'm dizzy from the blood loss. It's everywhere: on my hands, in my hair, and pouring from my mouth. The floor is slick with it, too.

"Where do you think you're going?" He grabs my arm and drags me right back while I scream and cry and sob and plead. Anything to make it stop. To make him stop.

He kicks me in the head. "Would you lie still, bitch."

Pain. So much fucking pain. The world spins in and out of focus. I cough, blood spluttering from my lips. I'm vaguely aware of my arms being toed with the boot until they're stretched by my sides. Then my legs. I cough again, struggling to breathe because of the blood in my mouth. The axe is lifted high. It hovers there as my eyes roll back into my throbbing head.

"This will only hurt for a minute."

The axe slices through the air.

KEIRA

I stare at my stepdad's veiny hand when he curls his fingers around the coffee mug. It disappears from view behind the newspaper.

Meanwhile, Liam chats animatedly to my mom with his arm outstretched behind me on the chair. I don't know why I agreed to let him come over for breakfast this morning. He wanted to stay over last night, but I said no because I had an essay to finish.

I didn't get around to completing it, though, thanks to the man across the table who is currently ignoring everything and everyone. I was too preoccupied with his fingers in my cunt.

I don't even feel bad for cheating on Liam. I mean, I should. But the truth is that I feel very little these days other than this constant longing to die.

I'm sick.

"Are you staying to watch my practice after school?" Liam asks, toying with the strands of my hair.

I breathe in his scent—amber and citrus and soap. My smile is half-assed at best. "Sure."

The last thing I want to do is pretend I give a shit about his football practice, but he keeps insisting.

The newspaper rustles, and my heart does a little jump. Some call it 'love' when anxiety is involved—that little spike of anxious anticipation.

I call it delusion.

My clit loves this particular delusion.

"I heard the season is going well," my mom says with a soft smile directed at Liam.

Tuning them out, I stare wide-eyed at the newspaper article before I launch myself across the table and rip it from my stepdad's hands.

"What the...?" he blurts, looking shocked.

I flip page after page with shaky hands until I stare at the photograph of Jessica's smiling face.

High school student murdered in a home invasion.

Liam takes it off me and scans his eyes over the text. "There are no details yet."

"It's too soon," I whisper, glancing at my mom. She has grown pale, sipping her coffee to distract herself.

"What's too soon?" Liam asks, handing the newspaper back to my stepdad.

"Details. It only happened yesterday."

We sit in silence while Mom drinks her coffee, and my stepdad reads the paper.

"I can't believe she's dead," Liam breathes out, easing back in his chair. "A home invasion? This is Blackwoods. Nothing ever happens here."

My stepdad clears his throat, lowering the newspaper.

Liam's eyes widen. "I mean, apart from..."

"It's fine." I scoot the chair back, in no mood to bring my biological father into this.

Liam follows me upstairs to my room, where I make a beeline for my bag on the desk chair. "Are you mad at me?"

I shoulder it, turning around. "Mad at you?"

"Well, you seem off."

I blink at him. "Jessica is dead, Liam. What do you want from me? She was your friend."

Dragging a hand down his rugged face, he breathes out a sigh. "I'm sorry. I just..." He drops his hand. "I can't believe she's dead."

I stare at a spot on the wall as he walks up to me and cups my cheek.

"Whatever you feel right now is fine. With your dad—"

I cut him off with a glare. "Don't bring him into this, Liam."

Holding his hands up placatingly, he crowds me against the desk. His white Henley stretches tight across his shoulders, and his light-blue jeans hang low on his hips. "I'm an insensitive dick sometimes." He lowers his hands and puts them on my waist. "I just want to make sure you're okay."

"We need to go to school."

"We can take the day off if you want. No one would blame you—"

Shouldering past him, I leave my room. Jimmy Hill has held me back for as long as I can remember. I refuse to feel this affected every time something bad happens.

But I can't help it. My stomach twists with unease as we step outside into the cool, autumn air. I haven't even put on my denim jacket. Instead, I'm carrying it in my hand on my way to Liam's black Range Rover.

He opens the door for me, rounding the car while I strap on my seatbelt. I'm lost in my own thoughts, memories assaulting me of the night my father was arrested, when Liam starts the engine. It roars to life, bringing me back to the present moment.

I scan the leather interior, the dice dangling from the rearview mirror, and the stack of CDs in the center console. Everything is the same except for one tiny detail.

Bending at the waist, I pick up the leopard print scrunchie in the footwell. "Whose is this?"

With a distracted frown, Liam looks at it. He doesn't miss a beat. "It's Sienna's. I gave her a lift to Miles's the other day."

"Huh... I'm sure Jessica had one just like it."

"Maybe she did. A lot of girls have scrunchies just like it."

I stare at it for a moment, then drop it in the center console with the CDs.

"You're not paranoid, are you? I was at your place last night."

Not all night. Not while my stepfather was fucking me like a whore. "I'm not paranoid."

His tanned, veiny hand lands on my thigh, and he squeezes firmly. "You can't let this get to you, okay? Promise me you won't."

Instead of replying, I stare out the window at the dark clouds in the distance and a derelict farmhouse. An abandoned, rusty car on the field, with weeds growing through cracks in the hood, passes by in a blur as we speed down the country lane toward school. I can feel Liam watching me, but I ignore him. This is what I hate; people are so quick to worry about me. Someone dies, and they all expect me to break like I'm a fragile crystal bowl.

I'm not.

"Pull over."

"What?"

"Pull over!"

The car slows to a halt on the side of the road, and Liam leans forward to press the button for the warning lights.

"What's wrong?" he asks, looking confused and worried at the same time.

"Nothing is wrong. Get your cock out."

His brows pull low, and he looks at me for a long moment. Then, as if kickstarted like an old engine, he unstraps his seatbelt, unbuttons his jeans, and lowers the front.

Reaching across the center console, I wrap my fingers around his slack dick and jack it. Liam breathes in a sharp hiss between his teeth, grabbing hold of the roof handle. It doesn't take long for his cock to harden.

Leaning back against the headrest, I stare at the empty road while jacking him hard and fast to the soundtrack of his labored breathing. I feel nothing. I'm so empty, I wonder if I even exist.

"Fuck, babe," he breathes out.

I jerk him faster, ignoring the cramp in my arm. Liam is panting harshly, thrusting into my hand in time with my movements.

I look down at his dick just in time to watch him ejaculate all over my fingers. I still feel nothing.

I'm as dead as Jessica, even though I'm still breathing.

Liam stares at me open-mouthed as I drag my tongue through his warm and salty cum on the back of my hand.

After licking off the last of his seed, I gesture to the road. "Are you driving us to school, or what?"

He shakes himself off, pulls his jeans back up, and fastens them. Then we're back on the road. Liam clears his throat, looks at me, then clears his throat again. "Are you sure you're okay?"

"Never fucking better," I mutter, staring out the side window at the trees.

KING

"Staring at the killer girl isn't going to win the dare," Hayley teases, pulling out the chair beside me in the cafeteria. She puts the tray down—tomato soup, a sandwich, and a bottle of water—then sits down. "When are you going to do something about it?"

"A girl was just murdered, and you care about the dare?"

"Well," her smile is teasing, "life moves on, as the saying goes."

Ava, wearing a pink top with white lace detailing at the neck, pulls a face as she tries the soup. "I don't believe for a second that it was a home invasion."

Seated beside Kit across the table, Kara eyes her. "Why not?"

With a careless shrug, Ava places her spoon back down and shoves her tray away. "It's too close to the anniversary and execution of Jimmy Hill."

I frown. "What makes you think the two are related to this girl's death?"

"Besides, she was a bitch," Hayley says, pointing her spoon at Ava. "She had it coming."

Dragging a hand through his unruly, blonde hair, Jasper slouches in his chair. He looks like a zombie after this morning's gym class. If there's one thing Jasper hates, it's exercise. He still manages to keep a trim physique, though. "Speaking of dares. I'm gonna move in on Mrs. Wadler this morning."

Kit chokes on his water, and Kara beats his back when he starts to cough. "I can't believe Ava challenged you to sleep with your married English teacher." He trains his amused gaze on Ava. "I think I have you pegged wrong. You come across as all shy and innocent with your cute little tops and your low pigtails and braids, but you're a psycho at heart."

"Why? Because I challenged Jasper to fuck his English teacher? It's the class he struggles in the most. Mrs. Wadler takes no prisoners."

Breathing a laugh through his nose, Kit shakes his head. "At least it makes for good entertainment to watch Jasper crash and burn."

"It's a fucking shame you're in a relationship, or I'd challenge you to fuck the receptionist."

Kit turns green. Beside him, Kara snorts a laugh. "She never smiles. The way she stares at you with those beady eyes..." Kit pretends to shiver.

"Even I want to watch you try to seduce her," Kara says, chuckling in Kit's oversized hoodie. "I might offer you a hall pass this once."

"I'll just close my eyes and imagine it's you, baby."

Hayley pretends to barf while Jasper slams his palm down on the table.

"Whipped motherfucker."

"Jealousy doesn't look good on you, Jasper," Kara says.

"Jealous? It'll be a cold day in hell when I tie myself to one pussy."

Half-listening, I watch Keira, seated on Liam's lap, pick at her food while her friends are deep in discussion. I know that dead look in her eyes.

No one else sees it.

Liam is blind to it. Too consumed by his own ego to see that his trophy girlfriend—the subject of too many true-crime shows on YouTube—is slowly dying inside.

I'm intrigued as fuck.

I want to play with the darkness in her gaze.

The atmosphere in the cafeteria is muted. Jessica, a loud, attention-seeking girl, was part of the popular cheerleaders, and her absence is loud. I never paid her much attention, but even I notice it. The way the school's jocks don't fill the cafeteria with raucous laughter for once.

I could get used to it. It's just a shame a girl had to die for silence to descend on Blackwoods' prestigious high school.

Soft fingers on my thigh disrupt my thoughts, and I look down.

"How did you manage to sneak a knife into school?" Hayley whispers, tracing the sharp blade inside my pocket.

"I have my ways."

She bites her plump lip like she always does when she's horny. It's her calling card. But for once, I'm more intrigued by the girl across the room than Hayley's poor attempts at seduction. But then again, when she strokes her hand over my cock through my jeans, it hardens. I keep my eyes locked on Keira while she stares at nothing, deaf to the conversation around her.

"Wanna go somewhere?" Hayley whispers, dragging her long nails over my rock-hard dick.

I don't look away from Keira. "No, you can touch me here."

She squeezes me, and I stare intently at the girl with the dead gaze. Those empty eyes flick up to mine, causing my dick to jump inside my jeans.

Hayley rubs me firmly, her calculating eyes following my line of sight. "You like her."

"You talk too much."

"You're never this hard with me."

Keira gets up from Liam's lap, whispering something in his ear, before walking out of the cafeteria.

I shove Hayley off. "That's enough."

Her smirk is cruel as she watches me leave the cafeteria. I'm pent-up and frustrated.

Maybe I should think this through.

Have a plan of some kind.

But the restless monster in me wants to sniff out her darkness. I don't even think as I set off after her.

She enters the bathroom, and I follow her inside, my boots soundless on the dirty floor. The air stinks of cheap, citrusy air freshener and damp walls. Keira has shut herself in the bathroom stall closest to the wall.

I stop outside the door and listen to the tinkling sound of her peeing, followed by the flush of the toilet. Strangely, I like to be this close to her while she does something as intimate as using the toilet.

The power I hold over her now, alone in a dirty toilet with Jimmy Hill's daughter—the girl with the dead eyes—has my dick throbbing.

Moving my hand down to my pocket, I palm the handle of my knife, anticipation curling around my heart.

She slides the bolt back and opens the door.

KEIRA

I step out of the cubicle and swipe at my wet cheeks. I'm angry with myself for crying at school. Jessica is dead. The papers call it a home invasion, but rumors claim it was something more sinister. In the meantime, there's nothing we can do but wait for the police report.

I'm shaken up and assaulted by memories at every turn. I wish my brain had an off switch, but it doesn't.

Stepping up to the sink, I switch on the tap and let the ice-cold water ground me. I keep my hands there until I lose feeling. Only then do I switch the tap off and reach for a paper towel.

My eyes widen as I look in the mirror. King stands behind me with his dark hood pulled low over his brown eyes.

I start to whirl around, but he's faster. My hipbones dig into the sink as he puts a sharp blade to my throat and fists my hair.

It hurts.

"One word," he whispers, watching me in the mirror. "One word, and I stop." The blade digs into my throat as he breathes me in. "What's it going to be?"

"Reaper," I reply, unsurprised by the pulsing in my pussy. Looks like a bigger predator than my stepdad found me, after all.

"Good choice." He spins me around, forcing me back with the sharp blade pressed to my throat. The sink digs into my lower back, and it hurts to bend this far.

Shoving his hand inside my jeans and panties, he rams two thick fingers inside me. It burns like hell, but I widen my stance like a whore.

"There she is," he breathes out, finger-fucking me so hard that I'm struggling to catch a breath. The sharp knife digs into my throat as warm blood trails a slow path down my chest and between my breasts. "I knew you were in there somewhere."

"Fuck you!" I hiss, and he pulls his hand out and slaps me hard across the cheek. Hard enough to stun me.

A shameless moan slips from my lips, and King grabs me by

the throat, trailing the knife down my chest. "You're gonna drop to your knees and suck me like a good little slut, understood?"

I try to fight him off, hitting and kicking anywhere I can reach, but he overpowers me with his big body before pressing the knife to my cheek. I immediately stop fighting, panting through my nose.

His smile grows, his eyes shadowed by the hood. "Fighting will get you nowhere but fucked raw in the ass."

Holy fuck... I ache everywhere, in the best way possible. I always knew King was dangerous, but I never realized how dangerous. "Anyone could walk in."

"Isn't that part of the thrill?" He puts his other hand on my shoulder, applying pressure.

"Why are you doing this?" I'm crying. Tears are streaming down my cheeks, but the single word that can stop this madness is far from my mind. For the first time in a long while, something stirs inside me.

My knees meet the sticky, hard surface, and I peer up at him when he uses the cold blade to lift my chin. Then he fists my hair so fiercely that I cry out.

"So fucking pretty." King taps my lips with the blade, ordering me to stick my tongue out. He drags the flat end of the blade over it, up and down, while I rub my clit against the floor, desperate for any kind of pressure.

His grip on my hair tightens, and he taps my tongue with the blade. "Stop that, or I'll cut your tongue out."

With his fingers in my hair, he unbuttons his jeans with the hand holding the knife before shoving the front down and bending his knees slightly to line his dick up with my mouth. "Show me how much you want it."

I slam my lips shut, trying to fight him off. The pleasure that shoots through me when he hurts me by pulling my hair and gripping me too hard is bringing me back to life for the first time since...

"Open your fucking mouth!" Fisting my hair tightly at the nape, he forces his cock between my lips.

I stare up at his shadowed face, tears cascading down my cheeks as he thrusts his cock down my throat. I choke, but he doesn't let up. He's a monster, and my suffering gets him off.

It gets me off, too.

"You like that, hmm? Such a filthy little slut, with your mouth stuffed with my cock." He trails the blade of his knife over my stretched lips, and I swear, I nearly come.

He stands with his feet planted wide, his cock thrusting in and out of my mouth in a maddening rhythm. My face is covered in tears and snot and drool. I'm a fucking mess.

"You don't think anyone sees you. But I do. I see how fucking dead you are inside."

My clit throbs painfully while I dig my nails into his jeans-clad thighs. The sounds of my choking and gagging are loud in the room and feed the darkness in him. In turn, it lures my monster out from the shadows. We circle each other, teeth bared.

"You're gonna let me fuck this pretty mouth anytime I want..." He slows down, pulling out and slapping his cock over my parted lips. "Something tells me one taste will never be enough."

I bare my teeth, my panties soaked through with arousal.

King grips my chin hard and bends down, plunging his tongue inside my mouth. His kiss is as savage as his touch.

Biting my lip hard and pulling it away from my teeth, he moves back in for another soul-destroying kiss. His teeth nibble, bite, punish.

Just when I think I'll die of oxygen starvation, he straightens up and rams his cock inside my mouth again.

He fucks my face with ruthless brutality.

As though I'm worth nothing.

A toy to be used and discarded.

And all I feel is relief.

Relief to finally be devoured by the devil.

"Such a good fucking girl!" he growls, pulling out and coming on my face, his hot cum squirting over my lashes and lips.

He milks his cock, his big hand stroking the thick length. I stare at it—at his veiny hand. It's big and tanned, covered in tattoos, with long fingers. The blue veins on the back of his hand disappear into the sleeve of his hoodie. I want to see the muscles in his forearm shift.

Shoving me away, he zips his jeans back up before picking up the knife off the floor. He must have dropped it when he painted me in cum.

Without another word, he walks out.

The little whore in me has found another plaything.

CASSIE

We're seated on the grass, watching the football practice. The bitterly cold wind seeps through my clothing. I pull my coat tighter around me, peering at Keira. She's distracted by her phone. When she notices me looking, she dims the screen and slides it back into her jeans pocket.

"It's not like you to be so engrossed in your phone."

The tips of her ears burn, but she shrugs her shoulders carelessly and looks out over the field. "Just checking something."

"Right." I stare at Liam's broad shoulders and blinding smile when he pulls his helmet off to slide a hand through his sweaty hair.

It pisses me off sometimes that Keira gets all of him while I get crumbs. And she doesn't even appreciate him.

"Do you believe the rumors?" she asks, tearing off a blade of grass.

I drag my eyes away and study her side profile, the way the breeze moves her blonde hair across her cheek. Tucking it behind her ears, she looks at me. Her cheeks are rosy from the cold, and her bottom lip is chapped from her constant biting.

"I don't know what to believe."

Tearing off another blade of grass, she nods. How she's not frozen to the bone in her denim jacket is beyond me.

"It's just..." I drift off.

"Just what?" Her eyes are intent on mine.

"The anniversary and the execution date... The timing is perfect, you know? Why a home invasion in Blackwoods, of all places? And why now?"

"Yeah," she agrees, worrying her bottom lip. "What are the odds?"

"Here in Blackwoods? Not high."

We stare at each other until I release a sigh and slide my gaze to Liam. He's running with the ball, his shoulders hunched protectively.

Last night he fucked me, then left to go be with her.

It never stops hurting.

I study her again when she brings her phone back out. What is it about her, aside from the allure of her notorious legacy? She's nothing special. I would even go so far as to call her dull. But Liam has some strange obsession with her, even when she treats him like shit.

I don't treat him like shit.

And what do I get for it?

Sex.

But that's where it ends.

Maybe I should ignore him and only throw him a bone every once in a while. Maybe then he would develop an obsession with me, too.

Even now, waiting for her boyfriend to finish football practice, she ignores him completely. He's the star quarterback, for fuck's sake. Girls line up to date him.

Maybe that's the secret.

Maybe his obsession with her has little to do with her father, after all.

I catch a glimpse of her phone and frown. "Is that King?"

Her head flies up, and she clicks the side of her phone to dim the screen. "Yeah, why?"

"Why are you looking at King's profile?"

"Research."

Confused, I pull a face. "What kind of research?"

Another cold breeze makes me shiver as a yellowing leaf blows across my legs.

Before she can answer, Madison joins us. She's wrapped up in her pink puffer jacket, with a white bobble hat pulled over her ears.

Sitting down, she stretches her long legs out in front of her. Her black jeans are destroyed at the knees, revealing pale skin, and her white Chucks are dirty and scuffed.

She pops her pink, strawberry bubble gum and lowers the headphones. "Liam's friend Miles is looking extra good today. Maybe I should become a cheerleader."

I snort. "Miles and Sienna predate the dinosaurs. Good luck with that one."

"I know that, and thanks." She flashes a smile.

Beside me, Keira laughs under her breath before climbing to her feet.

"Where are you going?" I ask.

"I need to use the bathroom. I'll be back soon."

She walks off, and I watch her go. When I look back at Madison, I find her staring at me with a smirk.

"What?"

"Oh, nothing," she says, wetting her lips. "You're so obvious, that's all."

"Excuse me?"

"Do I need to spell it out for you?" She leans in close, smiling a little too big to be genuine. "Liam."

Stiffening, I watch her closely. "I don't know what you're talking about."

"I'm sure you don't." She smiles at me for a moment longer, then eases back. "I wonder what Keira would say if I told her that her best friend is fucking her boyfriend?"

"I'm not fucking Liam."

Staring out over the football field, she slowly lets her eyes slide back to mine. Wisps of raven hair frame her face, and when she sinks her teeth into her bottom lip, I catch a glimpse of her pink bubblegum. "What if I told you," her eyes stray over my shoulder, "that I have proof?"

Keira is on her way back, her head bent low as she crosses the grass.

"What do you want?" I bite out.

Her smirk grows, and there's a taunting glint in her eyes. "Who says I want something? Maybe I just want to watch you squirm."

Loud hollers from the football field cause my heart to jump to my throat while I continue staring at Madison.

She's a fucking bitch.

"Everybody wants something," I reply through gritted teeth.

"You don't like it, do you? That someone knows your dirty little secret."

Keira is within earshot now. I lower my voice. "If you open your fucking mouth, it'll be the last thing you do."

Now she laughs—a rich, drawn-out sound that rubs me the wrong way. When she looks at me again, all humor is gone. "Now you listen to me, bitch. I've got you by the fucking balls. Don't threaten me. It won't end well."

"Someone stuck a fucking tampon to the wall," Keira says, plopping down beside me. "I had to stare at it the entire time I was peeing."

Madison's easy smile returns. She leans back on her elbows and draws a leg up. "I think your boy is about to score, Keira." Then she winks at me.

Fucking winks.

MADISON

I'm still chuckling to myself when I walk back inside the school building after practice to use the toilet.

The look on Cassie's face. She resembled a ghost.

So fucking funny.

The hallways are quiet, absent of students now that they've all gone home. There's something eerie about an empty school, the way my Chucks clap on the floor.

How it seems to echo.

Further up is an abandoned mop and bucket and a pool of soapy water on the floor. But I see no one.

Pulling my headphones over my ears, I take a right down the next hallway. At the top of my recommended music list is "Sweet Dreams" by Marilyn Manson. I press play and hum along to the haunting lyrics.

A broken light flickers overhead, adding to the spooky atmosphere as I shoulder the bathroom door.

Pocketing my phone, I enter a stall, shut the door, and pull the lock into place. The toilet lid is open, and the bowl is stained black with a thick layer of limescale and a line of dried shit.

I tear off strips of toilet paper and use them to cover the seat before placing the roll down and unbuttoning my jeans. No fucking way am I sitting my bare ass down on the toilet seat.

Hooking my fingers in my jeans and panties, I pull them down to my thighs before carefully taking a seat. My knee bounces while I empty my bladder, stopping short of whistling a tune. When I'm done, I wipe clean and stand back up, then flush the toilet and pull my pants back on.

My phone vibrates with an incoming text. I fish it out of my pocket, unlocking the screen.

> Mom: We're out of milk. Can you pick some up on the way home, please?

> Me: Sure. I'm leaving now.

Placing the phone back into my pocket, I exit the stall and come to a halt when my eyes land on a robed figure in a metallic, red devil's mask. In his hand is a knife, the blade glinting beneath the fluorescent lights.

"What the fuck is this?" My voice shakes as I pull my headphones down around my neck and inch back, closer to the wall. It's stupid. The only way out is through the door.

The door he's currently blocking.

My heart smashes against my chest the longer he stares at me through the mask. I break out in a cold sweat, darting my gaze around the room, then shout, "What the fuck do you want?!"

"I want many things," he says in a distorted, twisted voice that makes me pause. "But for now, I'll settle for your blood on these walls."

"What the hell?" I breathe out, ice cold with horror.

He steps closer, causing my heart to jump to my throat. I let out a whimper, holding my hand up in front of me. "Please, don't hurt me."

"You're a slut like everyone else," he says, slowly dragging the blade of the knife over the doors. "And like everyone else, you have buried secrets you don't want anyone to find out."

Salty tears prick my eyes and blur my vision. When he makes a slashing motion with his knife, I scream, cowering against the wall. "Like how your mom let the principal fuck her on top of your admission papers on his desk to secure your place here. And now that legacy falls on you, doesn't it?"

"You don't know fucking anything!" I scream, surprising myself with the level of anger in my voice and how it tears through my vocal cords.

"Every week, usually after biology, he calls you into his office for a chat, doesn't he?"

"SHUT UP!" I sob, lowering into a crouch. "Just stop!"

"At first, it was just your mouth, then your cunt. Until one day, he demanded to fuck your ass."

"Please..." My voice crackles with pain as I hug my arms around myself and stare up at him through my damp lashes. "Leave me alone."

"But that's not the worst part," the distorted voice says, back to dragging the knife over the stall doors. "A sick, demented part of you looks forward to your weekly visits with Mr. Byrne. It revels in the sting when you sit down in class, and your ass burns with pain."

My chest racks with sobs, and I press my hands over my ears to tune out his cruel words.

"Such a filthy little whore."

I scream when he launches himself at me, then kick out with my feet. I don't stop kicking, and he falls back with a heavy grunt. Jumping to my feet, I run for the door, but he tears the headphones from around my neck and grabs me before I can get there. Leather-gloved fingers dig into my throat from behind, bruising me.

I elbow him in the waist as hard as I fucking can, dashing for the door. It's locked.

It's fucking locked...

"No. No. No." My fingers tremble too much. I finally manage to flip the lock, but it's too late. The sharp blade sinks into my shoulder, and a searing pain steals my breath. He grabs my neck, pulls me away from the door, and shoves my head into it full force. My teeth rattle from the impact, my temple exploding with pain.

Dazed, I slump to the floor, vaguely aware of my headphones abandoned a few feet away. The monster crouches down in front of me and parts my hair with the knife.

The devil's mask grins at me.

"If it's any consolation, I admire your fighting spirit. It will be an honor to include you in this."

Swallowing through my dry throat, I wince. My head throbs and the dirty floor is sticky beneath my fingers. "Go to hell!"

He presses the knife to my throat, causing me to whimper as I push myself against the door. My heart has ceased to beat, and my stomach has dropped to the floor.

Loud, masculine voices echo through the hallway outside, and the monster in front of me shoots his head up to listen.

I don't hesitate. I scream, "IN HERE! HELP ME!"

Silence. Then the thunder of heavy footsteps on the floor.

The monster in front of me tears himself away, cursing loudly behind the mask.

Behind me, the door slides open, forcing me to drag myself across the sticky floor away from the entrance. I don't know how much blood I've lost, but it's pooling on the brown tiles.

When I push myself up to lean against the stall, the masked man is gone, and the window near the roof is wide open.

KEIRA

There's a cop car parked outside my house when Liam drops me off.

It can only mean one thing.

The past has come back to haunt me.

"Are you sure you don't want me to come inside?" he asks, one hand on the steering wheel, his body half-turned toward me.

My head shakes as I slowly unfasten my seatbelt. "No, it's fine."

It has started to rain, and the sickly scent clogs the back of my throat as I place my hand on the door handle.

Before I can push it open, Liam stops me with his fingers on my arm. "Babe, I'm here if you want to talk, okay?"

I look at him over my shoulder, then nod once before stepping outside into the drizzle. The walk to my porch feels like it's miles long. I try not to think back on that night when the police barged through the front door with their guns drawn, shouting for my father to drop to the floor. I also try not to think of the things they unearthed behind the shed when they dug up the yard.

Why the fuck did we not move?

According to Mom, we can't afford it.

Ascending the front steps, I watch my Chucks step on each one. I feel like I'm seeing myself from a distance. Like this is happening to someone else.

And not me.

But then the door opens, and a police officer greets me.

"Miss Hill, mind stepping inside for a moment?"

I walk past him, careful not to let my shoulder brush his chest, and enter the hallway. After toeing off my shoes, I make my way to the living room with the officer close on my heels.

My mom is seated on the sectional with my stepdad. One officer stands by the window, and a second officer is seated on the armchair.

As I enter the room, he stands up. "Miss Hill, why don't you take a seat."

I watch him carefully as I walk to the couch. My mom grips my hand when I lower myself down.

"I'm Officer Wells, and I am in charge of this investigation. We have already informed your mother, but she wanted you to hear this from us."

"Okay?" I respond, my voice barely audible above the thudding of my heart in my ears.

"The girl who was murdered last night was killed in the same way Jimmy killed his first victim."

I stop breathing. Images of a torso with all four limbs chopped off flick through my mind too fast for me to stop them. I never saw the pictures, but my brain is good at conjuring up its own imagery.

"Now, there's no reason to believe we have a serial killer on our hands. It could have been an isolated incident. But regardless, we want to station officers outside your house as a precaution."

His words go in one ear and out the other. I can't focus on anything besides the fear Jessica must have felt as the killer chased her down and slaughtered her like livestock.

And for what?

To copy my father?

"What are we dealing with here? A copycat?" I ask, looking between them all.

They exchange glances.

"As I said, we have every reason to believe this was an isolated incident. But if it's not, it's safe to assume the next attack will follow the same pattern and method your father used."

"He killed his next victim in a public bathroom," I whisper. "Sliced her throat before mutilating her vagina."

I feel sick.

"There's no need to panic. You will have two officers stationed outside your house at all times."

"What about when she's at school?" my mother asks. "Will someone shadow her then?"

"No," I blurt. "I can't live my life hiding away from some psycho. What makes you think he's even interested in me?"

The officers exchange another glance, and then the man on the couch clears his throat before rising to his feet and holding out a manila envelope.

"These photographs were found at the crime scene."

I stare up at him, unsure if I want to see whatever horror awaits me, then reach for the envelope. Holding my breath, I slide it open with my finger and peek inside. It's a lot of fucking photographs. "I don't think I can look at them," I reply shakily. "It makes it all real."

"Take your time."

With my heart in my throat, I tip one out.

It's a photograph of me leaving school, jogging down the front steps.

"You might want to see the rest."

Instead of pulling one out, I tip the envelope upside down. The contents spill onto my lap—too many photographs to count.

Mom looks away with her hand over her mouth.

I bite my lip so hard, I taste tangy blood in my mouth. The sharp pain is better than allowing this festering fear to take root. I can't live my life fearing my own shadow.

I carefully pick up a photograph from the pile on my lap. It's one of me fucking Liam in his car. It's lucky I was fully clothed from the waist up. As it is, it looks like we're kissing and nothing more.

Fear clogs my throat as I leaf through the photographs. Fear that one of these pictures might be of my stepdad fucking me.

Luckily, none of them are.

My dirty little secret remains buried for another day.

"Do you understand now why you need a police presence?"

I look up from a picture of me, fresh out of the shower and wrapped in a towel. It was taken through my bedroom window. "I understand."

"Do you have any questions?"

I look at my mom, but she's staring at a spot on the wall, her cheeks stained with mascara streaks.

"I... uh... Why is he doing this?"

"That's what we're trying to figure out." His beeper goes off and he looks down at it, then back at me. "I have to go. Officer Riley and Officer Nash will be right outside." To my mom, he says, "If you need anything, you have the contact details."

After collecting the photographs, they file out.

I stare at nothing, my bones nearly breaking from my mom's tight grip.

"It'll be okay, sweetheart," she says, but I know she's trying to convince herself more than me. Rising to her feet, she smooths down her skirt. "I'll... uh... I better get started with dinner."

As she walks out, my tears fall. Sniffling pathetically, I wipe my cheeks. I hate being weak. I hate it even more when my stepdad is here to see me crack open.

He rises from the couch, and his shiny leather shoes come into view. His fingers grab my chin roughly, forcing my eyes to lock onto his cold ones. He pushes his thumb between my lips, and I suck it like the obedient girl I am when he looks at me like that.

Anything to take the pain away.

I have no doubt that if my mom weren't clattering pans in the kitchen, he'd grab the nearest cushion and tell me to cover my face.

And I would strip out of my pants, lie back with the flowery cushion over my mouth and nose, and spread my legs.

I would be his little whore.

He pulls his thumb from my mouth and walks away.

As I look out the window, I spot the cop car outside. The officers are sipping coffee from travel mugs.

This is my life now.

Just one long fucking nightmare that never seems to end.

I walk back to my room and shut the door behind me before throwing myself down onto my bed. It smells of fresh bedding. Mom must have changed it before the cops came knocking.

Staring up at the ceiling, I listen to the rain on the window. It's coming down heavier now, punishing the glass.

With a sigh, I sweep my gaze around my room. The walls have been painted a deep purple and decorated with black-and-white photographs of gargoyles. The creepier they are, the better. It's a weird thing to collect, and I don't remember how it started. But I do recall Cassie sent me a photograph in the mail once when she visited Hamburg with her family. Ever since then, the collection has grown.

I dig my phone out of my jeans pocket, surprised to find a message waiting for me.

> Unknown number: I can't stop thinking about your lips wrapped around my dick while you cried.

I stare at it until I'm forced to blink.

> Keira: King?

> Unknown number: You could have used the safe word anytime you wanted, but you chose not to.

When I don't respond, another text message comes through.

> King: I jerked off as soon as I got home. I can't get the image of you on your knees out of my fucking head.

It's followed by another.

> King: Ignoring me won't make me go away. Not after the little show you put on.

> Keira: What do you want?

> King: Meet me down at Blackwoods Bay. Do you know the trail that leads through the forest?

> Me: Why should I meet you there?

Heat sinks to my clit when I remember how brutally he fucked my mouth. I shouldn't want him to do it again.

> King: You know why.

Chewing on my lip, I consider my options and then berate myself. I can't possibly want to play a game of consensual non-consensual sex with King when there's a killer on the loose. It's the definition of reckless.

> Keira: I can't... I have a police guard now. If I leave the house, they'll follow.

> King: Too scared?

> Keira: What if you're the killer?

> King: Maybe I am. Does that turn you on?

I start to type out a response, then delete it, staring at the screen. Does the thought of being chased and ravaged by someone who could possibly be the killer turn me on? I don't even want to go there with my mind. The truth is too shameful to admit, even to myself. Fuck... I need psychological help. But the last therapist my mom sent me to blinked at me, wide-eyed, when I admitted to some of my darkest secrets. I never saw him again.

I sit up and crane my neck to look out the window. The cop car is still parked across the road. I can't exactly leave the house... unless...

I bet no one is watching the back door. I could sneak out and take the trail that cuts through the forest.

Looking down at his latest text, I war with myself. While I'm intrigued by his dark side, I also know it's a bad idea to be in his spotlight. I try so very hard to act normal. To blend in. And along comes King, who sets me back at square one.

"Fuck!" I growl, falling back onto the bed.

Why am I torturing myself like this? I'm already acting recklessly by fucking my stepdad. Why am I considering this, too? But then I remember how it felt when he pressed the knife to my throat and told me I only got one word.

How freeing it was.

No, I'm not going there. Not when there's a psycho stalker on the loose. I'm staying right here. In my bed. Where it's safe.

My thoughts shatter when my phone lights up with another message.

> Cassie: Did you hear what happened? There was another attack. Madison is in the hospital.

Reading over the text, I shoot upright in bed, all thoughts of King gone.

> Keira: Another attack?

> Cassie: I heard it from Sienna.

Cassie: Apparently, it's all over the news.

"Fuck," I whisper shakily, palming my forehead, then louder, "Fuck!"

The rain is lashing at the window. I can even hear it on the roof.

Keira: Is Madison ok?

What a stupid question. Of course she's not okay.
What do I do?

Keira: I'm going to the hospital.

Throwing my legs over the side of the bed, I hurry downstairs and call out, "Mom, I need a lift to the hospital."

She's by the sink, pouring a dash of liquid dish soap into the hot water. As I come tumbling into the kitchen, out of breath and crying, she stops what she's doing and blinks at me over her shoulder before slowly turning. "What's happened?"

"I don't know... Madison was attacked."

Seated at the table, my stepdad stands up. "I'll take her, it's fine."

Mom says nothing as her gaze strays to the windows and the rain outside. It's darkening out there, and it won't be long before the streetlights come on. She turns back to the sink and puts a dirty pot into the water.

This is what she does.

She shuts down.

"Come on," Allen says, steering me out of the kitchen with his hand on my shoulder. "Let's go to the hospital."

OFFICER WELLS

The woman's voice on the car radio grates on my damn nerves with her endless chatter in between songs. Reaching forward, I switch it off, preferring silence. Especially now that I have so much on my mind.

Officer Riveiro, a Spanish woman in her late twenties with a severe bun, peers at me sideways as she drives. "What are your thoughts on the Madison girl?"

We briefed back at the station before heading to the hospital, so she already knows. Now she's making conversation to kill the silence that seems to stretch on while the wipers fly across the windshield. The seat warmers are on for the first time this year. So not only do I get to listen to the rain on the roof while my ass is slowly heating up, but I also get to work an endless amount of overtime, thanks to the lunatic. My wife is going to be so happy.

I throw my hands up in a helpless gesture. They settle back on the folder in my lap, filled with photographs of each crime scene. "It was a copycat killer right off the bat. We're sitting ducks, just waiting for the killer to make his move again. Thanks to Jimmy fucking Hill, we know what he'll do next time. We just don't know who he'll target."

Officer Riveiro nods, her grip tight on the steering wheel. "What about his daughter?"

Reaching for my lukewarm coffee in the center console, I take a sip and then wince. "Cheap shit."

Officer Riveiro manages a small smile.

"Our killer has staged Jimmy's daughter in the center of this. She's the queen on the chessboard. We have to assume that he intends for her to be his final victim." I hesitate, rubbing my beard. "I bet my yearly salary that he plans on killing her on the execution day."

Silence descends on the car before Officer Riveiro clears her throat. "What about you, Wells?"

The cup's logo stares back at me. I drag my thumb over it, feeling each groove of the ridged paper cup. The detective in charge of Jimmy Hill's case was brutally killed shortly before Jimmy was arrested. "I can't let my thoughts go there. Regardless of who is in charge, they'll be at risk. If not me, it'll be someone else."

Officer Riveiro stays silent.

Opening the folder on my lap, I straighten the photo on top and study the pool of blood on the bathroom floor back at the high school. This girl is lucky to be alive. The question now is, will he try to replicate Jimmy Hill's second murder again, or will he move straight on to the third victim?

"We need to speak to the kids."

"You think a high school student is behind all of this?"

"I don't know," I reply, looking at the next picture in line, "but it wouldn't surprise me if the killer is someone close to Keira. Someone who's had an obsession with her family for some time."

My phone rings in my pocket, so I fish it out and swipe the screen.

"What's wrong?"

I shake my head, dimming the screen and pocketing my phone. "Word got out, and now there's a media frenzy outside the hospital. Everyone is frothing at the mouth."

"And Blackwoods is once more back in the spotlight," Officer Riveiro mutters, her gaze distant.

"History repeats itself."

KING

There are some things I don't take well to, and rejection is one of them. Keira never replied to my last message, much to my friends' amusement. I didn't tell them outright, but they could tell.

It was kind of obvious when we met up at the movies to watch the latest horror flick. I spent the entirety of the movie with my feet propped on the seat in front of me while staring at my screen. Waiting and waiting and fucking waiting for a text message.

She ghosted me.

No one fucking ghosts me.

Which is why I'm now in her bedroom, soaking wet from the rain outside, hovering over her while she sleeps.

A lightning strike lights up her slender form on the bed. She's on her side with the quilt bunched between her bare legs.

Tilting my head to the side, I glide my gaze up her pale ankle, past her knee, all the way to her pert ass, hidden beneath a pair of pink sleep shorts. Her tank top has ridden up to reveal a sliver of waist and toned stomach.

The rumble of thunder outside masks the sound of my heavy Doc Marten's on the laminate floor as I step toward her. Rainwater drips from my coat and fingertips. I tighten my grip on the switchblade in my hand in anticipation.

She's so vulnerable and easy to hurt. Seeing her like this, asleep and barely dressed while there's a psycho killer on the loose, wakes the restless monster in me.

I take another step closer, the floorboard creaking beneath my heavy weight. Keira stirs, and my heart thuds heavily.

My soaked clothes are cold against my heated skin as I wait. Nothing happens. Keira's soft breathing evens out.

A part of me is disappointed she didn't wake up and scream. But that would alert her parents.

My legs meet the side of the bed. I lean down and carefully brush her hair away from her brow with the wet knife, trailing the flat end down her pale cheek. Her long lashes and parted lips stir my dick. Who am I kidding? I've been hard as a rock ever since I climbed through her window.

Leaning down further, I let my lips ghost her ear as I whisper, "I'm gonna fuck you up, baby."

My little toy stays sleeping while I dip the blade inside her sleep shorts before cutting them off her body. Another lightning strike lights up the curve of her pale ass, and the mattress dips beneath my weight. I straddle her thighs and unbutton my jeans, careful not to touch her yet. My clothes are cold. I don't want her to startle awake before I have her where I want her.

Slowly sliding down the zipper, the sound loud and erotic in the quiet room, I shove my jeans down until they're around my thighs. Precum beads on my dick as I wrap my fingers around the thick length, stroking once.

Pleasure bursts behind my eyelids. I'm so fucking aroused, touching myself while she sleeps in front of me, none the fucking wiser, with her bare ass right there for the taking.

Flipping the knife in my hand, I spit on the handle before dipping it between her ass cheeks. Still soundly asleep, she arches her back as a whimper slips from her lips. I jack my dick while rubbing the handle over her cunt and tight exit.

One day soon, I'm going to ram my dick in her ass and muffle her screams with my hand over her mouth.

I hiss a breath through my teeth, my balls tightening at the thought of her crying beneath me.

Maybe I should thank Hayley for making Keira my dare. Though the dare is far from my mind now. I no longer want to fuck this girl as part of some Halloween game. I want to feast on the dead look in her eyes. And the darkness in her that calls out to mine.

The knife is soaked with her arousal when I slide it out from between her ass cheeks. She's a slut even when she's asleep.

I lie down on top of her and clamp my hand over her mouth as she startles awake with a scream.

There it is.

The sweetest fucking sound in the world.

I don't breathe a word as I press the knife to her throat and sink my teeth into her neck at the same time I ram my cock in her cunt.

Ah, fuck! It feels so good to hurt her.

Her sweet screams beneath my palm and her panting breaths through her nostrils create a twisted symphony of depravity. I should let her know it's me, it's cruel not to, but the way her pussy strangles my dick speaks the truth of her own perversion.

Scented with the autumn rain, my cold, wet clothes soak through her tank top as I fuck her into the mattress. I fuck her so hard, the bed creaks loudly.

Then, when she's sobbing so hard that her chest racks, I growl, "Did you really think you could ghost me? That the cops could keep you safe up here in your little tower?" Sliding my hand from her mouth, I curl my fingers around her little throat, squeezing hard until she's wheezing.

Her pussy pulses around my dick, and she spreads her thighs wider, pushing back against me, forgetting herself. She wants to play the rape game, but with the knife pressed to her skin, there's nothing she can do but play by my rules.

Another rumble of thunder followed by a lightning strike

lights up her room. My elongated shadow looks grotesque on the wall, like a fanged devil, as it mounts hers.

"Your pussy is strangling my dick, little slut." I bite down on her ear, pumping my hips viciously against her ass cheeks. "Want to use your safe word yet? Want me to stop fucking you like you're worthless?"

Her head eagerly shakes no but then she remembers the game and opens her mouth to scream.

I only just manage to muffle it in time.

She's screaming herself hoarse while I chuckle in her ear. "The more you scream, the harder I'll fuck you."

Keira screams louder.

She screams so loudly, I remove the knife from her throat and slide it back between her ass cheeks. It has the desired effect; her screams fall silent as she stiffens.

"I'll cut you if you make a noise," I warn, straightening up onto my knees. Her puckered hole is revealed when another lightning flash lights up her bed.

While fucking her cunt with slow, deep strokes, I cover the knife's handle in her own juices before pressing it into her ass. "Relax, baby."

"King?" she whimpers shakily, her voice tinged with fear and lust.

I close my hand around the blade, feeling it dig into my fingers. "I wish you could see how fucking perfect you are, with your cunt stuffed with my dick and my knife in your ass."

The blade is sharp, and when I slide the handle back out, I cut myself. The burning sting and the sensation of warm blood dripping between my fingers are so fucking erotic. I hiss a breath through my gritted teeth as she releases a frightened sob, clutching the sheet.

I fuck her with the handle in time with my thrusts, high on the pain as I cut myself again. Keira comes, her cries muffled by the mattress.

"Yeah, such a good girl," I praise, removing the handle and sliding my bloodied hand over her pale ass cheek before grabbing it hard.

The pleasure mounts and mounts until I think I'm going cross-eyed. This girl is going to be the death of me with her twisted desires.

I pull out and coat her ass in cum, releasing a tortured groan deep in my chest. By the time the last squirt of cum rains over her pale skin, I'm spent and ruined. I slide back out through her open window like a shadow in the night before she can come down from her high.

KEIRA

F our days pass. Four days of King startling me awake at all hours of the night to ravish me after sneaking past the cops outside my house. I'm sore between my legs and tired as hell, but it's the perfect distraction. Especially now, seated in the church, staring at Jessica's white coffin. The murdered student in question smiles at us all from the photograph on top. I don't even know why I'm here. Not really. Jessica and I weren't friends; we merely hung out in the same circles because of Liam. If I wasn't dating the star quarterback, the cheerleaders wouldn't so much as look in my direction. I would be a blip on their radar.

The church is cold, and my legs are mottled with goosebumps. I dressed for the occasion in a black skirt and blouse, forgoing my denim coat. Liam notices and shrugs out of his suit jacket, placing it on my shoulders. It's warm and smells of him—amber and citrus. I pull it tight around me, staring blankly at the coffin while the priest reads a passage from the Bible.

Cassie cries softly on my other side. Even the boys—Miles, Chris, and Marcus—look pale with glassy eyes. There's not an untouched soul in the room. Jessica was popular and had a charismatic personality.

She was also a bitch, but that doesn't matter now that she's dead.

Now she was suddenly everyone's best friend. Students, even

the ones who used to sneer in her direction behind her back or shrink into the shadows when she walked past, cry softly in the pews. No one has a bad word to say about the queen bee anymore.

And I'm a bitch for finding it all so fucking hypocritical.

Jessica wasn't nice.

She played to win, and she didn't care who she hurt in the process.

Liam puts his hand on my cold leg, and the warmth of his skin burns through the thin layer of my skirt. My gaze slides away from the coffin to Liam's tanned, veiny hand and then over to my right.

King is watching me across the church, where he sits in a pew opposite, a few rows in front. He didn't know Jessica, but his father is close to hers. We may not move in the same social circles, but King's family is still one of the wealthiest families in town.

When I die, he'll be here, too. Pretending he gives a shit.

His lips tilt upward in a sinful smirk, the kind of smirk that brings back memories of last night, when he hauled me out of bed and fucked me against the window, in full view of the cop car. The icy glass licked at my bare tits while I came on his cock.

Again, and again.

King hides a monster behind those dark eyes. I have to admit, he looks hot in a suit and skinny tie, with his hair styled. Gone are the destroyed jeans, black T-shirts, and backward caps.

Liam's warm arm wraps around my shoulder as he leans in to place a kiss on my temple. It's for show more than anything.

Poor Jimmy Hill's daughter, who can't catch a fucking break from death and destruction. Isn't she so lucky to be doted on by the perfect, charming quarterback?

I can't read the look in King's eyes when he cuts them to Liam by my side, but I don't miss the shadows that flicker in their depths.

The girl by his side, Hayley, dressed in a black dress with white bows on the shoulder straps, leans in to whisper in King's ear. It's intimate, the way her lips curl back into a seductive smile despite the white coffin a few yards in front.

Something ugly rears its head inside me. I'm never possessive around Liam, but I don't like how this girl looks at King.

Not one bit.

I'm torn from my thoughts when Liam squeezes my thigh. He's staring straight ahead at the coffin, his fingers digging into my thigh as if he wants to hurt me.

I like pain.

It keeps the demons at bay.

As I shift in my seat to look behind me, my eyes collide with Mom's. She's emotionless. I want to fucking shake her, if only to crack her mask enough for a single tear to spill out. I know there are emotions buried deep inside her. Somewhere.

I face forward again, listening to Cassie's soft crying. Madison should be here too, but she's recuperating at home. It's been so quiet without her this week, and I've missed the ruffle of her pink puffer jacket and the fruity scent of her strawberry bubblegum.

Reaching out, I grab Cassie's hand and squeeze gently. She responds by interlacing our fingers. We both know it could be us next. The days have seemed grayer, and the wind has felt colder ever since Madison was attacked at school. The icy breeze slithers beneath my clothes like a whisper, but my winter coat remains at the back of my closet. I welcome the icy bite that has my teeth chattering every time I walk outside. Or as I pull my jacket closer to my body for a reprieve but get none.

The wake afterward is muted in both sound and color. The hum of conversation lulls my senses. It's late afternoon, and the sun has almost settled beyond the trees outside the tall windows. It's windy, but the rain has stopped for now. We're seated at one of the circular tables in the hall. Jessica's house is still a crime scene, so the wake is held at the local country club owned by Jessica's father. Luxury, rose-gold curtains frame the large windows that overlook a lake and the forest beyond. Waiters and waitresses, dressed in black and white, bring out the food while a projector screen at one end of the room plays a series of photographs of Jessica on repeat.

I'm seated with Liam to my left and Hazel to my right. Cassie sits on Liam's other side and, much to her chagrin, the seating plan put her between him and Marcus.

Hazel is quiet. Out of everyone at this table, she was the closest to Jessica. Amanda, Chris's on-and-off girlfriend, reaches out to squeeze her hand. "It's not the same without her."

Hazel nods, her bottom lip trembling. "I miss her."

Sitting across from us, Sienna and Miles watch her with soft, sad smiles.

I feel out of place amongst Jessica's friends. Sure, I fuck the quarterback, but I wasn't anything more than a hindrance to Jessica.

As if Liam can sense my thoughts, he slides his hand beneath my hair to massage my neck.

I seek out King in the room. He sits with his parents at a table near the windows. Hayley is there with her family too, and so is their friend Ava.

"I'm scared," Sienna admits, and Miles wraps his arm around her. She's beautiful tonight, with her curled, auburn hair and her lips painted a dusty rose color.

"We all are," Amanda replies before sharing a look with Chris.

Marcus snorts, leaning back in his seat when the waiter fills his plate with potatoes. "I'm not."

We all look at him.

"What?" Chris sounds incredulous.

"I'm not scared of some pathetic copycat killer who doesn't know how to be original but needs to draw on someone else's material to feel relevant. It's bullshit."

"Bullshit or not, he's killing people," Hazel bites out beside me. "Jessica is dead, Marcus."

They stare at each other for a long moment. No one speaks, and the hum of conversation from the nearby tables feels loud to my ears. I try to tune it out without much luck. It's pitch black outside the windows now. The club is situated in the countryside, away from the town, so there are no streetlights for miles.

Only the dark forest with its fanged trees and creepy animal calls.

I lean back as a waiter pours sauce over my minted potatoes and beef. It pours over the rounded edges and pools on the plate.

"It's my fault," I speak up.

It doesn't sit well with me that they're all in this situation because of me.

"All of this is my fault."

"No," Liam says, straightening in his seat. "Don't say that, babe. None of this is your fault."

"Of course, it is. If it weren't for my father, Jessica would be..." I drift off, my throat clogged with emotion.

Hazel remains silent, staring at an empty spot on the table. Though I can feel her thoughts. I can feel *all* their thoughts. Somewhere deep inside, Liam knows I'm right, and he has put his friends in danger by being with me. What started out as a novelty has turned deadly.

Marcus, smooth as always, says, "Who do we think is next?"

Sliding his arm around me, Liam glares at him.

"Someone insignificant." Miles reaches for his sparkling water. "Someone at this table who knows our main star." He looks at me, taking a sip and putting the glass back down. "But isn't a close friend."

"Someone like me," Hazel whispers, still staring at that empty spot as if it wields all the answers.

"You're not insignificant, Hazel," Amanda reassures her, but Hazel pulls her hand from beneath hers.

Hazel's voice is surprisingly strong. "I have never spent time with Keira. Never really talked to her. I sided with Jessica when she tried to freeze Keira out."

Marcus, with his mouth stuffed with beef, speaks around a mouthful. "That means nothing. I'm not close to Keira, either. We've exchanged what?" Placing his fork down, he looks past Liam at me. "Five words?"

My shoulders rise and fall carelessly while I slide a piece of potato through the sauce on my plate with the fork.

"It could be literally any one of us," Sienna butts in, pointing to herself and Miles. "We don't know Keira, either."

"The only one who's safe," Marcus says, taking a sip of his sparkling water, "is Cassie."

"Liam too, don't forget," Chris points out, his arm wrapped around Sienna.

Marcus shakes his head. "The boyfriend always dies in horror stories."

"The hell?" Liam chuckles uneasily beside me. "That's not true."

Marcus flashes him a smile, but it's Miles who speaks up. "He's right. You're a dead man walking."

Liam looks between them all, his arm slack around my shoulders. Then he removes it and sits forward, pointing to his chest. "I don't know what kind of shit movies you watch, but if anyone comes for me, I'll make them regret it."

"You mean they'll gut you." Marcus stabs a piece of potato.

Hazel is stiff. "Can we not talk about this, please?"

We're silent, the hum of conversation like that of a swarm of buzzing bees.

Amanda whispers, "What if the killer is here? Tonight? Watching us?"

"He is."

"Fuck you, Marcus," chuckles Miles. "You don't know that.

It's probably some perverted old man who lives in a trailer on the outskirts of town."

Marcus has almost cleaned his plate. He sits back and loosens his navy tie. "Copycat killer or not, this is a game to him, and we're sitting ducks. Jessica's funeral arrangements were plastered in every local newspaper. It's a safe assumption that the killer is watching us. It's not enough to just replicate Jimmy Hill's killing spree." He waves a hand dismissively. "This is not about good old Jimmy."

I inhale a sharp breath as he points at me.

"It's about her. This is Keira's stage, and Jimmy Hill is the backdrop."

"I think you're wrong," I answer him. "I think the obsession is with my father, and *I'm* the backdrop—or the excuse, if you will—to perform some sick celebration of his murders ahead of his execution."

"I guess we'll soon find out," Hazel mutters, stabbing at her beef before dropping her fork on the plate. She shoves the plate away and stands up. "I've lost my appetite."

As she starts to walk away, Marcus calls out, "Oh, come on, you know better than to run off alone when there's a killer on the loose. Unless it's you."

Hazel whirls, her honey-blonde hair sliding over her shoulders. "What the hell, Marcus?" She points a finger at herself. "Are you accusing me of killing my best friend?"

Marcus, being the dickhead that he is, simply shrugs. "It could be any one of us."

"Or no one. It could be a fucking stranger for all we know."

"It could be. But most likely, it's not. And if you walk out alone, you could end up dead. Unless, of course," his lips curve into a smirk, "you don't fear the killer."

"Marcus," Chris warns, "you're taking it too far, man."

"Am I? From where I'm looking, Jessica is dead, and Madison was attacked. That's two people from *our* friend group."

No one says a thing.

"We need to stick together, not walk off alone." Marcus trains his eyes on Hazel. "If you leave this room by yourself, you're asking for trouble."

"I'll go with her." Sienna scoots her chair back and smooths down her flared, black skirt. To Marcus, she says, "Safety in numbers."

"Unless Hazel is the killer."

"Give it a rest, man," Miles growls, glaring at Marcus before grabbing Sienna's hand as she walks away. He pulls her back for a kiss. "Be careful, babe."

"You're a dick sometimes, you know that, right?" Liam asks Marcus when Hazel and Sienna have left the room.

LIAM

The thing about funeral wakes is that they always start out demure, but the atmosphere changes as the night progresses and the adults consume more alcohol. The guests lose their inhibitions.

That's the part I like the most because no one cares that their underage teenagers have long since snuck off to consume alcohol.

That's where I am now, in the empty kitchen, raiding the cupboards for something to drink. This wake will carry on all through the night, and I don't intend to stay sober for the duration.

"Knock, knock," Cassie says with a smile as she appears in the doorway.

I show her my catch, wiggling the bottle of brandy in the air.

"You know we shouldn't walk around alone."

"You're alone," I point out, unscrewing the lid and taking a large swig. It burns my throat as she walks deeper into the room.

Her black dress, a little too short to be appropriate for a

funeral, swishes enticingly around her thighs. "I'm not alone anymore."

"Hmm." I take another swig, my gaze sliding down her body. "This is a bad idea."

"It is," she agrees, stopping in front of me. "But something about burying my dead friend makes me want to make reckless decisions, you know?"

With the bottle pressed to my lips, I shake my head. "I don't."

She drops to her knees and drags a hand up my thigh. The glint in her eye is one I've seen before. She's high, and I find myself wondering who supplied her with drugs.

Because fuck it, I want some too.

"You brought any?"

And like a devil masquerading as an innocent angel, she holds her hand up. There, on her palm, is a white pill.

Without a second thought, I reach for it and place it on my tongue.

"I've missed you," she whispers, biting her bottom lip. "You spend all your time with Keira."

The counter is sticky behind me as I curl my fingers around the edge. Cassie drags her hands up my thigh, squeezing the outline of my hardening cock.

"When did you last fuck her?"

"This morning."

Her touch never falters, even as a shadow falls over her face. She unzips me, slowly curling her fingers in my waistband.

"Did you like it?"

"Fucking her? Yes."

She slides down my suit pants, palms my throbbing dick, and leans in to drag her flattened tongue from base to tip before sucking on the crown. Her heavy, lust-filled eyes never leave mine.

Anyone could walk in at any moment. Maybe that's what makes this so hot.

Maybe Keira would finally give a damn if she walked in and spotted us.

"Yes, that's it," I grunt, letting go of the countertop behind me to palm the back of her head. "Suck me just like that."

Reaching down between her legs, she rubs her clit while jacking me one handed and sucking my dick.

The drugs are taking effect. Everything is a haze as she takes me to the back of her throat.

My head falls back between my shoulders. I release a loud groan and tighten my grip on her long hair. *"Jesus, fuck!* You sure know how to suck cock..."

When I open my eyes, I'm met with King's smirk as he leans against the doorframe. His suit is still pristine, not a crease in sight, but he has removed his tie. It hangs around the back of his neck. I'm so fucking gone, drugged up to my eyeballs, that I barely register him walking deeper into the room.

Cassie is just as gone, sucking my dick as if competing for an award.

The slide of a knife leaving the wooden block on the counter cuts through her gagging. King inspects it in the fluorescent light overhead before wetting his lips, his eyes returning to me.

Somewhere deep inside, I know I should push Cassie away. I'm the star quarterback with a spotless reputation to uphold. But my body won't obey me. Not when I'm about to blow my load down Cassie's throat. And not when the world is a blurry haze.

King points the knife at me with a cold smile, then slides it back into the wooden block and walks out. But before he leaves, he removes his phone from his pocket, unlocks the screen, and takes a picture.

My head falls back as my heart thuds wildly in my chest. I come, thrusting so viciously I accidentally slip out of Cassie's mouth and spray my cum over her face.

KING

I love secrets.

Secrets make me fucking happy.

I love brooding over how to best make use of them.

And walking in on Liam and Cassie?

Well...

I couldn't have asked for a better secret to gain leverage. The question is, when do I use it?

I watch Keira in the hallway between classes, the way Liam fawns over her as though he gives a shit.

The thing is, I think he does.

I think he's a starved puppy who seeks negative attention by fucking her friend. He just wants Keira to notice him.

In any fucking way.

If he struggled to get her attention before, he struggles even more now that I'm in the picture. Because let's face it, he doesn't know what his girlfriend craves, or the fact that she wants to pretend to be raped in her sleep. He doesn't know she gets off on humiliation and pain.

"What the fuck are you smirking at?" Jasper asks, shutting his locker beside me while I stare at her across the hallway.

I drag my eyes away slowly. So fucking slowly, Jasper waves his hand in front of my face.

"I think he fulfilled the dare," Hayley singsongs, nudging Ava's shoulder.

The stupid dare. I couldn't care less about their childish games.

"Not yet," Kit says, carrying Kara on his shoulders. "He needs to fuck her at the Halloween fair next weekend."

"I thought he just needed to fuck her?" Ava asks, scrunching up her nose. "Why the fair specifically?"

"That's a valid question," Hayley agrees.

"Because Liam will be there. It's not fun to just fuck her, is it? He needs to fuck her under her boyfriend's nose."

"I'm not even going to the stupid fair," I drawl, bringing my fist to my mouth and dragging my thumb over the swell of my lip.

Ava studies me with her books pressed to her chest. "Have you fucked her?"

"Of course he has," Hayley says, rolling her eyes. "Look at him."

"I thought they were serious," Ava says, referring to Keira and Liam.

"They are, but that doesn't mean the school's little princess can't enjoy dick on the side, too."

I ignore them all, annoyance flaring up inside me when Liam appears out of fucking nowhere, lifts Keira up from behind, and spins her around. That's a thing he does a lot, and it winds me up to hear her carefree giggles. If he only knew I had my fingers in her ass last night while she strangled my dick with her soaking cunt.

Instead, I'm forced to watch him push her up against the lockers and kiss her while his filthy fucking hands slip beneath her crop top.

I'm going to cut them the fuck off.

"Jealousy doesn't look good on you, King," Kara teases, winking at me from her spot on Kit's shoulders.

I tear my gaze away from the man I'm going to strangle to death with my bare hands. "I'm not fucking jealous."

"Sure," chuckles Kit as we start walking.

I ignore him.

Ava scrolls on her phone. "The police have finally agreed it's a copycat killer."

"Took them long enough," I mutter.

"I don't know," Jasper muses, his hands in his jeans pockets. His white hood is pulled over his head, and his blonde hair sticks out from beneath. "There hasn't been another attack for almost a week. It could be over."

Hayley shakes her head and loops her arm through mine. "My gut tells me it isn't over."

"Your gut?" laughs Kit.

"Don't make fun of me. We all have gut feelings sometimes."

We turn the corner. The hallway is bustling with students on their way to lessons, and we slow to a halt as we near the classroom. There's a commotion outside it, with tons of students shoving at each other to have a look inside.

I share a look with Jasper beside me before pushing ahead. The crowd parts when they notice it's me. Jasper crashes into my back as I come to a stumbling halt inside the doors.

"What the fuck?" he breathes out.

The others slide in beside us.

Scrawled on the whiteboard in bright, red letters are the words:

You thought it was over? The games have only just begun.

"It's a joke, right?" Hayley's voice trembles.

Ava has her hand clamped over her mouth, tears beading on her lashes.

"It's a practical joke," Kit growls, wrapping his arm protectively around Kara. "There are thousands of students here. Some pathetic dickhead thought it'd be fun to worry everyone." We share a dark look as a muscle tics in his jaw.

"We need to call off King's dare," Hayley says, turning her back on the writing and sweeping her eyes over our little group.

"Why?" Jasper asks, laughing incredulously. "What has this got to do with a stupid dare?"

She shuts the door and flips the lock to the soundtrack of annoyed, curious students outside who want to catch a glimpse for themselves. "Nothing. However, that," she points at the wall, "is directly related to Keira, and if King starts fucking her..." Hayley falls silent, swallowing thickly. "It makes us all a target."

Dragging my tongue over my teeth, I shrug. "Well, if that's the case, then we're already a target."

"I fucking knew it!" Kit blurts excitedly, punching the air. "You can't lie for shit, man." He slides his pointed finger over the group. "Who's ready to pay up?"

"No fucking way," Jasper argues. "So what if he's dipped it in her cunt? He has to fuck her at the fair."

"I'm not going to the fair," I tell them, but no one listens.

Hayley rolls her eyes. "Look, the dare is over. King has already fucked her." She studies me briefly. "And numerous times, by the looks of it. So it won't be a challenge at all to fuck her at the fair, will it?"

"Still not going to the fucking fair," I mutter.

Ava sighs. "Can we please try to focus on what's important?"

Jasper ignores her. "Let's up the stakes. He has to fuck her with Liam in the same room."

"It's a fair. There are no fucking rooms."

"Behind a tent. Whatever."

Rubbing a hand over my face, I growl, "Just fucking forget about it. I don't give a shit about the dare."

Kara winks at me at the same time Ava throws her hands up and walks out, unlocking and throwing open the door.

I look back at the whiteboard, unable to shake the unease inside me and the trickle of a shiver that trails down my spine.

The games have only just begun.

Just then, Keira, Liam, and their friends enter the room wide-eyed. Liam barely spares me a glance, but I know he remembers the wake two days ago.

I know because he stiffens when he spots me before wrapping his arm around Keira's waist and pulling her into his body.

He can pretend it's to soothe her worries all he wants, but we both know what it is. We both know he's secretly worried I'll show her the photograph I took.

And I will.

But not today.

I smirk at him when he glances at me again, letting my gaze skate down to the girl in his arms. The same girl who was spread naked beneath me a few hours ago.

When I look back up, he narrows his eyes.

I can't fucking help it.

I chuckle.

MADISON

Principal Byrne is not an attractive man. In fact, he needs to do something about his beer gut and receding hairline. Maybe he could pull it off if he had an interesting personality, but he's as boring as the dead plants on the windowsill in his office.

The only thing he has going for him is his decent-sized cock. And no student at this school should be as familiar with it as I am.

"How are you feeling?" he asks me, said cock in hand, unbothered by the sound of students outside his locked office door.

I watch his right arm move while he jerks his dick fast and viciously as if he wants to pull it off. I wouldn't mind if he did. Beads of sweat have formed on his big, shiny forehead.

"I'm healing."

"That's good."

Today is my first day back at school, and I should have known this sleaze bag wouldn't let me have a few days to recover from my ordeal. He called me in here as soon as he found out I was back. And now I'm watching him jerk off. He smiles, revealing yellow teeth. "Did you do your homework?"

A subtle nod.

"Good," he chokes out, his top lip glistening with sweat. "Bend over the desk and show me."

The other day, I received a text message from him late at night with a set of instructions he expected me to follow over the coming days. This was one of them.

I rise from the creaky chair and slowly step between his legs and the desk, while he continues stroking his cock.

"There's a good girl." He bunches my skirt in his hand—another instruction—and shoves it up. "Bend over. Let me see."

There's a reason I never wear skirts. It offers easy access to predators like Principal Byrne.

Swallowing my pride, I bend over and lift my skirt.

"No panties. Good girl."

A blush creeps up my neck as I feel myself grow wet. I shouldn't like this. It's fucking demented.

But I do.

The killer was right.

A sick, twisted part of me has come to crave Principal Byrne and his sweaty hands.

He palms my ass, teasing my clit before ordering me to pull my ass cheeks apart.

With the side of my face pressed to the paperwork on the desk, I stare at the closed blinds while spreading my ass. The nip in the air licks at my sensitive folds.

I hate myself for the throbbing in my clit.

Principal Byrne taps the pink butt plug in my ass. "So pretty. Now pull it out, let me see your stretched hole."

Reaching behind me, I grab hold of the flared base and slowly inch it out.

"Bear down. Open yourself."

I feel his fingers around my stretched asshole, circling the ring of muscles. He smacks my ass hard enough to make me yelp, and I bite down on my lip to stifle a moan.

The desk chair creaks. He opens a drawer, and the distinct click of the lube bottle cuts through the silence like a sharp knife. After I'm lubed up and my hole is teased, he grabs my dark hair and sinks his cock into my ass. Then he proceeds to fuck me on the desk like a rutting animal.

He smacks me, pulls my hair, calls me a whore.

And I take it all. Like I always do.

Both hating and loving every second.

I once saw another girl walk in here, and hot, fiery jealousy burned through me. That's how sick I am.

Someone tries the handle, and Principal Byrne clamps his meaty hand over my mouth, but he doesn't stop fucking my ass. If anything, he takes me harder, digging his sweaty fingers into my cheeks.

The stab wound on my shoulder throbs with pain, but it has little on the burning pleasure that steals my breath. My pussy weeps, making a mess of the front of his suit pants.

There's an urgent knock on the door. But whoever it is must think Principal Byrne is out, because the footsteps outside retreat.

I come. I can't fucking stop it as it surges through me with enough power to force a muffled scream from my lips.

"I told you that you weren't allowed to fucking come, you dirty little whore."

Principal Byrne releases inside me and slides his meaty finger from my cheek and into my mouth to tease the back of my throat. I gag while he fills me up with his cum.

And then he reaches for the pink butt plug on the desk, carefully slides his cock out, and plugs me. "There, you can keep my cum in your ass all day now for being such a greedy little whore. I'll know if you take it out before I tell you that you can." He drags a finger through the sticky arousal on the inside of my thigh. "Naughty girl."

With a slap to my reddened ass, he steps back and zips himself away. I know the drill. I stay bent over his desk with my ass in the air until he tells me I can leave.

As soon as the words leave his chapped, sweaty lips, I straighten up and pull down my skirt. I can still feel him in my ass, and the friction and weight from the plug shouldn't arouse me this much. But it does.

I hurry out of his office, keeping my head low as I make my way to my lockers with his cum trapped in my ass.

PRINCIPAL BYRNE

My office smells of sex, so I open the window for fresh air. Smirking to myself, I collect the crumpled papers on the desk and shove them all into my drawer before reaching for the remote tucked in the top one. I aim it at the hidden camera on the bookshelf and press the off switch. Over the last year, I've collected enough of these videos to start my own fucking movie company. Madison is my favorite, because, unlike the other girls, she enjoys it in her own twisted way.

In fact, I sold one of her clips to a porn site the other day. She's a little gem, that one. I expect she'll earn me a nice little penny on the side. But of course, there's always the risk of being found out. My office is recognizable, but the internet is a vast black hole, much like her sweet ass, so the likelihood is low.

Besides, if one of the teachers here found one of my videos, would they want to admit to watching it? Pausing and rewinding? Unlikely.

And how could anyone prove it's me?

So it's my office? Circumstantial at best.

The girls could talk, sure. But the secrets I have on all of them ensure they'll keep their pretty little lips shut.

More than Madison's ass and her choked whimpers, I enjoy the thrill of knowing I could get caught.

That it could ruin my career.

The forbidden always tastes sweeter.

There's a soft creak behind me, and a wire is dropped over my head and pulled taut around my neck before I can spin my chair around. My body jerks on the seat, and my legs kick out as I begin to struggle. I grapple desperately with the wire, my hands coming away slick with blood and my eyes bulging as I choke.

A cold mask brushes up against my ear, and then a distorted voice taunts, "So you like to fuck underage girls and sell the recordings online?"

He tightens the string with a hard yank, and it makes a wet sound when it cuts through my carotid artery.

"And now you get to die like a pig and have all of your dirty secrets exposed to the world."

My fighting stops, and my limbs fall helplessly to my sides. The last thing I hear before the darkness takes me is the blood that drips steadily from my fingertips.

Drip. Drip. Drip.

OFFICER WELLS

"What are we dealing with here?" I ask as I step into the office. The school has been cornered off while the crime scene is photographed and scoured for evidence.

I'm exhausted, having barely slept a wink.

Officer Riveiro nods her head towards where Principal Byrne lies bent over the desk, his dead eyes staring in the direction of the window.

I walk closer, careful not to step in the large pool of blood on the floor. Principal Byrne's pants and briefs have been pulled down to his ankles, and his hairy ass cheeks have the word *pig* written in blood on each side.

"Look at this," the crime scene investigator, Pinnegar, says, inching the ass cheeks apart with his gloved fingers.

I stare at the stapler that protrudes from his rectum. "Well, this is new. Jimmy Hill didn't do this to any of his victims."

Officer Riveiro speaks up. "He also didn't kill any of his victims this way. It's a deviation."

"The copycat is going off script," I mumble, bending at the waist to inspect the corpse's neck.

"That makes him more dangerous," Riveiro points out. "We're back at square one."

Pinnegar points his gloved fingers to the lacerations on the neck. "His head was almost severed in the struggle."

"What do you think?"

"Judging by the blood, he was garroted on his desk chair, and then the killer staged the scene."

"What about the stapler?"

"Personal," Riveiro says, pointing a finger at a stack of tapes on the desk. "They were placed there after the murder. I bet they will have some incriminating evidence."

I straighten up and scan my eyes around the room. "Entry point?"

Riveiro lifts her chin, and I turn to look behind me. "The killer most likely hid in the built-in cupboard."

Walking over, I stick my head inside. The floor-to-ceiling shelving is stacked with files and books. More importantly, it's big enough to fit a grown man. Maybe even two, if they squeezed together.

"So aside from the note on the whiteboard, which could have been a practical joke, we have nothing that suggests this is related to Jimmy or Keira Hill?"

"No," Riveiro replies. "Unless you count good old instinct. Aside from Jimmy Hill's murder spree, something like this is unheard of in Blackwoods. What are the odds we have two homicides and an attempted murder in less than two weeks by two different killers?"

"You're right," I reply, slowly walking the length of the room.

"But I can't go to the public with theories. We need proof. And until our copycat strikes again, or we find some evidence to tie this murder to that of the Jessica girl... Well... We're fumbling in the dark. We need to treat the murders as unrelated incidents while also keeping an open mind that it's most likely the same person." I remove a pair of gloves from my pocket, shake them out, and then slide them on. Pinnegar hands me a small, plastic bag with a zip.

Collecting the tapes, I seal them inside. "Let's get these looked at."

The door behind me squeaks open, and I press pause on the screen. Never in my fucking life did I think I would get paid to watch the principal of Blackwoods High fuck underage girls in his office. It's disturbing, and I will need a year-long holiday once the killer is behind bars.

Riveiro spares a quick glance at the screen, at the Madison girl bent over the desk.

Rubbing my tired eyes, I clear my throat. It's almost nine in the evening. I should be home with my wife, but I'm trying to wrap my head around how I'm going to keep this under wraps for the time being. It will overshadow the investigation once the media gets wind of Principal Byrne's extracurricular activities. Not to mention create another media frenzy.

One we could do without right now.

Riveiro puts a steaming cup of coffee in front of me before rolling over a chair and sitting down. "Found anything out yet?"

Dropping my hand, I gesture to the screen. "We know he fucked the Madison girl, and she left the office straight afterward. Byrne turns off the camera after straightening up his desk. Did Madison return to seek revenge?"

"But why now? Why not before? She's in lots of those tapes. And let's not forget our killer targeted her a week earlier."

"Which is what I thought. But I found this. Look..." Leaning forward, I rewind the tape, pointing to the screen. "See that?"

Riveiro squints, a tendril of dark hair sliding from behind her ear. "What am I looking at?"

I rewind it again, pressing play and pointing at the cupboard door behind Byrne. "See how it slides open a fraction?"

"Shit," Riveiro blurts, shifting forward to rewind the recording. "I see it. The fucking killer was in there the entire time, even before Madison entered the room."

"Biding his time," I reply.

"So Madison leaves..." Riveiro mutes the moans and grunts, her eyes wide as she looks at me. "Byrne opens the window, tidies up his desk, and switches off the camera."

"And then he sits down at the desk," I finish for her.

Her brown eyes flick between mine. "The killer strikes... He was in there the whole time."

Picking up the steaming coffee, I blow on it before taking a sip. "We just need to figure out who it is."

"What about security footage at the school?"

My head shakes as I place the cup back down. "Byrne didn't want any evidence of the girls that came and went. The security systems in the hallway where his office is based have been down for months. We have nothing."

"And no one knew?"

"Or maybe they knew but didn't question it."

The desk chair creaks as Riveiro leans back and stares at the screen, at the cracked-open door behind Byrne. "The killer must have known the cameras were down, right?"

"That would be my guess." I blow out a breath, rubbing my thumb and finger together. "We need to figure out who this killer is quickly. Before more people die."

I'm so fucking sore from King's nightly visits that I shouldn't shimmy my jeans down my ass when my stepdad tosses the couch cushion on my face and orders me to put it over my eyes. The marble floor in the hallway is cold, and I can feel the chill through my denim jacket.

No sooner had I returned home from school after Principal Byrne's murder than my stepdad stepped out from the living room in a crumpled suit and ordered me to lie down. Mom is away for two days at a conference, so I should have foreseen this.

I press the pillow over my face as I kick my jeans and panties off.

"Open your legs."

Of course I do.

I open them as wide as I fucking can, baring my pink cunt to his dark eyes. It's as if he knows I need this after another shocking murder.

My past is chasing me, and I can't outrun it.

Only pain can save me now.

Lots of fucking pain.

Unbuckling his belt, he pulls it slowly through the hoops. I shiver in anticipation, my heart thrashing wildly in my chest. My breaths come fast, too fast for me not to grow dizzy from the high. As he walks closer, I hear him wind his belt around his hand. I know what's coming even before he unwinds it and strikes my pussy.

The pain hurts so fucking bad, like a knife slashing my intimate parts. My hips buck, and I cry out, silently begging for more.

He whips me again, making my pussy scream in delicious pain. It's too much, but in the midst of the agony is demented pleasure. The kind of pleasure that requires me to let go. There can't be any thinking or worrying when he hurts me like this.

I can only feel.

The next strike lands on my bare stomach, where my crop top has ridden up. I gasp, clutching the pillow to my face.

If I accidentally remove it, he'll stop.

His monster likes to play hide and seek.

Unlike King's.

Fuck, why am I thinking about King now? He has no place in these dirty moments with my stepdad.

Any thoughts of the raven-haired boy with the cruel, cold smirk evaporate when another strike lands on my bare skin. This time, he used the belt buckle. And the pain is so immense, I let out a sob. He only leaves marks when Mom is away.

"Please stop," I whimper, shuddering on the cold marble floor.

I don't mean it though.

And he knows.

He knows nothing can satisfy this craving.

Dropping to his knees between my legs, he covers my burning, throbbing cunt with his mouth and proceeds to eat me until my sobs transform into sounds of unbridled pleasure. His teeth nibble and bite, and his stubble scratches in the best way possible.

My soreness from King only heightens the pleasure that mounts and mounts until I explode on my stepdad's tongue. My body writhes on the floor as he lies down on top of me and holds the pillow over my head while shoving down the front of his pants.

"Did you miss Daddy?" he whispers in a smoky, dark tone he only reserves for our playtime.

Barely able to breathe beneath the cushion, I claw at his shirt buttons. Anywhere I can reach.

I claw and scratch and scream.

The pain when he enters me has me gasping against the damp fabric.

"Fuck, so tight!" he growls, thrusting forward.

Curling his fingers around my wrist when I dig my nails into his chin, he shoves my hand hard against the marble, causing the bone to rattle from the impact.

The sounds he makes while fucking me on the entrance floor are nothing short of animalistic. My hands fly out, connecting with stray shoes. I pick one up and beat him over the head with it, if only to catch a sip of precious air. All the while, my pussy pulses, and my heart thrashes. I'm so fucking high on the humiliation and the depravity. The feel of his massive cock as it tears me apart.

And then, tonight, my second monster will seek me out to feast on what's left. Maybe he'll scent the other predator on me. And maybe he'll punish me for being a greedy little whore. Just the fucking thought has me coming again.

With a final grunt, my stepdad pulls out and covers my sore pussy and lower stomach in cum. Each spurt rains over me like a soothing balm accentuated by his strangled grunts.

His weight disappears, and I listen to him pull his trousers back up and tighten his belt. Just when I think the humiliation is over, he spits on my cunt.

Squeezing my thighs together, I let out a shameless moan beneath the pillow. His footsteps retreat, and I stay on the floor until the door to his office slams shut.

Only then do I remove the pillow and blink my eyes open against the harsh light that streams in from the window beside the front door.

Pushing up on my elbows, I gaze down at the red welts on my skin. Bruises are already forming from when he whipped me with the belt buckle.

I carefully slide a finger over a welt, feeling the sore swelling. *Fucking beautiful.*

Cassie blinks at me through a sliver of her curtain when I knock on her window. If I didn't know better, I'd say she gulps.

"Let me in."

Cassie pulls her curtains shut. I rub my hands over my freezing arms while I wait for her to open the window.

I could have knocked on her door, but I didn't want anyone to know I'm here, which is why I cut through the forest that lines the back of her property. That way, I could avoid the houses on the street and the nosy neighbors.

Sneaking past the cops parked outside the front of my house was easier than I thought. So easy, in fact, I should leave a formal complaint. But then they would know, and I don't want that.

Cassie finally slides her curtains open and lets me in through the window. Her bedroom smells strongly of air freshener, as though she sprayed some before opening the window.

"What took you so long?" I ask, my feet landing on the floor.

"What are you doing here?" she asks, ignoring my question as she shuts the window and pulls the curtains shut.

Hiding from King.

I can't possibly take another fucking tonight. I'm so sore that I can barely walk, and my welts burn and throb. I need time to heal and rest. "I wanted to spend time with you. With everything that's going on..."

Her eyes soften, and she pulls me in for a hug.

My nose pricks. "Did you spray on perfume just now?"

"I was stinky." She lets me go and takes a seat on her bed. "Where's Liam tonight?"

My pussy stings as I join her on the mattress. I lean back against the headboard, placing a pillow behind my back. "I blew him off." And then, as an afterthought, I add, "I wanted to see you instead."

It's not a complete lie.

"Can I sleep here tonight?"

"Of course you can. You're always welcome." She reaches for my hand, and we link our fingers.

"Can I ask you a question?"

"Sure."

"What makes a whore?"

Cassie chokes on her own spit. "What?"

"Is it how many partners you've had in the past or how many you fuck at the same time?"

"What do you mean *at the same time?* Like an orgy?"

"Well, I suppose..." I shrug. "But I meant if you have more than one sexual partner at any one time. Would you be a whore if you fucked three guys, but not at the same time?"

Cassie slides her hand from mine and scoots further up on the bed, her back against a poster on the wall. "I don't think a woman is a whore because she fucks more than one guy."

"What about the things she enjoys?"

"Positions?"

"Amongst other things. What about women with fetishes? Things like rape fantasies and fetishes for pain and degradation?"

"Where are these thoughts coming from?"

Chewing on my lip, I focus on the throbbing pain between my legs. "Us women, we like to think we live in such a sex-positive society, but is it true? Are we truly that advanced, or is the world still full of women who judge other women for the things they enjoy?"

"That will always be the case." Then she asks a question of her own. "What about women who fuck men in relationships? Are they whores?"

A few hours ago, I let my mom's husband fuck me on the vestibule floor.

My mom's husband.

Cassie and I gaze at each other.

"No," I shake my head. "They're not."

Swallowing thickly, she clears her throat. "Did you really walk here by yourself when there's a killer on the loose?"

"I didn't want anyone to see me. Besides," I rest my head back on the wall, "the killer won't kill me yet."

"You can't possibly know that."

"True, but life has to move on. What if they never find this guy?"

"They will."

My lips tilt upward. "You sound so sure."

Cassie gestures to her laptop on the bedside table. "Want to watch a movie?"

Cassie is fast asleep beside me, snoring softly.

I'm too warm.

Kicking the sheet off, I scoot up to sit, glancing at the alarm clock. It's almost two o'clock in the morning.

It's raining again.

While the soft pattering on the window is soothing, it's not enough to help me drift off to sleep. I listen to the grandfather clock in the hallway. Even with Cassie's door closed, it can still be heard.

My phone lights up beside me on the bed. I pick it up, already knowing who it is.

King: Where the fuck are you?

King: Think you can hide from me?

Keira: It's working great so far, wouldn't you agree?

> King: Wanna play games, baby?

> Keira: My pussy is sore. I need a break.

His response is immediate.

> King: Your ass isn't sore.

Why do I tingle between my legs? And why do I want him to hunt me down?

King sends me a short video recording. Pressing play, I clamp a hand over my mouth to muffle my gasp. He's masturbating over my bed.

> King: I like it when you hide from me like prey. It makes me so fucking hard.

I replay his video clip too many times, watching his tattooed, veiny hand move harshly over his dick. I have never touched a man so savagely. But it doesn't surprise me that King likes it rough as hell.

I've experienced it firsthand.

> King: I'm imagining you on all fours, looking at me over your shoulder with that lust in your eyes while you pretend you're scared.

My hand dips inside my panties. I'm so sore, I can barely touch myself.

> King: I know you're fucking that sweet pussy, baby.

I inch a single finger inside my sore channel, unable to take anymore.

Keira: So, what if I am?

King: Fuck... you drive me insane.

I bite my lip as the pleasure builds in my core. Sliding my finger back out, I rub my clit, imagining King.

Keira: I want you to lick my pussy.

King: Maybe if you're a good girl, and I'd say you're a very bad fucking girl since you're hiding from me.

Keira: You've never licked me before. Why?

Before he can reply, I type out another message to lure his monster closer to the surface.

Keira: Liam licks me. He loves it when I come on his tongue.

King: Careful, baby. You don't want to play that game with me.

I bite back a moan, rubbing myself harder. The orgasm is so close that I can taste it on my tongue.

Keira: I'm at his place now. I'm gonna give him a nice little wake-up call with my pussy on his face. Bye, King.

Before I can dim the screen, his reply pops up on the screen.

King: You're lying. Guess how I know?

Another video recording pops up on the screen. I click on it faster than I would like to admit.

Rubbing my clit, I watch King come all over my bedsheets. It pushes me over the edge, and I bite down on my hand as the orgasm stiffens every muscle in my body.

Despite my best efforts, a whimper slips out.

> King: Did you bite your hand so hard you bled?

Wait. What? Ice runs through my veins. My eyes fly up to the window just in time to watch his shadow step out from behind the curtains. He's on me before I've had a chance to make a noise. With his leather-gloved hand over my mouth, he puts a finger over his lips. His brown eyes glint in the dark.

I stay silent while my heart thrums wildly in my chest. If Cassie wakes up now, I'm screwed.

King sees the fear in my eyes, and a sinful smirk curves his lips as he lowers his finger from his mouth. It disappears between our bodies, and he drags it through my sore, soaking slit. His grip tightens on my mouth and I begin to pant through my nostrils.

My eyes tear up from the delicious sting when he slides two gloved fingers inside me. I'm sure my heart is about to explode as he finger-fucks me until tears seep from the corners of my eyes.

"Did you really think you could hide from me?" he whispers, scissoring his fingers.

My eyes roll back. I'm about to come again, but he wrenches his digits out of me, then shifts down the bed. His hot mouth is on me in the next second, and I press both of my hands over my lips.

Holy shit!

He puts Liam and my stepdad to shame.

Fuck... King knows what he's doing.

I strangle his head with my thighs as he sucks my clit between his teeth with vicious intensity. King eats me out as if he wants to erase Liam's—or any other man's—touch from my memory. He licks, sucks, and nibbles until he's all I can see and feel.

Oh, fuck, the sensation of his prickly stubble on my most sensitive part.

I come.

But the asshole isn't done.

He grips my thighs, pries me open, and tongue fucks me until I squirt my release.

What is it now? The third?

By the time he's done feasting on my pussy, the sun is rising in the distance, the birds are waking up, and Cassie's mom's alarm clock goes off in the room next door.

Only then does he sneak out, leaving me in my own ruins with his bite marks on my thighs.

CASSIE

I'm in the girl's changing room after PE, staring at the pile of clothing on the bench. It was the last lesson of the day. I know Keira has plans with Liam after school, and it's been eating away at me all fucking day. This festering jealousy inside me is growing stronger by the day. I don't know how to shift it.

But the lines are blurring.

I scan the changing room. Everyone else is gone. It's so typical of Keira to ignore common fucking sense and be alone while there's a killer on the loose.

Nothing ever fucking fazes her.

I grab her clothes and towel before I can talk myself out of it.

I'm a bitch.

A two-faced bitch who's willing to sabotage my own best friend if it means I can have her boyfriend to myself.

Stuffing her things into my backpack, I bolt.

With my head down, I hurry to the parking lot. There's a small niggle of guilt inside me, while I toss my backpack into the trunk before rounding the car. Though it's not strong enough for me to go back. Maybe Liam will finally have enough and dump her when she fails to turn up for their date.

"Why are you looking so sketchy?" Madison asks behind me as I slide my keys into the lock.

I jump, dropping them to the ground. After bending down to

retrieve them amongst the stray leaves that have blown across the parking lot, I straighten up and brush my hair out of my eyes. "You scared me."

Madison looks different without her pink puffer jacket. I let my eyes drift over her black body warmer and pink bobble hat. It's cold as fuck, and my own winter jacket is doing little to ward off the icy breeze.

Madison stares at me for a moment longer before scanning her eyes across the parking lot. "Where's Keira?"

"Why would I know?" I ask a little too defensively. Schooling my features, I slide my key back into the lock. "I haven't seen her."

"Why are you out here by yourself when the killer is still out there?"

"I could say the same about you," I point out, opening the door.

"I'm not alone." She lifts her chin toward the school entrance, where Hazel is skipping down the front steps. "We're heading to Blackwoods Bay. Want to tag along?"

"It's freezing," I answer her, strands of my hairs getting caught in my lip gloss.

Madison peers over at Hazel as she jogs to catch up with us, her cheeks stained red from the cold. "Liam is meeting Keira there."

I narrow my eyes on her but don't reply.

Stepping closer and tilting her head to the side, she studies me with a small smile. "The day I was attacked. Where were you?"

"What? I was on the grass, watching the football practice. You know that. We talked."

Madison hums, lowering her voice as Hazel nears. "Don't you think it's an interesting coincidence that I told you I knew about your little secret with Liam and then ended up stabbed in the bathroom while you *supposedly,*" she makes air quotes, "stayed outside to watch the football practice?"

"Hi, Cassie. Where's Keira?" Hazel asks as she joins us, out of breath and smiling big.

Shaken up, I look between them both before getting myself together and addressing Madison. "Fuck you! I didn't hurt anyone."

Smirking, she sucks her bottom lip between her teeth. "If you say so."

With a disgusted snort, I enter the car, put it in drive, and step on the gas.

Fucking bitch.

Who the hell does she think she is? Accusing me of murdering people?

KEIRA

Hot water runs over my tender skin, soothing my sore muscles. I tip my head back and open my mouth to catch the shower water. Between my stepfather's brutal fucking and King keeping me up all night, I'm aching everywhere.

I take my time as I wash my hair with my favorite apple shampoo. The others have left, and blissful silence has settled over the locker room. I shouldn't stay here this late, but my mom is still away, and I can't possibly face the monster at home two days in a row. I'm supposed to meet Liam, but I'm not in a rush to spend an entire evening with him.

The logical thing would be to dump him, but something stops me. He's the closest thing to normal that I have in my abnormal world. I don't want to lose that. What I have with King belongs to the night. That side of me, like a vampire, can't exist in the daylight. There's no room for my inner whore to externalize my emotional pain while the sun is up.

I need facades to help me survive.

The good girl.

The serial killer's broken daughter.

The perfect girlfriend.
The whore who comes out to play after sunset.

They all make up a part of me, like an individual piece of the tapestry. Without one, I'm an unfinished patchwork quilt.

As the door to the locker room creaks open, I stiffen and brush the water from my eyes. "Hello?"

Nothing else happens. No monsters dart out from the shadows to devour me whole. I turn the shower off and ease open the cubicle door. It's eerily silent without the chatter of girls and showers running.

Squeezing the excess water out of my hair, I walk up to the bench but stop short.

My things are gone.

"What the hell?" I turn in a circle, scanning the room.

They're gone. The towel is nowhere to be seen, and neither are my clothes.

My wet feet move across the floor as I wrap my arms around myself to keep warm. What the hell am I going to do? My clothes are gone. The school is empty.

I check each locker, causing them to slam shut while I open the next in line and repeat the process. They're all empty.

Every single one.

"Fuck," I breathe out, pausing as I slowly turn around. There, written in red on the closed changing room door, are the words:

"Guess who's next, Keira?"

My hand flies up to my mouth, and I stumble back against the lockers. Releasing a sob, I squeeze my eyes shut, but they fly open just as fast. What if the killer is still around? He was in here while I showered. He was feet away from me...

A whimper dances on my lips as I begin to hyperventilate. I steady myself with a hand on the locker. Now is not the time to panic. If he wanted me dead, he would have killed me already. The killer wants to scare me, that's all.

My eyes snag on a red item on the bench closest to the door. Lowering my hand from my mouth, I take hesitant steps closer.

It's a metallic, red devil's mask.

Bending down, I carefully pick it up, despite my better judgment. An evil smile reveals sharp teeth.

I swallow audibly, my eyes darting across the room for any sign of danger. "This isn't funny!"

Even now, my rationalizing mind wants to believe this is a practical joke.

A door slams shut somewhere in the hallway, making me jump as my heart nearly explodes inside my chest. Bent at the waist, I stifle a sob, tears pouring from my eyes. I'm not strong enough for this.

I don't know what to do. I'm naked.

My clothes are gone.

My phone...

I try to inhale a breath, but another sob rips loose when footsteps sound in the hallway. Inching back with the mask clutched between my fingers while my other hand presses over my mouth, I watch the closed door.

One step back, followed by a second.

Heavy boots thud on the floor, closer and closer.

I toss the mask on the floor with a whimper, unable to look at it anymore. My heart thuds in my head, my hands are clammy, and my breaths are too shallow.

I feel dizzy with the mounting panic.

The footsteps stop, shifting outside the door, and I hold my breath, not daring to make a noise.

Wrapping my arms around myself, I shift back while counting to ten in my head to force myself to focus on something other than the shadow in the gap in the door.

My attempts to control my mounting fear turn to ashes when

the handle is pushed down. It rattles once, twice, three times, as if the person on the other side enjoys my whimpers.

I can't control them.

I'm sobbing uncontrollably now, pressed up against the lockers. Is this what Jessica felt in her final moments? And Madison, before she was rescued?

I let out a scream when the door slams open to reveal a robed figure with the same devil's mask as the one on the floor. I stare, breathing harshly. My eyes sting with tears as he enters the room, his head cocked to the side. In his gloved hand is a baseball bat.

As I watch, he drags it over the tiled floor. The sound will haunt my nightmares if I survive this.

"Poor little Keira. The pathetic daughter of a serial killer."

The distorted voice sends my heart ricocheting.

"What do you want?" I choke, barely able to recognize my own shaky voice.

"I just want to chat with the main star of my little reenactment."

"Fuck. You!" I'm shivering from both the cold and the adrenaline, my teeth clattering violently.

My response must amuse him, because he laughs.

Loudly.

Then he rams his baseball bat into the nearest locker, causing me to scream. I try to dart past him, but he jumps in front of me and presses the bat to my sternum.

"Not so fast, Keira. I want to play a game."

"What game?" I ask cautiously, stepping back.

He follows until my spine meets the lockers again. With nowhere to run, I let my eyes fall closed. A loud crash to my left startles me, and I press my hands over my ears as he strikes locker after locker until all I can hear are my own hoarse screams.

"Now," he says with that distorted voice that shrivels my heart. "I want to play a game."

"Then fucking play," I bite out, shoving his bat away from my neck when he uses it to tap my chin.

"I want you to answer my question."

"What question?"

"The one on the door." Dragging the baseball bat down my chest, he pauses at the apex of my thighs. "Guess who's next, Keira. If you get it right, I'll spare them."

"Why would you do that?"

"Despite the mask, I'm not all devil."

I look away, but he slides the bat between my legs.

"Do not ignore me."

His red mask grins at me as the bat slides back out, only to return, dragging over my most sensitive flesh.

"You want me to guess?"

"Yes."

"And what if I refuse?"

"You remember the details of your father's third kill, don't you, Keira? How he gutted his victim with a machete before removing the heart?" Leaning in close, he adds, "Ripping it out with his bare hands."

"You didn't answer my question."

"I did. If you don't play my game, I'll gut them like a pig."

"You'll kill them anyway."

"Not true. Guess it right, and I'll spare their life."

"And deviate from the script?" I spit out. "I don't think so."

Removing the bat from between my legs, he brings it to his nose and breathes in my scent through the mask.

I refuse to cower anymore. There's no escape from the monster in front of me.

"If you don't guess, I'll kill them tonight. Do you want their death on your conscience? To lie awake in your bed tonight, wondering how many hours I spend torturing my next victim, all because you refused to give me a measly guess?"

My mind is racing a million miles a minute as I struggle to

come up with an answer. "It could be literally anyone. How could I possibly guess?"

"That's why it's a game of chance, and those are my favorite games." He points the bat at me again, the wood brushing my chin. "Now guess."

"Cassie." At least if I guess her name, I give her a chance of survival.

"Beep. Wrong. You should know better, Keira. Cassie is one of the main players. Consider her your bishop. First, I need to take out the pawns, then the bishops, knights, and rooks. Have you never played chess, Keira?"

I don't answer.

He tilts his head to the side, the mask smiling evilly at me, and trails the bat down the line of my jaw. "It's okay, Keira. You play the game well. It's an honor to make you the star of your father's movie. Just think. Soon your father will be executed, and I'll get to watch the light fade from your eyes as I inhale your last breath."

"You're sick," I bite out.

"So are we both." I can practically hear the smile in his distorted voice. "That's why you're so perfect for what I have planned." With a final tap to my pubic bone, he leaves the locker room. I stare unblinkingly at the red letters as the door slides shut behind him.

"Guess who's next, Keira."

LIAM

I burst into the locker room, out of breath and fucking panicked. "I came as soon as I heard."

Keira sits wrapped in a blanket, her damp hair stuck to her cheeks.

Officer Wells moves out of the way, patting my shoulder as I sit down beside her and pull her into my lap. "She's had a tough night. Look after her, kid."

It's terrible to admit that I'm relieved. I waited for her at Blackwoods Bay for hours while my friends chuckled about how pathetic I am. For a moment, I agreed with them.

But then Officer Wells rang me.

The killer stole Keira's clothes, taunted her, and made her play a game. Then he left her naked and cold in the changing room. It took her over an hour to build up the courage to escape the changing room and walk naked, wet, and shivering through the school on the hunt for a phone. She finally located one behind the reception desk and phoned the police.

I get to play the hero in this scenario, and I like that more than I'll ever admit.

Chin propped on her head, I keep her tucked into my chest. "Thanks, Officer. What do we know so far?"

Officer Wells flits his worried gaze to mine. "The killer never intended to kill her. He just wanted to frighten her."

My jaw tightens. When I find out who the killer is, I will personally beat the living crap out of him for thinking he can touch my girl.

Officer Wells nods his head in the direction of a female officer with dark hair and olive skin. "Let's take the mask back to the lab for testing. If we're lucky, we'll find something." To Keira, he says, "Don't be alone again, okay? None of you should be without a friend for protection. There's safety in numbers."

Just then, his phone rings. He fishes it out of his pocket, swipes the screen, and puts it to his ear.

"Officer Wells." There's a crease between his brows as he looks from the female officer to me. "Check it for fingerprints. In the meantime, she needs a new one." He hangs up and pockets his phone. "Her cell was traced to a field about a mile from here. We're keeping hold of it for now. In the meantime, we'll get Keira set up with a temporary phone. I don't want any of you kids to be without the means to contact the police."

They all file out.

"Are you okay?" I ask her, stroking her hair away from her face and scanning my eyes over her pale face. She looks exhausted.

Shaking her head, she stays silent.

"It's okay, baby. You're staying at my place tonight."

"Can we go, please?" she whispers, her voice barely audible. "I don't want to be here anymore."

I scoop her up and rise to my feet. I've never seen her so vulnerable, and I like it a hell of a lot.

For the first time, she looks at me as if I'm her hero. I guess I have the killer to thank for pushing her into my arms.

And now I get to take her back to my place, tuck her into bed, and take full advantage of her fragile state. She wants reassurance and to feel safe. I want to bury my cock in her pussy and pretend to be her hero.

It's a win for us both.

"Can you hold me?" she whispers as I fold the blanket up before placing it on the back of my desk chair.

Wrapped in my navy bedding, she looks so fragile in my big bed. Above the headboard hangs a poster of my favorite football player, and beside it is a photo of Keira and me that I pinned to the wall a year back. It was taken after I scored an important goal. I'm by the bleachers, helmet in hand, with Keira wrapped around me like a koala bear. I took her home that night and fucked her on the kitchen island while my parents were out at dinner with friends.

"Of course, babe." I strip down to my white boxers before sliding in beneath the quilt. She's still cold, so I pull her close.

"He's going to murder someone tonight," she whispers into the crook of my neck.

"He was taunting you, babe."

"He meant it."

I reach across her to switch off the light, but she shakes her head.

"Please, leave it on."

She must be spooked if she wants to sleep with the lights on.

I lie back down and pull her onto my chest. Outside, the wind rustles the bush beneath the window, and the tall branches scratch the glass. They need trimming back.

"He wanted me to guess his next kill."

I stay silent, sensing she wants to say more.

"I couldn't do it."

"But you gave a name?"

She nods, snuggling closer.

Rubbing my hand down my face, I stare up at the ceiling. Keira smells of apple shampoo and her own unique scent. I breathe her in, my cock stirring to life.

"I said Cassie... I knew it wasn't her, but I couldn't live with myself if he killed her."

Cassie...

I had my cock down her throat today after lunch. She makes it so fucking hard to say no.

Even though I know I should.

Especially after what happened at the wake.

I'm surprised King hasn't sought me out yet to blackmail me. What the hell is he waiting for? I've contemplated dispatching him, but it's not a good idea with an active killer in the area.

If I kill King, what's to stop Officer Wells from pinning the other murders on me?

I just won't let myself get caught.

"You did what you had to do," I reassure Keira. "You protected your friend."

"But now someone else will die."

I roll her onto her back and push up on my elbow. "Don't let the killer get to you. It doesn't matter what name you said, he won't stop killing people. He just wants you to stay up worrying about it, like you are now." I palm her cold breasts, loving their fullness in my hands. "Don't let him play these mind games with you."

The way she stares up at me has me throbbing in my boxers.

I roll on top of her and grind my cock against the inside of her thigh, letting her feel how hard she makes me. Her lips part, and then she wraps her arms around my neck and pulls me down to her mouth.

Shifting on top of her, I grind my dick against her pussy and whisper between kisses, "I need to be inside you."

"Someone is dying tonight. We shouldn't—"

"That's exactly why we should." Reaching between us, I shove my boxers down before kicking them off. "We can't let him win, babe."

She stares up at me, and her long lashes flutter as I press into her. This is what I wanted when I saw her crying on the bench in the locker room.

To bury my cock in her cunt and watch her lips part.

I like to fuck Cassie. She's good fun, and she has a tight pussy. But it feels like a fucking win every time I get to feel Keira, my own girlfriend, wrapped around me. I realize as I grind my hips against her pelvis while buried to the hilt inside her, that I like the chase as much as I hate it.

I like when she gives in.

I like this moment right now, when I get to pound her into the mattress and feel like a fucking king. And I also realize that I shouldn't have to feel like that with my own girlfriend. It's not healthy, but I keep chasing her like an addict.

Because when I win against her, it tastes so much fucking better than any other pussy on the planet.

"Fuck," I grunt, grabbing hold of the headboard. "I love how you take my cock so fucking well."

Her nails claw a path down my back, and a shiver runs through me.

But not from the delicious sting.

I can't shake the feeling of being watched.

And strangely, it makes me hotter to think that someone might be witnessing me fucking Keira to the soundtrack of her filthy little moans.

Watching my ass pump the air while her heels dangle off my shoulders.

I hope they're fucking jealous. Because this sweet pussy...

I'll kill to keep it.

KING

I open the fridge to pull out another beer while staring at the unanswered messages on my phone. I've sent my little toy numerous ones tonight, but they're still unread.

It makes me fucking restless to wait for a reply. Why the hell isn't she checking her phone? That's not like her.

"Hand me one, too," Jasper says, entering the kitchen with Ava and Hayley in tow. Kit and Kara are too busy making out on the couch.

Retrieving the bottles, I shut the fridge and place my phone down. As I root through the drawer for a bottle opener, Hayley lifts herself up beside me on the counter. Her long, bare legs dangle in the air, her ankles crossed, and her short, pink, leather skirt barely covers her panties.

Ava opens the fridge behind me and pulls out a leopard print can of gin and tonic.

"I like your parents, Jasper," Hayley says. "They always keep the fridge stocked."

After opening my bottle of beer, I toss him the opener, and he catches it one-handed.

"There are perks to parents who make lots of money and are rarely home."

"Besides the obvious abandonment issues?" Ava questions, shutting the fridge before pulling her denim skirt back down.

I don't know why she wears the damn thing because it keeps riding up her waist.

"There are those," Jasper replies with a smirk, winking at her as he presses the bottle to his lips. The innuendo in his voice is impossible to miss. I whack him over the back of the head.

With a surprised grunt, beer spilling onto his chin, he flips me off, then wipes the droplets away with the palm of his hand. "Thanks, man."

I sip my beer, eyeing him while he shakes out his hand.

Hayley lifts her chin in the direction of my phone. "What's with the long face?"

Instead of replying, I leave the kitchen. Kit and Kara are dry humping on Jasper's sectional, so I take a seat on one of the armchairs and reach over to pick up the remote control from the coffee table. The others sidle out of the kitchen, Ava and Hayley with matching gin and tonics.

Hayley plants herself in my lap, and Ava sits down on the edge of the sectional, as far away from Kit and Kara as possible.

The look on her face is comical. "There are bedrooms upstairs, you know?"

They're too lost in each other to care.

Ava scrunches up her nose when Jasper sits down and slides his arm over her shoulder. "What are you doing?"

"Trying his luck," I chuckle, sipping my beer.

There's nothing on the TV except for an old movie we've all watched before. I avoid the news channels like the plague. Blackwoods is back on the map, whether we like it or not.

"He's hot," Hayley whispers, leaning back against my chest.

I stare at my phone screen. There's still no reply, and my messages remain unread. Where is this unease coming from? Maybe she's busy. But then again, it's late, and she should be at home by now.

Besides, Keira checks her phone regularly. Maybe she's with him. I heard from a buzzing fly that they were meeting up at

Blackwoods Bay, and that thought annoys me more than it should.

"Did you hear what I said?" Hayley asks, her lips close to my ear.

I dim my screen. "You think the actor is hot."

"More than hot."

After unlocking my screen again, I open social media.

"What do you say, Ava? Do you think he's hot?"

"I prefer the guy who plays his dad."

"His dad?" Hayley all but shrieks. "He's in his fifties or something!"

In my periphery, Ava shrugs. "I like them older."

I click on Keira's profile at the same time Jasper bursts out laughing.

"Didn't I say you're hiding a dark side?"

"So I'm hiding a dark side just because I find an old man in a movie attractive?" She snorts, taking a sip of her gin and tonic. "Yeah, right."

Keira hasn't posted in a few days. The latest photograph is a selfie of her and Cassie out on the quad between classes.

I scroll down, pausing at a picture of her and Liam. Against my better judgment, I follow the tag to his profile.

Big mistake.

Liam likes to show her off on his profile as though she's a fucking prize.

While she only posts the occasional picture of him, he posts a fuck ton more of her.

There are only so many pictures of them, smiling and kissing, that I can take before I want to smash my phone against the wall.

So maybe I like her more than I want to admit to myself.

And maybe that's why I avoid her in the daylight, away from the protection of night. Because despite me fucking her in every position imaginable while threatening her with a weapon or making her bleed with my blade or teeth, she goes back to him.

Every. Fucking. Day.

All the while, he's nothing but a fucking asshole who fucks around behind her back. Liam doesn't deserve her. He doesn't even know how to fuck her properly.

"You're thinking too hard," Hayley whispers, her breath scented with gin and tonic.

Grinding my teeth, I drop my head back against the couch, taking another sip of beer. The bottle is almost empty, but there's enough for another three large swallows.

Hayley watches me lean over the edge of the armchair and place the bottle on the coffee table.

"I'm not thinking too hard."

"You are. Let me guess. Keira."

"Keira again?" Jasper says, his arm still wrapped around Ava's shoulders. "Does she have a golden pussy or something?"

Hayley laughs, her shoulders shaking against me.

Staring at the TV, I press my thumb to the tip of each finger, back and forth.

"She has something," I admit.

JASPER

"Smoking will give you cancer," Kit teases, as he exits through the patio doors. It's cold as fuck tonight, and my breaths puff out in front of me. I take another deep drag of the cigarette pinched between my fingers, then blow the smoke out to the side and smirk. "What's the saying? You only live once."

Kit peers in through the patio doors to make sure no one is watching before taking the cigarette from between my lips. He takes a drag, his eyes squinting in the darkness. Then he tosses it to the ground and crushes it beneath his shoe.

"What the—" I chuckle disbelievingly, but he cuts me off as he shoves me back against the side of the house and sinks his teeth into my bottom lip. My cock jumps in my jeans, and my hands land on his hips.

"You're looking too fucking irresistible tonight," Kit growls.

I brush his brown hair away from his brow and kiss him again before whispering against his lips, "You should leave her."

His head shakes, and then he deepens the kiss as he snakes his arms around my neck. "It's more exciting to sneak around, don't you think?"

I hum into his mouth and palm the hard outline of his big cock through the rough fabric of his jeans. Spinning us, I press him up against the wall. "You this hard for me?"

Laughter drifts from the partially open patio doors while I kiss him slow and deep. Kit and I first hooked up about a month back when we had both had a few too many drinks one night.

I like him.

Probably more than I should.

But he's good fun and partial to dick when he's not pretending to be straight.

"Where did Kit go?" Kara's voice rings out from the living room.

"Fuck," he grits out, breathing harshly against my lips. "She'll come looking for me soon." His big hand fumbles with the button of my jeans, and he snakes it inside my boxers and palms my length.

Choking on air, I fist my hand and bite the knuckles. "Fuck, Kit..."

"I love it when you do that."

I lower my hand and crane my neck to look in through the patio doors. If anyone finds out about this, my fun with Kit is over. I don't want that to happen. I would rather sneak around with him than not get to have him at all.

"Do what?"

"Groan my name like that."

He nips at my neck with his sharp teeth before dropping to his knees in front of me.

As he lowers the front of my jeans, I bang the back of my head against the side of the house. "You're killing me."

Stroking my veiny cock, he flashes a dirty smile. "Have I ever told you that you talk too much?"

"Once or twi..." I trail off as he takes me into his hot mouth.

Holy fuck...

My thighs shake while he sucks me like a fucking pro.

I pull his short hair, too fucking aroused to make this last.

That's the thing about Kit. I can't control myself when he's on his knees in front of me.

The sight itself is so fucking erotic.

The way he looks up at me with his dark eyes that glint with a sparkle of amusement at seeing me so pent up.

But fuck... Kit has no idea how hot he is with his mouth full of my dick. And that silver ring on his thumb as he strokes my veiny cock.

I don't know what it is about that ring. But one thing is for sure: Kit has nice, masculine hands.

"Fuck, Kit," I grunt. "Suck me just like that."

He takes me down his throat, the way he knows makes me weak at the knees. My skin breaks out in a cold sweat.

I'm so fucking close.

I've been sucked off by a lot of girls, but none of them have gone down on me with half as much enthusiasm as Kit. It's wet, sloppy, and fucking noisy. He's on a mission to suck my soul from my body.

"Dammit," I grunt as my hips jerk.

I try to hold it off, but it's fucking impossible when he handles me like he was born to suck dick.

My balls draw up tight as pleasure pools low in my stomach. I come down his throat, biting back curses.

Rising to his feet, Kit makes a show of wiping his mouth with the back of his hand. "You look a little flustered."

The amusement in his voice makes my lips twitch. I roll my head on the back wall as I button my jeans back up. "You're enjoying this, aren't you?"

"Trust me," he chuckles. "I enjoyed it a fucking lot."

I fish a lighter and my packet of cigarettes from my pocket, biting one out. Kit watches me light it. I hold the packet out. "Want one?"

"I better go back inside."

The embers crackle as I inhale a breath, watching him through the curling smoke. "Alright."

He slinks back inside, and I exhale a sigh before bringing the cigarette back to my lips. Kit has never allowed me to make him come. He seeks me out to suck me or jack me, and then he leaves. He'll let me paint him in my cum, but he never wants me to return the favor.

And they say women are complicated.

I take a final drag and then crush the cigarette beneath my boot. The TV surround sound is loud. And from what I can hear, my friends are watching a car chase or something similar.

I turn to go inside but pause as the clouds part to let the moonlight slip through. Something red dangles from a branch in one of the fir trees.

Tilting my head, I squint. I still can't make out what it is, so I round the empty pool and walk across the sprawling lawn that's covered in a layer of frost. The grass crunches beneath my shoes as the clouds slip in front of the moon. The light gets snuffed out. It's too dark to see properly.

I retrieve my phone from my pocket, switch on the flashlight, and angle it toward the trees.

As I near, my steps slow. Dangling from the branch is a metallic, red devil's mask.

I pull it down from the branch, brows knitted, and scan my

flashlight over the forest. The silence is eerie out here, away from the blaring TV. Chills run down my spine as I scan the trees one more time before angling the flashlight at the mask. There's something written inside it.

I squint, looking closer.

You're next.

My head explodes with pain, and I fall to the ground. My cheek meets the frosty grass as a bloody rock rolls in front of me before coming to a stop a few inches away from my face. Groaning pitifully in the dark, I fade in and out of consciousness. I can't move. My limbs won't obey me.

"Time to die," a distorted voice taunts. My ankles are grabbed, and I'm dragged further into the forest, away from the lawn and out of sight. Pine needles and sharp twigs cut the skin at my stomach, where my T-shirt rides up.

I try to speak, to call for help, but my voice is nothing more than a pained murmur.

I fade out for a moment. When I come to, I'm on my side with the scent of damp moss and earth in my nostrils, while he ties my hands together behind my back. I try to scream, but there's duct tape over my mouth and eyes.

He rolls me over onto my back, and I kick out with my feet as he tries to grab them.

What the fuck is happening? I can't fucking breathe through this agony. My nostrils flare while I kick and scream, the sound muffled beneath the duct tape. I shuffle my shoulders, desperately trying to wriggle away. I can't see, which only heightens the fear.

He kicks me in the ribs, causing me to double over with pain. I sob, my sore wrists rubbing against the rope as I try to wrench free.

Despite my feral kicks, the monster finally overpowers me and ties my ankles together. Silence falls once more before his weight lands on my thighs. He straddles me and slips something cold beneath the hem of my T-shirt.

What the fuck? I lift my neck off the ground and kick out with my bound ankles, trying to buck him off me.

Fed up with my struggle, he grabs hold of my head and whacks it against the ground. The impact rattles my brain. I'm dizzy, my head lolling as the cold feeling returns.

"Lie still," he demands in his distorted voice. "Let's cut this T-shirt off your body."

The icy, cold scissors slide up my stomach and chest. He puts them down, and then something sharp is pressed to my belly button.

I begin to scream uncontrollably, and my chest constricts with panic. *Please. Please. Please. I don't want to die.*

My body jerks as red-hot pain rips up my belly and spreads up my chest like liquid fire.

His mask brushes against my ear. "This is how your friends will find you. Gutted like a fucking pig, in a sea of your own innards."

OFFICER WELLS

I t's icy cold, and the threat of snow hangs in the air. I pull up the police tape and duck beneath it, careful not to knock over any of the evidence markers on my way over to Riveiro, who crouches in front of the gutted, decapitated corpse.

The flash goes off as she takes another picture.

"What have we got?"

"Young male. Cut open from the stomach to the chest. The killer removed both the heart *and* the head."

I nod, scanning the corpse covered in pale innards, and the blood-soaked ground. The chest cavity has been pried open.

It's nothing I didn't expect.

Jimmy Hill did the exact same thing to his third victim.

Well, almost. "The removal of the head is a deviation from the original crime."

"Yes. Jimmy Hill removed the heart and kept it in a freezer in the garage, but he never decapitated any of his victims."

I scan the nearby vicinity. There's a flurry of movement as men and women, covered head to toe in white, scour the ground for evidence. "Where did you find the heart and the head?"

"We didn't."

My head snaps in Riveiro's direction. "What do you mean?"

"They're missing."

Rubbing a hand over my face, I let it drop by my side. This

case is proving to be too much. Whoever this killer is knows how to cover his tracks. Everything is perfectly planned out.

"And the victim?"

"The friends who found him confirmed his name is Jasper Massey." She rises to her feet and hands me a plastic zip bag. "This was found on the lawn, by the tree line."

The plastic rustles beneath my fingers as I shine a flashlight on the devil mask inside. "It's identical to the one in the changing room."

"There's writing on the inside."

I turn it over. "What did we find out about the mask?"

"Generic. Two of the leading retailers stock it, so it's impossible to track it down. By this time tomorrow, kids all over the country will have masks just like it. Sales have already sky-rocketed since the news first broke."

"And with Halloween around the corner..." I look up. "No DNA on the mask in the changing room?"

Riveiro shakes her head.

"You're next," I read aloud. "The killer likes to play games."

"Another deviation from Jimmy Hill."

I hand her the mask back. "Let's get the kids back to the station for questioning." After throwing one last glance at the corpse on the ground, I rub my hand down my face and add, "Let's get them counseling, too. God knows they'll need it."

KEIRA

King's lunch table remains empty for the rest of the week. None of them return to school for days.

According to the news, Jasper's friends found him murdered in the woods. The cops are tight-lipped about what happened to Jasper, but we all know it was bad.

The atmosphere at school is demure, and the other students give me a wide berth. I don't blame them. None of this would be happening if it weren't for my father.

Jessica, Principal Byrne, and Jasper would be alive. How can I not blame myself?

I stare at King's locker across the hall while Liam shuts his. Cassie is reapplying her lipstick in a pocket mirror, and Madison is leaning with her shoulder and temple against the locker beside me.

"They'll be back soon," she says quietly, as if she can see the worry on my face.

Slowly dragging my eyes away, I let my gaze trail over her raven hair. I'm so used to her bobble hat that I had forgotten what she looks like without it. She now has thick bangs that are slightly too long.

I reach out and finger a few of her silky-smooth strands. "Two of our classmates are dead because of me, and I never once spoke to them."

She leans in, lowering her voice. "Babe, you can't think like that. It's not your fault, okay?"

Releasing her hair, I punch her in the arm gently. "I like your new puffer jacket."

"You know me, it's my staple item."

I grab the straps of my backpack and lean my temple on the locker. "I miss the pink."

With a simple shrug, she smiles. "Red stands out more."

"True."

"I'm serious, Keira. You can't blame yourself for what's happened. It's not your fault!"

Before I can reply, Liam slides his arm around my waist from behind and pulls me into his chest. "I think we need a party this weekend."

"Did someone mention a party?" Marcus says as he joins us.

"It's nearly winter, and you're dressed in your letterman jacket?" Madison questions, removing a packet of bubblegum from her pocket. There's only one left. She pops it into her mouth, crumples up the empty packet, and tosses it at Marcus. "It's snowing outside."

"It's not snowing," Cassie says, rolling her eyes.

"It sure feels like it."

Marcus sidles up next to Madison and leans his back against the lockers. "I'm only young once, and wearing a letterman jacket is a privilege. One day, I'll be in my forties and reminiscing about the time I was a young, popular football player in high school."

Rolling her eyes, Madison pops her gum.

Marcus lifts his chin to the lockers across the hallway. "So, King and the rest haven't returned yet?"

"Do you blame them?" Cassie asks, pocketing her mirror. "One of their friends was murdered."

"They were close," I say quietly, and they all look at me.

Madison reaches out to squeeze my arm gently with a soft smile on her lips. Liam buries his nose in my hair and breathes me in before putting his lips to my ear and whispering, "Want me to stay with you after school?"

"No, I have that thing..." I don't. I just want to be alone.

He seems to understand because he steers me down the hallway. The others follow behind. Liam and Marcus discuss an upcoming game that was canceled at today's assembly. Their deep voices fade into nothingness as I walk toward the front doors looming up ahead. The rain outside lashes against the glass. It's a gloomy and miserable day.

Liam slides his arm from around me and walks ahead to open the door. I'm vaguely aware of Marcus's aftershave as he guides me forward with his hand between my shoulder blades.

We step outside into the chilly autumn afternoon. It was freezing this morning, but now it's milder. The weather forecast predicted a flurry of snow, but it's raining instead.

Wet, mushy leaves get crushed beneath my shoes as we hurry across the parking lot to where Liam's blue sports car is parked.

Cassie shrieks, holding her backpack over her hair. Marcus's warm hand is still on my back, and the heat in that one spot right between my shoulder blades remains my main focus as he opens the passenger door.

"Get inside, Keira."

So maybe I'm a mess and have been since the news broke. I got the name wrong in the changing room. If I had guessed Jasper's name, he would be alive now.

But he's not alive.

He's dead.

Marcus straps me in while Liam tosses his backpack in the backseat, where Cassie runs her fingers through her wet hair.

"See you tomorrow," Marcus says to Liam. "I'm driving Madison home."

The passenger door shuts and then Liam, seated sideways with his forearm on the steering wheel, clears his throat. "Are you sure you don't want to come back to my house, babe?"

"I'm sure."

Liam directs his attention to Cassie in the backseat. "You going straight home?"

While they talk, I stare out the window at the school building. It's dark outside because of the gloomy weather, so the lit-up windows look bright, but inside those gray walls dwells evil.

The principal was brutally murdered in his office, and a student was attacked in the bathroom. The killer has walked those hallways, blending in with the students.

As I look away, a shiver crawls down my spine. I can't help but feel like I'm being watched.

With a final glance in my direction, Liam starts the engine, but my gaze stays locked on the metaphorical blood on my hands.

"Play the game, Keira. Guess a name."

The central heating slaps me in the face as I walk through the doorway and toe off my shoes before kicking them to the side. The house smells of curry and a scented vanilla candle that sits on the console table in the lobby. Mom is cooking in the kitchen, and my stepdad is seated in the armchair in the living room, watching a replay of last night's football game.

I walk upstairs and hurry to my room, the steps creaking beneath my feet. My hair is soaked, and the strands have clumped together.

Pressing my shoulder to the door, I emerge into my bedroom and drop my backpack to the floor. It's dark, so I reach out to flip the switch while combing my fingers through my wet hair.

As I turn, I nearly jump out of my skin.

King sits at the edge of my bed with his elbows on his knees and his face in his hands. My room smells of him—bergamot, leather, and a hint of peppermint. How did I not notice it when I walked in?

He looks up when I cross the floor and, without speaking a single word, he reaches out, palms the backs of my thighs, and guides me between his legs. He's hauntingly beautiful, dressed in ripped jeans, a red T-shirt, and a worn leather jacket.

And maybe I'm a horrible person, but I like how destroyed he looks.

I like that his pain brought him here.

"You don't blame me for what happened to Jasper?" I whisper, stroking my fingers through his black hair. It's dry, unlike mine, so he must have been here for some time.

Instead of replying, he reaches up to pop the button on my jeans, and I hold my breath as he slides the zipper down before curling his fingers inside the hem of my jeans and panties.

King yanks them down my legs, and the momentum makes me gasp. I almost collapse against him, but he keeps me upright. His dark, haunted, and sinful eyes never leave mine. Not even as he leans in to taste me.

A deep rumble rings out in the silence as he burrows his tongue in my soaking slit. Every time he touches me, I fall more in love with his pain.

Reaching up, he digs his fingers into my ass and spreads me apart while continuing to nibble and suck on my clit. I can feel the lick of cold air against my exit and the fire that spreads closer when he drags a finger through my arousal before applying pressure to my asshole.

This time is different from the other times he snuck into my room and fucked me senseless. He brings me to the edge slowly. Licking and nibbling on my puffy cunt like it's his favorite pastime to eat me out.

I inhale a sharp breath when he forces two fingers inside my ass, his arm banded around my waist to keep me frozen. The sharp pain, along with his sinful tongue—currently buried so deep in my pussy that I'm shaking—create a symphony of demented pleasure that holds my heart in a vice.

"I'm gonna bury my cock so far up your ass, you'll feel me for a week."

The way he whispers the words against my clit before dragging his teeth over it has me moaning out loud. I clamp a hand over my mouth, so I don't alert my parents.

King unbuckles his belt one-handed while priming my exit with his fingers.

Just then, my stepdad shouts at the football on the TV. I should stop this. My parents are downstairs. I shouldn't let one monster fuck me in the ass, right under the nose of another monster.

Anticipation swirls in my veins when King slides his fingers from my ass and turns me around. His warm hand trails up my spine and applies pressure. I bend forward, placing my hands on my knees. As he spreads me apart and leans in to lick at my asshole, a satisfied groan rumbles in his chest.

"Oh, fuck," I whimper, pressing back. The pleasure is so

fucking intense, I'm struggling to stay upright. Liam has never eaten my ass. He's never even licked my cunt this dirty.

With a final slap to my backside, King orders me to lie down on my back on the bed.

After kicking off my jeans, I slowly lower myself down, careful not to collapse in a heap. King hasn't even fucked me yet and I'm already experiencing full-body trembles.

As soon as my back hits the mattress, he grabs my ankle and yanks me down to the edge of the bed. Then he bends me in half until my ankles are by my ears and instructs me to loop my arms around the backs of my knees. It's awkward at best, and I'm completely exposed to King with my cunt and asshole on full display.

I'm only naked on the bottom half, but King doesn't seem to care about my crop top or damp denim jacket. Not when my pussy is weeping with need and my cheeks are flushed.

"So fucking beautiful." Placing a knee on the edge of the mattress, he sinks two fingers inside my pussy and hooks them just right. "Did you miss me?"

"Yes…" My voice shakes. "I missed you, King."

It's true. I kept looking for him, hoping to see him in the hallways or in the cafeteria. I missed him even more at night as I lay awake, staring longingly at the windows. But the hours ticked by, and King never showed.

Now he's knuckle deep in my cunt, finger-fucking me like he's as starved for me as I am for him.

Removing his fingers, he smears my mouth with my own pussy juices. When I try to snatch his digits up with my teeth, he slaps my clit once, twice. "Naughty girl."

"King," I whimper, bearing down, and his eyes flick to my pussy as more desire seeps out and trickles between my ass cheeks.

"You're so fucking dirty," he groans, shoving his jeans down to his thighs. His hard cock bobs free, and I crane my neck to watch him stroke it. "Want me to fuck your ass, baby?"

I don't even hesitate as I nod. "Please..."

King fingers my cunt slowly and deeply, using my own arousal as lube while my stepdad shouts downstairs. The mattress shifts as he climbs on and rubs the head of his cock over my clit and through my slit until he's right *there*. "Ever been fucked in the ass before, Keira?"

My head shakes no. I'm too aroused to speak coherently. I just want him inside me.

King lets go to grip hold of my chin, pulling my bottom lip away from my teeth with his thumb. It's rough and dirty, just like him. "A virgin ass, I like that." As if to prove his point, he spits on my puckered hole and inserts a finger while watching me closely.

"King," I whimper, my clit pulsing almost painfully.

"You're a dirty little slut for my cock and fingers, aren't you, babe?"

I don't feel ashamed for being bared to him like this while he fingers my ass. Not when he looks at me with such raw lust in his heavy eyes.

While Liam fucks me and makes me come, King, on the other hand, devours me whole. He sees my perversion and matches it with his own.

His finger retreats, and he palms his dick, pressing into me. "Relax, don't push me out."

I hold my breath as burning pain rips through me. But it's a good kind of pain. The kind of pain that makes me forget all the other bullshit in my life.

At least while my ass is on fire, my heart ceases to hurt, and the pressure on my chest eases.

"You're taking my dick so well," King chokes out, one hand on the back of my thigh and his other on his cock.

"It hurts, King," I whimper, but he doesn't ease up on me or stop. If anything, he feeds on my pain and tears.

The head of his cock pops inside, and I squeeze my eyes shut against the burning pain. My ass feels like it's been doused in gasoline and set on fire. How can pain feel so fucking good? And why do I get off on it?

Why do I get off on knowing King likes to inflict pain?

Releasing the back of my thigh, he presses his palm over my mouth to muffle my soft sobs. "There's a good girl, keep fucking quiet for me."

Tears seep out from the corners of my eyes, trailing a path to my hairline while he rips through my virgin ass. I'm close to coming just from the degradation of being impaled by his cock while he keeps his hand over my mouth to keep me quiet.

"Sshh," he whispers, digging his fingers into my cheeks. "Quiet!"

Just when I think I can't take it anymore, he rams his cock all the way inside me, causing the headboard to crash against the wall.

Eyes flying open, I cry out. My nostrils flare as I pant through the excruciating pain and pleasure. There's something seriously wrong with me. I'm loving every single fucking moment of this.

"Look at you crying like a pathetic little whore while I fuck your ass. You think I can't see how much you love it? How greedy you are for my dick?"

I come.

Holy fuck...

His cock tears through me with each brutal thrust, and my cunt pulses while he fucks me hard and fast. I come again, cum leaking from my empty pussy.

King chuckles, ramming his fingers inside my throbbing, soaked cunt while his hips slam against my ass cheeks. "That's it, strangle my fingers with that greedy little cunt."

Each slide of him steals a piece of my soul. I stare up at him while he moves inside me like a revengeful god. His darkness wraps around my heartstrings, squeezing so tight that I can hardly breathe. King leaves no part of me untouched. Not my body. Not my soul.

"That's it," he growls, grinding his cock deep inside my ass. "Look at me like that. Let me see how much you want it."

Another relieved sob rips through me. My chest racks while the tears pour freely from my stinging eyes. I can finally let the darkness free that suffocates my soul. King nurtures it, coaxing it out to play as though he never wants to see it caged.

Sobbing uncontrollably, I come again.

With a final thrust, King collapses on top of me, spent and breathing hard. His cock twitches in my ass as his deep groan vibrates his chest. He rolls off me and drags a hand down his face, his dick glistening with my cum against his T-shirt. "You killed me."

We both stiffen, out of breath and sweaty. His cum seeps out of me when I lower my legs.

"I'm sorry. That came out wrong."

"It's okay."

"It's not." King pulls his jeans back up and fastens the belt. "It was fucking insensitive of me." Instead of leaving, he rolls over onto his side and pulls me into his body. I'm so shocked, I don't dare breathe. King always leaves after sex. Without exception. I don't know what to do, so I breathe him in—bergamot, peppermint, and a hint of sweat. I'm still naked from the waist down, but King makes no move to retrieve my jeans off the floor. Instead, he slides his hand down to my leg and hooks it over his hip. Using his arm as a cushion, he searches my face. "I couldn't face school this week... Jasper's empty seat in the cafeteria... The haunted look in my friends' eyes."

I press my finger over his lips. "You don't need to explain."

He nips it with his teeth, then replies, "I haven't slept for days. I have nightmares every time I close my eyes."

My heart hurts, and the urge to make his pain go away and soothe it somehow overwhelms me. Pushing up on an elbow, I slide my fingers into the silky, damp hair at the nape of his neck. "I'm sorry."

It's an inadequate thing to say. Especially when I wasn't there that night. I don't know what they stumbled upon in the forest, but the haunted look in King's eyes tells of unspeakable horrors.

Stroking my hair away from my brow, King swallows thickly. "What are you sorry for?"

"A lot of things..." I kiss him softly, inhaling his breath. When I lean back, I struggle to look him in the eye. "I'm sorry you're going through this. I'm sorry your friend died. I'm sorry that I can do nothing to help or make it stop. But most of all, I'm sorry to have put you in this situation."

His calloused fingers glide down my cheek, following my jaw line. He cups my chin. "You didn't put me in this situation."

"If you weren't fucking me—"

King cuts me off with a hard kiss. The kind of kiss that tells me to shut up.

Shoving him off, I throw my legs over the side of the bed and swipe up my jeans, but King steals them from me, wraps the pant leg around my neck, and proceeds to choke me with it. His gravelly voice rumbles in my ear. "None of this is your fucking fault."

My hands fly up, clawing at the denim fabric.

"Stop blaming yourself for shit you have no control over." Breathing me in, his nose dragging over my cheek, he whispers in my ear, "Besides, no one can keep me from your pussy. Not even you." With a sharp pull, he tightens the denim around my throat until I begin to struggle. In the midst of the sick depravity, one thought screams in my head: I love his strength and how he uses it to subdue me; his lust for violence and how he doesn't hold back when he's with me; the fact that he just fucked me in the ass and now he's strangling me with my own jeans because he can.

"Fuck, I missed you," he whispers as I gasp for air. "I missed the way you tuck your hair behind your ear when you concentrate on a task in class, and the sound of your laughter in the hallway between classes. It's rare, which makes it even more special. And it also makes me jealous of whoever made you happy enough to let your laughter bubble up from your chest. I want it for myself. I want it to be for my ears only, just like your moans and whimpers. I hate it when others get to see you smile or cry. All of your emotions belong to me. Each and every one. If you're horny, it's because I made you horny. If you're scared, it's because I'm chasing you through the forest. And if you're happy, it's because I make you happy."

My feet kick out on the bed as my nails claw my skin in the process of trying to pull the denim away from my throat.

I just need a breath.

My lungs scream with pain, and my cunt gushes. I'm so fucking horny.

King slides my pants from around my neck, and oxygen rushes back into my lungs. I cough and splutter, tingling all over.

When I finally look at King, it's with unrestrained desire in my eyes. He's lying back and stroking his hardening cock again, his arm behind his head, one leg drawn up. "I want your mouth on me."

KING

There's a cold draft coming from the windows, despite the thick curtains. I bet I'd see snow if I looked outside.

I should leave.

Keira is with Liam.

But like an addict, I watch her sleep as the first sliver of light crawls along the bed.

I have never stayed the night with Keira before. Never slept beside her. Not that I got much rest since I stayed awake all night to watch her sleep.

Call me a creep, but I can't get enough of her.

The thought crosses my mind of killing Liam. It's not the first time my mind has conjured up ways of getting rid of the boyfriend problem without incriminating myself. I could think of a hundred different ways, and they all end with Liam buried six feet under, where he belongs.

I want Keira to myself, and I hate the thought of him putting his hands on her or watching her sleep.

I like that when I'm with Keira, the rest of the world fades away, and all the other crap is just annoying background noise when she's around.

Keira's mine.

Not Liam's or anyone else's.

Only fucking mine.

My phone inside my jeans pocket burns my leg. The easiest way to eliminate Liam would be to forward Keira the picture I have of him and Cassie, but I don't want to use it just yet.

And maybe I like the idea of killing him? He has fucked her, after all.

I fucking hate knowing another man has felt her wrapped around his dick. The damn thought buzzes in my head like an annoying mosquito I need to crush beneath my palm.

Buried beneath the quilt, Keira stirs beside me before snuggling close. I don't dare breathe, and the foreign feeling inside my chest chokes me more than any hands could.

Until Liam is out of the picture, I can't let myself wake up next to Keira. I just won't let myself be that fucking vulnerable with her, and I refuse to let her see the power she holds over me. Not until he's gone.

With those thoughts swirling inside my head, I carefully extract myself from beneath Keira's arm that's wrapped around my waist.

It's easy to slip away when I'm already fully dressed. It's even easier to go unnoticed when the cops are asleep in the cop car.

KEIRA

I'm cocooned in the quilt as the bright morning sun rouses me. I wake to a rancid smell, and my nose scrunches up when I glide my hand across the cold mattress.

King is gone.

"King? What's that smell?" Blinking my eyes open, I push up on an elbow and rub my tired face before lowering my hand back down.

I stare at the empty pillow beside me.

Only it's not empty.

Buzzing flies.

Mottled blue, rotten, and maggot-eaten skin.

Empty eye sockets.

A gaping mouth.

Scrambling off the bed, I release a terrified scream, and my hand flies up to my mouth as I begin to retch at the sight of the severed head on the pillow. Footsteps sound on the stairs, and then my mom and stepdad burst through the door and come to a stumbling halt, their eyes widening. I'm still naked from the waist down, dressed in my crop top and denim jacket. The insides of my thighs are coated with King's crusted cum, but that's the least of my worries.

Collapsing to the floor, I empty my stomach's content. It churns violently while my stepdad runs to alert the cops outside.

He soon returns, pale and shaking, clutching the house phone in his hand. "They're dead..."

Crouched beside me and rocking me in her arms as though I am a toddler in need of comfort, Mom looks up at him. "What?"

"They're dead. The fucking cops are dead! There's blood everywhere..."

"What the hell are you talking about?" Her voice shakes.

My stepdad phones the emergency services while Mom leads me out of my room and downstairs to the kitchen. She guides me to sit at the table before putting the kettle on. Then she returns, pulling out the chair next to mine and taking my hands in hers.

"Everything will be okay, sweetheart."

"He was in my room," I whisper shakily, staring at the flowery tablecloth. *And King? Where is he? Is he okay? Did the killer murder him, too?*

Instead of replying, Mom stands up and proceeds to pour us each a coffee. She flurries around the kitchen while my mind replays the moment I opened my eyes and saw Jasper's severed head.

On my pillow.

The same pillow King slept on.

Mom disappears, returning a few minutes later with a pair of jogging bottoms. "Put these on, dear."

"The killer was in my room." My voice is stronger now. I look up at my mom as she holds my pants out. "When will it end, Mom? When will this nightmare be over?"

Her voice crackles with pain. "I don't know..." Then, weaker, "I don't know..."

Without looking away from her blue, glassy eyes, I accept the pants and get dressed in silence.

It doesn't take long for the house to swarm with police.

Officer Wells exchanges a few words with my mom and squeezes my shoulder reassuringly before disappearing upstairs with Officer Riveiro.

I'm lying on the hotel bed, gazing up at the ceiling, when my phone lights up with a message.

King: Why the fuck are you not at school?

I stare at the message for too long before letting my gaze trail to the large windows. The sky has clouded over, and the gloomy, gray weather matches the emptiness inside me.

I can't shake the image of Jasper's severed head. Every time I close my eyes, it's there. My room is now a crime scene, so Officer Wells set us up at a hotel for a few nights while they scour my room for evidence.

Mom is sitting on the bed beside mine and staring out of the window too, while my stepdad pours a cup of instant coffee.

The teaspoon clinks against the mug as he stands with his tense back to us.

No one speaks.

More messages light up my screen.

> Liam: Are you okay, baby? I'm getting worried.

> Cassie: Sienna and Amanda said your house is swarmed with cop cars. What happened? Are you okay?

> King: If you don't answer my messages, I'm gonna hunt you the fuck down. Why are there cop cars outside your house?

> Madison: Are you okay, babe? We're all worried about you.

I don't respond to a single one.

The guilt that festers in my heart is slowly eating me up from the inside. None of my friends are safe until I'm gone. I wish the killer would come after me and end this nightmare.

"I can't just sit here," Mom whispers.

My stepdad puts the spoon down carefully on the saucer, then slowly turns and takes a sip. "What are you going to do? Go to work and pretend like your daughter didn't wake up with a damn decapitated head on her pillow? Are you going to pretend everything is fine? That we're not displaced in a hotel room while the police dust every surface of the house for fingerprints?" He slurps his coffee, his tie hanging loose. "You're not a fucking robot."

With a scoff, Mom gets up off the bed and storms into the bathroom, slamming the door shut. She flips the lock and runs the bath.

My stepdad chuckles bitterly under his breath as he puts the scalding hot coffee down. His eyes land on me and his hand comes to his leather belt.

Like a tiger on the prowl, he stalks up to me and quickly unzips his pants. He leaves them open, and I spot the soft curls that peek through. He's commando.

"What the fuck are you waiting for?" he barks out, and my eyes flit to the bathroom door before I swallow thickly.

Mom could walk out at any minute, but that thought gets muffled beneath the storm of emotions that floods to the surface.

I finally feel *something*.

Against my better judgment, I flip over onto my front, shift onto my knees and reach for the pillow. It smells strongly of laundry soap as I place it over my head and wait for my stepdad to slide my jogging bottoms down.

He doesn't waste any time, pulling them halfway down my thighs and gripping my hips before slamming into me. It hurts like hell since he has made no effort to make me wet.

I keep quiet while he fucks me hard and dirty from behind to the soundtrack of slapping skin. The water sloshes in the tub behind the closed door, but my stepdad doesn't stop to make sure the coast is clear. He keeps fucking me, chasing his release like a crazed madman. His fingers dig into my bony hips as he finally rams into me one last time and shudders through his release.

As he steps back and tucks his dick away like he didn't hurt me in the best way possible just now, his cum seeps out of me. "Pull your pants up."

I obey, keeping the pillow over my head. There's a wet patch on my crotch. I can feel it.

"Good slut," he says, picking his coffee back up. I listen to him drink it in silence while my mom soaks in the tub until the water grows cold.

And when she finally emerges from the bathroom, wrapped in a towel, I'm asleep on the bed with the pillow still over my head.

OFFICER WELLS

Riveiro shakes me awake with a gentle hand on my shoulder. "Wells, you need to get home and rest."

I groggily lift my head off the desk. I'm back at the station, surrounded by paperwork and empty cups of coffee. I count at least three. "I'm fine."

Her dark eyes dance over my messy desk. Riveiro knows I haven't slept for days. Not more than an hour here or there. "What's on your mind, Wells? What's keeping you from going home to your wife?"

With my elbows on the desk, I rub my eyes. "The heart."

"The heart?"

"It's still missing."

Riveiro sighs, rubbing the back of her neck, her other hand on her hip.

"The killer is planning something with it. But what? Why wasn't it left with the head?"

"Maybe he simply wants to keep it as a souvenir."

The old desk chair creaks as I sit back. My shirt smells of sour sweat. It's been days since I had a shower. "The killer is always one step ahead of us."

Watching me carefully, Riveiro says, "Go home, have a shower, and get some rest."

"I need to read these reports." I fish them out of the pile of paperwork. There's a coffee stain on one.

"We won't get any further unless you sleep, Wells."

"You nag me more than my own wife."

Her lips twitch, and then she waves me off on her way out of the office. "Phone me if you find anything. I'm going home to catch a few hours of sleep."

Reaching for a coffee cup, I put it to my mouth and frown when I realize it's empty.

"Fucking typical."

KEIRA

It's fucking freezing tonight. Liam insisted I watch his game, so here I am, regretting my choice to wear my denim jacket. The red and black checkered scarf does little to keep the icy wind from creeping in through the fabric.

Beside me, Cassie unscrews the cap on her bottle of soda. She's been in a strange mood lately, even more so after my mom sent me to stay with Liam for a few days. She thinks it's healthier for me to strive for an ounce of normality than to stay locked up in a hotel room with my parents.

Though she fails to realize that by staying with Liam, I put him at risk.

I don't want anyone else to get hurt because of me.

"Have they said when you can return to your house?" Cassie asks, wrapped up in a thick, warm coat that reaches her ankles. It reminds me of a sleeping bag. I'm jealous.

"Not really. In the next few days, hopefully." I watch Liam, dressed in his navy blue, red, and white football uniform, sprint across the field with the ball. He gets tackled at the last minute.

"I can't believe your mom thinks it's a good idea for you to stay at Liam's."

The bitterness in her tone has me looking away from Liam on the field. "What do you mean?"

"You should stay with me."

She offers me a torn-open packet of Sour Punch, and I slide one out. Needless to say, it's sour as hell. I don't get how she can enjoy this stuff. It hurts my teeth and makes me scrunch up my nose.

The crowd around us erupts in cheers as Liam scores, and we stand up with them. Cassie cups her mouth and hollers while stomping her feet, but I can't shake the feeling of being watched. My eyes scan the immediate crowd but come up empty.

Even so, it's claustrophobic to be surrounded by so many people.

"Lighten up," Cassie tells me, nudging my shoulder with hers. "The killer isn't going to murder you in a crowd of thousands of people."

Her words are insensitive, considering two students and the principal are dead, but Cassie has always been someone who doesn't think before she speaks. Sometimes, her mouth moves before her brain has caught up. And sometimes, she notices.

But not today.

Her eyes stay glued on the football field, where Miles and Liam chest bump. The masculinity on show has me rolling my eyes.

Reaching for another Sour Punch, I fish my phone out of my pocket and angle the screen away from Cassie.

> Madison: I found this jacket online and it made me think of you. It has Keira written all over it.

I follow the link, smiling to myself when an image of a puffer coat designed to look like a denim jacket pops up on the screen.

> Keira: If you had it your way, everyone would wear puffer jackets.

> Madison: Admit it, it's perfect. You get to continue your love affair with denim while also staying warm. It's a win/win for everyone.

"Are you talking to Madison?" Cassie asks, her voice thick with distaste.

"I don't get why you dislike her so much."

"She's an entitled bitch."

Chuckling, I take another bite of the piece of candy in my hand. It's still just as sour. "I think you're a little hard on her."

"You just like her because she's *quirky.*"

"Or maybe I like her because she makes an effort? Friends are hard to come by when you're Jimmy Hill's daughter."

"You're dating the quarterback," Cassie points out, staring at the football field. "You're popular by default."

"Popularity doesn't equal friends. Besides, Liam is only with me for my notoriety."

"I thought you didn't want friends?"

"I don't want *false* friends."

The crowd erupts in cheers again, and I reluctantly rise to my feet. I'm frozen to the bone by now, my lips turning blue.

"You don't want false friends, but you'll date a boy that you claim is only with you because of your family history."

"You're very judgy today."

We sit back down.

"You're contradicting yourself."

My teeth chatter as I jiggle my knee to keep warm. "We've had this discussion before, Cassie." I nudge her shoulder with mine again. "It's easy with Liam."

I expect her to laugh like she always does, but she stays silent, and her lips curl back into a sneer before she trains her gaze forward.

It gets my back up. *Fuck her!* I should ask her what's wrong and why she's so off with me, but I just don't have the damn energy to care. She can sit on her soap box somewhere fucking else.

I rise to my feet and push past her legs. Of course, she doesn't offer to move out of the way. I don't know what the hell her problem is. I've had a shit week, and the last thing I need is for her to sit and tell me how I should live my life. She can make her own mistakes and leave me to make a fucking mess of my own life.

My phone vibrates in my hand as I mumble apologies, bumping into people's knees on my way to the side stairs.

Unknown number: Let's play a little game.

I pause as my heart jumps to my throat. The person in front of me grumbles, shouting at me to move. I shuffle sideways out of the aisle.

Another incoming message has me pressing a hand over my mouth. It's a picture of Madison, seated at the movies, with her hand in a bag of popcorn and her ankles crossed on the seat in front of her. Trust her to go to the movies by herself after she was attacked in the bathroom.

I quickly bring up her latest text message, but another text pops up on my screen before I can type out a response.

Unknown number: Warn her, or anyone else, and she dies.

My hands shake violently as my breaths puff out in front of me.

Me: What do you want from me?

Unknown number: Leave the stadium and take the trail that leads through the woods toward the gas station.

I consider my options before walking down the steps with trembling legs. The cold doesn't register anymore. Nothing does, except for my hammering heartbeat.

One step. Two. Peering to my left, I stare blindly at the hundreds of faces on the bleachers. No one notices the tears on my cheeks or the fear that is slowly strangling me. I gulp down breaths as I reach the ground. The noise from the football game on the field fades out until it's nothing more than a hum.

Exiting the stadium, I look left to right. The parking lot is empty. An empty soda can rolls across the ground, and the sound is so loud to my ears that I jump.

Unknown number: Now walk.

I swallow down a whimper, clutching the phone in my hand. The walk across the parking lot seems impossibly long.

Keira: Don't hurt Madison.

Unknown number: Play the game, and I won't.

The icy wind licks at my cheeks and creeps beneath my clothes. I shiver, but not from the cold. Eyes follow me as I slowly walk through the parking lot.

Unknown number: The movie finishes at 9:30 tonight. Plenty of time to pay her another little visit. Walk faster unless you want your friend to die.

The whimper that I swallowed down earlier bubbles back up and slips from my lips. Another sob follows, and I press my hand over my mouth as I quicken my pace.

The tree line is just up ahead. Blackwoods' trail is popular with middle-aged dog walkers and families with young kids, but not on a night like tonight when the game is on.

Football is a huge thing here in Blackwoods, and it's sacrilege not to attend the games, which is also why Madison is alone at the movies. She's the only one who doesn't care about sports.

Sticks break beneath my shoes as I enter the trail, the parking lot at my back. It's so dark in here that the moonlight struggles to break through the canopy of leaves overhead.

With trembling hands that are cold and wet from wiping my cheeks, I unlock my phone and scan the path up ahead with the flashlight. Tall spindly trees with branches that resemble crooked, fanged demons seem to reach for me. Each step I take is accompanied by the violent thuds of my heart in my head.

He's playing with me. I know he is.

Feeding on my fear while hiding in the shadows.

"Show yourself," I shout, my voice cracking. "You're a fucking coward!"

Silence reigns thick and heavy as I spin in a circle, imagining shadows crawling out from between the spindly trees. I release another sob, my chest constricting with icy-cold dread.

My phone vibrates in my hand.

> Unknown number: Who should I kill next? Madison or Miles? But think long and hard before you answer. If you spare Madison, someone else you care dearly about will also pay the price.

I grow even colder, if that's possible.

> Unknown number: Your friend or your boyfriend's? Pick one.

My numb fingers fly across the screen. In my panic, I mistype several times.

> Keira: I'm not choosing.

> Unknown number: Then you'll have both of their deaths on your conscience.

> Keira: You promised me you wouldn't hurt Madison if I played the game.

> Unknown number: And I won't. If you spare her life.

But then someone else I care about dies.

It's an impossible situation, and I lose regardless. If I don't pick, he'll go after Miles and Madison. If I spare my friend's life, he'll kill Miles and someone else close to me.

If I pick Miles, Madison dies.

No matter what I do, someone dies.

> Keira: please don't do this.

> Unknown number: Tick tock.

> Keira: I can't choose. Don't make me choose.

Sobbing, I scan the trees again.

> Unknown number: Is that your final answer?

> Keira: Fuck you!

A picture of the outside of the movie theatre comes through.

> Unknown number: You have made your choice.

"No. No. No," I whisper, typing.

> Keira: Miles, I pick Miles.

> Unknown number: Good choice.

"FUCK!" I roar, my hands flying to my hair.

A leather-gloved hand clamps over my mouth, and I release a

startled scream, trying to wrench free as warm, moist lips whisper against the side of my cheek, "Calm down, it's me."

I break free from King's grip and spin around. "Get away from me!"

Puffs of cold air leave his lips while he studies me with a small frown between his eyebrows.

"It's you. You're the killer. All this time," I point an accusing finger at him, "it was you."

"What the fuck are you talking about?" he growls, stepping closer when I inch back.

Wet leaves stick to the soles of my shoes, and the shell of a snail gets crushed as I pocket my phone and slowly back away. "What are you doing here, King?"

"I saw you leave the football stadium."

"You don't attend the games." One more step. I don't take my eyes off him.

Dressed all in black, King blends with the shadows and moves with lethal power. "Do you seriously think I'm the killer? That I murdered my own friend?"

"You tell me, King. Isn't it convenient that you show up at the same time the killer is taunting me through text messages?"

King's face twists with anger. "He's doing what?!"

"Don't play innocent with me. I'm not that fucking naive."

He moves toward me, but I take two steps back. King pauses, watching me closely before charging for me. His thick arms band around my waist, and he easily overpowers me as I continue to struggle.

"Calm the fuck down."

I kick, claw, even fucking bite.

King grunts from the effort of restraining me, and I soon tire, growing listless in his arms.

"Why are you doing this? Playing these games?" My voice is as choked as my sobs.

Spinning me around, King grips my shoulders. "What are you talking about, Keira?"

"The text messages."

With a sharp huff, King digs his phone out of his back pocket, lights up the screen, and angles it at my face.

Squinting, I grab hold of the phone and scroll through the history of messages. There's nothing there. The latest message is from the other day when I left him on read.

King snatches the phone from my grip. "Satisfied now?"

"You could have another phone in one of your pockets."

King glowers at me, a muscle clenching in his jaw. "Why don't you go ahead and strip search me?"

When I fail to respond, he shoulders off his jacket and tosses it to the cold ground before pulling the back of his T-shirt over his head. It falls to the sticks and leaves on the damp, trodden trail. His hands come to his jeans button, and he pops that, too.

"What are you doing?" My voice is barely above a shaky whisper.

"Showing you that I have nothing to hide. I'm not the fucking killer."

"It's freezing out here, King."

"Maybe you should have thought of that before you accused me of killing my own fucking friend." He shoves his jeans down his thighs, then his boxers. "You're not the one who found him in the woods. I am." He points at his chest. "I found his gutted and decapitated body."

I stare dumbly while he kicks off his jeans and boxers and cups his junk.

"Go ahead and check my clothes. Maybe you want to check my ass, too? Maybe I hid it in there."

I feel stupid now. It's so cold that my breath puffs out with every exhale as King stands naked before me, visibly shivering.

"Check them."

"King..." I whisper.

"CHECK THEM!" he roars, and I flinch.

"Fine, okay." I crouch down, wiping my wet cheeks with the denim sleeves of my jacket. King waits silently while I search his pockets.

Except for a house key, a wallet, and a packet of chewing gum, there's nothing.

Rising to my feet, I hand him his clothes, and he pulls them on while I sniffle pathetically.

"Can we move past your paranoid shit now?"

I start to reply but then I remember the choice I made, and my eyes widen.

I set off running.

"Keira?" King calls after me.

"He's gonna kill Miles. We have to stop him."

LIAM

We lost. The atmosphere in the changing room is about as quiet and tense as you can imagine. It was an important game—one we couldn't afford to lose. But lose, we did.

Chris sits with his head in his hands, not in any hurry to have a shower while the rest of us strip out of our clothes.

Miles and I exchange a look.

"You okay, man?" I ask Chris, pulling my sweaty jersey off and letting it drop to the floor.

Chris shakes his head as the room fills with steam and bare asses. "You won't believe what I did."

Miles runs a hand through his dark hair, the towel around his hips threatening to slip to the floor. "You told Amanda that you want a threesome?"

"I made a bet with Rodrigues that we would win the season."

I pause, towel in hand. "Rodrigues? *The* Rodrigues? The fucking drug mule?"

Rodrigues is a well-known dealer here in Blackwoods. He's the type who has a hand in everything and not someone you want to get involved with.

Chris nods, breathing out a ragged breath behind his hands.

"What do you mean, you made a bet?" Miles asks carefully, and we exchange a glance.

"I scored some drugs off him last year. He invited me to meet some of his cronies, and we drank alcohol and smoked weed. I thought he was alright."

"And?"

"He pulled a fucking gun on me and demanded I pay him $200,000. Said my trust fund was good for it."

"And then what happened?"

Chris finally lowers his hands. "I don't fucking have that kind of money, so I made a different deal instead."

"What deal?" I bite out, sensing this is going nowhere good.

"I didn't want to die, okay? I wasn't fucking thinking clearly. I just agreed to anything to get out of there."

"What deal did you make, Chris?"

Swallowing thickly, Chris puts his elbows on his thighs and pulls sharply at his hair. "He said he'd give me an out: win the season and walk away unharmed." His eyes are wide when he looks up at us. "We murdered the competition last season, so I thought we had it in the bag."

I slam a locker shut. "You're so fucking stupid sometimes, Chris."

"I wasn't fucking thinking clearly. What part of 'I had a gun pressed to my temple' didn't you fucking get?"

"What would happen if we lost the season?" Marcus asks, shutting his locker and turning around.

Chris's face drains of color, and he goes back to pulling his hair. "He and his friends get to take turns with Amanda for a night."

"What the actual fuck?!" I blurt.

Miles is speechless, staring at Chris.

Pulling his T-shirt over his head, Marcus chuckles.

"Say something," Chris mumbles, and Miles snaps out of his stasis.

"You offered your own fucking girlfriend up as a cash price?"

"No, I didn't. It was Rodrigues's idea."

"Of course it was." Miles shakes his head, rubbing his hand over his mouth. "Jesus fucking Christ. Does she know?"

I walk over to the showers. "Do you think they'd still be together if she did?"

I'm about to step into the shower when the door to the changing room flies open, and Keira stumbles through. Her eyes widen, and she covers them with her hands.

I would ask her why the fuck she's in the boys' locker room, but my eyes catch on King as he steps through the doorway. He looks like a fucking serial killer, dressed head to toe in all black, those dark eyes of his skating over the room until they land on mine.

The fucker smirks.

I tie the towel around my waist and stride over to Keira, gripping her arm tightly. "What the fuck are you doing in here?" I lower my voice. "With him?"

Her wide, glassy eyes lock on mine as she lowers her hands from her face, and the panic in their blue depths makes me pause. "The killer messaged me. He's going after Miles next."

Miles's head snaps up in my periphery.

Looking past her shoulder at King, my gaze darkens. I bring the full beam of my attention back to Keira. "Are you sure about this?"

Her tears spill over, and she nods. "I'm sure."

"Fuck..." I point an accusing finger at Chris. "As if we haven't got enough shit to deal with."

"In my defense, Rodrigues scored me drugs before it all kicked off."

"He was probably just messing with you," King drawls, his hands in his pockets.

I sneer at him. "Stay out of it, King. You don't even know what the fuck the deal was."

"Let me guess. Rich boy here scored drugs, Rodrigues pulled a gun on him and made some weird bet. If your boy lost, Rodrigues would fuck his girlfriend?"

We all stare at him. Well, everyone except for Keira, who's gazing at the floor.

"What are you saying, King?" Miles asks carefully, reaching for his clothes. He's clearly given up on a shower.

"Rodrigues has no shortage of willing pussy. He just wanted to see your friend here sweat. Probably laughed about it for days after."

"So he's not gonna come after Chris's girlfriend?"

King shrugs. "Unlikely."

I step closer to King. He's a few inches taller than me, which pisses me the fuck off. "How do you know this? You close to Rodrigues?"

King's lips tilt and then he steps closer, too. "We run in different circles, you and I."

My eyes narrow, but Keira's shaky voice breaks our stare-off.

"We need to call the police."

"I'm already on it," Chris replies, phone held to his ear.

"Something about this doesn't feel right," I mutter as Chris talks to the person at the end of the line.

"What do you mean?" Miles asks, sliding his gray hoodie on over his white T-shirt.

"Why would the killer announce who's next? Why make it harder for himself? He knows we won't leave your side now."

"Maybe because it's a distraction," King drawls again.

His voice is starting to get on my last nerve. I turn on him. "Why the fuck are you still here? And why are you hanging around my girlfriend?"

There's that smirk again, the one that whispers, *I know something you don't.*

"I found her outside, visibly shaken up."

I grind my teeth so hard I worry I'll do damage. "And now you can leave."

King slides his dark gaze to Keira, so I pull her into my arms. Her freezing cold fingers dig into my bare chest. King's smirk falters, but he masks it well.

Without another word, he walks back out.

"What did they say?" Marcus asks Chris when he pockets his phone.

"They'll send someone over, and you'll be shadowed by an officer."

"Because that went so well for Keira," Miles mutters, sitting down on the bench to tie his shoelaces.

"It could be worse," I point out. "If King is right, then at least we don't need to worry about Rodrigues."

"Can we go back to your house?" Keira whispers quietly. "I want to leave."

I guide her down onto the bench, reaching for my clothes, which are crumpled in a pile beside her. "Let me get dressed first." To Chris, I say, "Are you okay with staying with Miles and Marcus until the police get here?"

KEIRA

Liam snores beside me in the bed, asleep on his front with his muscular arms beneath the pillow and one knee peeking out through the quilt, where it has tangled itself around his legs.

I admire his ability to sleep after everything that's happened. While he's been snoring away, I have stared at the windows for too long, listening to the sound of a fox barking outside and clutching my phone in my hand until my fingers went numb.

The killer has my phone number.

In the end, after hours of anxiety, I powered down my phone and placed it beside the half-empty glass of water on the nightstand. I haven't looked at it since.

The killer said someone close to me would die if I spared Madison's life, but what if King was right? What if it was a distraction? What if someone else gets murdered tonight?

The longer I lie awake, the more the haunting thoughts taunt me. I try to snuggle up to Liam, but he's too warm, so I flop onto my back and stare at the long shadows on the ceiling.

When that doesn't work, I roll onto my front and watch the minutes tick by on the digital clock. No sooner have I started to drift off after hours of tossing and turning than a heavy weight presses me down on the mattress, and the smell of bergamot, leather, and peppermint swirls around me like a heady concoction.

Warm, moist lips smirk against my ear. "Did you miss me, baby?"

King fists my hair with one hand and pulls the blonde, tangled strands at the same time he shoves Liam's jersey up over my ass. "Did you let him fuck you tonight?"

My boyfriend snores softly beside me as King slides his calloused fingers between my ass cheeks, then lower until he circles my entrance. He shoves three digits inside me, finger-fucking me with abandon.

"Did you?" he whispers gravelly again, his thumb pressing into my asshole.

My scalp prickles, my ass stings, and my pussy burns. I want more. With a shake of my head, I arch against him, silently begging for more.

Maybe it's wrong to let King finger-fuck me while my boyfriend is fast asleep next to us, but the truth is that I need King's depravity. I need him to hurt me and call me names while dicking me into the mattress.

I don't even care that Liam is right next to us.

It only excites me more.

And King knows it.

He gets off on it, too.

"Listen to the wet sounds your pussy makes. It's a greedy little cunt, isn't it?"

I bite my pillow. If I don't, I'll moan out loud and wake Liam.

"What do you think he'll do to me if he wakes up and finds me fingering his girlfriend's cunt? And what do you think he'll do to you for being such a slut?" King shuffles behind me and slides his fingers from my cunt before shoving the front of his jeans down. He slaps his hard dick over my slit and then takes me in one go. His hand snakes beneath my body to rub at my clit, while he fucks me nice and slow so as to not wake Liam. Each delicious slide of his big cock has shivers racing up and down my sweaty spine.

I turn my head and stare at Liam's face. Drool slips from his partially open mouth, and his long lashes rest against his tanned cheeks.

King's lips find my ear, his ragged breaths hot on my skin. His hand presses down between mine and Liam's face on the soft mattress as he picks up his pace, fucking me harder as if he, too, doesn't give a shit if Liam wakes up.

Maybe he wants him to.

Maybe he wants Liam to watch him fuck me.

But Liam doesn't wake up. He stays asleep the entire time.

King slides his cock out, climbs off the mattress, and guides me to kneel beside the bed on the cold, wooden floor like a good girl performing her nightly evening prayers. And then his hand is back in my hair, and his fingers dig into my hips while he fucks me so hard from behind that my tits bounce wildly inside Liam's jersey.

By the time he finally pulls out and spins me around, coming all over my face, my knees have friction burns and my scalp stings with pain.

He slips back out through the window like a burglar in the night, leaving me ruined and throbbing between my legs from multiple orgasms.

After wiping my face clean with one of Liam's discarded T-shirts, I climb back into the warm bed, sated and exhausted from the adrenaline of doing something so forbidden. Within minutes, I'm fast asleep.

"How much have you had to drink?" Jasper laughs as I struggle to pour the vodka into the two plastic mugs sitting on the counter. Most of it spills on the already sticky surface. The music in the living room is loud, but the sound is muffled here in the messy kitchen. Jessica's dad will be pissed if she doesn't get this place tidied up before he arrives back tomorrow. Red plastic mugs litter every surface, along with empty bottles of alcohol and an empty package of string cheese.

"Here, let me pour it." Jasper moves me out of the way, but he's just as drunk and high. We soon end up laughing almost hysterically. I don't even know what's so fucking funny.

I take the bottle from him, place it on the sticky countertop, and grab his muscular arm to steady myself. My fingers dig into his bicep, and I'm suddenly aware of how good he feels. Something inside me stirs, and my dick jumps in its denim confines. He slides his hand behind my neck and slams his lips to mine before backing me against the counter. It's so sudden and violent that I gasp into his mouth as undeniable, fiery pleasure pools low in my stomach.

Thoughts of my girlfriend, Kara, who is somewhere around— probably dancing with Jessica, Hayley, and Ava—are far from my mind as Jasper's fingers dig into my trim waist and tangle in my short hair. My own hands slide up his hard chest, the soft fabric creasing against my palms. I explore every muscle, every dip and curve. Where Kara is soft and smooth, Jasper is hard and defined and so fucking broad.

"Fuck, Kit," he groans, kissing me so deeply that my lungs start to

burn. As our rock-hard cocks grind together through the rough fabric of our jeans, I swear I nearly come. I always thought I was straight, but this is on another planet entirely. I want my mouth on his veiny cock. I'm burning up beneath his skilled hands, prickly stubble, and warm lips.

A light tap on the window steals me away from my memories. Ever since Jasper's murder, I have been a shadow of my former self. Jessica's death shook us all, but Jasper's...

We had hooked up for a few months when the killings started happening. I knew Jasper wanted more, that he was willing to wait while I sorted out whatever internal bullshit was raging a war inside me. But in all honesty, I don't think I would have ever left Kara. Jasper and I wouldn't have stood a chance in a small, backward place like Blackwoods. It takes a certain type of character—someone like Jasper—to be brave enough to go against the grain.

I always admired that about him. He was unapologetic in many ways, and stepping out of the closet was his last hurdle. He would have done it in a heartbeat if I had left Kara.

I always touched him—never the other way around. I would suck his dick but not let him return the favor.

While I wanted to, it was my way of keeping distance between us. I was falling for him. But I'm not brave, unlike Jasper.

And now I'm riddled with guilt.

Amongst all of my fucked-up emotions keeping me up at night, I miss him.

I miss how we laughed until we cried when we were alone and how he used to brush his fingers against mine as we walked into the classroom. It was only a light touch, but I felt it down to my core.

Sliding out from beneath the sheet, I place my feet on the cold floor. One look at the alarm clock confirms it's three in the morning.

With my elbows on my knees, I drag my hands through my

dark hair before sliding them back down over my face and blowing out a ragged breath. Sleep deprivation is now my nightly visitor.

Every time I close my eyes, I'm assaulted with memories from the night when we found him in the woods. I struggle to merge that vivid image of horror with the laughing, blonde-haired boy I fell for.

"Screw this," I mutter, rising to my feet.

As I step out into the hallway, I'm met with the sound of my father's loud snoring. It's a mystery how my mom can sleep in the same room as him.

I make my way downstairs to the kitchen, bleary-eyed and exhausted. The cold air bites at my bare skin, and I regret leaving my room in my boxers.

After switching on the light, I pause when I spot a box on the kitchen island in the middle of the room. It's a small, square box wrapped in black tissue. It sits there, ominous and chill-inducing.

I hesitate, looking left and right. My eyes sweep over the tall windows. It's pitch-black outside. Darkness presses in against the glass, lined at the edges with a layer of frost, like thick smoke.

Inhaling a steadying breath, I walk up to the island with slow, careful steps.

On top of the box is an envelope with an image of the devil. I stare at it for too long. The crimson face contrasts brightly with the crisp white envelope, and the cruel, sinister smile reveals fanged teeth and a slithery forked tongue.

I recognize it for what it is—the killer's calling card. A devil's mask was found near Jasper's body.

Against my better judgment, I reach for the card, turn it over in my clammy hands, and slide a finger beneath the sealed flap. A blood-red card peeks out from inside, and I slide it out while my heart pummels my chest.

As I open the card, a polaroid picture falls onto the marble surface. I stumble back, staring wide-eyed at the photograph of Jasper bound on the ground. Strips of gray duct tape cover his mouth and eyes. He was still alive. The killer stands over his body, photographing him.

My eyes flick to the card that lies beside the photograph. Icy dread slithers down my spine as I carefully pick it up and read the scrawled handwriting.

You stole his heart and toyed with it like a selfish little fuckboy, and now you get to keep it, like your very own souvenir.

With a shaky hand, I place the card back down and reach for the box, the tissue crinkling loudly in the silence while I carefully unwrap it.

My heart beats viciously behind my ribcage, and my throat is so clogged with a mixture of gnawing fear and trepidation that it's a miracle I manage to slide the lid off and place it down carefully beside the photograph. There's more tissue inside, hiding its contents.

A rancid, stomach-churning smell hits my nose, and I press my hand against my mouth, gagging behind my palm. My insides twist and coil.

Lowering my hand, I hold my breath so as to not empty my stomach content on the kitchen floor while I shift the tissue out of the way.

Inside are the remains of a rotten, decomposing heart.

Jasper's heart.

My own heart slams its fists against my chest, and I scramble back, only to fall on my ass. The pain in my tailbone is the last thing on my mind when I roll over and proceed to puke until my stomach lining burns and there's nothing left but bile.

I should hear the approaching heavy footsteps as they cross the kitchen floor to where I lie in a pool of my own vomit, but I don't.

Not until it's too late.

A sharp blow to my head knocks me out, my body collapsing to the floor. Darkness seeps in at the corners of my eyes, blackening my vision. A pained groan slips from my lips as my ankles are grabbed, and I'm dragged through the kitchen, leaving a trail of half-digested carrot pieces and sweetcorn behind.

I wake to the sound of an insistent drip. To my left is a hole in the roof, where the rain is leaking through. My head throbs, and blinding pain shoots through my skull when I look around the empty room.

Where the fuck am I?

It's an abandoned shed, large enough to fit a car. An icy, cold wind is blowing in through a hole in the roof, and I shiver. I'm still in my boxers, with my wrists and ankles tied to a metal chair. My fingers and toes are so numb I can barely feel them. How long have I been here, tied to this chair?

When a red light flicks on in front of me in the darkness, I pause. It's a video camera, I realize. Mounted on a tripod.

I'm being filmed.

Glacial, cold panic flares up inside me, and I begin to struggle against the restraints, pulling and tugging. Coppery blood beads on my wrists and ankles, the pinching pain drawing sharp hisses through my clenched teeth.

In my struggle, the chair topples over, and my temple connects with the wooden floorboards in a hard blow. I groan with pain as the sickly scent of damp, rotten wood settles in my nostrils.

Precious minutes tick by while I try to shake off the dizziness. I'm vaguely aware of a devil's mask peering down at me and gloved fingers trailing over a bleeding cut on my cheek before fisting my short hair and forcibly pulling me up. My scalp screams with agonizing, prickly pain. I don't recognize the tortured sounds escaping my lips.

I also don't recognize the stream of pleas that dance on my tongue and crackle in the cold darkness.

The masked man walks around me, the coldness of his mask brushing up against my bleeding cheek as he whispers, "Look in the camera, fuckboy. Let's play a little game."

A nip of teeth, and then a warm tongue slides up the inside of my thigh. I'm powerless when his heated breath glides over my soaking slit like a filthy lover's caress. I cry out and arch my back off the mattress as he blows on my pussy. Fuck, I need more.

"Please," I whimper, my hips lifting off the mattress in search of more pressure.

Warm hands clamp down on my thighs and spread me wide open as a distorted, twisted voice taunts, "Let's play a little game."

I startle awake with a gasp, my eyes flying open as an orgasm steals my breath. It's so strong and unbidden that my cunt jerks against Liam's hot mouth. The sensation is too much, and I bite down on my hand to stop myself from waking his parents with a scream.

He pops out from beneath the quilt with a look of masculine satisfaction on his face, his mouth wet with my cum. "Morning, babe."

"What the hell?" I check the time. Four hours ago, I came on King's cock, and now I came on Liam's tongue. I'm spinning a web of lies and deception. And I know I should come clean, but I can't bring myself to do it.

Not with Liam.

Not with King.

And certainly not with myself.

Climbing up the bed and flopping onto his back, Liam palms his hard cock. "My turn."

I watch him stroke it, a salty drop of white precum forming on the thick head. As I slide out from the quilt, the bead trails down the girthy length, following the line of one of the protruding, purple veins on his cock.

His big hand moves up and down the shaft with skilled strokes. He kicks off the quilt and grabs the back of my neck. "Come here, babe."

I let him guide me down, his fingers gripping me tight. It hurts, but it's what I need to feel alive when all I want is to succumb to the darkness.

Sliding further down the bed, Liam puts an arm behind his head while watching me suck his cock. "I'm so fucking lucky to have a girlfriend who knows how to suck dick."

He says it every time I give him a blow job. I'm sure it's supposed to be a compliment, but it makes me feel cheap.

King's words come back to me. *"What do you think he'll do to you for being such a slut?"*

If only Liam knew...

"Fuck, yes, that's it."

I love to suck cock, and I do it a lot. But for the first time, I wish it was King instead of Liam.

And that thought worries me more than I want to admit to myself. I can't afford to grow attached to King, or anyone, for that matter.

So why do I tune out my boyfriend's praise, imagining King in his place? Why do I almost come just from the thought of sucking off King?

Why do I wish it was King I woke up next to? And why do I consider breaking up with Liam?

I've lived this unfulfilled, safe life for a long time. So, I don't love Liam. What's the problem? He's good for me. He brings me out of my shell, forcing me to be social when it would be so simple for me to become a hermit.

And he's safe.

Unlike King, Liam isn't in love with me, despite what he thinks. Obsessed, maybe. But not in love.

I'm not so sure about King... The way he looks at me sometimes at school when he thinks I'm unaware... And the fact that I want him to keep looking at me like that...

It needs to stop. I'm not someone to fall in love with.

I'm the daughter of a monster. Deep inside me, waiting and watching, lurks the same evil that runs through my father's veins.

I'm a monster in my own right. Maybe I haven't murdered people *yet,* but I hurt them.

I break hearts.

I use others.

I'll do anything to put a balm on my own hurt.

"Fuck..." Liam grunts, his cock jerking at the back of my throat. I stare up at him, my mouth stuffed with his dick. At least while his cock is twitching on my tongue, I won't question why I dreamed about the killer and the kinds of fucked up that makes me.

Glad to be rid of the heavy books, I place them in my locker. The others aren't back from the library yet. It's just Cassie and me. She hasn't spoken a word to me since the game, but I can feel her watching me now while she worries her lips. She wants to say something but doesn't know how to. Cassie has always been proud, and it's her biggest weakness.

Surprising me, she sighs and leans her shoulder on the locker next to mine. "I shouldn't have said what I did."

I inch mine closed and look at her. Cassie has dark circles under her eyes, and her straight, red hair is up in a messy bun.

Her face is absent of makeup except for a thin layer of clear lip gloss.

"I get it," I reply. "Things have been shit lately with everything that's going on."

"I feel like we're stuck in a nightmare." Her green eyes follow a group of students walking past us.

"Me too..."

She clears her throat and brings her attention back to me before pushing off the locker. "I hope we can catch up properly when all this is over, and emotions aren't running so high."

Nodding softly, I watch her as she scuffs the floor with her sneakers.

"I need the bathroom."

I let out a shaky breath when she walks off. Everything is such a mess, and I don't know how to fix it. I'm losing my best friend; I can feel it.

As I open my locker again to grab a notebook, a shadow falls over me from behind. I breathe in the addictive smell of peppermint and leather. My body responds in earnest with an insistent, warm throb that starts up between my legs. I hold my breath, and when King slides my hair away from my shoulder in plain sight, my heart kicks into overdrive.

He shifts closer, his heat pressing up against my back. "I want to fuck you against these lockers while everyone watches."

"You shouldn't be here," I whisper shakily. "Someone could see."

"Don't pretend like you don't enjoy the thrill." King leans in, and his soft lips brush the shell of my ear. "You proved as much when you let me fuck you in the same bed as your quarterback boyfriend."

Vicious tingles spark between my legs. I slowly turn around and press my back against the locker. It's a big mistake. Now I'm caught in his dark gaze that holds me hostage, and what I see in those brown orbs squeezes my heart in such a brutal vice that I'm left powerless. He trails his fingers over my cheek and tucks my hair behind my ear in a deceptively gentle touch.

Looking left and right, I scan the hallway for potential witnesses. He digs his calloused fingers into my jaw. "You can play your little games with the quarterback, but we both know you belong to me. And when he's fast asleep beside you tonight, I'll fuck you raw in the ass until you scream my name. That's the only time you feel alive, isn't it? With your ass in the air and my cock in one of your tight little holes."

I snap out of whatever trance I'm in and shove him off. "The only time you feel alive is when you inflict violence on someone else."

With his hands in his pockets and his head tilted to the side, he's the depiction of calm. "Not someone. You."

"Is that supposed to make me feel special?" I ask, keeping my voice low when a group of students walks past. King is still too close. My eyes slide over his tanned arms, the ink curling around his biceps and disappearing beneath the stretched sleeves, and the veins in his forearms. Halloween is around the corner, and he's in a black T-shirt with a white print on the front. How is he not cold?

"I think it makes you feel very special," he drawls tauntingly, wetting his lips. "You wouldn't like it if I inflicted my violence on some other equally depraved girl."

I set my tense jaw and shoulder my bag higher up on my shoulder. The urge to argue with him sparks inside me like hundreds of little popping bubbles, but I force them down. King is right; just thinking about him fucking some other girl draws the darkness inside me to the surface. The urge to inflict damage makes me flinch.

"Leave me alone, King." I walk off, feeling his dark gaze burn my back.

LIAM

"Here he comes," Miles says.

I peer around the corner at King, who is walking down the crowded hallway with his phone in his hands. After I spotted him at the lockers with Keira, I knew there was something going on between them. He was touching her as if he has the fucking right to, but he doesn't.

Only I do.

"You're on the lookout," I tell Jones and Simon. "Make sure no one enters the classroom."

King turns the corner and slows to a halt when he's met with a wall of footballers.

I step forward with my arms crossed and smirk as his gaze slides in my direction. "We're gonna have a little chat, you and me."

Instead of cowering or running away, he begins to slide his phone into his back pocket. I jerk my chin at Chris and Miles, who move forward to restrain him. A scuffle breaks out. King is a savage motherfucker, but he fucked with the wrong guy this time.

Panting harshly, he tries to wrestle free from Miles's and Chris's grip on him. I slide his phone from his back pocket and hold it up in front of his face to unlock it.

"Take him into the classroom," I instruct, tapping into his messages.

What I find makes me see fucking red. King, the soon-to-be-dead motherfucker is screwing my girlfriend. Text after text describes in detail all the fucked up shit he wants to do to her. There are videos of him jerking off in her damn bedroom, too.

One clip, in particular, has me stopping in my tracks as I enter the classroom. I taste sick on my tongue, watching King fuck Keira from behind. His big hand palms her pale ass while she writhes with pleasure. The camera phone shakes in his grip as he slips his dick out and slides the glistening length over her puckered asshole before entering her tight cunt again.

How long has this been going on for? The text messages go back weeks.

After I'm done deleting his photo evidence of Cassie and me that he took at the wake, I slide the phone into my back pocket. King grinds his teeth while watching the movement. His eyes collide with mine. I crack my neck, my veins pulsing with the need for violence. I'm going to beat him to a fucking pulp. Once I'm done with him, he'll never look at *my* girlfriend again.

"You thought you could touch my girl and get away with it, hmm? That I wouldn't find out and come for you?"

King is breathing hard through his nostrils, but his face remains a blank mask except for the slight tilt of his lips. Even now, seconds away from meeting with my fist, he looks cocky. It rubs me the wrong fucking way.

I study his dark hair—tousled from his scuffle with Chris and Miles—and his broad shoulders, sharp jawline, and the "I don't give a shit" attitude oozing from his pores. It's time to teach the untouchable King a lesson. His rich parents can't help him wriggle his way out of this.

"You know," I start, dragging my tongue over my bottom lip as I walk closer. "Falling for someone like Keira was a bad move on your part, King. While she might open her legs to you, she will always pick me. When she's done with your sorry ass, she'll crawl back into my bed after she has picked you to pieces. It's what she always does."

Scoffing, King shakes his head. "And yet, she let me fuck her in your bed last night while you were asleep *right there* beside us. Maybe it's the other way around, quarterback. Maybe it's me she crawls back to after she's done picking you apart."

Red is all I see. I want to beat this fucker up so badly that Keira will never look in his direction again.

"You think she cares about you, King? Keira cares about no

one but herself. She gets that trait from her killer father. She's selfish at heart. Do you think you're special, King? That you have somehow wormed your way through her shell? After you supposedly fucked her last night, she sucked my dick this morning." I laugh a taunting breath through my nose. "Looks like we're both nothing but playing pieces on Keira's board game. But unlike you, I always win. Keira is mine!"

Before he can open his mouth to retort, I ram my fist into his smug face. It feels so fucking good to see his nose explode with blood and to watch him crumble to the floor while I kick his ribs, his stomach, his fucking face.

I crack my neck again. "We're just getting started, lover boy."

HAYLEY

The cafeteria buzzes with noise and rowdy laughter. Except for our little corner, where we sit gathered around the table, staring at the two empty seats.

"Where the fuck are they?" Ava asks, her voice laced with concern.

"Kit has been missing all morning," Kara says. "He hasn't read my messages yet, and no one answered when I rang the house phone."

"When did we last see King?" I ask, giving up on my food.

"This morning."

"He's probably fucking Keira in a bathroom somewhere," I mutter, picking up my fork and stirring it through the sloppy pasta on the plate.

"No, he's not," Ava says, nudging her head in the direction of the football table, where Keira sits on Liam's lap. The latter is smiling too big, looking far too pleased with himself. Keira is a ghost—pale, distant, and washed out.

Knowing your serial killer father is months away from being executed is bound to have that effect on anyone. Not to mention the brutal murders taking place here in Blackwoods.

My eyes skate to Jasper's empty chair. His silence still screams loudly, but it's even worse now that Kit and King are missing too.

Madison walks past in a cloud of fruity perfume, and I circle my fingers around her bony wrist and pull her to a stop. "Have you seen Kit today?"

"Not yet, no," she replies, eyeing us all before placing her tray down and sidling in beside Ava. She wears silver hoop earrings that brush her shoulders, and her chin-length hair is hidden beneath her bobble hat. I wonder briefly if she ever takes it off.

"Where's King?" she asks, unscrewing the lid on her apple juice.

Madison is one of the rare girls here at school who flits between friend groups. She fits in everywhere and nowhere all at once. While she's social by nature, she's also a lone wolf. And only Keira seems to have made it past her highly erected walls.

Ava leans back in her seat and slides her fingers over one of her braids. "We haven't seen him since this morning, and he isn't answering his phone."

"Maybe he went home?"

"It's not like him not to tell us," Kara points out, her eyes watery and wide with silent pleas. "He always lets us know."

Madison reaches across the table and takes her quivering hand. I follow suit, and we all hold hands in the middle of the table in solidarity. As I look out the window, my heart frosts over. Ambulances and police cars are lining up outside, their sirens falling silent.

"What the hell?" I breathe out, slowly rising to my feet.

Exchanging a look with Ava and Kara, I hurry out of the cafeteria. Something really fucking bad has happened. My gut instinct tells me as much.

As I run down the hallway, shoving my way through groups of students congregated near the front doors, I see King. He's bloody and unconscious on a stretcher.

The paramedics wheel him out into the gray afternoon and load him into the back of the ambulance.

"King!" I shout, rushing down the front steps and nearly falling on my face in the process. It's drizzling, but the cold rain on my cheeks barely registers as I stumble into a wall of officers who tell me to step back.

Ava pulls me into her arms, while Kara tries to get answers from anyone willing to divulge what the hell happened.

As the ambulance's sirens blare to life, Madison's glassy eyes meet mine. We're truly stuck in a nightmare with no end in sight. Kara looks visibly shaken up, and Ava lets me go to soothe her, too.

Out of all of us, I was the closest to King. Yes, we fucked from time to time before the dare changed it all, but I considered him my friend. I trusted him more than anyone else.

And now the killer got to him, too?

Is King even alive?

Though we're not close, Madison pulls me into her arms. She smells of strawberry bubblegum, fruity perfume, and coconut shampoo.

I cling to her fleecy jumper inside her unzipped puffer jacket. "I don't know what to do."

She stays silent, hugging me closer, and that's what I need more than reassuring, soothing words.

Stepping back, Ava looks from Kara to Madison and me. "Let's go to the hospital."

"I'm not close to King," Madison points out, releasing me and throwing her thumb over her shoulder. "I'll head back inside. See if I can find out some information. Someone must have seen something, right?"

We watch her leave, and then Kara wipes her wet cheeks and says, "Even if we go to the hospital, they'll never let us see him."

"It doesn't matter." Ava's voice is thick with conviction as she tightens her khaki wrap coat. "They'll let him know we're there for him. For when he comes out."

She's right. We need to be there for him. "Try Kit's phone again," I call out, crossing the parking lot.

One of our friends is missing, while the other one is in the back of an ambulance. My heart is in knots, but now is not the time to fall to pieces.

Liam drives me home in silence. It's so quiet that a spike of anxiety zips through me when he finally inhales a ragged breath.

King is in the hospital after the killer attacked him in a classroom. I can't process all the information. I've tried texting him numerous times, but all of my messages go unread. Not that I'm surprised; he's in a hospital bed.

I don't even know if he's dead or alive.

All I know is that my heart hurts something fierce.

Everyone around me is dying.

My father's legacy has created a ripple effect that holds the whole of Blackwoods in a chokehold.

Is this what the killer meant when he said someone else close to me would die? Did he target King?

Liam puts his clammy hand on my thigh, and I look down at his cracked knuckles. They're red and raw as if he has...

I stiffen, my head snapping in his direction. I study his side profile while he continues driving. His beard needs a shave, and his sandy hair sticks to the thin layer of sweat on his forehead. It's cold in the car—the heat hasn't kicked in yet—but his hair is damp as if he's had a recent shower or maybe washed his face in the sink at school.

"Where were you earlier today?"

His steel-gray eyes slowly slide to mine. "What?"

"When King was attacked. Where were you?"

The left side of his lips inch upward, and then he flicks on the wipers as the rain starts to pelt against the windshield.

"Why won't you answer me?" I ask, dread gnawing at my insides.

Liam takes a left down a dirt road, cuts the engine, and turns in his seat. He digs a phone out of his pocket—*King's phone*—and wiggles it in the air. "Did you enjoy his cock, babe?"

My eyes widen. "You..."

"Yes, me." He pockets the phone and relaxes back against the car door. "Someone had to teach him a lesson about what happens if you go after what's mine."

"So, you did what?!" I all but shriek. "Beat him up so badly that he had to go to the hospital?"

"He deserved it."

I stare at him unblinkingly while the rain hammers on the roof, not recognizing the calm facade gazing back at me. "What the hell, Liam? What the actual hell?! How sick can you be?"

He's on me in a flash, gripping my jaw so tightly that I can feel bruises forming. "Now you listen to me, you fucking whore. You don't get to humiliate me. I will not tolerate my own girlfriend treating me like shit and spreading her legs for other guys."

Batting him off, I reach for the door handle. "Luckily for you, I'm not your girlfriend anymore. It's fucking over between us."

I manage to get the door open, but I'm wrenched back by my hair before I can step outside. A yelp escapes me as Liam grips my jaw from behind, his other hand still in my hair. He snarls, "It'll never be over between us. You think I'll let you go just because you decided you've had enough? Think again. You can fight me all you fucking want, Keira. You're my girlfriend, and I'll kill anyone who so much as looks at you."

"Fuck you," I hiss, fighting him off. My jacket hangs halfway down my shoulder as I stumble out of the car, my knees connecting with the damp, muddy patches of grass. The rain is bordering on sleet, and the frigid cold slithers inside my thin denim jacket and jumper.

Behind me, a car door slams shut, followed by the sound of heavy footsteps. I've never seen Liam so enraged. The golden boy with the dimples and charisma hauls me to my feet, drags me kicking and screaming to the back of his car, and shoves me into his trunk. It slams shut, shrouding me in darkness. For one brief moment, my quivering breaths and thundering heartbeat penetrate the sound of the heavy rain on the trunk.

Curled up in the fetal position, I let out a hoarse scream that rips through my lungs and tears them to shreds. While the inside of the trunk is not big enough for me to get any real power behind my kicks, I still try.

Stop it, a voice inside me whispers. *You're tiring yourself out. Wait until the car stops.*

But my panic screams louder than my common sense. I lash out with my hands and feet, kicking and screaming.

The rumble of the car as it starts up sends my heart into overdrive. I begin to hyperventilate. Why is it so fucking warm in here? Or is that my panic? It's so dark, I can't see anything. Every bump and rocking movement has me inhaling ragged breaths deep into my lungs. It doesn't help.

Nothing does.

By the time the car finally rolls to a stop, I'm a sobbing mess.

The trunk opens, and I blink against the bright light as Liam grabs hold of me and pulls me out. He throws me to the grassy ground, cocks the gun in his hand, and points it directly at my face. There's no warmth in his eyes. Nothing but cold emptiness, void of humanity.

Rain drips off my lashes and beads on my lips. I stare up at him, framed by the naked trees with their crooked, spindly branches stretching across the cloudy sky.

"Stand up."

"Liam?"

"Stand the fuck up!"

Slowly climbing to my feet on shaky legs, I hold my hands up in front of me in a surrendering gesture.

Without taking his eyes off me, he opens the passenger door to the backseat and leans in to grab something. He tosses it at me, and I stumble back.

"Now walk."

Shivering from the cold and wet, I blink down at the spade clutched to my chest. "What's this?"

"It's a fucking spade. Now stop asking questions and fucking walk."

Grabbing me roughly, he shoves me forward towards the woods. My pulse thuds in my ears the entire walk. I focus on the softness of the wet moss beneath my shoes, the sound of the rain as it falls around me on the forest floor, and the breaking of sticks underfoot. Liam doesn't speak a single word, but I can sense him behind me. The gun digs into my head every time my steps slow.

By the time we finally stop walking, my legs are aching, and the sun is setting beyond the trees. We're in a clearing, and the rain is falling freely. I'm frozen to the bone, my teeth chattering.

Liam jerks his chin when I slowly turn around to look at him. "Start digging."

"What?" My voice is a shadow of a whisper, but he hears it.

The gun in his hand remains steady—a solid threat. "Are you deaf all of a sudden? Start digging."

"Please, Liam," I plead, my eyes blurring with stinging tears. "Don't do this."

"Did I stutter? Dig a fucking grave!"

My chest constricts as I release a sob and slowly turn from him. I grip the wooden handle with my numb, icy fingers. Despite the sleety rain, the ground is hard, and it takes me an excruciatingly long time to get through the first layer of soil. My arms burn from exertion as Liam remains a threatening shadow behind me.

I dig for hours. Liam doesn't speak. He never moves. When I think my legs will give out from beneath me, he reaches forward and slides the spade from my hands. Tossing it to the ground, he orders me to step into the hole.

My heart jumps to my throat, where it beats wildly. Dread resurges, creating panicked words that pours from my frozen lips. "Please don't do this, Liam. Please don't. I'm sorry, okay? I'll do anything... please just don't—"

"Shut the fuck up. You're embarrassing yourself."

Panicked sobs rack through my chest, the icy wind burning the insides of my lungs as I try and fail to breathe through the mounting fear.

"Step into the hole."

When I hesitate, he beats me over the head with the gun. Pain slashes through my skull. I fall forward, but before my knees connect with the ground, he grabs my arm and shoves me into the freshly dug grave.

My shoes sink into the soft mud as he tosses me the spade and orders me to keep digging. My frozen hands slip on the wet, wooden handle. The potent smell of damp mud is thick in the fresh air while I continue shoveling dirt. After many exhausting hours, I fall to my ass on the wet ground. The rain has created a puddle of water in the hole that's now soaking through my jeans.

"Hand me the spade."

"Please stop," I plead, beyond exhausted and cold.

I'm numb.

Blissfully numb.

"Hand me the fucking spade, or I'll blow your brains out."

It's a herculean task to lift it up to him where he crouches at the top of the hole while looking down at me.

Liam stands up, pockets his gun, and starts to shovel mud on top of me. The panic is back and swarming my chest before I can stop it. I throw myself against the side of the grave to escape the dusting of dirt tossed into the hole. Mud crumbles away beneath my fingers as I claw at the wall in my bid to climb up. I can't do it. The hole I dug is too deep, and I'm too weak.

"This is what you get for being a cheap whore," he taunts, tossing more wet mud at me.

I splutter and cover my face while sliding to my butt in the dirt. "Stop, Liam. Please, stop."

"Why don't you tell me all about how good it felt to fuck King in my bed, huh?"

More mud rains over me, and I roll into a ball.

It's a nightmare. Nothing more than a bad nightmare.

"Did you not think I would find out, babe? Or did you secretly wish for this? For me to bury you alive out in the woods, where no one will find you?"

"Please, stop," I whimper, my cheeks coated in tears, mud, and rain.

"Maybe it was a cry for help."

Shooting to my aching feet, I point an accusing finger at him. "Fuck you, Liam! You don't know shit. Does this make you feel good, huh? To see me scared and begging for my life? You wanna kill me, *babe?*" I taunt. Fuck it, at this point, I have nothing left to lose. "Then go ahead. Do it. Kill me."

He shovels more dirt on me, but I stand my ground even as wet mud fills my mouth. He keeps shoveling, and the rain keeps falling while I silently cry.

Just when I think he'll never stop, he stands up, cocks his gun, and takes aim.

Bang!

Letting out a startled scream, I begin to sob all over again. I want to be strong, but how can I when he tortures me like this?

I always wanted to die, longed for it even. But this...

Liam disappears from view, and I wait.

I wait as the moon rises high in the sky, and an owl starts to hoot in the distance. I'm broken beyond repair, convinced he'll let me freeze to death in the middle of nowhere, by the time he finally shows his face.

He helps me out of the hole and takes me back to his car with a warm hand clasped around the back of my neck. As soon as we're strapped in, he starts the engine and says, "If you ever so much as look at another guy, I *will* bury you alive in that grave. That's a fucking promise. Don't test me."

And I believe him.

If I ever betray him again, it'll be the last thing I do.

LIAM

I like how pliant my girlfriend is over the next couple of days. When I try to fuck her before school, she lets me. Okay, so she lies there and stares at the window like the thought of watching me fuck her is appalling, but I find that I strangely like that, too.

What I don't like is how her eyes seek out King's empty chair at school. What the hell will it take to get that fucker out of her head? Maybe I should simply pluck out her eyes so that all she'll know is me.

Seated beside Amanda and Chris, Madison is watching me strangely across the table. It seems like I'm the only one who doesn't give a shit that the loser kid, Kit, is missing. We're not even friends with that group of kids, so it's beyond me why everyone at my table is so demure.

"You haven't let her out of your sight for days," Madison says, flicking her gaze from me to the girl on my lap.

"What's your point?" I ask, popping a fry into my mouth. Keira is still staring at King's empty chair, and the urge to shove my fingers into her eyeballs returns.

"Yeah, what's your point?" Cassie asks tiredly, dropping her silver fork to her plate. It clinks loudly in the silence that reigns over our table.

"My point," Madison says, looking at me accusingly, "is that I have seen marked change in my friend this week, and it's not a good one."

Chewing, I shrug my shoulders and band my arm around Keira's waist. "Why don't you ask her yourself? She's right here."

A muscle twitches in Madison's cheek. She looks at my girl-friend. "If you want to talk, I'm here."

"That's enough." My voice is sharp enough that Madison's spine snaps upright. "You should stay out of shit that doesn't concern you."

Madison shoves her plate out of the way before placing her elbows on the table and leaning in, her eyes fixed on mine. "You see, that's the thing, Liam. It *does* involve me. Keira is my friend." She trains her eyes on Cassie. "And yours, but you don't seem to care much lately."

Cassie sneers at her, and when Keira shuffles off my lap while mumbling some excuse about needing the bathroom, Cassie palms my dick through my jeans beneath the table. "You only pretend to care, Madison. In reality, you're nothing but a psycho bitch beneath that mask you wear."

"Is that so?" Madison smirks, flicking her eyes to my lap hidden beneath the table. "I guess you and I define the word 'bitch' differently."

I'm about to open my mouth when she scoots her chair back and walks off. Beneath the table, Cassie's fingers come to my button.

KEIRA

I'm lying on my bed, surrounded by schoolbooks. Music plays in my ears while I try and fail to read the page in front of me. I have an exam later this week, but I can't focus, no matter how hard I try. The concept of school seems so meaningless right now. My father's execution is nearing, King is still in the hospital, one of his friends is missing, and Liam has shown his true colors.

Everything else is just noise.

At least I was finally allowed back home yesterday. I couldn't have handled another day with Liam. If I never have to see him again, it won't come soon enough.

Mom is at a dinner party with friends, and my stepdad is on a business call in the office. His voice drifts through my floorboards while I switch songs.

My phone lights up on the bed. I reach for it before sitting up and swiping the screen.

A text message waits for me.

> **Unknown number:** It's time to play a little game.

My eyes fly wide open, and I drop the phone as though it's on fire. A video clip pops up on my screen. I click on it even though I know I shouldn't. What I see has my hands flying to my mouth and my heart roaring in my ears.

Kit sits tied to a rickety, metal chair, wearing nothing but his black boxer shorts. It's too dark to see where he is or to make out details. What I can see, clear as day, is a cloaked figure in a blood-red devil's mask. He grips Kit's hair before exposing his throat and putting a sharp, curved blade to it. "Play the game, Keira, and Kit gets to live."

My fingers fly over the screen.

> **Keira:** Don't hurt him. What's the game?

> **Unknown number:** Walk downstairs to the kitchen. There, you'll find more instructions.

> **Keira:** How do you know I'm upstairs?

There's no response. He leaves me on read, and precious

seconds pass as I stare unblinkingly at the screen. It finally dims, bringing me back to the present moment.

Kit is alive.

Shooting out of bed and hurrying downstairs, I come to a tumbling halt in the kitchen when I see the items laid out neatly on the table. I take careful steps closer to the folded cloak with a red devil's mask on top.

The phone vibrates in my clammy hand.

> Unknown number: You have an important choice to make, Keira.

> Keira: What choice?

My eyes flit up to the contents on the cream tablecloth. The mask is taunting me with its nefarious smile.

> Unknown number: Before we get to that, let's discuss the darkness in you. Have you ever fantasized about killing someone in cold blood the same way your father did?

A breath rushes out of me, and my hands shake so violently that I can barely hold the phone. I listen for sounds in the house, but it's eerily silent except for a car passing by outside.

> Keira: I'm not sick like you.

> Unknown number: That's what I thought you'd say.

Another video clip pops up on my screen, and I watch in horror as the distorted voice cuts through the roar of my pounding pulse in my neck. "Every time you lie, I will hurt your friend."

And then he drags the blade slowly down Kit's cheek. Blood pours from the deep cut, and I let out a choked scream when Kit roars.

"Oh, god, no, no, no!"

> Unknown number: Have I got your attention now? It's time for the truth, Keira. For every lie you spin, I will cut your friend.

> Keira: I won't lie again, I promise. Don't hurt him.

> Unknown number: Now answer the question, Keira. Have you ever fantasized about killing someone in cold blood?

I squeeze my eyes shut and inhale a breath.

> Keira: Yes.

> Unknown number: Very good.

> Unknown number: Do you believe your father's sick tendencies run in your blood?

> Keira: I don't know.

Another video message pops up. I release a whimper, shrinking back against the fridge while watching the masked man drag the knife down Kit's arm. The slice is so deep that yellow fat protrudes from the wound.

Gagging, I angle the phone away for a second.

> Unknown number: It was a yes or no question. You don't get to tap out with "I don't know."

> Keira: Yes, okay. I believe my father's sickness runs through me. I can feel it.

> Unknown number: Feel it how?

"Fuck," I whisper shakily, sliding down the length of the fridge until I'm seated on the floor. He'll hurt Kit if I don't tell him my deepest, darkest secrets.

> Keira: I like pain. Humiliation. Degradation. And I sometimes want to inflict it on others, too.

> Unknown number: What's stopping you?

The tears in my eyes spill over, and I hastily wipe my cheeks dry, but more tears seep out.

> Keira: I can't let the darkness inside me win. I'll end up locked away in a mental hospital or on death row like my father.

> Unknown number: Ah! Your father. The famous killer of Blackwoods. Tell me, Keira. Does a small part of you enjoy the popularity you gain by being his flesh and blood?

More tears fall, and the salty liquid seeps between my lips when I wet them.

> Keira: Maybe.

My thumb hovers over the send button, but then I delete it.

> Keira: Yes.

> Unknown number: Admit that you almost willingly tapped out that time because a sick and twisted part of you—the darkness that you hide from the world—wanted me to sink the knife into Kit's flesh.

Lowering the phone, I stare at the windows. Darkness is settling outside, and the streetlights have come on.

Typing out a response, I wait with bated breath.

> Keira: No.

> Unknown number: Did that lie taste sweet?

My stinging, bloodshot eyes fall shut when another video pops up on the screen. I breathe through the swirling sickness that thickens and grows stronger as the seconds tick by. If I let it, it will sniff out the story I have created for myself. The story where I am a good person.

A normal person.

Not a person who opens her eyes and draws in a breath in anticipation before pressing play.

Spine-tingling screams of agony ripple through the air as I watch him savagely cut off one of Kit's ears. Blood pours unhindered down Kit's face, and his head slumps forward. He's weak, succumbing to the pain.

> Unknown number: Did it, Keira?

Gripping the phone tightly in my hand, I squeeze my eyes shut for a second. The self-hatred I feel at this moment matches the sickness in him. We're two demented, sick individuals feeding off each other. But I'm not him. While this urge to indulge in my father's illness runs through my veins in time with each solidifying heartbeat, I refuse to become my father.

> Keira: Yes, it tasted sweet.

> Unknown number: Ready to play?

Climbing to my feet, I brace my hand on the fridge and type out a response.

> Keira: Let's play.

> Unknown number: I like your spirit, Keira. See the cloak and the mask?

My eyes skate to the table where the mask stares up at the ceiling.

> Unknown number: Put it on.

I want to ask him why or argue, but I refrain. I either play his game or let him kill Kit.

Placing the phone on the table, I gingerly reach for the mask and the cloak. The mask is cold to the touch, the material reflecting the dimmed roof light overhead. I put it back down and pull on the black cloak with trembling hands before reaching for the mask.

With my fingers inches from the red metallic, I pause. There's no going back if I do this. In order to beat this monster at his own game and get to his queen, I have to embrace the killer inside me. He knows that. It's what he's banking on.

Before I can let my thoughts steal the last of my courage, I swiftly put the mask on. The elastic string is tight at the back of my head, and my breaths soon dampen the lower half of my face.

Swiping my phone back up, I stare at my reflection in the dimmed screen. A shudder runs through me, raising the hairs on my arms. I take a picture and send it.

His response is immediate.

> Unknown number: How does it feel?

The urge to lie through my teeth is almost too strong.

> Keira: I'm torn. I feel sick to my stomach, but I also feel closer to my father than I ever have, as if I can finally connect to the depravity in him that now runs through me.

> Unknown number: Look at you playing the game so well.

> Unknown number: Choose a weapon.

A weapon? I grow cold, my breath fanning against the mask. My face is warm. It's almost panic-inducing. I look around me, unsure of what I'm searching for. What does he mean by a weapon? A knife? A gun? My eyes snag on the kitchen counter. I storm up to it, pull open a drawer, and extract a pair of scissors.

> Keira: What's next?

> Unknown number: What weapon did you pick?

My fingers tighten around the symmetric handles.

> Keira: Scissors.

> Unknown number: Interesting choice.

> Keira: Cut the bullshit. What's next?

> Unknown number: Careful, unless you want me to hurt your friend again.

Another text comes through. At the same time, there's a thud somewhere in the house.

> Unknown number: Walk to your stepdad's office.

The floorboards creak loudly beneath my feet as I pause.

> Keira: Why?

Unknown number: Play the game, Keira.

Mustering up my courage, I walk out of the kitchen, past the stairs that lead up to my room. The dark hallway seems to stretch on for miles. I search the cold wall for the light switch, but the hallway remains creepily dark when I flick it.

A light floods the floor from beneath the closed office door, and haunting classical music drifts through behind it. I have never once known my stepdad to listen to that type of music.

Or any music, for that matter.

But now it plays, the crackling sound reminding me of a record player.

Tightening my grip on the dull scissors in my hand, I walk closer, as softly and as quietly as I can. All the while, the music plays.

I stop and listen outside the door. It's the type of music that you would expect to listen to at a circus or a ghostly fun fair.

Icy shivers splash down my spine as I reach forward to curl my fingers around the curved, black, iron door handle. I push it open, the hinges creaking loudly. With bated breath, I take in the scene in front of me.

Plastic sheeting covers the room from top to bottom. It's everywhere, not a single surface untouched except the ceiling.

As I step over the threshold, the plastic sheeting crinkles beneath my bare feet and sticks to my soles.

My stepdad is on the floor, naked, bound, and gagged.

Seeing such a powerful but dangerous man reduced to this sparks a tingle of excitement that starts at the center of my chest and spreads outward before settling at my fingertips. I stroke my thumb over the blade of the scissors in response.

Unknown number: If you want Kit to live, you need to unleash the monster inside you.

His next text message sends my heart into overdrive.

> Unknown number: Kill him.

Kill him? What the hell? My eyes fly up to my stepdad, who's lying with his neck craned and his wide, terrified eyes staring directly at me. I quickly type out a response, sweating beneath the mask.

> Keira: I can't kill someone.

> Unknown number: It's in your blood, Keira. You were born for this.

> Unknown number: Think of how good it will feel to kill someone beneath the protection of someone else's identity. You're not Keira anymore. You're the devil.

> Unknown number: Should I cut off another ear as an incentive? Or maybe I should let your mom be my next plaything?

My heart skyrockets.

> Keira: No!

> Unknown number: Look up at the corner, near the bookshelf. See the camera?

Lowering the phone, I lift my weary gaze to the small, square camera while the tinny music continues playing its haunting circus notes.

> Unknown number: Welcome to the games.

KEIRA

I inch closer, a thin layer of sweat coating my skin beneath my clothes and cloak. The scissors threaten to slip from my fingers, so I tighten my grip until my knuckles turn white.

The sickening anticipation in me curls my toes as it whispers secrets to the beating valves of my heart.

This is the man who has unleashed his demon on me more times than I can count. Little did he know that mine was slumbering in the darkness, soon to stretch its limbs and climb out from the shadows.

A smile plays on my lips, one I'm thankful stays hidden behind the mask. My darkening gaze drinks him in, vulnerable and scared on the floor.

The music. The crinkling plastic. The sounds of his whimpers. I feed on it all like a starved vampire fledgling thirsting for blood and chaos.

After placing my phone down on the sheet-covered desk, I let the cloak drag over the floor as I hunt him like prey, circling his prone body on the floor. I can taste his fear in the air and the confusion when he gazes up at me.

His wide eyes slide down to the blunt scissors in my hand, and he shakes his head violently, as if the act alone will force my predator back into the shadows.

Tilting my head, my gaze dances over every inch of his naked skin. His knees are drawn up to his chest, and as I walk around him, I let my attention wander over his hairy balls that protrude from between his thighs. Balls that have slapped against my ass for the last time.

I'll miss the way his unhinged monster toyed with my need for pain and punishment. But at some point, like tonight, the punished has to become the punisher.

The scales need to balance.

But maybe there can never be a balance between two sick people like us, whose only drive in life is to seek destruction. Maybe the scales will always tip too far toward one end or the other until we take it too far one day.

Like tonight.

Shoving him onto his back and straddling his waist, I grip his stubbly, sweaty cheeks. He tries to talk with the gag in his mouth, to plead with me to let him go, and I wonder if he knows it's me.

A calm, so unlike anything I've ever known, settles over me as I stare down at him through the holes in the mask.

This feels so *right*.

Is this what my father felt when he let go for the first time?

This euphoria at finally being free?

Sliding my mask up, I smile down at my stepdad as the cool air kisses my damp face. "Hi, Daddy. Let's play a little game."

Eyes wide, he cranes his neck off the floor even more as I wriggle down his body until I'm seated on his flaccid dick. And to think that something so impressive when it's erect can look so pathetic now.

His nostrils flare while I gently use the scissor blades to play with the dark curls on his chest. He begins to make screaming noses behind the gag, which makes me curious to see what other interesting sounds I can draw from his body.

"Come here, sweetheart," my daddy says, gesturing with the knife for me to join him at the head of the table.

I scoot off my chair, my pigtails swaying, and run up to Daddy, who pulls me in front of him. The large turkey is bigger than my head, but Daddy said it would definitely fit in the oven when I asked him. And now, here it is, cooked and seasoned.

Mom and Grandma smile softly at me from across the table, wineglass in hand, as Daddy leans down to whisper in my ear. "There's an art to carving, sweetheart."

I love my daddy. Sometimes even more than Mommy.

Maybe because he doesn't shout at me when I dirty my knees outside or tell me to stop burning ants to a crisp with Mom's magnifying glass. And he has also never spanked my butt for disturbing a swarm of buzzing flies while poking the insides of a dead squirrel with a stick.

But Mom has.

Dad puts the carving knife in my hand before closing his long fingers around mine. "Now, a good blade will slice through meat like it's butter."

We saw off a chunky piece together, and I smile wide when it flops onto the plate.

"There's a good girl. Let's do a couple more."

Dipping the scissor blade into his belly button, I channel some forgotten darkness I have forced down and stifled for too long in order to fit in.

"That's it, baby girl, let's put some force behind it."

I press down gently at first. When he starts screaming like a squealing pig, I put my entire body weight behind it until the scissors sink deep into his gut. Daddy was right, it does slide through flesh like butter once the tough barrier has been broken. Unfortunately, these blades aren't sharp, so I have to really bear down to cut through his flesh.

The plastic sheeting soon pools with blood that soaks through the fabric of my cloak. My fingers ache from the effort of cutting him open. All I manage are jagged cuts of flesh. I want to see what's inside, like that time with the squirrel.

Mommy isn't around to spank my butt this time.

THE DEVIL

Unknown number: I hope you enjoyed yourself as much as I enjoyed watching. Now strip out of your clothes. All of them. Then step into the slippers by the door and walk back to your room, careful not to touch anything or brush up against any surfaces. Take a shower and don't come out of your room until further notice.

Unknown number: If you fail to comply, Kit dies.

KEIRA

The warm water scalds my pale skin and turns it a bright pink, not so unlike the pink water swirling down the drain.

I stay in the shower until my fingertips resemble prunes and the adrenaline from what I just did wears off. And then I turn the temperature up even more to punish myself. I shouldn't have enjoyed killing my stepdad. I shouldn't have derived such perverted pleasure from it. I'm the true monster here, and it would seem the killer is playing dangerous mind games.

After washing my hair for a third time, I step out of the shower and dry myself off with a fluffy towel that smells of laundry soap.

As I enter my bedroom, wrapped in a towel, I stop to listen. The house is quiet except for the wind outside and the creaking of the floorboards beneath my feet. The music downstairs has fallen silent, and I wonder what will happen now. I was told to come in here and wait.

Now what?

I busy myself by getting dressed in my pajamas and drying my hair. I even read a chapter in a book before giving up because of the flashing images that assault my mind.

When I unlock my phone, I have a new text from Liam. I ignore it and dim the screen. He can fuck off for all I care. He stole my power from me when he made me dig my own grave and threatened to bury me in it if I go against him again, but I took it back tonight. I feel brand-fucking-new, and I guess I have a certain psychopath to thank for that.

My screen lights up again, and I breathe out a heavy sigh, swiping up my phone and expecting to see another message from Liam.

> Unknown number: Kit is waiting for you outside the back door. You better hurry, he's cold.

I fly out of bed and run so fast down the creaky stairs that I fall down the last three steps. My tailbone explodes in pain, but I'm back up on my feet, sprinting toward the living room.

I'm out of breath and breathing hard by the time I reach the patio doors and flick on the light outside. The cold air hits me in the face as I finally get the doors unlocked and step outside. I'm barefoot, and the pavement slabs are icy beneath the soles of my feet.

I take careful steps closer to the settee and slow to a halt when I step on something cold. Like a trail of breadcrumbs, body parts lead a path to the wicker chair that sits by the garden table.

As I step over a hand with each finger severed, my stomach cramps violently. But before I can make it any further, I double over and puke. Acid burns my esophagus on the way up, and my eyes water from the violent cramping. The air reeks of rotten flesh, decomposition, and feces. By the looks of it, Kit has been dead for days.

I played the devil's game and lost.

And just like last time, I never stood a chance at winning.

Furious, I dig my phone out of my pocket.

> Keira: You promised you wouldn't kill him.

His response is immediate, and I can picture him smiling behind the creepy mask.

Unknown number: I lied.

Keira: Fuck you!

Message failed to send.

I release a scream that rips from my vocal cords. I'm so fucking angry and frustrated and betrayed. Kit is dead, and I murdered my own stepdad in cold blood. The killer played me right from the start, and I fell right into his trap.

Again.

Blaring sirens draw nearer in the distance, their blue and red lights flooding the side of the house. They're everywhere—a flurry of motion and loud voices barking orders. I'm led inside and then Liam is there too, playing the role of the doting boyfriend.

They find no trace of my stepdad's mutilated body. His office is as if nothing happened. Even the camera up in the corner is gone. I should be relieved to know I'm important enough in the killer's twisted games to keep me alive for another round, but relief is far from my mind when I'm stuck in an endless nightmare I can't escape.

Sunlight pours in through the windscreen. The weather app on my phone confirms it's barely above freezing temperatures, but streaks of sunshine warm my cheeks.

"Do you want me to come inside with you?" Liam's voice drags me from my thoughts, and I quickly shake my head before reaching for the car door handle.

"It's fine. I need to do this on my own."

Liam watches me closely, unhappy with my unwillingness to let him help me, but I need to face this part of my life on my own.

My father is a part of my past, but recently, his legacy has been bleeding into my presence.

Tainting me.

I smile weakly at Liam before stepping outside and pulling my denim jacket closed. With one last look at Liam behind the steering wheel, I walk up the path to the high-security prison.

After I'm buzzed inside and taken through security, they guide me to sit in front of a small booth, one of many. My tired, haunted reflection stares back at me in the glass in front of me.

My father looks exactly how I remember him, but he also doesn't. He's now ten years older with a receding hairline, a gaunt face, and sunken cheeks, and his once-dark beard is speckled with gray hairs.

I scan my eyes over his white jumpsuit as he lowers himself down onto the chair on the other side of the glass and removes the phone from the cradle. I try to remember what his voice sounded like. It's been so long since I last heard him speak that I can't remember it anymore.

Curling my fingers around the phone on the wall, I pick it up and press it to my ear.

"Hey, sweetheart."

The organ in my chest ceases to beat as memories of my father reading me bedtime stories flood my mind. Suddenly, I remember it all—the slight rasp to his voice and his booming laughter.

"Hi, Dad."

We stare at each other until he breaks the moment by scratching his temple. "What are you doing here, sweetheart?"

"We haven't spoken for over ten years, and that's the first thing you want to ask me?"

Releasing a soft breath that rushes down the phone line to caress my ear, his eyes soften with regret. "You wouldn't be here after all this time if you didn't feel trapped in a corner."

I study his face, every crease and wrinkle, trying to see the monster in him that killed all those people, but all I see is Dad.

My dad...

My childhood hero until he became the villain.

"I needed to ask you something."

He clears his throat, scratching his beard. "You can ask me anything."

Hesitating, I look around for listening ears. "Your blood runs in my veins, and I... I did something... and... How can I stop myself from turning into you?"

Jimmy Hill, as the world knows him, blows out a deep sigh and looks around. He pins his blue eyes on me and leans in, his nose close to the glass. "You have to fight it, sweetheart."

"But what if it's already too late? What if I'm already like you."

"You can never be like me, Keira. Do you know why?"

With a shake of my head, I whisper a quiet, *"No."*

I want to memorize every inch of his face. His execution date is set. Soon, I'll be all that's left of Jimmy Hill and his stain on Blackwoods.

"Because you're so much better than I ever was. So much *stronger.*" He sits back and fiddles with the coiled cord. "I heard there's a killer on the loose in Blackwoods."

"Yes..." My voice is weak and shaky. "He... uh..." I clear my throat, straightening my back. "He plays evil games."

"You're his obsession?"

"The main star of the show, as he calls it."

My father studies me intently as if he wants to memorize me. His actions broke our family, and there are so many questions I want to ask.

So many things I want to try to understand.

"Dad..."

His eyes collide with mine as I wipe wretched tears from my cheeks. I don't want to be here, talking to my dad in a place of death and misery. I want to go for a walk along the river, feel the sun on my face, and maybe hold his hand like I did when I was little.

I want to be the only person on this entire planet who sees past the serial killer Jimmy Hill. The one person who sees the soul residing behind all that evil, but I dismiss that thought.

After he was arrested, my mom forbade any contact. As I grew older, I started to resent him and the heavy burden of his legacy. It's too late now to mend any bridges.

My voice crackles with pain. "Why am I so broken, Dad?"

"You're not broken, sweetheart."

"Remember when I was little, and my mom spanked me after the squirrel incident?" I chance a look at him, finding him grinding his teeth. "The curiosity is like that now, but so much worse." In the silence that follows, I admit something to my father that will soon be buried with him. "I'm scared, Dad. I'm so fucking scared."

"I know," he replies, his voice thick with regret. "If I could have turned back time..."

"Would you have stopped yourself from killing all those people?"

He lowers the phone for a beat, wiping his wet eyes before putting the receiver back to his ear. "No, sweetheart, I don't think so."

His words soothe me like the balm I've been seeking. At least I don't have to live with the what-ifs now that he has admitted his ugly truth. Even in retrospect, my father would have still murdered. He was always destined to rot in this place.

"It was never a choice," he tells me, and I get it.

My father can't possibly know how much I understand the meaning behind his words. The look in his blue gaze, the slight sparkle, lets me know he sees me, too.

"It was a drive for you," I whisper, placing my fingertips on the cool glass. "An all-consuming urge."

His fingertips press against mine, and despite the barrier, I feel him. I feel each and every one of his unspoken words.

"You'll be fine, sweetheart," he assures me.

I look from our hands on the glass to his sorrow-filled eyes. "I'm sorry I never came to see you sooner."

"I don't want you to lose a single moment of sleep over it. I made my choices, and I had to live with those. I need you to know that losing you was the hardest part of all. I don't regret a lot of things, no matter how cruel or sinister they may seem, but I regret hurting you. I'm a monster that deserves to be put to death, but my love for you was always real."

"Don't say that," I whisper.

"Think of all the people I killed and the suffering their families endured. They deserve their justice."

"Dad?"

"Yes, sweetheart."

"Will I be okay?"

"You'll be fine."

I nod, swiping at my wet cheeks with the denim sleeve. It comes away black with mascara.

"As long as you don't feed the monster."

Staring at our hands on the glass, I let my heart bleed for the young girl who lost her father.

For the lost teenager who has done unspeakable things.

"Before I go," I start, locking my gaze on my father. "I need you to tell me how to beat the killer at his own game. You know how he thinks, Dad. Only you can help me."

The heating blasts straight at my face as the rock music blares through the car. I glance at the time on the dashboard. Keira has been in there for over an hour now, and I'm getting fucking tired of waiting. Besides, why wouldn't she let me come with her?

When will she let me in?

Okay, so maybe I went too far when I locked her in the trunk and forced her to dig her own grave, but she fucking cheated on me. And sure, I cheat on her too, but it's not the same thing. I only let Cassie into my bed because Keira fails to see me.

For as long as I have known Keira, she has only given me crumbs. I thought that maybe with time, she would open up and let me in.

I'm the star quarterback, for fuck's sake, but that means jack squat to Keira. Everyone worships at my feet except for her.

Leaning forward, I turn off the heating and straighten back up. I don't even know why I switched it on in the first place, when the sun outside is beaming through the windshield.

I do a double take when I glance in the rearview mirror, but before I can react, a broad arm wraps around my throat from behind and begins to choke me. I'm assaulted with the smell of leather and peppermint. The horn blares, but there's no one around to watch me struggle.

"Did you think you got rid of me, quarterback?" King taunts

in my ear. His hot breath is deceptively calm despite his effort to choke me. "You were wrong when you said you always win."

I let go of his forearm and stretch my jerking arm out in front of me to grab hold of something, *anything*, I can use to beat him over the head. But we're in my car, and there's nothing here.

"I always win, quarterback. When you're rotting in a cold grave tonight, I will ram my cock so far down Keira's throat that she'll gag and choke while making a mess of the sheets, and then I'll fuck her sweet pussy."

The sick fucker breathes me in as if he savors the stench of death. I'm weakening, and the agonizing urge to breathe burns my lungs as my feet kick out in the footwell. I'm back to clawing at his arms, but my movements are sluggish now.

"Do you have any idea how much I love her tight cunt? The great lengths I will go to ensure no one takes her from me?" His lips spread into a smile against my temple as he tightens his grip around my neck. "I think you do, quarterback." He slides his arm from around my throat and pistol-whips me.

KING

Keira's reaction when she walks out of the prison doesn't disappoint. She slows to a halt and stares at me for a beat, where I sit in the front seat with a small smirk and my hand hanging over the steering wheel.

Come to me, baby.

And then—while Liam struggles, bound and duct-taped in the backseat—she sets off running toward the car, her blonde hair flying behind her.

Wrenching open the passenger door, she climbs inside and throws herself at me, crushing her lips to mine. "King!" Her arms wrap around my neck as she straddles my lap behind the steering wheel. Despite the loud groans, Keira doesn't even look at Liam in the backseat. "You're okay."

With my hands in her soft hair and on her hip, I tongue-fuck her mouth until she's a panting, writhing mess in my arms.

Breaking the kiss, she moves back and skates her eyes over my face as if to reassure herself that I'm alive. Aside from the faint bruising on my left cheekbone and the cut on my lip, I'm almost fully healed.

"Hey, baby." I reach up to slide a few strands of hair away from her moist lip before slipping my hand behind her neck and braiding my fingers in the cascading hair. As I pull on it sharply, the harsh breath that slips from her tempting mouth has my hard cock twitching inside my black jeans. "You didn't think you could get rid of me that easily, did you?"

I'm aching to be balls deep in her now, but we're outside the prison. Liam's muffled scream behind the duct tape could draw attention if anyone entered the parking lot.

With a tap to her sweet ass, I tell her without words that it's time to get the show on the road.

She climbs off and straps herself in, taking a quick peek into the backseat. Her eyes sparkle with something heady and delicious when she looks at me again.

Putting the car in drive, I step on the gas to the soundtrack of Liam's angry, hoarse screams.

As soon as we're out of there, I reach for Keira's fingers. We fit together perfectly, like two missing puzzle pieces. Her pale hand looks so tiny in my tanned one. I quite like that I'm physically bigger and stronger than her, and she's so small compared to me. It makes me want to hurt her in the best way possible.

"Hey, quarterback," I call out, sparing him a glance in the rearview mirror. "I have a special surprise for you today."

His nostrils flare aggressively as his eyes fly up to meet mine. He's pissed and scared.

"The thing is..." I grip the steering wheel tighter, my knuckles white against the dark leather. "You hurt my girl."

Thick and heavy silence settles over the car while Liam glares at me. I have come to appreciate it a lot lately: how it heightens anticipation or fear.

My voice comes out deadly calm. "No one touches my girl and lives to tell the tale."

Keira's gaze burns the side of my face, but I don't look at her. Not while I have Liam's full attention.

"You fucked with the wrong person, quarterback."

"King?" Keira's soft voice draws my attention away from the asshole in the backseat, and I reach out and wrap my fingers around her slender throat. If for no other reason than to soothe the restless monster inside me that wants to tear the quarterback to pieces and fuck his girlfriend in his blood.

Keira's hands fly up to my forearm, but I don't miss how she squeezes her thighs together to alleviate the ache building inside her. She loves the depraved just as much as I do.

"Baby," I breathe out, caressing her pulse point with my thumb while watching the road. "I'm gonna bury your boyfriend. You sure you wanna be there to watch it? I can drop you off somewhere."

Unfastening the seatbelt, she shoves my hand off her neck and leans across the center console. Her warm, soft lips find my ear. "I want to watch, King."

My throat jumps as goosebumps dot my arms. I'm fucking aching for her.

As if she knows her effect on me, she palms my throbbing cock through my jeans and licks a path up the side of my neck all the way to my earlobe. Sinking her teeth into it, she squeezes the outline of my hard dick.

"Such a fucking tease," I grit out, wringing the steering wheel.

"Just drive, babe."

I smirk at Liam in the rearview while Keira makes swift work of my belt with her sweet ass in the air.

I must be a sick fuck, because I get off on knowing he's about to watch the object of his obsession, his precious girlfriend, suck me greedily, while he roars and screams in the backseat like a pathetic loser.

Her warm mouth envelops me, and she takes no prisoners as she begins to deep-throat me right away.

"Fuck," I hiss out, one hand in her hair, the other wringing the steering wheel until I worry my knuckles might pop out of the skin. How I get us to our destination in one piece is beyond me. But I do, by some miracle.

Cutting the engine, I kick out my legs in the footwell and sit back to enjoy the show. "I have missed this mouth," I tell her before sucking on my middle finger, getting it nice and wet, and slipping it inside her jeans. "Greedy little pussy, huh?" I slide it knuckle-deep into her cunt, then back out to circle her tight exit. She stiffens when I press forward but soon relaxes back against me. "There's my good girl, let me in."

With a quick glance in the mirror, I wink at Liam before closing my eyes with a grunt. "Fuck, that feels good."

Keira licks and sucks and teases until it fucking hurts to hold back.

Defeated, Liam's angry roars die down, and he rolls over onto his back and stares up at the roof.

I come with a deep grunt, and my girl greedily swallows every drop before sitting back and wiping her mouth while she scans the clearing where I parked.

There's nothing out here on this rarely used dirt road except for overgrown, dried grass and tall trees.

I know the moment realization dawns. Keira's wide, blue eyes collide with mine, and I smirk as I reach for the door handle. "You sure you wanna do this, baby?"

Her response is to exit the car.

Fuck me. I stare at her ass in her denim jeans for too long before opening the car door and joining her outside in the chilly air that smells of freshly fallen rain and wet moss. The cold instantly seeps through my leather jacket, but I don't bother zipping it up. Instead, I throw open the passenger door to the backseat, hauling Liam outside. After cutting the zip ties around his ankles, I step back and pull the gun from my jacket's inside pocket.

"Get up, quarterback."

Keira is slowly rounding the car, watching me carefully with no small amount of intrigue and lust in her eyes.

I raise the gun. "Get the fuck up!"

Glaring daggers at me, Liam climbs to his feet. I know that look; we're past simple beatings. Now it's kill or be killed.

Placing my arm over Keira's shoulder, I lift my chin toward the thick tree line where he took her the other week, when he made her dig her own grave. I jostle the gun. "You know where we are, quarterback. Lead the way."

Liam wants to make a run for it, but one look at the gun in my hand and he must think better of it. He sets off walking like an obedient puppy.

With my arm extended in front of me, the gun aimed at Liam's head, I place a kiss on Keira's temple. She smells of her apple shampoo and something uniquely her that I can't get enough of.

Tightening the grip on the gun, I call out, "Did it make you feel good to take her out here and scare the living shit out of her? Did you feel like a man?"

His head hangs, and his shoulders slump. I'm a bit disappointed that he isn't putting up more of a fight, especially since he's walking to his death. But we're teenagers, so he probably thinks I won't kill him.

Naive fucker.

Sticks break underfoot, and we have to duck beneath branches a couple of times before reaching the clearing where the grave greets us. It has since rained, and the bottom has a soggy puddle of water that won't dry out until the temperature drops below freezing.

Liam stiffens as he looks at it, and then he turns slowly. His eyes come to mine, watching me carefully.

Pulling Keira into my chest, I ask him, "Did you not think I would have you followed every minute of the day? Come on, Liam. I'm King Knight, for fuck's sake. My family has more money than sense. We're fucking royalty here in Blackwoods."

His gunmetal gaze flits to Keira, and I pull the trigger, making the fucker shit his pants when I aim just to his right. "Don't look at her, or I will fucking shoot you."

His chest rises and falls rapidly, but he remains mute behind his gag.

"Get in the grave."

His eyes widen, and his nostrils flare.

"Did I fucking stutter?"

Liam looks at the grave behind him, then his eyes are back on mine. For the first time today, raw fear reflects in their depths. He starts to shake his head, so I shoot him in the kneecap.

His pained, muffled screams bounce off the trees as he topples to the ground.

Beside me, my girl giggles.

Fucking giggles.

I chuckle too. What a fucking loser he is, sobbing and rolling around on his back while clutching his bleeding knee in his hands. Blood pours between his fingers, bright crimson against his skin.

Fed up with his weeping, I stalk up to him, aim the gun at his uninjured knee and shoot that, too. The loud gunshot sends birds erupting from the treetops.

I kick him into the grave to the sound of his agonized screams, watching the mud stain red while he cries like a fucking baby. "Not such a man now, are you?"

Keira spots the shovel propped against the nearest tree, and I keep the gun aimed at Liam while she retrieves it. Not that he can try to escape with both of his kneecaps blown to smithereens.

When she returns, she sneers down at him as she begins to shovel dirt. It rains over his face and chest. "Doesn't feel so good, does it?"

More dirt rains over his tear-streaked, muddied, and terrified face. I almost want to jump down there and remove his gag so I can listen to him beg for his life.

"You're an asshole, Liam," Keira hisses, aiming straight for his face. "Do you know how fucking scared I was?"

I study the cold fury in her eyes and the curl of her lips.

"It's only right that you get to experience what I did when you forced me to dig a grave for hours, not knowing if I would live or die."

Keira is a goddamn goddess coated in sin and sadistic pleasure.

Because she *is* enjoying this.

It's there in the cold, callous sparkle in her eyes. For a moment, I imagine this is what her father looked like when he feasted on his victims' fear.

She has his eyes. When she looks at me, with the spade gripped tightly in her hands and strands of her blonde hair stuck to the sheen of sweat on her temple, I know I'm looking into the eyes of a monster. I like what I see—that she feels safe enough with me to show me her true nature.

I kill the distance between us, palm the back of her damp neck, and crush my lips to her soft ones. My tongue delves into her mouth to tangle with hers while she fists the hem of my T-shirt beneath my leather jacket.

I'm so fucking obsessed with Keira.

The need to unearth all of her secrets and the hidden layers she keeps safely guarded has me hungering for more. I'll never get enough of her. Not while there's breath in her lungs and whimpers to be coaxed from her lips.

I take the shovel from her fingers with one hand, the other

tangled in her long hair, and nip her bottom lip with my teeth before releasing her.

The blade sinks into the wet ground again and again as I proceed to bury the fucker alive. It takes a long fucking time, but I have all the patience in the world.

Especially when Keira wraps her arms around my waist and grins down at a terrified Liam, who's on his side in a pool of blood, screaming himself hoarse. As if that will save him.

Nothing will.

Liam thought he could hurt her.

Scare her.

He doesn't deserve to live.

My arms burn with pain when, finally, only patches of his pale face peek through the mud. He's snorting desperately as it gets in his nose, and I know the next shovel of dirt will be the last before he slowly suffocates to death.

A sick sense of anticipation swirls low in my stomach, heightened even more when Keira peers up at me from beneath her long, wispy lashes with a look of cold-blooded detachment.

She wets her plump lips and reaches down to cup me through my jeans.

To see her true, hidden self like this—dark, dangerous, and deadly—has my heart thudding heavily in my chest, and it's not from the exertion of burying her boyfriend alive.

It's from the intimate connection between Keira and me. Something was cemented here tonight.

I scoop up more dirt and toss it over Liam's face. Silence settles over the woods while I stare at Keira's pale face and flushed cheeks. The icy wind has caused her lips to chap, and she's shivering.

"Fuck me, King," she pleads, her teeth chattering. "I need you."

This girl...

While Liam slowly suffocates to death in his grave, I pick Keira up by her waist, guide her legs around my hips, and carry her over to the nearest tree.

Once there, I help her out of her jeans and panties before freeing my aching dick and grabbing hold below her knee. I lift it up and align the thick head of my dick with her soaking, pink cunt.

Leaning back slightly, I stare down between our bodies and watch my dick tear through her tight pussy. The killing must have riled her up because she's so fucking wet that I meet no resistance. My dick disappears inside her tight cunt, and when I slide it back out to the tip, it glistens with her arousal.

I ram my cock back inside her and guide her ankle to my shoulder before placing my thumbs on each side of her pussy lips and spreading them apart to reveal all of her.

"Fuck," I groan, staring at her puffy slit. While I have seen and fucked a lot of pussy in my life, hers is hands down the prettiest I've come across.

"King," she moans. With her eyes on me, she reaches down between her legs and begins to circle her clit, while I hold her open. "You're so big..."

"Keep talking like that, and I won't last."

It's true; the heavy look in her eyes and the way she licks her lips are my undoing.

"It feels so good..."

I thrust forward, all the way to the hilt, and grind my hips. This girl, *my girl,* is fucking perfect.

"Kiss me, King," she pleads, and I let go of her pussy lips to wrap a hand around her slender throat, feeling her pulse flutter erratically beneath my thumb. I ravage her mouth, kissing her deep and slow, until needy whimpers dance on her tingling, swollen lips, and her pussy floods my dick.

I inhale her trembling breaths, while Liam fades away in a grave he made his own girlfriend dig. Karma is funny like that. It has a way of biting you in the ass when you least expect it.

Keira's pussy strangles my dick as she wrenches her mouth away. "I'm coming."

With my lips pressed to hers, I fuck her harder, faster, chasing my own release while she moans through her climax. And then, with a final groan, I come, pumping her cunt full of cum as her pussy continues pulsing.

We're both breathing hard, clinging to each other, when the first raindrop falls from the sky, followed by more.

Keira blinks as one strikes her cheek, and then she lets out a breathless laugh.

A laugh I want to hear again.

Lowering her ankle from my shoulder, she wraps her arms around my neck, presses her chest against mine, and pulls my mouth down to hers. This kiss is different from earlier. It's slow and sensual, but dirty nonetheless. It's a promise and a commitment. *We killed together.*

The rain comes down heavier, soaking through my clothes and cementing the loose soil in Liam's grave.

My hands slide over Keira's wet cheeks. I palm them and suck her bottom lip between my teeth, tasting her for all the times I couldn't while I was confined to a bed in the sterile hospital room.

All the times I wanted to rip my IV line out and leave, hospital gown or no hospital gown, and hunt Liam down.

But patience is a virtue.

So I bided my time, like a predator crouched in tall grass.

OFFICER WELLS

The rain patters against the windows to my left while I stick a picture of Liam on the whiteboard. I uncap my pen and write 'missing' in red.

There's a clearing of a throat behind me, and I turn in time to spot Riveiro entering the room, dressed in black pants and a white, silk blouse. She eyes the whiteboard with a small smile, and I wave a hand dismissively. "Forgive an old fart for preferring the old ways of doing things."

Riveiro is a modern woman of the world and prefers to use a whiteboard app on her sleek tablet. Gone are the days of traditional ways.

"I never said a word."

The teasing lilt of her voice draws a smile from my lips. Rubbing my neck, I breathe out a tired sigh. "Four dead and two missing, and we're nowhere closer to catching this guy."

As she comes to stand beside me, I breathe her in—laundry soap and a discreet, feminine perfume with hints of jasmine and blackcurrant. It's better than the stench of frustration and failure.

"The killer is only human; he'll make a mistake."

"What do you think?" I ask, gesturing to the whiteboard, and the numerous photographs of mutilated bodies. Before she can reply, I continue, "What I don't get is why the last three victims went missing when the first two were left for us to find. Kit, on the other hand, was left for Keira to discover—almost as if all of this is for her and her alone."

"So, rather than a crazed killer playing copycat, the killings are done with a personal motive that involves Keira?"

"Which means the killer is close to her." With another sigh, I step closer to the whiteboard. "The killer kept Kit alive for days before finally slicing his throat—"

"*Barely* alive," Riveiro cuts in. "The results from the autopsy indicate a lot of the body parts, like the ears, fingers, and toes, were removed before death.

"Alive nonetheless, which means there's a good chance Liam is still alive. We need to double down on our efforts to find him."

Riveiro slides her phone out of her pocket and taps into it. "On it." After she has pocketed it, she says, "But, Wells, you need to prepare yourself that it's probably too late already. If the killer wanted you to catch Liam alive, you would. If we know one thing by now, all of this," she gestures to the whiteboard, "has been carefully planned out."

"That's what I'm afraid of," I mutter, capping my pen.

As I place it back down on the nearest table, the door opens, and one of the lab technicians enters with an envelope clutched in his hands.

"We have a match to the fingerprints found in Keira's bedroom on the day the head was discovered on her pillow and the two officers were killed outside."

Riveiro perks up, accepting the envelope when he holds it out. Her eyes find mine, and then she lifts the flap and pulls out a sheet of paper.

"Well?" I ask.

"It's King Knight."

The morning sun filters in through the curtains. One look at the alarm clock confirms it's nearly time to grab a shower and get ready for school, but the last thing I want is to leave my bed *and King*.

It was the first time I'd woken up beside him. Like a creep, I watched him sleep. In fact, I could stare at him forever. At the way his dark bed hair falls across his dark brow and how good his muscular, tanned back looks in the morning light. I can't believe he's here. In my bed.

It's a shame for reality to intrude on this moment when I want nothing more than to stay here all day and fuck. Even if my pussy is already so sore this morning that I can feel him every time I shift.

"Are you sure you don't want to come with me to school?" I ask, my chin propped on his bare chest, while he traces the bridge of my nose with a finger.

"You know I do, but I have a few things I need to take care of first."

"Sounds ominous," I tease.

"I need a new phone, for starters. Besides, we need to stay low for a few weeks."

I pull a face. "Fuck that."

It makes him chuckle, his chest vibrating. "I don't like it either, but we need to play it smart. It will look suspicious if we're seen together so soon after Liam goes missing."

"Since when did you become the sensible one?" I pout, even though he's right.

King rolls us over, pulling the quilt over our heads and nuzzling my neck. He tickles my ribs, and I squeal with laughter while he shushes me.

"Quiet, baby." His smile is as wide as mine. "You don't want your mom to come in here."

Wrapping my thighs around his trim waist and my arms around his neck, I stare up at him. Framed by the white quilt, his dark hair curls at his nape, and his soft lips are parted. "I can't think when I'm around you. You make me stupid."

That has him chuckling again, and it's a sound I love. "That's good, isn't it?"

"Sometimes." I lift my head off the pillow to taste his lips, then whisper, "Sometimes, not so much."

"No? Why's that?" His lips are back on my neck, stealing my train of thought.

"The killer is still out there."

King peppers kisses up my neck, chin, and lips. "He won't go anywhere near you. I'll kill him myself."

"King," I whisper, and he stiffens slightly before leaning back to look me in the eyes. "I'm sorry about Jasper and Kit."

A muscle works in his cheek, but aside from that, his face remains a careful mask.

"Can I tell you a secret?"

It's hot beneath the quilt, but I'm grateful for the cover it gives us. Secrets spill easier when it's just us, hidden inside our cocoon.

"You can tell me anything, baby."

His tone is sincere enough that I relax a little while playing with the silky curls at the nape of his neck. I focus on them, whispering, "I killed my stepdad."

King says nothing, so I chance a look at him.

"The killer threatened to kill Kit and my mom if I didn't murder my stepdad." My voice shakes. "He made a game of it."

"A game?"

His stubble rasps beneath my fingers as I drag them down the sharp line of his jaw.

I nod. "Yes... but that's not the worst of it."

"What is?"

It takes courage to confess this next part. Courage I don't really have, but I force the words out anyway. "I enjoyed it."

King's breath whooshes over my face, and then he rolls off me, settles on his side, and drapes his warm arm over my waist. He pulls me closer, burying his nose in my hair. "Tell me everything, baby. From the beginning."

So that's what I do. I snuggle close to my new anchor and bare the deepest, darkest parts of me.

The fear of becoming my father.

The fear of losing control.

But instead of retreating and calling me a monster, he slides his fingers into my hair and crushes his soft lips to mine in a searing kiss.

"You're fucking perfect," he growls, nipping at my bottom lip with his sharp teeth. "So fucking perfect."

"You're not afraid of me?"

He squeezes my bare waist and digs his calloused fingers into my skin. "Of course I'm not scared of you. I want you more, if anything."

"Because I'm a killer like my father?"

His head shakes, and he leans in to sink his teeth into my neck while rolling his hips against me. It's unfair how nice he smells in the morning. I breathe in the hint of sweat on his skin. It would be gross on anyone else, but on King...

"Because you're brave. It takes a lot of fucking guts to do what you did. Do you think your friend Cassie, Madison, or even my friends, Ava and Hayley, could do it? No fucking way."

"Don't be sexist," I tease, causing him to chuckle and roll on top of me again.

"Fine, how about your friends, Miles and Chris? Think they could kill someone in cold blood to save someone like Kit—a guy they're not close to?"

"I don't know."

"I'll tell you now, from what I witnessed when they held me down while Liam pummeled me, they're both scaredy cats who would crap their pants if faced with the same situation."

"I was fucking furious with him for hurting you," I grit out, but he cups my jaw and presses his hungry mouth to mine in a deceptively tender kiss that makes my heart turn to putty. He kisses me again, just as painfully slow, his tongue delving past my lips to dominate mine.

I pull away, breathing heavily. "And then I couldn't get ahold of you. I was scared, King."

I haven't admitted that to anyone. Not even myself.

It's easier to pretend to be strong than it is to be vulnerable. The world feasts on vulnerability. It tears into it like a pack of vicious hyenas until nothing remains but fleshy bone.

"I was always coming back for you."

"What if I'm a psychopath?"

"Then we can be psychopaths together. The new Bonnie and Clyde."

It's meant as a joke, but behind the sparkle in his dark-as-night eyes resides a promise that I'm driven to reciprocate as I pull him down to me and ravage his mouth.

When we break apart for air, he says, "Don't hold back on me, baby. I want all of you—the good and the bad. I want the angel and the demon, got it?"

My head nods, and I smile against his tempting mouth that I want on my cunt. "Got it."

As he pulls the quilt back, the morning light assaults my eyes, and he chortles at my less-than-impressed reaction. But I soon melt into the mattress when he trails biting kisses down my quivering body.

Let's just say I'm very late for school.

HAYLEY

"Who was that?" Ava asks when I pocket my phone as we enter the cold library.

"Don't they ever put the fucking heat on in here?" I mutter, setting off down the aisle, on the hunt for the girl who has leashed King as though he's a lap dog.

Ava scurries after me, her pink-and-black, checkered skirt teasing her thighs. The colors are so bright that she could stop traffic. I wonder briefly how she isn't freezing to death. I mean, sure, her white winter jacket is puffy enough, and her earmuffs help, but she has nothing on her legs.

If that was me, I would've caught frostbite by now.

No, thanks. I'll stick to my bootcut jeans, combat boots, and a black, turtleneck sweater.

"Was that King?"

"It was." I look left and right down each aisle. Books and more books greet me, but no Keira.

"When is he coming back to school?"

"Tomorrow. He said he has a few things to take care of first."

"He'll have eyes on him when he returns."

I slow to a halt and frown.

Noticing my reaction, she explains, "Everyone knows he was fucking Keira behind Liam's back. They kept it quiet, but you know how fast rumors spread in Blackwoods. As soon as the news broke about what Liam did to King, speculations were flying wild." She shrugs. "And Liam liked to brag."

I grind my teeth, scanning the nearby area. Ava is right. Everyone knows. The looks the other students have thrown Keira's way today have been nothing if not wary and hostile. Now that Liam is gone, everyone is blaming her for his disappearance. She's Jimmy Hill's daughter, after all. The murders are happening because of her. People are scared. No one wants to be next.

"Revenge is a strong motive."

I pull a face. "What are you saying, Ava? That King killed Liam? He's missing. Not dead."

"Missing or dead, King should stay low for a few days."

"I disagree," I reply, setting off walking again. "It looks more suspicious the longer he stays away."

I finally find Keira at one of the study tables toward the back, where she sits with a book open in front of her while she stares out the window to her side at the flurry of snowflakes. Her denim jacket and scarf are draped over the chair beside her. Keira is another seemingly crazy person who is immune to the cold, but at least she has on an oversized, cream, cable-knit sweater.

Striding up to her with Ava in tow, I plant my hands on the desk. Keira turns her head to look at me, and I breathe the scent of her apple shampoo. Beneath it is something sweeter and warmer, like vanilla.

Her sky-blue gaze slides from me to Ava and back again. "Can I help you?"

I scoff. "That's the first thing you want to say to me? I'm King's closest friend."

"Are you here to intimidate me? To tell me to stay away from King?"

My glare is met by a smirk on her end. She leans back in her seat, picks up the pen by the book, and taps it on the desk. "Let me guess. You're jealous now that he isn't fucking you anymore?"

Tap. Tap. Tap.

"You little shit," I grit out. "You think this is a joke? Jessica, Jasper, and Kit are dead because of you. Dead! That's two of King's friends murdered in cold blood. So yeah, I will tell you to stay the fuck away from King before he gets hurt, too."

Her smirk falls as her face drains of color. I've hit a sensitive spot.

"I had nothing to do with those murders."

Ava plants her butt on the table. "Does King like your naivety? I think it's tiresome."

Keira snaps her gaze away from Ava when I say, "The killer is obsessed with you, or have you forgotten that? King started fucking you. Soon after, people started dying."

She stays quiet, so I add, "Dump him. I don't care how you do it, but if you care about King at all, break his heart."

"You're callous."

"I'm protecting him. The same can't be said for you. Can't you see how fucking selfish you are?" I snarl. We're so close that our noses nearly brush. "You'll happily put him at risk so long as you get a good dicking. You don't care about him. You only care about yourself."

"Selfish," Ava sneers, tittering.

Relaxing back into her seat, Keira crosses her arms and looks from me to Ava before releasing a soft snort. "And you think King would leave me alone if I dumped him? You think he would just walk away?" She looks me in the eye, baring her white teeth. "Who's the naive one now?" She points a stern finger at Ava. "And you should shut your mouth! You don't have a fucking backbone, so don't stand here and pretend you wouldn't quiver like a fucking leaf in the wind if Hayley weren't here."

A peal of laughter slips from my lips. The girl has some nerve, I'll give her that. I can see now why King is so obsessed with her.

Ava, on the other hand, is less than impressed. "You think you're so special? King wouldn't have looked twice at you if it weren't for the dare!"

I briefly close my eyes.

Stupid girl.

"What dare?" Keira asks carefully, bouncing her gaze between us.

"It's nothing," I reply before aiming a pointed look at Ava, mouthing, "Shut up!"

If King finds out—which he will now—that Ava told his precious Keira about the dare... I don't even want to think about the consequences. He'll rip into Ava until there's nothing left but a sobbing mess. King can be ruthless when provoked, which makes me wonder if he has something to do with Liam's disappearance.

"You're nothing but a dare, sweetie," Ava taunts gleefully. "Hayley challenged him to fuck you behind Liam's back. Did you really think he would be so fucking persistent otherwise? Think about it. Has he ever looked at you twice beforehand?"

Keira stares at Ava, her eyes glassy with emotion. It's the first crack in her brave facade. "You're lying."

Ava smirks and I glower at her. "You know I'm not."

The chair scrapes on the marble floor as Keira slowly rises to her feet. She collects her bag, then her denim jacket and her scarf. Not once does she look at either of us.

I stare after her as she walks out without another word, holding her head high.

While I sought her out with King's best interests at heart, I never meant for Keira to find out about the dare. It was just a bit of fun banter between friends. A challenge to cure our boredom, or, more accurately, *my* boredom. King wasn't interested at first.

Ava turns to leave, but I grab her by the arm. "What was that?"

Her eyes flick down to my hand on her jacket, where my fingers dig into the puffy, white material. "I thought you wanted her to break up with him. Now she will."

My fingers twitch while I try to control my influx of emotions. "Not like this."

Ava wrenches free of my grip as a male student hurries past

with his head bent low. "Newsflash, Hayley. There's no right or easy way to break up. You don't get to play the devil's advocate *and* the angel. Pick one."

"King will have your head for this when he finds out."

She shrugs carelessly. "At least he'll be alive, right? And that's what matters."

As she walks away, I pull my bag up onto my shoulder. Begrudgingly, I can't argue with her.

She *is* right.

KEIRA

I skip classes.

I shouldn't let someone like Hayley and her minion, Ava, get to me. But the truth is, I'm hurt.

I'm hurt King would do something like that, but I'm also not surprised. Ava was right when she asked me if King had looked at me twice before. King never noticed anyone. He was above everyone and everything. So why would he suddenly pursue me?

I'm so fucking stupid.

The bell above the door tinkles, and Madison walks in, shaking off a layer of snowflakes. She looks around the small cafe until she spots me seated at the back, where it's easy to blend in. This is my spot—the one place I come to when I'm down.

Even Claire, the owner, knows something is up when I order a skinny latte and hide away in the back. As soon as I entered, her lips turned down, and she asked who'd hurt me this time.

"Long story," I'd mumbled, my cheeks icy cold and red from the bitter wind outside.

Madison waves at me before walking up to the counter and ordering a slice of carrot cake and a pumpkin-spiced latte. I can smell it from here when she walks over, precariously balancing the items on the tray.

She places it down on the table and says, "I'm honored you called me instead of Cassie."

I can't exactly speak to Cassie about this. I'm sure she's heard the rumors like everyone else at school—it's impossible not to— but she wouldn't understand. Not like Madison. Unlike Cassie, she never judges.

Removing her white bobble hat and shrugging out of her puffer jacket, she smiles at me. "What's the emergency?"

My cheeks redden. Now that she's here, I feel stupid. "Ava admitted I'm a dare to King."

"You are or you were?"

"What do you mean?"

She unrolls her fork and knife from the napkin. "The dare. Are you still one? You and King have been an unofficial thing for some time. He must have completed the dare by now, right? So why is he hanging around if he doesn't like you?"

I stir my half-drunken coffee, the spoon clinking against the side of the glass. "I don't know how to feel about the fact that I was a dare to begin with."

"You'd been going steady with Liam for a long time."

"Your point?"

Madison cuts her carrot cake into small pieces—a weird habit of hers whenever she eats cake. "Why would you be on his radar when he knew you had a boyfriend? Unless," she shrugs, "he had a reason to."

Laughter bubbles up from my chest. "That's a bit harsh, don't you think?"

"Is it?" she says, deadpan. "King doesn't have to work for pussy."

"I'll have you know mine is prime-time pussy."

Madison's shoulders shake with laughter. She munches on a

piece of carrot cake, brushing stray crumbs off her lips. "I love how humble you are."

Watching her with a wide smile, I jerk my head at the cake. "Is it good?"

"You have no idea." She grows serious. "You can't let Hayley and Ava hurt you like this because of their stupid dare. King is obsessed with you. Trust me when I say that you're more than a dare to him. The poor guy can't take his eyes off you when you enter the room. You're all he sees."

The tips of my ears heat, and I lower my gaze to my lap. "Maybe."

Shaking her head, Madison stabs a piece of carrot cake, then points the fork at me. "No maybe. Trust me on this. The boy is crazy about you."

"But what if they're right?" I wave a dismissive hand when she lowers her fork and looks sternly at me. "Forget about the dare. Yes, I'm hurt about it. But in the grand scheme of things, it pales in significance."

"What's the problem?"

"Well..." I worry my bottom lip, hunching forward a little with my hands trapped between my knees. "It's dangerous to be associated with me. Just look at you..." I lift my hand and gesture to her. "You were nearly killed."

"But I survived." She puts her fork down, reaching for my hand and inclining her face so we're level. "You can't blame yourself for everything that's happened. And you can't distance yourself from everyone just to keep them safe. Besides, Jasper and Kit were friends with King, not you."

Tears sting my eyes, and I quickly release her hand to wipe at my wet cheeks. "I'm sorry I dragged you away from classes for this."

"Are you kidding me?" She takes another bite of carrot cake, smiling around a mouthful. "I get to gossip and eat cake to my heart's content. This beats school any day. Just don't let my parents know."

I reach for my coffee and take a sip of the now lukewarm drink. Madison cleans her plate in seconds.

"I couldn't talk to Cassie about this."

Madison scoffs, wiping her mouth with a paper napkin before crumpling it up and tossing it on the plate. "No kidding. That girl loves her seat atop the soapbox she guards with her misplaced morals."

There's bitterness in her tone, but I don't question it.

I love how relaxed Madison is. A few weeks back, she was stabbed by a madman. But here she is, listening to me rant.

"Thank you," I whisper as I reach for the paper napkin and begin tearing it into strips.

"For what?"

"For listening." I line the stripes up, three in total, then tear off another. "For making me feel better. I'm hurt about the dare, but... I don't know... It feels stupid to make it into a big thing, you know? Four people are dead. I don't have it in me to make a big drama."

Madison drains the last of her coffee. "Hayley was fucking King before you, wasn't she?" She puts the cup down and wipes her mouth with her hand. "Maybe she just wanted you out of the way. Plain old jealousy masquerading as concern."

"You think? It didn't seem to me like she wanted Ava to tell me."

"I don't know, but don't let it get to you either way." She slides the plate forward and puts her forearms on the table with a coy smile. "Even if you broke up with him today because of some juvenile dare, he wouldn't leave you alone. He'd corner you and fuck you silly."

"Madison," I laugh. "You're so crude sometimes."

Her eyes sparkle with humor. "Are you denying it?"

I bite down on my lip to stop myself from returning her

simpering. My head shakes as I relent with a soft laugh. "He wouldn't leave me alone if I broke up with him."

"There you go. So why give the dare any more of your energy? You like him, don't you?"

There's no point denying the truth. I'm crazy about King.

"Yes, I like him."

"Problem solved. Now you can tell Hayley and Ava where to stick it."

"I thought you were friends with them?"

"I have a lot of friends," she says with a small shrug. "But I'm loyal to few."

"I hope I make that list."

She snorts, her arms crossed. "You're my closest friend, Keira. If anyone messes with you, they mess with me."

That makes me laugh. "I think you're my closest friend, too."

"Did I knock Cassie down a step?"

I wet my lips, looking out through the window at the snowflakes outside. "She took care of that herself."

"Do I sense some animosity?"

A waitress clears our table and asks if we want anything else. Madison shakes her head.

When she's gone, I reply, "It's hard to be friends with someone who judges your decisions, you know? Of course I know it was wrong to cheat on Liam. I never claimed to be a good person." I sit back and scrub my face before looking at Madison again. "Liam and I weren't in love. He was using me as much as I was using him. So I guess it didn't seem like a big deal to keep my thing with King a secret."

"Girl, you don't have to explain yourself to me. Liam had some strange obsession with you, but it was an unhealthy one."

"You don't think King's is?" I ask curiously.

"He's in love with you, Keira."

I nearly choke on my own spit. "He's not."

He can't be.

I know he likes me. But in love?

How anyone could love me is a mystery. Especially after coming face to face with the twisted side of me.

I don't know what this thing between King and me is, but to finally admit that he's in love with me? It feels like such a big step.

"Ask him yourself if you don't believe me."

"But the dare—"

"Screw the fucking dare. Screw Hayley and Ava. Don't let anyone mess with your head," she spits out. Then her eyes soften, and she asks, "What about Liam? How do you feel about his disappearance?"

I inhale a deep, steadying breath, crafting my lie carefully. "I don't know how to feel, to be honest. He beat King up and put him in the hospital. I can't just forgive him for that. But despite the bad blood between us, he's also my friend and I want him to be okay."

She reaches for my hand, squeezing reassuringly. "I'm here if you want to talk, okay?"

KEIRA

Darkness has settled on the sleepy town of Blackwoods. The cutlery clinks on the plates while Mom and I eat a ready meal at the kitchen table. It's bland but too salty at the same time.

My stepdad has been missing for almost a week, but Mom still sets out a plate for him as if she expects him to walk through the door at any moment.

I should feel guilty for murdering him, and maybe I do *a little,* but only because Mom looks so lost and broken without him here, even though he was a waste of space.

It's strange to sit here alone with my mom. We haven't been alone together since that night when the police hauled my dad away. Shortly after that, my grandparents turned up. From that moment forward, there's always been someone else around.

I guess, in a way, I lost both my parents that night.

I push my plate away, my appetite gone. Ever since we murdered Liam, the thought of food has made my stomach churn. The way he screamed himself hoarse and the raw panic in his eyes. How he fought for his life, tied up and injured. Somehow, I disconnected from my human side as a suppressed, dangerous part of me surfaced—the part my father passed on.

It's strange, though. I should feel something, right? Guilt and shame? Disgust toward myself for enjoying it? But I feel nothing when I think about it now.

Not sadness. Not regret.

Not even relief.

Just nothing.

The same goes for the dare.

I can't even summon the strength to feel hurt anymore. Not after my talk with Madison earlier.

We killed Liam together.

Why would King go through all that trouble for a stupid dare?

Maybe it started out that way, but we became something more somewhere along the line.

"You should have told me," Mom mutters, giving up on trying to spear an overcooked piece of carrot with her fork. She drops the fork on the plate before reaching for her glass of red wine. She's been drinking a lot lately as a way to drown her emotions. I don't blame her. I wish I had a poison of choice, too.

"Told you what?"

"You went to see *him.*"

"My dad, you mean? Yes, I did."

She drinks her wine, downing it in one go before refilling the glass. "You need to forget about him. Nothing good comes from dragging up the past."

The wine glugs loudly as she refills the wine glass to the top. Any more, and it will spill over the sides. She puts it down and looks at me. "Do you hear me, Keira?"

"Four people are dead, Mom. Liam and Allen are missing. Unlike you, I can't ignore what's happening."

Mom looks like she's tasted something sour. "You think visiting your father is going to change things? Bring answers? No, Keira. Your father is a cold-blooded murderer who deserves what's coming for him."

"We might not make it out of this alive, Mom. You do realize that, right? The killer isn't done yet with his little reenactment or whatever psycho bullshit this is. If my incarcerated father can shed any kind of light on what's going on, I'm willing to listen. Not only that... I'm lost. Despite what you may think, you're not the only one who's struggling. I was there that night, too. I loved Dad, too." I stand up and leave the kitchen. She can drown herself in her misery for all I care.

We all deal with trauma differently. Maybe it works for her to bury her head in the sand and pretend everything is fine, that her husband isn't missing, but it doesn't work for me.

I can't just pretend that something dark and scary isn't growing inside me, that *maybe* I'm more like my father than I let the world see.

Entering my room, I make a beeline for my phone on the desk. Before Mom called me downstairs to eat with her, I was trying to get an assignment done. That's how cruel life is; four people are dead and two are missing, but life doesn't stop.

We're still expected to show up.

To perform.

To give a shit about math tests or geography assignments.

The desk light is off, so I switch it on and lean with my hip against the desk while tapping into my phone. I open social media and click on King's profile. It hasn't been updated since he was taken to the hospital.

I bring up a picture of him at the local burger joint, taken from across the table by one of his friends. King is looking directly at the camera with a small smirk on his lips, dressed in a maroon T-shirt with the sleeves cut out and a black, backward cap.

Heat sinks to my clit as I zoom in on his face, staring for too long at his brown eyes that are so dark, they sometimes look black. Especially when he's horny and lets his monster out to play.

I guess a deeply buried part of me is happy that Liam got what he deserved after putting King in the hospital. He beat him up when King was powerless to defend himself, and that's the definition of weak. Liam liked to think he was all that but when push came to shove, he felt bolstered by his football friends. He wasn't man enough to go head-to-head with King without his backup.

As I scroll through the rest of King's posts, there's a knock on the door, and I nearly jump out of my fucking skin.

Mom pops her head inside. "I'm heading out."

I straighten up from the desk with a frown. "Heading out where?"

"To see a friend."

"There's a killer on the loose, and you think it's a good idea to leave the house alone?"

"I'm a grown-up."

"You're not acting like one."

Mom hangs her head and then, with a tired sigh, she responds, "I'm sorry I can't live up to your expectations of me, Keira. With everything that's happened... Allen is missing... I can't sit around and wait. The silence... It's too much."

"I'll be alone in the house. Do you think that's a good idea?"

"I'm only going across the street to Esme's. Besides, the cops are right outside. You're safe, Keira."

I snort disgustedly. "Last time we had police outside, they were brutally murdered. I feel *so* safe."

Mom ignores my sarcasm, inching the door closed. "I'm only across the road at Esme's. Call me if you need me."

As soon as the door clicks shut, I flip her off. What a fucking role model she's turning out to be.

I'm seated on the sectional in the living room with the TV on.

"And she left you home alone?" Cassie asks, inhaling deeply. The crackle of her cigarette filters down the line.

I can picture her seated on her bed with the window open—despite the cold—while she smokes. When she's done, she'll flick the blunt out the window and spray her room with a cheap air freshener that reeks of peony in the hopes that her parents won't find out.

"I couldn't believe it either," I reply, toying with the remote control in my lap. I'm not even watching the car chase on the TV screen. "She's not coping at all with Allen's disappearance."

It's strangely easy to lie and to call it a *disappearance*.

Well, it's technically not a lie since I don't know what happened to his body *after* I killed him.

Cassie smokes in silence, her breaths trembling. She took the news of Liam's disappearance worse than anyone.

In fact, the whole of Blackwoods is in a state of shock. The star quarterback—the town's own golden boy—is missing.

"Are you okay?" I ask when the silence stretches on.

We're still not there yet after our arguments lately, but she phoned me tonight, so we must be moving in the right direction.

"Shouldn't I be asking you that? He was your boyfriend."

I slide down further on the couch, my woolly, gray, sock-clad feet on the coffee table. "That doesn't mean you're not sad, too."

"Are you, though? I haven't seen you shed a single tear."

Chewing on my lip, I continue toying with the remote. "Just because I don't cry doesn't mean I'm not sad."

The sound of her window closing travels down the line.

"Besides," I continue, "I think I'm numb."

"Yeah?"

"I woke up to find Jasper's severed head in my bed, and then, a few weeks later, I found Kit hacked to pieces in my backyard. And now Liam is missing, too. I think that maybe some part of me shut down."

"I'm sorry," Cassie replies regretfully, and the bed creaks as she shifts on the mattress. It's followed by the hiss of the air freshener can. "I can't imagine what you've gone through lately. I feel like such a bad friend."

I switch the TV off, drop the remote control by my side, and rub my tired eyes. "I think we've all been caught up in the mess over the last month."

"Maybe," she agrees.

We fall silent as I stare at the TV screen. The living room is dark except for the single lamp sitting in the window behind me. Without the flickering of the screen, it's barely enough light.

"It'll be so weird at school on Monday."

"I know," I breathe out softly. "It won't be the same with so many people gone."

"Liam was the star of the show, you know? Our table will be so quiet without him."

He was an asshole toward the end.

"Anyways," she blows out a long breath. "I have to go now. Talk tomorrow?"

"Sure."

She hangs up, and I dim the screen before tossing the phone beside me on the couch.

"I haven't seen you shed a single tear."

Her words play on repeat in my mind. Am I a psychopath for not grieving Liam, my own boyfriend? He was an ass in the days leading up to his murder, so should I be a blubbering mess now?

Cassie always thought he hung the moon when, in fact, he was selfish and narcissistic. I'm not saying he was bad, but we used each other for selfish reasons.

I run my hands down my face, then reach for the remote again. The TV won't switch on, so I bang the remote control on my palm. Why do we do that? Will the batteries magically work? I sit forward, arm stretched out in front of me as I press down hard on the button. Nothing happens.

"Stupid thing."

Just as I'm about to give up, I'm wrenched back by my hair, and a sharp knife is pressed to my throat from behind. I'm assaulted by the smell of bergamot, leather, and peppermint—my favorite combination in the world.

"Did you miss me, baby?" King's dark, raspy voice rings out in my ear, his warm breath gliding down the curve of my neck. I swallow against the cold blade. It nicks my skin, the sharp bite of pain drawing a soft whimper from my lips.

"You didn't think I'd let your sore pussy have a break, did you? That I wouldn't come back tonight to fuck you raw? I'll always come back to you, night after night, no-matter-fucking-what."

My clit tingles deliciously at the dark promise in those words.

"Let's play a little game, baby. I'm gonna let you go, and I'll count to ten. And you're gonna run like a good, frightened little prey. If I catch you, I'm gonna fuck you and fuck you up."

Holy shit... My pussy clenches in anticipation as I squirm on the couch in hopes of catching myself on the knife.

"Remember your safe word?"

Arching my back off the couch, I wet my lips. My voice comes out heavy with breathy lust. "Reaper."

"Good little whore." The knife slowly slides from my throat, the blade kissing my skin. "Now, run."

KING

Without hesitation, she sets off running. My cock hardens inside my jeans in anticipation of the chase. I've been away from my little rabbit for a couple of hours too long. Now it's like I have my oxygen source back.

I wanted her taken by surprise, thinking that I wouldn't come back tonight. That *maybe* I was done with her for the day.

She doesn't know that she has crawled beneath my skin like a parasite feasting on my heart, and now I need my daily fix. She's my drug, my downfall, and my sweetest addiction. The monster in me wants to indulge in the darkest parts of her psyche.

"Eight," I count out loud, cupping my erect cock through my jeans to alleviate some of the pressure. "Nine."

With my head tilted slightly to the side, I listen for any sound of her. The house is eerily quiet. My little whore knows how to mask her fearful, shaky breaths. She knows how to lure my demon out of Hell.

My lips lift in a smirk, and I make sure my voice carries through the house as I call out, "Ten."

The floorboards creak beneath my loosely tied Doc Martens as I walk slowly through the living room. I love this part of being extra noisy so that she'll hear me coming. If I'm really fucking lucky, she'll bolt from her hidey hole like a rabbit.

And like a cunning fox, I'll take chase.

"I can hear your racing heartbeat, baby. Is your pussy dripping for me?" I crack my neck and flex my hands.

I swear I can fucking smell her fear scenting the air like an aroma designed to entrap me, and it makes me wonder who the real hunter truly is.

She knows how to coax me out to play.

"Come out, come out, wherever you are."

The wooden floorboards creak again as I enter the dark hallway, looking from the kitchen to the staircase that leads upstairs.

As a diversion, I walk up to the staircase. Then, at the last minute, I turn around and enter the kitchen. Moonlight shines in through the window above the sink, which is stacked with dishes. The trashcan beside the kitchen island is filled to the brim, with two takeout boxes at the top.

Walking up to the counter, I pick up a fork and wait for a beat to let the silence settle over the room before dropping it to the floor.

The loud clank assaulting the quiet as it collides with the marble flooring doesn't disappoint. I bet my little rabbit's pounding heartbeat jumped up to her throat.

Tongue darting out to wet my bottom lip, I slowly turn and slide my gaze over the dark room. She's hidden in the shadows.

I can sense her.

And my dick throbs in response to her fear thickening the air.

"You're naughty, baby, toying with me like this. Do you have any idea how hard it makes me to think of you hiding somewhere, terrified, wet, and needy?"

There's a sound behind me, and I whirl around just in time to duck when she throws an empty glass at me. "I was a fucking dare to you, huh?!"

The loud crash is followed by another one as she grabs the vase of lilies on the counter and tosses that, too. "You're an asshole, King!"

So she found out about Hayley's stupid dare? I knew it would happen sooner or later, but that doesn't mean I'm not fucking pissed that someone, most likely Hayley or Ava, snitched.

I take chase when she sets off running blindly through the house. "You think your anger is gonna stop me? Think again."

Keira flies up the stairs to the second floor, and I smile to myself. What a rookie mistake.

"Never run upstairs, baby, when there's a predator on your tail. You'll get yourself cornered and fucked."

"Go fuck yourself!" she shouts, out of breath.

Grabbing the railing, I take the steps slowly. Keira trips and bangs her knee halfway up, but I make no move to grab her yet. Let her think she stands a chance at getting away. "I would much rather fuck you."

She hauls herself up the last steps and onto the landing. Then she sets off running down the carpeted hallway. I take a moment to watch her hair fly behind her in the darkness before releasing a slow chuckle and taking off after her. To heighten her fear, I tap the knife on a picture frame of Keira and her parents.

"Which one of my friends snitched? I bet it was Hayley. She was always jealous." I keep talking, if only to get her to engage in conversation. Keira makes bad decisions when she's distracted. Like now, when she enters one of the bedrooms and slams the door shut. The lock clicks into place, the sound loud in the silence.

My dick likes it a lot.

Stopping outside the door, I tap the blade against it. "Open up, baby."

Of course, she doesn't. It's not like I expect anything less.

"If you don't open up, you leave me no choice but to kick the door down. And somehow, I don't think your mom would like that."

"You're a fucking psycho!" she shouts from the other side.

"Says the girl who slaughtered her own stepdad and enjoyed it."

"I also fucked him and enjoyed it," she sneers.

Stiffening, I glare at the door as if it will magically incinerate if I glower at it for long enough. "You did fucking what?!"

"You heard me."

A low, bitter chuckle rises from my chest before gaining strength and ripping through the echoing silence like a deadly threat. "Just you fucking wait until I catch you, baby. I'm gonna fucking destroy your cunt."

"Fuck you!" she screams, causing my chuckle to die a swift death.

"I'm coming in, baby. You better start praying now."

"King, you crazy psycho! Don't you fucking dare kick that door."

I drive my boot into the wood, causing Keira to cry out behind it. "I'm sorry, baby, I can't hear you." I kick it again and again, putting my full weight behind the blows until, finally, with one last, hard kick, it breaks off its hinges and topples to the floor with a resounding thud. "Hi, baby. Did you miss me?"

Staring down at the broken door on the floor, she breathes out, "You're fucking crazy..."

"I do remember our date when we killed your boyfriend together. Just going on a hunch here, beautiful, but I think your crazy likes my crazy."

She lifts her startled gaze, blinking so slowly that it's almost comical. Then she turns and jumps up on the bed before grabbing a pillow and throwing it at me. It flies over my head as she scurries off the mattress, looking for more objects to throw in my direction.

As if that will stop me.

Her gaze darts around the room, and then she picks up the alarm clock on the bedside table.

I tut when it crashes to the floor. "Don't you think you're overreacting?"

The look on her face turns murderous. "Overreacting, King? Really? You're the one who kicked down my goddamn door!" She points at it on the floor. "How do I explain that to my mom?"

My shoulders rise and fall in a careless shrug. "You're putting obstacles between us. What did you expect to happen?"

"Not that," she all but squeals, and it's too cute not to smile.

I grow serious, rounding the bed. Keira jumps up on the springy mattress and darts across it like a sprinting rabbit that barely escapes my clutches. I launch myself at her, but she gets away just in the nick of time.

Then she's gone, running back down the hallway. Before she can fly down the staircase, I grab her by the hair and yank her back. I'm not gentle, but I know she wants me to bring her my worst so that she can fight me and pretend she hates every second.

I bet she would soak my hand if I touched her cunt.

Her breath gets knocked out of her as her back collides with my hard chest. She continues to struggle, so I band an arm around her waist, effectively trapping her arms against her sides. I slam my other hand over her mouth to muffle her screaming. The last thing we want is to alert the cops outside. Keira sure fucking knows how to scream like a banshee.

"You like to tease me with your pathetic screams, don't you? Taunt my dick with your fighting?"

Her nostrils flare, and she immediately stops struggling, which makes me chuckle.

"Mind games count as fighting, too. You think I'll grow bored and let you go if you turn weightless in my arms? Wrong." I seize her arm, hauling her down the hallway toward the bathroom, where I shove her inside.

"What the fuck are you doing?" she asks as I switch on the overhead light before walking over to the bathtub.

She makes no move to run, though, and her intrigued eyes follow my every movement while I plug the bath and turn the taps.

As the water begins to fill the bath, I straighten and half-turn. "If you're smart, you'll run."

Drawing in a shuddering breath, she retreats a step but makes no move to escape. Her eyes never once leave the bathtub. "What are you doing, King?"

"You like to play games." I bend at the waist, looking at her over my shoulder while testing the temperature with my fingers. "So tonight, we'll play."

Her throat jumps, and she slowly slides her gaze up to mine. "You're scaring me, King."

"You know the safe word." I grab her by the arm and pull her to me, making her yelp as she collides with my chest. Her scared, blue eyes flicker with uncertainty for a brief moment, but she stays silent, even while she tries to fight me off. Her hands lash out and slap my chest, my face, my arms, anywhere she can reach until I grab her wrist so hard that the bones grind together. Her terrified whimper drowns out the running taps and the sound of the sloshing water. Her eyes fly up to mine, silently pleading with me to stop.

To continue.

The mixture of emotions in her gaze is a heady concoction of drugs. I'm an addict, and she's my fix.

I bring the knife to her throat, the blade glinting in the muted overhead light. "You're gonna be a good girl for me, or I'll be forced to use this on you, understood?"

Her pulse hammers wildly in her slender wrist, which feels so small and breakable in my hand. The urge to snap it swirls in my veins.

"Understood?" I ask again as she glares up at me from beneath her long, wispy lashes. Even now, with a knife pressed to her throat, she's defiant.

That's what I love the most about her.

She never backs down.

And she stares evil in the eye without cowering.

Wait a minute...

Love?

I shake that thought off.

236

"What are you doing?" she blurts out when I lower the knife and spin her around.

With a hand on her bony shoulder, I shove her down to her knees and bend her over the bathtub's edge.

Now, my little whore isn't stupid.

Or meek.

She sees my intent and lashes out, trying to elbow me in the gut. Her fight turns vicious, primal, and so fucking euphoric that my balls ache from restraining her.

She still hasn't uttered her safe word.

I grab a handful of tangled hair and pull so fucking sharply, she cries out. "You wanna fight me, whore? We can do this all fucking night. Either way, I'm gonna drown you while you strangle my fingers with your cunt."

She bares her teeth, her eyes spitting fire. "You're so fucking sick in the head, King. You need psychological help!"

Using sheer strength, I force her head over the rippling surface at the same time I yank down her jeans and panties. Her pale ass will soon be painted red with my handprints.

I slap her once, the sharp sound bouncing off the walls along with her startled scream. "Want me to stop, baby? Want me to treat you like a good little girl? Fuck you real nice and slow, missionary in the bed?" My next hard slap makes her yelp. "Or do you want me to treat you like a dirty little slut? A fuck toy to ruin and break?"

"Fuck you!" she hisses, her tone venomous and thick with lust. "You don't know how to purge this darkness out of me. Do you think spanking will do it? You pathetic assho—"

With my hand in her tangly hair, I shove her face beneath the surface while she thrashes. My fingers trail through her soaking slit, pressing down on her swollen clit, and I chuckle to myself.

Keira's fucking perfect.

When I finally let her up for air, she's coughing, spitting, and spluttering. "What the fuck, King? What the actual hell is wrong with you?!"

"Don't pretend it didn't make you fucking drip for me." To prove my point, I drag a single finger through a trail of pussy juices on her inner thigh.

She tries to fight me off again, to escape my fierce grip on her hair, but she soon stops when I press the flat end of the cool blade to her soaking folds.

Her sharp inhale of breath has a nefarious smile spreading over my lips.

"Scared I'll hurt you, baby?" I taunt. "Now be a good girl and take a deep breath for me."

Before I force her underwater again, I press my lips to her temple and slide two fingers inside her tight hole while whispering, "I might not stop this time." I shove her down, submerging her head completely underwater, and she immediately begins to thrash. Even as she pushes her cunt against my hand.

With her hair fisted tightly in one hand, I finger-fuck her drenched, tight pussy.

"That's it, baby," I taunt as her hands slide desperately over the bathtub's wet edge. "Strangle my fingers with your cunt."

I let her back up for air, listening to her sweet sobs. Her drenched hair lies plastered to her face, and mascara runs in streaks down her cheeks.

She's a beautiful, ruined mess.

"Your pussy is pulsing around my fingers, baby."

"Stop. Please, stop!" she sobs, her body shaking from the force.

I don't stop.

Instead, I push her back under and keep her there, thrashing and splashing water over the sides, while I unbuckle my belt one-handed and free my aching dick.

Cracking my neck, I palm my cock and push into her needy pussy.

Fuck...

She's pulsing around me rhythmically as I begin to pound her tight cunt, giving zero shits that her hip bones crash against the bathtub's edge with every brutal, feral thrust.

I yank her head back up, fucking her while she inhales sharp, gasping breaths amidst coughing and spluttering.

"Do it again," she whispers, her voice so haunted, I almost lose my shit. This girl is fucking perfect. "Drown me."

"Ask nicely, and I'll consider it." My hand slides from her hair to her neck, and I curl my fingers around the slender column. Her pulse is thundering beneath my fingertips, and her knuckles turn white on the tub's edge.

I slam into her so hard that she yelps.

"Please, King, drown me while you fuck me."

"With pleasure." I push her back down, fucking her harder.

The sounds of her wet cunt, the splashing of the water, and my deep grunts create a symphony of animalistic desire. Of demented pleasure and twisted kinks that would make most people squirm with unease and clutch their pearl necklaces. My little whore thrives on the depraved and of having her power confiscated. Even now, with her face submerged beneath the surface and her greedy cunt swallowing my dick, she weeps with relief. That's what humiliation and degradation bring her—euphoric relief from her demons.

Sliding my hand from around her neck, I pull her exhausted body from the bath.

I strip her out of her jeans, spread her over my lap on the soaking floor, and band my arms around her trembling body. "You did so fucking well, baby. So fucking well."

Her heart races against my chest as I lift her hips and sink back inside her.

"I'm so fucking proud of you," I whisper in her ear. "You're fucking perfect."

Keira slides her wet arms around my sweaty neck and holds on tight while I fuck her sweet cunt.

"Thank you, King," she breathes out, her breath tickling my throat. "Thank you for leashing my demons."

"My demons play nicely with yours." I place a kiss on her temple.

We fuck and fuck.

Nice and slow.

Deep and unhurried.

Her lips find mine in a searing kiss, and her soft tits inside her damp sweater press up against my chest.

Pulling down the collar, I pepper her shoulder with biting kisses. "I love how fucking good you feel wrapped around me, baby. It's like you were made for me."

"I want you to force yourself on me," she whispers quietly against my lips, as though she's nervous. "I want you to hurt me."

Fuck me... This girl...

"You're tired, baby," I point out, unsure why I'm suddenly so concerned about her well-being. I like this girl a fucking lot. I don't want to hurt her.

Not for real.

"Please," she pleads.

I tap her bare ass in a silent command to stand up, and she obediently climbs off my lap, her eyes skating down to my erect, glistening cock.

I draw my leg up and rest my arm on my knee. "Run, babe."

Despite how tired she is and how much her legs tremble, she darts for the door and wrenches it open. Then she's gone, and my lips kick up in a smile as I climb to my feet.

Unlike her, I'm not tired.

I'm so fucking amped up on the adrenaline of chasing and fucking my little rabbit that if she wants to play, I'll fuck her all night long, while her mom sips cheap martinis with her friend.

Keira barely makes it halfway down the hallway when I collide with her back. She screams and kicks and flails, but I'm soon buried to the hilt inside her sore cunt, fucking her so hard against the worn carpet that she'll have friction burns in the morning.

This time, it's not sweet or gentle.

I fuck her from behind like she means nothing to me.

Like she's a stranger that I grabbed down a dark alley.

Her sweet, haunted sobs spur me on, and when I press the sharp blade against her throat and nick her skin on purpose, she comes. Fuck does she come, pulsing around my throbbing length like a slut.

My slut.

"Fuck, yes," I grunt, slamming my hips into her pale ass cheeks one last time before releasing inside her with a choked sound deep in my chest.

It goes on for fucking ever.

By the time I roll off her, I'm fucking spent.

KEIRA

It's not even five in the morning when I kiss King goodbye. The freezing morning air has my nipples puckering inside my thin, baby-pink tank top. I can't believe he dragged me out of the warm bed for this.

"You can stay," I reassure him as he climbs through the window. "My mom won't be home for hours."

We've fucked all night. I'm sore everywhere, but the part of me that aches the most is the organ in my chest. It feels too full, and it's agony to watch him leave. Happiness like this frightens me the most because it can so easily be snatched away.

When I'm with King, my father's execution, the killer that's on the loose, and everything else fades away. I love that he gives my heart a rest from all the drama.

"I'll see you at school, baby." He gives me one last kiss.

"You can use the front door."

"I would have to sneak past the cops."

"Don't you think they will have nodded off by now?"

King's smile is naughty. "You're cute when you're trying to convince me to stay." He starts to climb down, and I lean over the ledge, noting the thin layer of snow on the ground. It's still coming down, but only slightly. As King jumps from the trellis, his Doc Martens sink into the snow, and white flurries stick to his inky, black hair.

With my forearms on the ledge, I smile down at him. "I'm gonna slip back into bed and play with my pussy."

He breathes a laugh. "The fuck you are. Don't make me climb back up."

My heart clenches with emotion, and the sensation feels so good but strangely frightening, too. It wasn't all that long ago, I wanted to disappear. Now here I am, ready to lock King away in my bedroom so that he won't leave. I miss him already, and he's still here, staring up at me from beneath my window.

"I'm gonna fuck myself and think of you."

"You're so damn evil," he says with a chuckle and a shake of his head. "Get back into bed. It's freezing."

The breeze moves my hair off my shoulders as I watch him walk down the sidewalk, away from the cop car.

When he's out of sight, I glance back at the car that's only just visible from here. There's movement inside, so at least my guards survived another night.

I pause as I let my gaze trail over King's footsteps in the snow. His aren't the *only* footsteps. A second set of footsteps steers off in the opposite direction, down the side of the house, toward the entrance that leads to the kitchen. My heart kickstarts in my chest, going into overdrive as my gaze dances across my bedroom to the closed door.

It snowed all night, so those footsteps are fresh.

Chewing my lip, I debate my options. Stay here and cower, or investigate?

Walking up to my wardrobe, I pull a gray, oversized hoodie off a hanger and slide it over my head. The sleeves are so long that I have to fold them up over my wrists.

I pad up to the door, the wooden floor cold beneath my feet, and carefully push the handle down to stop the hinges from creaking. With bated breath, I peer outside. The empty hallway stretches on for miles. At least, that's what it feels like when I sneak outside and take slow, measured steps toward the staircase.

Inhaling a shaky breath, I pause and listen. Nothing but thick, oppressive silence surrounds me. My own heartbeat roars in my ears with my next step.

I reach the top of the stairs, closing my eyes briefly before descending the steps, careful to step where it doesn't creak. It's freezing down here. As I cross the landing into the kitchen, I find out why. The backdoor is wide open, allowing the cold breeze to blow through the first floor.

While my heart was racing earlier, I'm sure it has stopped now, but it soon jumps back to life, thudding heavily in my chest.

Against my better judgment, I step into the kitchen and wrap my arms around myself to ward off the cold. The floor is wet from the snow that has drifted inside and melted on the marble tiles. My eyes skate up to the window and the cop car visible outside. The officers inside look bored out of their minds.

Crossing the kitchen, careful not to step on the broken glass from when I threw the vase at King, I quickly shut the door and lock it. Then a thought occurs to me. I open it back up, staring down at the footsteps in the snow leading back into the kitchen. My shaky breath comes out in a puff. I shut the door on autopilot before backing away. He's been in the house.

Maybe he's still here?

As I step away from the door, my back meets the kitchen island. I let out a yelp, my heart jumping to my throat, and turn around.

My phone is upstairs. I could run back outside and alert the cops, but they're proving as useful as a sack of potatoes. Too busy drinking coffee and taking turns napping while the other plays Angry Birds or something equally lame on their phone.

I swipe a knife from the block on the kitchen counter. The sound it makes as it leaves the block soothes my mounting fear. It's better than nothing. At least, that's what I tell myself as I exit the kitchen and enter the hallway.

A gust of icy wind shifts my hair off my shoulders, and the

hand clutching the knife begins to shake. "What the hell?" I whisper, staring at the wide-open front door. Another sudden gust causes it to slam into the wall. My heart explodes in my chest.

I run over and shut it, then whirl around with my arm outstretched in front of me. My grip tightens on the knife until my knuckles feel as if they might pop.

The killer is toying with me. Scaring me on purpose.

Slowly inching forward, I peer inside the living room. The morning sunlight casts streaks on the floor as it shines in through the half-closed blinds.

My gaze snags on the couch, and my cheeks heat at the reminder of how King snuck up on me from behind and pressed a knife to my throat. He's the Lucifer to my Hell. Or maybe I'm the Lilith to his Lucifer?

The living room is empty, so I make my way back upstairs to check each room. I find nothing. If the killer was here, he's gone now. Maybe he entered through the kitchen and hid in the living room while I went downstairs before escaping through the front door. Maybe I forgot to lock the doors properly last night, and I'm imagining all of this because I'm paranoid.

Pressing my shoulder to the door, I blow out a breath as I enter my room. The stress is getting to me.

As I shut the door and turn around, I pause.

There's a red mask on my bed.

And not just any mask.

A red devil's mask.

The last time I found a mask, the killer made me play a deadly game. A game I couldn't win.

I grab my phone from where it's plugged in on the bedside table and quickly type out a text to King's new number.

> Keira: The killer has been in my house and left a mask on my bed.

As I read it over, I realize how stupid it sounds. I delete it and type out a different message but delete that, too. Why am I messaging King? I don't want him to come back and put himself at risk.

Tossing the phone on the bed, I reach down to grab the mask before I can change my mind. I know this is the beginning of another game, and I can't deny the unwelcome excitement that accompanies the fear.

A folded-up note slips out as I lift the mask. I pick it up with trembling fingers and unfold it.

Your father is nearing his execution, rattling the bars of his solitary cell while praying for absolution. But it won't come. Not for men like him. Not for scum.

Poor Keira, the daughter of a serial killer.

What do you say, sweetheart?

At least your pathetic sob story makes for a good thriller.

But we both know what lurks beneath. The lies and secrets buried deep.

So grab your shovel. It's time to dig yourself into more trouble.

Who am I, you ask? Do you need another clue?

Welcome to the third act, Keira, where no one is safe. Not even you.

I read it over more than once, and my heart does a double beat each time.

"What the hell?" I whisper, staring at the words until they begin to blur.

The killer knows about what I did to Liam.

He knows I buried him in the woods.

246

"Oh, fuck." I swallow thickly, carefully folding the letter back up. I somehow manage to place the note inside my bedside drawer and slide it closed, despite my trembling fingers. Common sense tells me I need to show Officer Wells this note, but I know I won't.

If I do, Wells will ask dangerous questions.

I deleted my string of text messages with the killer, but I've watched enough crime documentaries in my time to know those can be retrieved, which is why I can't give Wells any reason to be suspicious.

And this letter raises questions.

Questions I'm uncomfortable with. The killer knows that.

I draw in a steadying breath. In through my nose and out through my mouth. The killer won't stop. Not until the game is finished, and we've crowned a winner.

I need to beat him at his own game.

Somehow...

KING

Something that annoys the living fucking daylight out of me is that Liam is barely cold in the grave, and his friend Chris is already all over Keira now that he's off again with Amanda.

And I'm forced to watch him put his arm around her shoulder during gym class and whisper in her ear with a shit-eating grin.

What does Keira do, the little troublemaker? She slides her gaze to me and smirks.

She's fucking begging for a chase and a spanking.

I exact my revenge on Chris by throwing the ball full force at his face. And when the gym teacher blows his whistle, throwing me a death glare, I simply shrug my shoulders and extend my arms by my sides in a helpless gesture. "Sorry, Teach. Thought we were playing dodgeball."

Chris pinches his bleeding nose while his friends fuss over him, including Keira. I'm going to spank her so fucking hard tonight that she won't be able to sit for a week.

"We *are* playing dodgeball, King," Teach booms, "but I'll have you thrown out of class if you put my students in the hospital. Keep it out of my classroom, whatever bad blood is between you and Chris."

I scoff, striding past Kara, Ava, and Hayley to stand at the back.

"Chris, go see the nurse."

He walks out, flipping me the finger as he goes.

It's with no small amount of satisfaction that I look back at Keira and raise a challenging brow. She looks too fucking good to eat in her tiny, navy-blue gym shorts and a gray T-shirt. Her long, pale legs go on for miles.

Of course I'd noticed her before Hayley made the dare that day. How could I not? She's stunning. I didn't openly drool over her, though, like the other male students. She was Liam's trophy, and the allure of a serial killer's daughter didn't appeal to me then. But now that I've seen her darkness with my own eyes, I want more.

Teach, however, with his red cap, whistle on a string around his neck, and graying hair, looks fed up as shit with me. He has slugs for eyebrows and a beer gut, which is not big but noticeable. His creased T-shirt bears the school logo, and his blue joggers have seen better days.

Still, I respect him for putting up with the likes of me.

As Keira narrows her blue eyes on me, I put my index and middle finger to my lips and flick my tongue between them. It's fucking adorable how she can't stop the blush that creeps up her chest and neck.

Yeah, baby, I'll be licking your sweet cunt later until you scream my name.

"King!" teach all but shouts. "Are you going to behave, or do I need to give you a detention slip?"

Smirking in his direction, I hold my hands up placatingly. "The trash has been taken out. I'll behave."

I don't miss how Keira puts her hands on her hips and glowers at me. It's too much fun to rile her up.

I stick to my word and try to keep a low profile, but it's fucking hard when other boys flirt with her now that Liam has been missing for less than a week.

They've all come out of the woodwork, behaving as if Keira is fair game now that the untouchable golden boy, Liam, is out of the way. For all they know, he has gone on an extended holiday without telling anyone and could walk back in tomorrow and cut off their balls for looking in her direction.

It's tempting, I have to admit.

One day soon, when the drama has settled, I'll claim her in front of the entire student body. She can smirk at me all she wants then; if another man flirts with her, I'll slaughter him.

I'm feeling irate just thinking about it.

As I pace on the spot, imagining all the ways I'm going to kill any guy who so much as dares to smile in Keira's direction, Kara and Ava exchange looks.

"Why are you behaving like a caged bull?" Kara asks, taking up position beside me.

"Why are you asking questions?" I reply. "Teach is about to blow the whistle."

"It's dodgeball. Not the army."

I chuckle, grateful that Kara is finally looking a bit brighter after Kit's death. She has been a ghost of her former self lately.

It won't last, though. Kit's funeral is soon, and that will hit us all like a sledgehammer.

"You need to be less obvious," Ava points out. "Now is not the time to be out in the open. Not while Liam is missing."

Hayley stretches her arms overhead, nodding in agreement. "Yeah, rumors are flying about his disappearance."

"Rumors fly regardless," I reply. "Everyone knows Liam beat me up for fucking his girlfriend."

"Well, maybe not fucking, but definitely flirting," Kara responds, tightening her ponytail. Black tendrils frame her face as she continues, "Liam would never openly admit his girlfriend is cheating on him."

I scoff. "There's not a chance the entire football team kept their lips sealed. Trust me, the truth is out there."

"You're quoting The X-files now."

Pulling a face, I open my mouth to reply, but the whistle blows before I can get a word out, and a ball comes flying at my face. I duck at the last minute.

Miles.

Stupid fucker.

He smirks threateningly, walking backward a few steps. His blonde hair is on the longer side and pushed back with a red headband. It makes him look like a dweeb.

That's pretty much how the game goes. Miles has it out for me, and I have it out for him. Teach blows the whistle several times and shouts at us until I'm sure he's sporting a migraine and a ticking vein in his temple.

The class finally ends.

Miles walks past me in a cloud of deodorant and sweat, whispering, "If you think we'll let you anywhere near Keira just because Liam isn't here, you're wrong. You don't want a repeat of what happened last time, do you?"

"Careful, Miles," I threaten. "Come between Keira and me, and I'll make you regret it."

He stops and strides back over. "Is that what you did to Liam? Make him regret it?"

Clasping his shoulder hard, my fingers dig into his flesh through his damp T-shirt. His face remains a blank mask, but I don't miss how he stiffens beneath my touch. "I don't know what you're talking about, Miles."

He stares after me as I release his shoulder and saunter away.

Keira waits for me across the hallway, pretending to scroll on her phone.

When she spots me, she walks off.

That's my cue to follow.

Her cute little butt looks far too fucking tempting in those short shorts. I don't like to think of the other guys checking her out, but now that the thought has entered my head, it won't leave.

She enters an empty classroom to the right, and I slink in after her. No sooner has the door closed than she flips the lock and shoves my joggers down until they're around my knees. She palms my cock. "I like making you jealous. You look like you want to hurt me."

"I fucking do. You're a brat when you taunt me openly like that."

"Yeah?" Her teeth sink into her bottom lip while she begins jacking me fast and hard. "I should taunt you more often. If only to see the promise of pain in your eyes." She nips at my jaw, whispering, "Will you hurt me later?"

"I'm gonna smack you so fucking hard, baby."

"Ass or face?"

"You want me to smack your pretty face?"

She cups my balls, her other hand working my dick like she's on a mission to bring me to my knees. "I want you to slap me while you fuck me. Call me dirty names. I want my cheeks to sting and be bright red when you're done."

"You're so fucking naughty," I grunt, my fingers tangling in her long hair.

"Slap me now, King."

"Now? Are you sure?"

She leans up on her tiptoes and nips at my lip. "Yes. Slap me hard."

I wrench her back by her hair, my hand flying out like it has a life of its own. The loud, resulting smack rings out in the room, and for a brief second, I worry I hurt her. But then she bites her plump bottom lip to the point of drawing blood as an erotic whimper slips from her mouth. It's so fucking filthy that a shot of pleasure shoots straight to my dick.

Keira jacks me faster, her small hand pumping my cock with expertise. "I want you to come on my face."

"Fuck," I groan. "You say the filthiest things."

Dropping to her knees, she sticks her flattened tongue out, and I stare down at her while she strokes my throbbing length.

"Pull my hair, King." She sticks her tongue back out and cups my balls.

Fisting a handful of her long hair, I pull on it sharply, tangling my tattooed fingers in the blonde strands. Her blue eyes stare up at me with so much lust and adoration.

I come with a choked grunt.

Strings of white cum coat her perfect face, raining over her lashes and plump lips. She keeps stroking me, aiming for her mouth, and the last squirt beads on her pink tongue. Keira rises to her feet and leaves me standing there with my gym joggers around my knees.

I take her in while she wipes my cum off her face with the hem of her T-shirt as though it doesn't bother her to walk around with cum stains on it.

But then again, she'll change into her normal clothes after this.

After pulling my joggers back up, I drag a hand down my face. "You're gonna kill me one of these days."

"Maybe," she purrs, walking up close to me and unlocking the door. "I am my father's daughter, after all."

Stepping out of the way, I stare after her as she leaves the room. I should wait to avoid anyone seeing us walk out together but fuck it. I don't care.

She strolls down the hallway toward the locker rooms before

turning and winking at me over her shoulder. Her gaze soon slides past me, and the flirty sparkle in her eyes dims.

Frowning, I turn around and pause.

The man in front of me clears his throat. "I'm Officer Wells, and this is my colleague, Officer Riveiro. We need you to come with us to the station."

Keira starts to walk over, but I hold my hand up behind me, silently telling her to stay back.

"Why?"

"I think it's best that we discuss it in private," his eyes skate past me to Keira, "away from here."

I half turn to Keira. "Get back to class."

"Mr. Knight, with all due respect, we need you to come with us," Officer Wells says, getting on my last nerve.

I plead with my eyes for Keira to walk away. "I'll catch up with you later, okay?"

Officer Wells clears his throat. "You can either leave with us peacefully, or we can cuff you."

Turning back around, I pull a face. "Cuff me? The hell?"

"We have an arrest warrant."

"He didn't do anything," Keira speaks up behind me, her tone thick with worry.

"Miss Hill, please stay out of this."

"The hell I will!" Shouldering past me, she glares at Officer Wells and Riveiro. "What's this about?"

"Miss, step out of the way."

"Not until you tell me what evidence you have."

We're starting to attract a crowd now. Students hover nearby, whispering to each other with their phone cameras out.

I pick Keira up by the waist and physically move her out of the way before gesturing toward the entrance at the end of the hallway. "Lead the way."

As I start walking, Keira wraps her small fingers around my wrist. "King? No. Don't go with them."

"It's okay, baby." I keep my voice low. "I'll see you later."

Her hand slips away as I walk off, following Officers Wells and Riveiro out the door.

I don't look back.

If I catch sight of her sad eyes, I'll burn down the fucking town to get to her.

King exits the school building and enters the cop car parked on the sidewalk. I want to run after him. To plead with Officer Wells to let King go. To convince him that he has the wrong guy.

But my feet stay rooted to the floor, and my breath stays lodged in my thick throat. I try to swallow past it. To inhale a breath. But all I manage is a choked sound that sounds surprisingly like a sob.

"Keira!" Madison runs up to me with Hayley, Ava, and Kara in tow. I'm wrapped up in an embrace, breathing in the comforting scent of strawberries and minty bubble gum. Madison soothes me like I'm a baby.

"What happened?" Hayley asks, stroking my hair away from my wet cheeks.

I *am* crying.

"Why are they taking King?"

Ava shoves Hayley out of the way and clicks her fingers in my face. "Earth to Keira. This is important. Why did they take him?"

"Can you at least try to be a bit more sensitive?" Madison asks sternly.

Kara simply stares at us with wide, worried eyes.

"They said they had to ask him questions down at the station,"

I mumble, my face squashed between Madison's generous breasts. Her wooly, mustard sweater is prickly.

I'm still in my gym clothes, but they don't look twice at my cum-stained, creased top. Not now that the cops came for King. Did they find out what we did to Liam? Did they find his grave?

Breaking out in a cold sweat, I step out of Madison's embrace. What if they found the grave and collected enough evidence to arrest King? My father's fate comes to mind.

No, I can't let my mind go there.

"Did they say anything else?" Ava asks, furrowing her brows.

I look between them all. It dawns on me that the girls that are here for me are King's friends. Not Cassie. She's absent again, like she has been since Liam disappeared. We haven't spoken much, except for the phone call yesterday.

Well, Madison is here, and she's my friend. Maybe even my only true friend.

As if she can read my thoughts, she squeezes my arm. "They'll release him, babe. I promise. What incriminating evidence have they got to keep him locked up? I know as much as you that it wasn't King who stabbed me in the bathroom."

Kara finally finds her voice, her face drained of color. "What do we do?"

"What can we do?" Hayley asks, throwing her arms out helplessly. "Absolutely nothing."

Now that show is over, the crowds are thinning. The bell rings, but we make no effort to move. Not until a teacher comes along and orders us to get to class.

I don't know how I walk to classroom 304.

But I do.

Coming to a stop outside, I stare at the numbers on the doors. I stare and stare, but the reality is still just as fucking awful.

Madison guides me forward with her hand in mine. "We just need to get through the next two lessons, and then we'll be out of here. We can come up with a plan, okay?"

Kara, Ava, and Hayley pull out chairs in the back row, and Madison seats me in the row in front of theirs.

Are we friends now?

Bonded over tragedy?

Madison sits sideways with her elbow on the desk. Her soft touch slides my hair behind my ear as I stare unblinkingly at the table. There's a groove in the wood about half an inch long. Someone has filled it in with a red marker.

"How long can they hold someone before an official arrest is made?" Hayley asks.

They all look to each other for the answer, and when it becomes abundantly clear that no one knows it, Kara says, "We should contact his parents. They'll get him a good lawyer."

"He's innocent. He doesn't need a lawyer," Ava blurts.

"Innocent or not, never ever talk until you have asserted your right to have a lawyer present. It's the golden rule."

Scrubbing a hand over my face, I blow out a long breath. I'm still in my gym gear. King's cum has dried on the hem of my T-shirt. It's crusty now.

"What if he did do it?" Ava asks, and we all glare at her. Even me.

"What the fuck?" Hayley blurts, her eyes popping wide open. "Why would you say that?"

"Well," Ava swallows, "he has a motive." Her eyes land on me, and I do a double take.

Turning fully, I lean over the back of my chair and hiss, "Fuck you, Ava! King is innocent."

"We know he is," Madison soothes, stroking my back as if she's worried I'll cause a scene and get myself thrown out of class.

"Do we?" Ava challenges.

This time, Kara stares at her disbelievingly. "This is King you're talking about. Our friend. Or have you forgotten?"

"I haven't forgotten. I'm just trying to look at this from the cops' perspective. Think about it for a second... Keira fucks King behind Liam's back. Liam retaliates and puts King in the hospital. Then Liam goes missing soon after King is released. Innocent or not, of course the cops are going to look in King's direction. He has the perfect motive."

"Only he doesn't," Kara emphasizes while Madison continues stroking my back. "King is a lot of things, but he's not a murderer."

I feel sick. There's a good chance I'll throw up all over the classroom if this nightmare doesn't end soon.

"Can we just drop this discussion now?" Madison asks, sensing my discomfort. She shoots Ava a stern glance. "Let's drop it, alright? This is stressful enough for us all."

Why do all classrooms look the same? Rows of seats, a whiteboard with barely eligible notes, and vertical blinds that sway in the slightly cold breeze. Why do all teachers insist on keeping the windows open? Even a small crack makes a big difference. As a result, the classroom has a nip to it.

I'm shivering from the cold.

"As soon as class is over, we'll head back to the locker rooms, okay?"

I nod, even though the thought of sitting here and doing nothing turns my stomach.

I hate feeling this powerless.

OFFICER WELLS

I enter the interrogation room and place the thick folder down on the desk before pulling out the chair and taking a seat opposite King Knight. The young man in front of me, with arms covered in ink and unruly, raven hair, watches me steadily from beneath his dark lashes. It's unnerving how collected he looks, considering the reason he's here. His brown eyes lazily slide from me to Riveiro and back again.

"We want to ask a few questions."

"My father's lawyer is on his way," King drawls, and I know we're almost out of time. As soon as he arrives, he'll tell King not to say another word.

"We just want to ask you a couple of questions," I repeat, sliding the folder toward me.

King's eyes flick down to it. "Why am I here?"

Straight to the point. This kid is smart.

After sharing a glance with Riveiro, I release a breath through my nose, closing the folder again. "Alright... Your fingerprints were found in Keira's bedroom."

King slowly lifts his gaze to mine. "And?"

"Keira never mentioned you, son. Your set of fingerprints was found at the crime scene after Jasper's head was discovered and two of my officers were brutally murdered."

King stares at me for a long moment, his face a blank mask.

"Care to tell me why your fingerprints were in Keira's bedroom on the day of the discovery?"

"Isn't it obvious?" His voice is a deep drawl, each word sliding off his tongue with ease. "We fuck."

I say nothing. Officer Riveiro says nothing.

"After dark, I climb in through her bedroom window and fuck her."

A shiver slides down my spine at the detached coldness in his tone. King smirks, shrugging a little. "And then I climb back out."

"So you were having an affair with Keira?" Riveiro asks.

His eyes home in on her. "Maybe... You found her boyfriend?"

I don't doubt they had an affair. Not after how protective she was of him today.

I try to understand why, though. Liam was, *is,* the golden boy —the popular football star with a rich family and colleges vying for him. King, on the other hand, is untamed, despite his privileged upbringing. There's a darkness surrounding him that has the hairs on the back of my neck standing on edge.

"No, we haven't found him," Riveiro admits, keeping her tone carefully even. "Now answer the question."

"Yes, we're having an affair."

I make a few notes in my notepad. "How did it start?"

"What are you accusing me of here?" he counters. "So you found my fingerprints in her bedroom? How about the severed head? Or anywhere in or around the cop car?" He leans in, holding my gaze. "I didn't kill Jasper or your officer friends, so you have nothing on me and no reason to keep me here. No DNA evidence to link me to the murders."

"With all due respect, Mr. Knight, you do have the perfect motive."

He frowns.

"You were having an affair with Keira."

"And? How is that a motive for killing my friends? Kit, Jasper, and Jessica? The fucking principal? You're clutching at straws, Officer Wells, and you know it."

"Okay, fine." I hold my hands up placatingly. "Who do you think has the motive to go on a murder spree?"

King stares at me as if I have three heads. I'm only asking because sometimes, not always, killers are more comfortable talking about their crimes in the third person.

"How the fuck would I know?" he snaps.

It's the first crack in King's mask. The first sign of emotion.

I tap the thick folder in front of me. "We have good reason to believe the killer is someone who has access to Keira."

King says nothing as he continues staring at me.

"Her stepfather and her boyfriend are missing. Two people who are close to her."

Riveiro speaks up. *"You* are close to her."

"What are you saying?" King asks, his unrelenting gaze landing on her stern face. "That I'll go missing or that you think I killed all those people?"

"I think you know more than you let on."

"And I think you're under so much fucking pressure from the media frenzy that you're willing to throw just about anyone under the bus at this point. But the truth is, you're nowhere near catching this lunatic. You hauled me in here because you found my fingerprints in Keira's bedroom, and I've told you that we fuck. So naturally, my fingerprints will be all over her room. If you don't believe me, ask her yourself."

"Do you fuck any other girls from school, King?"

I bite back a laugh at the unimpressed, no-nonsense tone in Riveiro's feminine voice.

"No, I don't," he replies, drawing out the vowels. "But if you're going to point fingers, Liam fucked around behind Keira's back. The guy is not short of enemies or girls that are obsessed with him."

Riveiro looks in my direction, but I keep my gaze solely focused on King.

This is new information to us.

"Who did he sleep with?" I ask carefully.

"You assume I know?"

"It was a bold statement to make."

The right side of his mouth lifts. "This is Blackwoods. Rumors fly."

"Rumors are mere hearsay," Riveiro points out, reaching for her cold takeout coffee.

"Aren't you trying to pin the murders on me based on hearsay?"

"Fingerprints aren't hearsay, boy."

"They are when they're absent from the actual crime scene."

Riveiro takes a sip, puts her cup back down, and levels him with a serious look. "Look, your fingerprints weren't absent from the crime scene. We found them in Keira's ro—"

"Did you find any of my DNA on the head? Any fingerprints at all in or around the car?"

"That means nothing," she grits out, losing her patience. "Despite the blood, the crime scene in the car was immaculate. The killer knew how to cover his tracks."

"So... I litter Keira's bedroom with my fingerprints but keep the head and the car immaculately clean? Wouldn't it be more reasonable to fuck Keira and leave as little evidence as possible of me entering her bedroom in the first place? At least that way, I'd avoid being here now, listening to your farfetched bullshit."

Beside me, Riveiro crosses her arms and huffs a breath through her nose. She opens her mouth to retort, but the door flies open and a man in a gray suit walks inside. He throws a brown folder down on top of mine, puts his leather satchel on the steel desk, and starts to unzip it. "The name is Mr. Morton, and I'm representing Mr. Knight. My client will not answer any further questions."

Blowing out a sigh, I scrub a hand over my face. Time's up, and we have nothing. "There's enough evidence to keep him overnight," I say, scooting my chair back and sliding my folder out from underneath his.

"The fuck there is!" King blurts, but his attorney shoots him a stern look.

"Your client's fingerprints were found in Miss Hill's bedroom on the day of the homicides of two of my colleagues."

"Because we fuck," King emphasizes, his eyes wild and angry. "I didn't kill anyone."

His attorney ignores his outburst, sliding his hands into his pockets. To me, he says, "Circumstantial at best and won't lead to a conviction."

Riveiro grabs her cup and walks out of the room. I was hoping to coax a confession out of him without all this hassle, but it looks like I have no choice but to pull out the big guns.

I open my thick folder and slip out a handful of printed

photographs—a small selection from the disturbingly large collection we unearthed on King's phone.

King's eyes pop wide open when I place them down in front of him.

"What the hell?" he breathes out.

I point to the picture on top—a photograph of Liam and Keira having sex in Liam's bed—and say, "Did you or did you not spy on her through Liam's window?"

"Where did you get this?"

"One of Liam's friends handed in your phone to the police after he was reported missing." I let the words sink in before adding, "What we found on it was disturbing, to say the least. You've had an obsession with Keira for quite some time. Years even."

"That's enough," King's attorney barks, motioning for King to stand. "We're done here, Mr. Wells. I need to speak to my client in private."

"That's fine." I swipe up the photographs before addressing King. "I'll be seeing you again soon. I'm glad you have good representation, son. You'll need it."

S taring blindly at my open window, I wait up for King all night. I don't even care about the freezing cold turning my fingers numb or the possibility of the killer climbing inside. All I care about is King.

I check my phone, but of course there's nothing from King. His phone is still missing.

Seated on the settee in her gown, Mom drinks wine in front of the TV when I finally emerge from my bedroom the next morning on the hunt for something to eat.

We resemble each other now.

Living ghosts.

As I step deeper into the living room, my eyes skate to the TV. Mom is watching her and Allen's wedding video.

It was about a month later when he first entered my room and leashed my darkness.

Or maybe he unleashed it.

Allen was a horrible man but fuck if he knew how to humiliate and hurt me in the best way possible.

He was even so cruel as to send me to therapy for my twisted tendencies before using them against me in bed to make me crave his sickness. He loved to play mind games, and I guess I did, too.

I guess I miss the pillow over my head and the rush of the forbidden.

The lashings of his belt.

Mom looks so happy on the TV.

So unlike the shadow that drinks directly from the bottle, with her gown sliding off a bare, bony shoulder. Mom has lost a lot of weight recently. She's gaunt, haunted, and tired.

"You're a whore," she whispers on the couch, not taking her eyes off the screen, and I freeze. Her head slowly turns my way, and she sneers before rising to her feet. "You're a spoiled little brat and a fucking whore."

I step back, breaking out in a cold sweat at the crazed look in her bloodshot eyes. Mom is beyond drunk, stumbling and swaying her way over to me.

"A greedy little whore," she hisses, reminding me of a coiled snake. Without taking her eyes off me, she stretches her arm out behind her and clicks a button on the remote in her hand. Loud moans and the slapping of skin on skin ring out loudly.

My heart stops beating in my chest as my gaze skates over her shoulder to the screen. There I am, with my pale ass in the air and a pillow over my head, while Allen slams into me from behind, his thick thumb buried deep in my ass.

It's not pretty.

It's fucking ugly and depraved and sickening.

I always wondered what Allen looked like when he fucked me. Always wanted to see his face.

Now I finally do.

He looks like a monster with his face screwed up and lips peeled back.

Mom's trembling hand flies out and connects with my cheek in a hard blow. "You fucking whore! You disgusting slut!"

She slaps me again, and I let her.

I fucked her husband.

I deserve each and every blow she doles out.

At least now that she has seen him for what he really was, a predator, she can stop mourning him. But her rage and pain are aimed at me. I want to beg for forgiveness and tell her I'm sorry, but I keep the words locked firmly behind my lips. I'm not sorry. I enjoyed her husband's dick. I enjoyed how good he felt and how he hurt me when I needed it.

I'm grateful that he kept the darkness inside me at bay, because now that he's dead and King is gone, I don't have a leash. No monster to stalk me and hunt me and choke me. No one to stop me from carrying on my father's legacy.

Mom hits me one final time, breathing harshly through her nostrils before she steps back and takes a swig from her wine bottle. "I want you gone."

Barely daring to breathe, I grow deathly still.

"You're not my daughter. I don't want to see your fucking face ever again. I didn't birth a fucking whore."

"Mom," I whisper brokenly. "Please..."

"You have ten minutes to pack a bag and get the fuck out of my house."

Mom's robe has slid open, revealing a pale breast. She pulls it closed, tightening the belt before turning and giving me her back. "Don't ever come back here."

Swallowing thickly, I let my gaze wander back to the screen, where Allen milks his cock over my ass, his cum raining over my skin in quick squirts. I don't even blame her for turning me away. I am a monster, and I know it.

I know I'm sick. Even my therapist told me as much before Allen stopped sending me. I'm a spreading disease, infecting everyone I care about.

After packing a backpack, I throw on my denim jacket and toe on my Chucks. It's too fucking cold outside for what I have on, and my toes are soon frozen as I head down the snowy sidewalk. I don't care if I freeze to death at this point. At least, I'd finally get some mercy from my own fucked up mind. Faulty people like me shouldn't be alive.

As I walk down the sidewalk toward town with no direction in mind, a black Hummer slows to a halt beside me. The passenger window slides down, and Miles flashes a smile. Chris is driving, one hand hanging over the steering wheel. He doesn't look at me, though. Simply stares straight ahead.

"Where are you heading?" Miles asks, his blond hair hidden beneath a red, backward cap.

I shrug, coming to a slow stop. "Nowhere."

"Jump in the back. It's warmer in the car than it is out there. We'll drop you off somewhere."

Uncertainty makes me hesitate. I'm not friends with Miles and Chris. We know each other through Liam, sure, but friends? No.

"We'll drive you to Madison's."

Chewing on my bottom lip, I scuff the crunchy snow with my shoe. I suppose I could always ask Madison if I can stay for a night or two. It's not like I have anywhere else to go. "Sure, okay."

"Cool," he replies, rolling his window back up.

I open the passenger door, toss my backpack inside, and slide in. The heat is on, which is a welcome change from the freezing temperatures outside.

"Psychosocial" by Slipknot blasts through the speakers, and Miles moves his head in time to the beat. Chris still says nothing, but his eyes land on me in the rearview mirror. His brown hair is kept short at the sides but longer on the top, and his eyes are dark brown with specks of hazel.

"Where's Sienna?" I ask Miles over the top of the music.

"Not here," he replies with a smirk, turning the music up even louder.

I look out the window and stiffen when I realize we're driving in the wrong direction. Madison doesn't live this way. "You're going the wrong way," I call out, but my voice gets lost in the music.

Chris takes a right turn, his eyes sliding to mine in the rearview mirror. The hazel specs in his eyes are nowhere in sight now. His eyes are dark, almost black in the fading light.

We turn down a dirt track, and I begin to panic. Something is very wrong. I try the handle, but it's locked.

Chris lowers the volume, spinning the wheel. There's a sadistic drawl to his voice when he says, "You can't unlock the door from the back."

My eyes fly up to the rearview mirror, and my heart stalls in my chest for a brief moment while I stare at him. Lashing out at the door, I push and shove and pull, but it stays locked.

The boys laugh and bump fists at my futile attempts.

Outside the car, the trees grow denser, and the weeds on the dirt road grow thicker. Chris pulls over at a clearing and cuts the engine.

Without hesitation, I push open the door and tumble out of the car with my heart in my throat. I sprint back down the dirt road, but I don't get far before Miles's muscular arms band around my waist. With a dark chuckle, he carries me back to where Chris leans against his Hummer with a cigarette between his lips.

I'm dumped unceremoniously on the cold ground. Scuttling back on my ass, I blink up at Chris, who smokes in silence, his black jacket rustling in the quiet.

The snowy ground is icy cold beneath my palms as my eyes dart around the clearing. My shaky breaths puff out in a big cloud in front of me, and my nose and ears burn from the sharp bite of cold in the air. I should at least have worn my scarf. "Why did you bring me here?"

Miles checks his phone, while Chris crushes the cigarette beneath his sneaker. "You're gonna tell us where Liam is, beautiful."

My eyes widen. "What? I don't know where he is."

Stalking up to me, Chris grabs my chin so hard that I whimper. His fingers will leave marks on my skin. I can feel it. "You know exactly where he is, and it's time to fucking talk."

"You can't make me," I hiss, wrenching free of his grip. "I don't know anything."

"No?" His chuckle is cold and cruel. "You're so damn innocent, right? Fucking King behind Liam's back. We watched the videos. All of them."

Miles releases a loud laugh. "Jerked off to them, too."

"Point is, you're a whore, Keira." Chris releases my chin only to grab me by my throat. "And you like cock."

A choked bubble of laughter rips from my vocal cords. "I have needs. So what? Women like sex, too."

Chris ignores my barb. "Where's Liam, Keira? Tell me now, and I'll take it easy on you."

It's snowing again. A thick flurry of snowflakes dusts Chris's hair as he glares down at me.

"I don't know where he is," I bite out.

Chris jerks his head to Miles, who walks back to the car. He returns seconds later with a small bag of white pills.

"What are you doing?" I ask, struggling against Chris's grip on me.

Miles opens the bag, slides a pill out, and pinches my nose. "It's time to swallow, princess."

I hold my breath for as long as I possibly can. It's not long enough. Nothing can ever be. My burning lungs finally give in, and I part my lips to inhale a ragged, desperate breath. Miles shoves the pill down my throat.

Chris drops me to the ground like I'm a worthless rag doll and fishes his phone out of his pocket. "It'll only be minutes before the drug takes effect." He wiggles his phone for me to see. "You'll be begging us to fuck you, and Miles here is going to film it. You see, the beauty of this particular drug is that it makes you horny beyond belief. You won't care who fucks you as long as you choke on cock. It'll make for a nice little video, don't you think? King will appreciate it the most."

I grow colder than the snow on the ground. I can't feel my

fingers or my toes. My clothes are soaked through, but all of that fades in comparison to the fucking horror of what's staring back at me.

"Unless, of course, you tell me where we can find Liam. I promise I won't lay a finger on you if you tell me. We'll drive you straight back to Madison, and you can beg her to fuck your throbbing cunt instead. I'm sure King won't mind if you give a girl a spin."

I climb to my feet, my knees quaking so badly that I struggle to stand up. "I can't tell you where he is because I don't know."

No way in hell will I tell them shit.

If Liam's body is found, so is his car.

And while we burnt it, I'm not willing to take chances.

King's safety is more important than his feelings toward me. Besides, I don't believe Chris when he says he'll take me back to Madison. Not when he's staring at me like a fucking predator with injured prey. He'll fuck me regardless.

He just wants me to think he won't.

Swiveling around, I set off through the trees to the sound of their taunting laughter. The drug is kicking in. The ground is coming up to meet me. My hand flies out, and I grab hold of a tree branch at the last minute. I'm laughing now.

Everything seems lighter somehow.

Big, warm hands grip my waist.

Hands that feel so fucking good as they slide beneath my denim jacket and sweater.

Hands that can make the ache between my legs disappear.

"There's a good girl." Chris's warm breath teases my ear. "We'll look after you. Miles changed his mind. He wants a turn, too. Isn't that great?"

Jelly in his arms, I laugh harder as he picks me up and hauls me over his shoulder. My hair swishes while he walks, and blood collects in my head. I'm vaguely aware of the pulse thrumming against my temples.

I'm tossed on the snowy ground with nothing but trees overhead. They remove my jeans as I continue to laugh, salty tears streaming down my bright-red cheeks.

"What the fuck is so funny?" Miles asks, his voice far away but too close at the same time.

"It's the fucking drug."

My panties are snapped off, and the freezing snow underneath me begins to melt.

"Look at that pussy. Even better up close."

"King," I whisper, reaching in front of me for his big body. I want him to drape himself over me. To whisper sweet nothings in my ear.

His weight presses me down in the snow, and his soft, moist lips curve into a smile against my ear. "King is here, baby. King is gonna make you feel so fucking good. Where's Liam?"

I try to kiss him, but he moves out of reach and curls his fingers around my throat. His unbuckled belt, cool against my tingling skin, rubs the inside of my naked thigh.

"I'll kiss you when you tell me where Liam is, baby."

I'm confused. Why is he asking me this? We killed him together. Cold fingers sink inside me, making me moan shamelessly loud.

"Tell me you're recording this, Miles?"

"Of course. Every second. If she refuses to speak, we'll post it to every porn site in the country."

"King, please," I whimper. I'm so cold. So, so cold.

"Does it feel good, Keira?" The voice is wrong. It's taunting, cruel, and vicious.

"So good," I slur, despite the blaring alarm somewhere at the fringes of my consciousness.

"Why don't we go and find Liam, baby?"

I try to kiss him again. This time, he lets me. His cold tongue tangles with mine, and he grunts into my mouth.

But something isn't right.

His taste is wrong.

Gone is the peppermint.

Replaced by tobacco and deception.

He wrenches away. "Enough with the lies, whore."

I laugh again, and he releases an angry, fed-up growl before scooping up a handful of snow and forcing it into my mouth. He flattens his palm over my lips and nose, leering down at me while I convulse, drowning in the melting snow that clogs my throat. "Where's Liam?"

"She can't speak with snow in her mouth," chuckles Miles, his red sneakers disturbing the snow near my head. "Let's just kill her. She's useless."

"I'm gonna destroy her cunt first. Liam got to fuck it for long enough. Never let any of us have a taste. I want to see what the fuss is all about." His fingers slide out from inside me, and he shifts onto his knees, shoving his unbuckled jeans down.

I roll over on my side and retch, expelling the snow and whatever food I've had.

"Fuck." He jumps back to his feet. A sneaker connects with my shoulder, forcing me onto my back. Grabbing my arm, he drags me away from the pool of vomit before covering me with his body again.

"King?" I ask.

He looks strange. Not dark like I have come to expect. His hair color is wrong. His clothes are, too.

And his scent...

There's a sickening, gurgling sound behind me, followed by a heavy thud. The weight on top of me disappears, and I lie there with my legs splayed and my pussy on full display, vaguely aware of the cold nip in the air and the melted snow between my ass cheeks.

A shadow falls over my shivering body, and a red mask with a sinister smile bends over me. I whimper as the bloody knife in their hand glides over my wet cheek, smearing it crimson red.

The drug is not making me feel so good now. The lightness inside me is quickly morphing into terror.

Something is placed over my face—a mask, I realize.

A distorted voice rings out in my ear. "Let's play a little game I like to call Revenge."

*M*y *bloody hands slide over warm, slippery flesh as I pry the chest cavity open. It's not easy. I have to put weight behind it to get the ribs to break and snap.*

I don't know when my stepdad died and can't pinpoint the exact time, but it doesn't matter. His death was minor compared to the euphoric excitement that runs through me when I lay eyes on his heart.

The air is thick with the stench of copper—a scent I have come to love tonight.

A scent I want more of.

Reaching in, I let my fingers curl around the slick organ almost lovingly. I want to cut it open and look at each chamber. I want to smell it, too.

Taste it.

Frozen to the bone, I startle awake with a sharp gasp. I sit up and try to look around me, but I can't because of the thing on my face. My hands fly up to investigate.

It's a mask.

I push it up on my head and look around the dark clearing in the forest, my eyes darting from tree to tree until they land on the pale figure that sits hunched against a trunk.

I recognize those red sneakers and that cap. His head is almost severed, and flops to the side, his dead eyes staring right at me. There's blood everywhere—a pool of frozen red in the snow.

Slowly climbing to my feet, I release a tiny whimper. As I step back, I trip over an ankle and almost fall on my ass.

Chris, who is out for the count by the looks of it, is tied to the tree behind me with a leather glove rammed into his mouth.

Orange pumpkins carved with grotesque faces sit dotted around the clearing. Their flickering lights dance over the blood-speckled snow, providing the only source of illumination in this place.

There's a letter on Chris's lap with my name written on the front. I look around, but there's no one out here, and the footprints have since been buried beneath a fresh layer of snow. My fingers are so numb, I have long since lost feeling in them.

Bending at the waist, I pick up the letter and carefully unfold it, while Chris begins to stir. He sounds like he's in pain, but I can't see any visible injuries on him. No blood.

Nothing tastes sweeter than revenge.
Are you ready to play another game?
You'll find what you need inside his pocket.

With a thick swallow, I read over the words again. Chris groans, his eyes fluttering open slowly.

He blinks at me and tries to focus.

What pocket?

Folding the note back up, I crouch in front of him and search each of his pockets until I find a phone and a knife.

I'm about to leave the phone when I feel another folded note. As I remove the items, he tries to talk before realizing there's a glove in his mouth. His nostrils flare, and his eyes fly up to mine as I rise to my feet.

My Chucks and socks are soaked. I'll invest in snow boots if I'm still alive next winter.

Unfolding the note with a slight tremble in my fingers, I read over the sentence.

Watch the first video clip in the photo album.

Chris's muffled, indistinguishable words sound behind the gag.

Ignoring him, I hold the phone in front of his face to unlock it. When it doesn't work, I reach out and remove the glove. It unlocks, letting me open up his photo album.

I push the glove back into his mouth as I click on the first video. Tied to the tree, Chris is starting to get distressed. He kicks weakly at the ground, shuffling the soft snow.

"What's this?" I whisper, watching him pull my jeans and panties down while I'm clearly drugged to my eyeballs. "You raped me?"

His head shakes no, and his muffled words start to irk me. Disgusted, I look away from the screen when he fingers me in the snow.

Miles sniggers behind the camera.

I hate that sound.

I hate that they're humiliating me while I'm drugged up and unable to defend myself.

My attention gets drawn back to the phone, and the anger and revulsion inside me reach a boiling point. No one else gets to play with my darkness except for King. No one else gets to chase me and catch me and fuck me. Yet Chris's fingers have been inside me, coaxing moans from my lips.

I feel sick.

The video ends abruptly, and I pocket the phone. I stare at nothing, unsure how long I stand there amidst the flickering pumpkins. Darkness creeps in between the skinny trees.

The branches resemble demonic, gnarled limbs above our heads.

Knife clutched in my hand, I tighten my fingers around the handle and look down at my thumb as it slides along the blade. The blood from earlier has long since dried.

Inhaling a deep breath, I welcome the darkness into my starving lungs and let a smile spread across my lips. It's different from any other smile. It lacks warmth and oozes sinister intentions.

Crouching down beside him, I tap his cheek with the flat end of the knife to gain his attention. Whatever he sees in my eyes must be evil because he physically recoils, pressing himself against the tree. I shift the handle in my hand and dig the blade's sharp point into his cheekbone.

Chris instantly stills.

I like that.

I like that he fears me.

"You want to know what happened to Liam? Is that why you dragged me out here and tried to rape me?" I tut, applying more pressure until a beautiful, scarlet bead of blood forms on his cheek. "You're out of your depth, Chris. These are not children's games. They're games with deadly consequences. Look at your friend."

On cue, his eyes flick past me to Miles, slumped in a pool of his own blood against the tree.

Reaching up with my free hand, I pull the mask back down. The movement draws his gaze back to me, and his eyes widen when he stares at the grotesque devil's mask.

I can't help the taunting smile that spreads over my lips. There's something so deliciously alluring about taking on the killer's identity. Or maybe it's an excuse to let the real monster inside of me resurface from the shadowy depths of my soul.

"People who place their chess piece on this board die, Chris. I figured out right from the start that we can't win. Not you. Not me. Not anyone." I push the knife further in, meeting soft flesh and pained screams.

Chris pisses himself, soaking through his jeans at the front.

Lowering the knife, I cock my head and listen to him sob. The sweet melody of anguished fear.

The power of inhaling it and tasting it.

"Liam is dead. I buried him alive," I gesture around us with the knife, "somewhere in these woods."

I had King's help, but he doesn't need to know that.

Leaning in close, I breathe him in—the scent of tobacco and citrus. Underneath the sharp tones lies something far sweeter.

Bloodlust courses through me. I want to watch his coppery life force pour from his veins. To cut him and make him bleed.

But first...

I grab his hand, push it flat on the snowy ground, and ram the knife into it, nailing him in place.

His hoarse scream is so loud that I have to press my hands over my ears, but I love how it threatens to burst my eardrums.

"That's what you get for touching what isn't yours."

Chris is sobbing now, his entire body trembling almost violently. I watch him for a moment, intrigued by his fear, his pale hand impaled by the knife and the blood flowing freely around the embedded blade.

"What did you think would happen when you decided to drag the daughter of one of the country's most notorious serial killers out here?" I scoop up a handful of snow and force it into his eyes. "I'm sure most offspring of serial killers grow up to be perfectly normal, healthy human beings. But me... I have never been normal. Ever since I was a little girl, I have felt a stirring at my very core. A curiosity, if you will. I suppressed it as much as I could, but the darkness would occasionally surface, demanding to be fed. I found ways to cope and ways to cause a little chaos, but nothing beats the euphoric relief of unshackling my sinister legacy. Then you happened to stumble along on my path." I walk my fingers in the air to emphasize my point. "You thought you could touch me against my will? I'm not a damsel in distress, Chris. My father may be the devil, but I'm his spawn. And boys like you should be very careful who you play with."

His bloodshot eyes stare up at me from beneath dark lashes that are covered in a dusting of snow.

I pull the knife out from his hand, and he roars behind the gag, fighting against the restraints. It's useless. Whoever tied him up did it thoroughly. Chris is mine until I'm finished with him.

As I reach for his bleeding hand, he tries to fight me off the best he can while tied to a tree. In the end, I have to sit on his forearm and trap his injured hand between my thighs. It's awkward at best. His blood is also ruining my favorite jeans.

Grabbing a finger, I begin to saw. He had his digits inside my body, finger-fucking me against my will.

This is the least he deserves.

But anger is not what I feel as I sever it with great difficulty. It's excitement and a rush of adrenaline. I'm alive again.

Alive in a way, I only am when I'm embracing my true, monstrous self. It's so fucking exciting that I release a crazed, haunted laugh. The kind of laugh that belongs in horror movies.

As I look over my shoulder, I realize that Chris is already fading in and out of consciousness. The fucker can't deal with pain at all. I turn around on his lap, his severed digit gripped in my hand, and tap his cheek with my blood-soaked index and middle fingers. "Hey, hey, wake the fuck up. We're only getting started."

Chris is dead, and I'm panicking. The sun is slowly rising in the distance. I'm covered from head to toe in blood and gore with no fucking clue what to do with the bodies. When I killed my step-dad, the twisted person behind these games took care of it all. This time, it's just me.

King isn't here to help me burn the car or bury the bodies

either. My DNA will be all over the place. Not only that, I don't even have anywhere to go.

"What the hell do I do?" I look down at my clothes. I need to burn them, but I have nothing else to wear. I can't go back to the car; I'll smear it with blood.

Pacing, I clutch my matted hair.

In the end, I return to the car after retrieving the keys from Chris's jeans pockets. I can't think when I'm frozen to the core.

We didn't walk far, so it doesn't take me long to reach the vehicle. I climb in behind the steering wheel, place the key in the ignition, and put the heat on full blast. My frozen cheeks slowly warm up, and my fingers and toes soon start to tingle. It hurts, but it feels good, too.

Flipping down the mirror, I take in my pale face beneath the caked-on blood. Dark shadows circle my eyes, and my lips are chapped. Not my best look, in other words. I look like a monster.

Reaching into my denim pocket, I retrieve Chris's finger, studying the short nail and the fingerprint. This is what experts refer to as collecting souvenirs. Is that what I'm reduced to now? A killer to study and analyze?

Besides, this finger will soon rot. But maybe I could keep the bone if I strip the flesh off? I know nothing about that process.

Resting my head back against the seat, I scrub a hand over my face. I'm in deep shit.

When the killer said it was time to dig myself into more trouble, he wasn't joking. I first thought it was a play on words—a hint toward the sin buried somewhere in these woods. But now, I'm not so sure.

As I lower my hand, my eyes snag on the backseat in the rearview mirror, or, more accurately, my phone that must have fallen out of my pocket.

My eyes widen, and I bolt upright, twisting my body between the seats to retrieve it. I smear blood over the screen as I quickly bring up my contact list, debating who to call. It comes down to

Cassie or Madison. Who of those two friends knows how to keep a secret as dark as this one? I know it's a risky game to call for help, but I have no other choice. Not when I have nowhere to go and no clean clothes to change into.

I'm stuck here.

I press the phone to my ear and wait for her to pick up.

KING

My lawyer, Mr. Morton, is a serious man in his early fifties with a receding hairline and graying beard. In all the ways that count, he's in good shape. No beer gut in sight and no bald spot yet.

My father smooths down his slim, black tie and sits down beside me in the small room. His gray suit is freshly pressed, and he reeks of expensive aftershave and cigars.

Mr. Morton sits down, too, across from us. He looks almost... nervous. "The news isn't good. They will press charges against King soon for first-degree murder."

"What the hell?" I blurt at the same time my father says, "What evidence do they have to tie my son to these murders?"

"Nothing of real significance, and it's all circumstantial at best." He gestures a meaty hand at me. "King's fingerprints in her bedroom, which we can argue are there because of their affair. The photographs found on his phone are the most damning evidence." Before I can open my mouth to retort, he holds his hand up and adds, "Photographs that prove your son had an obsession with Keira."

"Circumstantial again," my father says calmly. "It's far-fetched to link his apparent obsession with Jimmy Hill's daughter to the murders of his friends."

"Yes, and my job will be to convince a jury of that."

I swallow past the thick lump in my throat. This is all a fucking nightmare.

"They will present their theory, claiming the killer harbored an obsession with Keira and her dark legacy." His eyes land on me. "The obsessed student with a troubled past goes after the popular quarterback's girlfriend. He eventually gains her trust. They start an affair, and she's clueless about the fact that her new lover is watching her from afar, photographing her with her boyfriend. I'm sure we can all admit that it looks bad. King, you photographed Keira and her boyfriend having sex."

Averting my gaze, I gnash my teeth.

Sure, I have an obsession with her. An unhealthy desire to watch her and fuck her and love her. Maybe I wanted Liam gone and out of the picture. So fucking what? I didn't murder my friends.

"A jury won't take kindly to that. They could even be so clouded by the images the prosecution presents them with, that they look past the fact that your fingerprints or DNA were nowhere near the dead bodies."

I say nothing else.

Beside me, my father scrubs a hand over his face. "Why did you take those photos, son? Why?"

My shoulders shrug a little. "I got a rush from it. Wanted to feel close to her. I felt like... like I got to know her a little bit better every time I snapped another picture."

Neither man speaks. They both watch me like I have a screw loose.

"What about when you photographed Keira having sex with her boyfriend? Did you like that, too?" my father asks, his voice strained.

"No," I admit. "I wanted to kill him for touching what was mine."

"That's the conclusion the jury will come to," Mr. Morton

says. "Liam is missing. They'll be out for blood until he is found—hopefully alive."

"Did you have something to do with it?" my father asks me.

The lie slips easily from my lips. "No. I didn't kill anyone."

If they believe me or not, I don't know. I don't even care.

"When can I call her?" I ask.

They exchange glances, and Mr. Morton clears his throat. "It's best if you don't contact her."

My gaze slowly lifts to his, then I look at my father. "When can I call her?"

"Son," my father begins, his eyes flicking briefly to my lawyer before colliding with mine, "you can't contact her again."

Frowning, I stare at him.

He continues, "Not until after the trial. We can't give the press any more material to froth over. The most damning evidence against you is your obsession with Jimmy Hill's daughter. You can't be seen contacting her."

His words go in one ear and out the other. He says them, but they don't register. I refuse to think I won't be able to talk to her again.

"She is waiting for me to contact her," I reply more firmly.

"That's not going to happen." My father crosses his arms. "You need to forget about her." He digs his finger into Mr. Morton's folder on the desk. The folder with copies of the photographs I took. "This stops today. Keira is no one to you."

I shoot up from my seat so fast, the chair topples over. I'm pacing like a caged tiger, dragging my fingers through my greasy hair. I need a shower, a hard fuck, and Keira's screams in my ears. Only then will I feel somewhat in control again.

I remember the first time I noticed her darkness.

How it called to me.

And now my father says I have to remove my new oxygen source? Fuck him. Fuck them all. I'm going to get out of here and hunt her down and make her hurt, just how she likes it.

Liam could never give her what she needs. But I can. I know how to wrangle that monster inside her until it submits to me.

"You need to calm down," my father says sternly.

"You're telling me I have to stay away from the girl I fucking love, and you want me to calm down?" I snort loudly, throwing a dismissive gesture in his direction.

"It's an obsession. Not love."

"What the fuck do you know about love?" I snarl, back to pacing. "You cheat on Mom every time you travel, and she turns a blind eye as long as you pay for spa weekends and expensive jewelry. That's not love, so don't come preaching to me."

"I haven't always been the perfect role model, sure, but can't you see how unhealthy this is? To stalk a girl, seduce her, and carry on an affair with her behind her boyfriend's back?"

"She wasn't going to leave him," I bite out, throwing my hands out. "I just wanted a fucking piece of her, okay? I didn't care at the time about Liam. I was too high on her every time she let me touch her. It was worth all the other bullshit."

"But you soon grew resentful, right?"

"Wouldn't you?" I shoot back. "I gave her everything she wanted, everything she *craved*. But she still returned to him. Why? Because everyone revered him, and it distracted from who she really is at the fucking core. The truth she hides from the world. The truth *I* saw and fucking loved." I point to myself. "The truth *I* brought out in her."

My father never takes his eyes off me as he asks, "And what's that truth?"

I realize my slip-up and clamp my lips shut.

"We're just trying to help you," my lawyer says, playing the devil's advocate. "It will help if we understand your motives."

"My motives were simple. I wanted to wet my dick."

"For fuck's sake." My father rubs his tired eyes. "We all know there's a lot more to it than that. You don't collect photographs like stamps of a girl you only want to use for sex. Maybe you think you're in love with this girl, maybe it's an obsession, but regardless, you're about to stand trial for replicating her father's killings. You're lucky you're still a minor, so the death penalty is off the table, but you'll still go away for a very long time if you're found guilty. So, I repeat, we're trying to help you."

I plop back down onto the chair, defeated and exhausted. "I don't know what you want from me."

"You can start by telling us about the truth you saw in Keira."

My chuckle is bitter. "No, I can't. That's between her and me."

"Are you willing to get locked away for a girl you barely know?"

I know her better than anyone. I'm the only one who sees her.

"Are we done here?"

My father stares at me. *Glares* at me. Then he slams his hand down on the table. "I wish you were a grown man so that I could beat some fucking sense into you."

"If you want me to talk, you let me contact her."

My father's chuckle starts out slow, a vicious kind of sound that soon grows in volume. "No, son. You're about to ruin your life for pussy. You don't get to call the shots here. If you don't talk, I'll make sure you never get to lay eyes on her ever again." He rises to his feet and puts his big hands on the table. His dark eyes narrow on me. "How long do you think it'll take before some other guy comes along and spots her, huh? How long until someone tries to seduce her? How long until someone is success-ful? Weeks? Months? In the meantime, you'll be rotting away behind bars, unable to do anything but torture your mind."

My gaze slides to Mr. Morton, who looks almost sheepish. "You can both fuck off. I'm done here. I'm not throwing Keira under the bus for something she didn't do just to save my own skin."

Standing up and walking over to the door, I bang on it hard enough to make the hinges rattle. It doesn't take long for it to creak open. I don't look back as the officer stationed outside returns me to my holding cell.

I don't care about my father's intense glare that burns the back of my head as I'm led around the corner. He'll have to let me talk to Keira if he wants me to cooperate, or I'll continue to be a pain in the fucking ass until I can hear her sweet voice again.

KEIRA

Madison throws herself out of the car door when she sees the state of me, covered in blood from head to toe, like something straight out of a horror movie. "What happened?"

I'm shaking like a leaf. Whatever adrenaline kick I was on is long gone, and now I'm in a state of shock. She tries to take me back to her car, but I shake my head. "I can't. I'm covered in blood."

Brushing my hair away from my bloodied cheeks, she skates her worried eyes over my stricken face. "What happened, Keira?"

"Did you bring a spare set of clothing?"

"Of course."

"I did something terrible." Dread gnaws at my insides. I hand her my phone. "It's better if you watch it. It'll make sense."

There's a slight tremble in her fingers. She presses play on the video and watches, horrified, as Chris and Miles abuse me.

"Oh, my God," she whispers, pressing a hand over her mouth. Lowering it again, she looks at me. "Are you okay?" She must regret the words, because she hurries to add, "I'm sorry, of course you're not okay."

"When I woke up," I reply as she pulls me into her body, "they were still there, and I..."

"You what?" Her voice is equally weak. I think she knows where this is going.

"They're dead."

Her eyes fall shut, and she holds me closer. "It's okay."

"It's not okay. I've made a mess of everything. My mom... She kicked me out. I have nowhere to go."

"It'll be fine," she reassures me. "You can stay with me."

"Their bodies. The evidence..."

Madison shushes me, rocking us side to side. "We'll get it sorted. Together. This is what friends are for. We stick up for each other. No matter what."

My trembling finally starts to ease off, and my breathing regulates, so she untangles herself from me and walks over to her car.

Opening the trunk, she lifts out the bottle of gasoline she keeps spare in case of emergencies that generally involve not getting to a gas station in time, but I think this classifies as an emergency, too. "Let's grab the bodies and put them in Chris's car."

It turns out that dead bodies are not so easy to move. They're heavy, so it takes both of us to finish the job. Madison doesn't question why all of Chris's fingers are gone or why I stabbed him in excess of thirty times. She asks no questions at all.

But I think she gets it.

He touched me when I was drugged up.

He tried to rape me.

Chris deserved what he got.

We place them both in the car and pour the gasoline over their mutilated bodies, the seats, the dashboard, and the doors.

Everywhere.

When the bottle is empty, Madison puts it back in her trunk and returns with a yellow lighter with a smiley face motif.

Pinning her eyes on me with a secretive smile on her lips, she strikes it, the sound loud in the brooding silence of shared secrets that thickens the air. The flame flickers wildly between us. I step back as Madison lights up the gasoline trail leading to the car. It shoots across the damp ground, despite the snow, and the car is soon aflame, a great cloud of smoke rising into the air.

We watch it burn and crackle.

Madison's hand finds mine, squeezing gently. The stench of burning flesh, melting plastic, and polyester fabric fragrances the cold air. "We'll never tell a single soul about this."

I rest my temple on her shoulder through her puffer jacket. "I'm sorry I dragged you into my messy life."

"Are you kidding me? This beats whatever mundane shit I had planned. Maybe it's not what I would envision when I think about an exciting day trip with a friend, but at least you're full of surprises."

"You don't think I'm sick? For what I did?"

The fingers. The stabbing.

"No," she replies, bringing our joined hands up to her mouth and pressing a tender kiss to the back of mine, letting her soft lips linger for a brief moment. "I think you're brave."

"I think I'm broken."

"All the best things are." Her words float in the air between us. I guess I've never considered my brokenness something to be admired and cherished. I have always thought of the cracks in my facade as ugly, less than perfect.

"Can we go?" I ask as Madison lowers my hand from her mouth.

"I'll get you your change of clothes."

Madison continues staring at the tall flames while I change into a pair of jeans that are slightly too big and shredded at the knees. The geo-patterned, wool sweater smells of Madison. Like strawberries and her coconut shampoo.

She slowly turns, letting her ice-blue gaze float down my body and back up before bending at the waist and picking up my discarded sweater, soaking it in the snow. She takes her time wiping my face and neck clean of blood, her eyes never trailing from my face.

There's something between us.

Something almost sexual, but not quite.

As if she can't help herself and wants to test the icy waters, she leans in and presses her soft, cold lips to mine. I don't move. I don't even breathe, but I do taste her strawberry lip balm, and I like it. I also like her frozen fingertips on my cheeks as she cradles my face. I like how she holds me, so softly and tenderly, as if I'm an autumn leaf that might crumble if she applies the slightest hint of pressure.

Her tongue darts out, warm against my parted lips, and she bites down hard, tasting my blood. It's such a contrast to the gentle way she's cradling my face.

She breaks the kiss, then takes my hand and leads me to her car. "You can have a shower when you get back to my house. So you can wash the blood from your hair."

Nothing is said about the kiss, but I feel it tingle on my chapped lips.

KEIRA

Madison turns on the TV and throws herself on top of her waterbed, causing the mattress to bounce. The water gurgles inside it.

I'm seated with my back against the upholstered headboard, staring at my phone.

She flops down beside me, pulls the pillow from beneath her ass, and puts it behind her head. I breathe her in with my next inhale and let her comforting scent wrap itself around my clenching heart. I wish King would contact me.

As if she can sense my thoughts, she takes my phone from my hands and sets it down on the bedside table. "He's probably not allowed to contact you."

"I'm worried about him."

Madison says nothing, but her hand finds mine again, and she strokes her thumb over my knuckles in a soothing, back-and-forth movement.

"Why have they not released him yet? He didn't do anything, so why won't they let him go?"

"I wish I had the answers for you."

"Don't you ever worry the mattress will break and flood your room?" I ask to distract myself from the thoughts that won't stop screaming in my head.

Madison's room is painted a light gray. Movie posters with

black frames line one wall, and a large corkboard with countless movie ticket stubs is mounted to the other. She's the only person I know who prints out her tickets and keeps them.

Her bookshelf to the right has more movies than I can count. The age of DVDs might be giving way to the digital age, but Madison likes old traditions.

"Not really." She lies down and shifts onto her side, her head cushioned by her folded arm. "Tell me about King."

"What do you want to know?"

"What's so special about him?"

Drawing a leg up, I extend my arm and rest my elbow on my knee. "What you saw today... He's seen that side of me, too. He didn't run or tell me I was a monster like my dad."

"You're not a monster."

I look at her black hair on the pillow and her woolly, red, turtleneck sweater that sits below her chin. The large, golden hoops in her ears, one of them lying half across her cheek. Her socks are fluffy and red to match her top. "I'm more like my father than you think." It's a soft admittance, whispered delicately in the ensuing silence.

Madison's fingers dance across the sliver of exposed, pale skin where my sweater meets my jeans, and then she grips my hip. Her touch is warm. Like an anchor to steady me. "You don't need to hide from me. I'm your friend."

"Probably my best friend."

"I like that." Her red-painted lips part in a smile that I respond to with a small one of my own.

I fidget with my nail beds, not really paying attention to the TV.

"Does King fuck good?"

A nervous chuckle slips from my lips, but then I nod.

Madison lifts her head and rests her cheek on her fist. "What do you like about fucking him? Is it his cock?"

Sucking my bottom lip between my teeth, I bite down until it hurts. It slips free, throbbing with pain. "I like his cock. And his hands."

"They're big," she admits, gripping my hip a little tighter. "His fingers are long."

"You've studied him?" I ask, but it's not really a question.

"He paid attention to you. It made me curious about him."

"Why?"

She leans in, rests her head on my chest, and drapes her arm around my midsection. "I don't know."

My fingers find her hair, tangling in the silky strands as I brush them away from her dark brow.

"You're special, Keira."

"I'm not." My voice is haunted. Shaky and a little breathy.

"You don't see it. Liam saw it and took advantage of it. Of you." She props her chin on my chest and stares up at my face. "Are you in love with King?"

I chew on my lip. "I don't know. Maybe."

Reaching up, she pulls it away from my teeth. "They're already chapped."

"Why are you the closest to me?" I ask. "You flit between friend groups, but you always come back to me. Why?"

"Why did you call me and not Cassie?" Her fingers are back on the sliver of exposed skin above the hem of my jeans. They slip beneath the fabric and tease the small of my waist.

"Cassie doesn't get me."

"But I do. I get you, Keira."

Her fingers come to my jeans button and pop it open before sliding the zipper down.

"Why didn't you tell me before?"

"Tell you what?" The mattress shifts under her weight as she lowers herself down until her mouth is right *there*. Between my legs.

"You never tried anything with me before. Why now?"

Her fingers hook in my jeans.

I should stop her. I should do a lot of things. But King is in prison, and I'm selfish.

I'm selfish because I want her to take away my pain. Even if I'm not into girls.

Madison yanks them down my thighs before sitting back on her knees and sliding my pants off my ankles. She lowers back down between my legs and covers me with her mouth. There's nothing between us except a thin layer of lace. She soaks it with her tongue, pressing it over my slit.

Or maybe my cunt soaks through the expensive fabric?

I don't know anymore.

All I know is that it feels good. The heat of her mouth through the fabric. The bite of her nails on my thighs.

"We can't tell anyone about this," she says, hooking a finger in the lace and pulling it aside.

I spread my legs as wide as I can, my pussy on full show. "Friends don't do this."

"Maybe we were never friends?"

She licks me then, and the reply on my tongue dies a swift death. Madison feels different from King and Liam. The prickle of a beard is absent, and she's patient in a way boys are not. She enjoys this. She enjoys bringing me pleasure.

My eyes drift closed as she licks and sucks and nibbles on my pulsing cunt. Pleasure builds in my core until I'm panting and fisting the sheets and her raven hair—anything I can reach.

"That's it, Keira," she whispers against my clit while teasing my tight hole with a finger. "Let me have you." She sinks a finger inside slowly until it's knuckle deep. It disappears just as fast, and she climbs up my body, shoves down the front of her boyfriend jeans, and shuts me up with a hard kiss.

I'm stretched to the limit, confused as fuck for a brief second, before she whispers into the kiss. "You like cock, Keira. I want to fuck you like King does."

I lift my head and stare down between our bodies, at the pink strap-on dildo buried deep in my cunt.

She slides out, slams back in, and steals another kiss.

I'm so confused and so unbelievably turned on by this.

"Is this how King fucks you?" she whispers, finding a rhythm. The bed creaks as she grabs hold of the bed frame and takes me harder. The way King would.

"He fucks you hard, doesn't he?"

"Yes," I choke out, clenching around the dildo.

"I have always fantasized about what you look like when he fucks you. Or when Liam fucked you. The reality is even better." She grabs my face, slides her fingers down my throat, and holds me like that, my chin clutched in her palm while she pounds into me.

I wonder briefly what it's like for her. If she can feel any pleasure at all. Or if she gets off on the power.

Madison always seemed meek to me.

Quiet even.

A people pleaser at heart.

I'm sweating in my wool sweater, and so is she in hers. Strands of her black hair stick to her temple.

"What's your favorite position?" she asks, removing her fingers from my mouth.

"From behind."

Madison flips me over on my front and enters me from behind. "You have a perfect ass."

I wonder what we look like.

What King would think if he saw this. Would he be jealous?

Straightening up, Madison pulls me up by my hair until her soft tits are against my back. She fucks me like that, rough, hard, and deliciously dirty.

Her hand snakes beneath my sweater and bra to palm a breast. "You like to be fucked like this, Keira?" She enunciates it with a hard thrust, and I moan my response.

Maybe I'll regret this later when I realize what we did.

What I let her do to me.

As for now, I'm too far gone to care about anything but the way she slides her hand out from beneath my top, slaps my soaking pussy, and presses down on my throbbing clit. I come apart, climaxing so hard that I collapse forward on the bed.

She continues to thrust inside me, her eyes riveted on the spot where she enters my pulsing cunt.

Only when I begin to laugh does she slide out and collapse beside me on the bed. The strap-on is still on. Thick, pink, and glistening with my cum against her sweater.

"When did you put that on?" I ask, rolling over onto my back.

She's laughing now, too. "Just before I joined you in here. Remember, I went to use the bathroom?"

"You're fucking crazy." I'm still laughing, my pussy on full display.

"It was worth it. I got to fuck you, something I've fantasized about for a long time."

My laughter slowly dies in my throat, and I close my legs. "Why?"

"I don't know." Madison shrugs, leaning over me and collecting my jeans off the floor. She hands them to me and flops back down. "There's something about you."

Sliding the jeans back on, I stay silent. Reality is sinking back in. I let my friend fuck me just now.

And I liked it.

"I won't tell King."

I swallow, and she notices, reaching for my hand. "I know you're not into girls."

"And you are?"

"I'm into you, Keira. I really liked fucking you. Straight girls don't get off on fucking other girls."

"But you got off on fucking me?"

"Very much."

"But you didn't come."

"It doesn't matter... I'd do it again in a heartbeat if you let me."

Why am I so tempted by that thought?

I roll over onto my front and slide my arms beneath my pillow. Madison removes the dildo and hides it inside the bedside table before mirroring me. We stare at each other.

"Are you in love with me?" I ask her.

"Would it make a difference? You're with King."

"I betrayed King just now."

"He won't find out."

I search her face, seeing her in a new light. Madison looks at me with a small smile, her long lashes brushing her cheeks every time she blinks.

"Go to sleep," she whispers. "You're tired."

Even though it's only early afternoon, I drift away into peaceful calm, vaguely aware of Madison's soothing touch on my forehead, my nose, my lips.

OFFICER WELLS

I'm on the phone when Riveiro bursts into my office. Her eyes are wide and urgent, so I hang up and drop my feet from the messy desk littered with paperwork, empty coffee cups, and family photographs.

Riveiro, dressed in dark jeans and a black cashmere cardigan, nudges her chin at the door. "We got a call from dispatch. They found another body."

I'm up on my feet in the next second, reaching for my winter coat on the back of my chair. I sling it on, follow her into the hallway, and shut the door.

Her raven ponytail sways as she walks speedily toward the main entrance of the building. I can barely keep up.

"What did they find?"

"Man in his early fifties, hacked into pieces. He's been dead for some time."

"Keira's stepfather?"

"I'll bet my salary on it."

We step outside into the cold evening air. It's been dark for a while. I promised my wife I would be home early, but that won't happen now.

"Where was he found?"

Riveiro unlocks her car with the key fob. "Placed in neat little piles on a bench in the local park. It was in a remote area, so God only knows how long the remains have been there."

We get in the car, and Riveiro steps on the gas. The roads are quiet at this time. We get there in no time.

It has started snowing again now, and the forensics are running around in a flurry of movement to erect a tent over the remains before the weather ruins whatever little evidence we may find.

I pinch my nose when the rancid smell hits me.

"You weren't joking. He's been dead a fucking long time."

Riveiro pinches her nose too as she crouches in front of the bench. Death doesn't faze her at all. She points to the head. What's left of it, anyway. Most of the flesh has rotted away. "Look at these marks here. The body parts were wrapped in plastic bags for a prolonged period of time."

"The humid conditions are probably why there's so little left."

Riveiro slides her gaze to the left. To the torso. The limbs are all missing, and the chest cavity is pried open. She looks at me over her shoulder with a pointed look. "Does Jasper come to mind? His heart was removed, too."

"The mask," I say, gesturing to where it lies propped up in front of what used to be the arms and legs. "Think it has prints on it?"

Since my colleague always comes prepared, she removes a set of gloves and a zippy bag from her pocket. After sliding on her gloves, she picks up the mask, careful not to disturb any potential evidence, and slips it into the bag.

"Only one way to find out. Look at the chest," Riveiro says, rising to her feet. "This is different from the Jasper case. This is almost like the killer was... curious."

I stare at Riveiro, who stands with her head cocked, studying the grisly sight in front of her.

"What makes you say that?"

Her shoulders rise and fall. "It's sloppy. Look at the cuts. It makes me think of a five-year-old serial killer in the making who starts out experimenting with cats and birds."

"Remind me never to attend a kid's birthday party with you," I mutter, wincing at the reek in the air.

Riveiro ignores my barb, a crease deepening between her brows as she looks closer. "Why the heart specifically? Why not the lungs or the liver?"

"I don't spend my days delving into the ins and outs of why killers prefer hearts over spleens or whatever."

"It matters," Riveiro says, sliding her rubber gloves off and stuffing them back inside her pocket, "because the heart is personal. It's an emotional connection to the victim."

"And the liver is not?"

She gives me a bored look and rounds the park bench. "It should be Keira's stepdad, but we'll need to identify him through dental records regardless since the remains are this decomposed."

"Let's get the mask back to the lab. Run it for fingerprints and DNA."

"We might get sufficient evidence to put King away for good. A rock-solid conviction."

Riveiro is thinking the same thing I am; this is the boost we both need for our careers.

To be the officers responsible for catching the second most prolific serial killer in Blackwoods' history.

We'll be classed as national heroes and get to feature in future documentaries.

We're so close to solving this case. I can taste it.

KEIRA

It's Saturday, and Madison takes me to the movies to cheer me up. I haven't been since I went with Liam, but Madison goes almost weekly. It's her happy place, hiding away at the back with a bag of popcorn on her lap.

She's in a pair of boyfriend jeans, a knitted, black-and-white sweater, and a pair of chunky-soled white sneakers. I have already sneaked a peak at her crotch, and there's no strap-on today. I'm sure the twinge inside me is not one of disappointment. My mind is simply looking for ways to escape reality.

I feel like the killer is watching and waiting. Somehow, he has made me the main player. And now he's waiting to see what I'll do next.

Nothing.

That's what I'll do.

I'm in limbo, waiting for King to be released.

The air is thick with the smells of popcorn and cheesy nachos. A candy bag rustles behind me over the sound of the movie.

Madison sits with both of her feet on the seat in front of her, her eyes wide as she stuffs more popcorn into her mouth. She offers me the bag, and I shake my head before rising to my feet. "I need the bathroom."

She nods, watching the movie, her fingers back inside the bag of popcorn to grab more.

I walk out, shuffling past strangers' legs in the narrow aisle. The movie music rises in crescendo just as I exit the movie theatre. It's empty out here beneath the dim spotlights. Stray popcorn surrounds an overfilled trash can.

I walk down the carpeted hallway, past the movie posters on the wall. As I enter the bathroom, I check my phone. I have one missed call from Cassie, but that's it. My mom hasn't tried to message me since she threw me out.

Pocketing my phone, I go to use one of the toilet stalls. The hot tap doesn't work, so I have no choice but to clean my soapy hands with cold water. I bang my hand on the dryer. Same story. Doesn't work. There aren't any paper towels, either. I return to one of the stalls and pull off sheets of toilet roll to dry my hands with. It's thin and breaks easily.

Tossing the wet tissue into the toilet, I pick stray pieces off the top of my hand before reaching out to flush.

A warm hand clamps over my mouth when I straighten up, and the heart-clenching smell of bergamot, leather, and pepper-mint surrounds me.

Fuck, I've missed him.

So fucking much...

"Missed me, baby?" he whispers in my ear, echoing my sentiment.

I nod eagerly, pressing my ass against him.

His nose drifts down to the crook of my neck, and he breathes me in, his arms wrapped around me. "I told you I'd come back to you."

I want to ask him how. If they're still suspecting him. But the prickle of his beard on the side of my neck has my full attention now.

"Have you been good?" he asks, nipping me as he lowers his hand from my mouth. The sharp bite of his teeth draws a gasp from my lips.

My first instinct is to lie, but the truth flows from my lips. "No, King... I haven't been good."

He stiffens, his hot breaths fanning the slender curve of my neck. "What did you do?"

"I fucked Madison."

Well, Madison fucked me.

A beat passes before King bursts out laughing. It shakes his diaphragm, the sound rich in the narrow stall. He spins me around, cups my chin, and tilts my eyes up to his. "You had sex with your best friend?"

"I was feeling vulnerable."

What a pathetic excuse. I cringe inwardly.

"You can't fuck other people every time you feel vulnerable."

"I know. I was scared. Scared they wouldn't let you out."

His brow comes down on mine, and he sinks his teeth into his bottom lip to hold back another blinding smile. "I told you, baby. I'll always come back to you." He bends at the knees, kissing me gently. "I'm obsessed with you."

"You're not mad?"

"About Madison?"

I nod, gripping the lapels of his leather jacket, which is still cold from his walk here.

"No. Just don't do it again. I wouldn't want to kill your friends."

"King..." I whisper, stepping closer.

His arms come down around me and he kisses my forehead, my cheek, the tip of my nose. "Yes, baby."

"I killed Chris." Hesitating, I look up at him. "Miles is dead, too."

His brows pull down low, and I see the question in his eyes.

"My mom, she, uh... she kicked me out—"

"She did what?!" he snaps, his tone laced with anger.

"She found out about my stepdad and me."

King cradles my cheeks, his hands warm and soothing against my skin.

"As I was walking down the sidewalk, Chris and Miles drove up beside me and offered me a lift to Madison's house. They took me out into the forest and drugged me, demanding I tell them what happened to Liam."

"Then what happened?"

This is the part I dread to speak out loud. "Chris tried to sexually assault me." King's face turns to stone, so I rush out, "He didn't get that far. The killer murdered Miles and tied Chris to a tree while I was unconscious."

His calloused, warm fingers brush a strand of wavy hair away from my cheekbone. "You killed Chris?"

"The killer plays games. When I woke up, there were instructions on what to do. He left me a knife." I don't need to tell him the rest. King sees the truth in my eyes and blows out a soft breath through his nose.

"You did the right thing."

"I was so angry King. He touched me... He..."

"You don't need to explain. I get it. I'm just so sorry that I was in prison, or I would have been there to protect you."

I swallow down the lump in my throat, pushing up on my tiptoes. His lips are soft against mine, and his stubble prickles my skin. Clutching his lapels, I moan into his mouth. It's only a soft sound, but he devours it like he's waited a long time to taste me again.

I break away first, and our lips hover inches apart. "I didn't know what to do afterward. I had no home to return to, I was drenched head to toe in blood, and I had two dead bodies to take care of. Madison helped me."

"It should have been me you called for help."

"You're here now."

His lips come down on mine, more urgent. Then he breaks

away and a mischievous smile pulls at his lips. "At least tell me I'm better in bed than her."

Throwing my head back, a peal of laughter bubbles from my chest. "No one beats you in bed," I reassure him, sliding my arms around his neck and pulling him down to my level. "You're the only one who knows what I need."

"The chase, right?"

I smile as our breaths mingle between our swollen lips. "And the pain."

"The humiliation." He buries his fingers in my hair when he says it. Then he pulls, and it hurts.

"I like Madison. She's nice but can't give me what I need like you can."

"No one can." His teeth sink into my lip, and he licks up the blood rushing to the surface. "And no one can give me what I need like you can."

My breath comes out in a shudder. I whisper, "I like the sound of that," so quietly that it's a miracle he hears it. King lifts me up and guides my legs around his waist as he presses me against the graffitied wall. His lips are hot on mine, his big hands slipping beneath my sweater to trail over my ribs.

"Madison will wonder where I am."

"Do you know how much I missed you?"

"Tell me."

King nips my jaw. "I was going fucking crazy in prison. They wouldn't let me call you."

Craning my neck, I stare up at the fluorescent light overheard while King peppers kisses over my neck. "Why did they release you? Lack of evidence?"

His lips trail back up to my mouth, and he kisses me once. "They were going to press charges against me. But then they came to my cell this morning and said there had been a development in the case, and that I was free to go."

"Did they say what?" I'm curious now. Maybe this nightmare will be over soon.

King shakes his head and lowers me to my feet before discreetly adjusting his hard dick. "They wouldn't say."

"At least they let you go." I reach for his tattooed hand.

"It was only a matter of time."

My hand looks so small in his. Small and pale.

"You sound so sure."

His thumb strokes over my knuckles as I chew on my chapped lip.

"After my dad was arrested..." I flit my gaze up to his face, needing him to understand why I'm so broken and why I sometimes make such shitty decisions. "I got really scared when you left with them. Then I didn't hear from you..."

He pulls on my hand, and I step into his embrace. "Baby, I'm sorry. I'm not going anywhere."

"What if we get caught? What if they find Liam?" I whisper, curling my fingers in the hem of his black T-shirt.

"We're not gonna get caught."

"You sound so sure. I've killed people, King."

He inhales my scent, his nose buried deep in my hair, his arms wrapped tight around me. "I am sure. Bonnie and Clyde, remember? We'll be fine, baby. No matter what."

KING

As we exit the bathroom, Madison is discarding her empty bag of popcorn in the overfilled trashcan outside. The movie is over, and the other visitors are filing out of the theatre behind her.

Looking up, she narrows her eyes at me as we walk over to her. Keira can't see it, but Madison is a rat. Manipulative, smart, and cunning. She's certainly not as innocent as she wants everyone to believe she is. She's not that loyal, either, which means she hopes to gain some leverage over Keira by helping her out.

When we near, she tosses a big, toothy smile in Keira's direction. "Look who got out."

Keira is beaming beside me, still glued to my waist, as if the thought of letting me go physically hurts her. "There's been a development in the case, so they let him go."

Madison's eyes briefly land on me before she steps away from the trashcan and walks closer. "What development? Did they find out who did it?"

"We don't know," Keira responds with a shrug. "Hopefully, they'll arrest the killer, and this nightmare will be over."

"Hopefully," Madison agrees.

Keira pats her pockets, looking in the direction of the bathroom. "Shit..." She peers up at me, tucking her blonde hair behind her ear. "I forgot my phone in the bathroom, I think. I'm gonna check."

I watch her walk off, and when I turn back around, I spot Madison staring after her, too. Closing the small distance between us, I stare down my nose at her before scoffing tauntingly. "Thought you'd try your luck while I was gone, hmm?"

Madison doesn't let my tall, broad build intimidate her. If anything, she rises to the challenge and inches even closer. "I didn't have to try, lover boy. She needed a shoulder to cry on, and you, well... you were indisposed. Who do you think will be there for her when they finally arrest you for good?"

Madison's cold smile rubs me the wrong fucking way.

"While you're rotting away in a cell," she continues, "I'll be filling the void you left behind. Quite literally."

"You're presuming a lot of things. What makes you think I'll be arrested for crimes I didn't commit? And the last time I checked, Keira isn't into girls."

"She was pretty into it last night."

My hands fist by my sides. I'm holding on by a fucking thread.

"I always saw through you, Madison. You're nothing but a cold bitch."

"We're alike, you and me." She brushes imaginary lint off my shoulder, and I jerk back, out of her reach. "We both play dirty to get what we want. Besides, there's something quite special about Keira, isn't there? Something that makes lying and cheating worthwhile."

I glower at her when Keira exits the bathroom.

"It was on the toilet seat lid. Gross, but at least it wasn't stolen or lost."

"I'm glad you found it," I reply, pulling her into my body with my arm around her slim waist while keeping my eyes glued on Madison.

"I'm hungry. How about we go for some food?" she asks, beaming at us both.

"Madison has somewhere to be," I answer, glaring at the girl in question. "Don't you?"

"Actually, no," she replies with a sly smile. "I think food sounds like a great idea."

We go to the burger joint. Kara, Hayley, and Ava are here, too. After several hugs and loud, excited squeals from the girls, we pull a few chairs over and join them.

Kara is already halfway through her meal, consisting of a burger, fries, and onion rings as an extra side. Hayley sips a banana milkshake, and Ava picks at her nachos.

It's busy on the weekend. Today is no different. The restaurant is buzzing with noise, and mouthwatering food smells drift over from the kitchen.

"Do you know how fucking worried we were?" Hayley asks. "You scared the living daylight out of us all."

Ava nods in agreement, biting down on a nacho covered in a thick layer of cheese sauce and salsa.

"They wouldn't tell us anything," Kara speaks up. "Your girl here," she points to Keira, who's perusing the menu, "was a wreck."

"It's true," Madison agrees, stroking Keira's hair behind her ear in a move that makes me want to chop her hand off. She looks at me over Keira's head, and there's an undeniable challenge in her gaze.

"What happened while you were in prison? Did they bring you into one of those rooms with a mirrored wall?" Hayley's eyes are wide and curious. The milkshake slurps as she takes a long sip.

Breaking eye contact with Madison, I nod and rest my elbow on the back of the chair. "Yeah, they tried to pressure me into admitting to murders I didn't commit."

"But based on what grounds? What evidence did they have?" Kara takes a big bite of her burger.

I shrug. "My fingerprints were in Keira's bedroom."

"That's it?" Kara asks around a mouthful of food. The words come out muffled.

"That's it."

"It makes no sense," Ava speaks up. "Of course your fingerprints are in her bedroom, you f..."

"Fuck," Keira finishes for her when she trails off, lowering the food menu. To me, she says, "What are you having?"

I point at something random, and Keira scrunches up her nose in an entirely adorable way.

"Triple spicy burger? Really?"

"I like a challenge." The hidden meaning behind my words is not lost on her as the tips of her ears heat.

"Bork." Hayley pretends to puke. "That was cheesy, King."

The waitress comes over to our table to take our orders.

Hayley's eyes soften as soon as she's gone again, and she says to Keira, "No news about Liam yet?"

Warm fingers slide over my thigh beneath the table and curl around my knee, tracing the skin beneath the shredded denim. "Not yet."

"It must be so difficult for you... with all the rumors flying around."

I narrow my eyes on Hayley, but she ignores me as she takes another long sip of her banana milkshake.

"The rumors are brutal," Keira agrees, meeting her gaze. "But I'm used to it... I'll never escape my surname, after all."

"Unless you get married," Kara jests, winking at me.

"Even if I change my surname, people will still know who my father is. It's a legacy I can't escape."

Sliding my fingers beneath her hair, I gently massage her slender neck, which is slightly damp with sweat beneath the big wool collar. The waitress arrives with our food, and Keira's hand leaves my knee. I instantly miss her heat, teasing fingers, and the slightly sharp scratch of her nails.

Madison talks to her while I take a bite of my burger. It's fucking spicy, I'll admit as much.

"You look like you're struggling," Ava says with a smirk, dipping a nacho in the red salsa.

I quickly shake my head, fighting the urge to fan my mouth. "This is nothing."

Keira sniggers, gazing up at me with her baby-blue eyes.

We talk about everything and nothing for the next half an hour, and for a while, it almost feels normal, like our group isn't missing three people.

"Will you be going to your stepdad's funeral?" Hayley asks carefully.

Fucking smooth thing to ask while we're eating.

Keira picks at her food for a long moment before lifting one shoulder and looking up at Hayley. "I doubt my mom will want me there. She threw me out."

"Threw you out? Why?"

"Stop being nosy," I say, stealing her milkshake and taking a sip.

Hayley snatches it back, scowling at me as she makes a show of drinking the last of it.

"It's Kit and Jasper's funerals soon too," Kara says, dipping a fry in the ketchup on her plate, but she doesn't take a bite. "I lie awake at night, thinking about them in a morgue somewhere."

Keira drops her burger onto the plate, looking green.

Beside her, Madison stops chewing. "Nice. Now I'm not hungry anymore."

Unbothered by the topic, I wolf down my burger while they stare at me.

Kara looks at me disapprovingly before resuming dipping her fry in the ketchup, smearing it around the white plate and through the dusting of salt. "I don't know how to move on from here. How to be a normal teenager again."

"No one expects us to be normal," Madison says, reaching for her glass of coke. "I have recurring nightmares about what happened in the bathroom. The way the killer taunted me and dragged the knife along the stalls."

"I struggle, too," Keira admits, looking around the table. "Every time someone dies, we're expected to move on after a day. I had two exams this week. *Two.* It's safe to say my grades are tanking."

My thumb soothingly rubs the slender column of her neck. I wish I could take her pain away.

With a soft smile in my direction, she leans in close, resting her head against my shoulder. I inhale her apple shampoo, kissing the top of her head. It's safe to say I'm more than obsessed with this girl. I'm falling for her.

Sirens outside draw nearer, and the interior of the burger bar lights up with blue and red lights. Keira straightens up and looks out the window as two cop cars pull up in the parking lot.

The doors open, cops draw their guns, and Officer Wells holds up a megaphone. "Keira Hill. Step outside."

"What the hell?" Madison whispers, and for once, we're on the same wavelength.

Keira is shaking beside me as she scoots her chair back and slowly rises to her feet. I seize her wrist before she has a chance to leave. We don't speak, but I see the truth in her eyes. The defeat. "I'll see you soon, King."

Without another backward glance, she walks out. The bell sounds above the door, grabbing me in a chokehold and throwing me violently back into the present moment. I'm up on my feet in the next second, tearing through the restaurant.

As I stumble through the door with the others hot my heel, Officer Wells is reading Keira her rights.

"You have the right to remain silent. Anything you say can and will be used against you in a court of law..."

The words fade out. *Everything* fades out except for the glistening, delicate tears on Keira's lashes.

Her biggest fear has come true.

She has become her father.

"What the actual fuck?" Madison shouts, shouldering through two officers. "What are you arresting her for?"

Officer Riveiro guides Keira into the back of the cop car with a hand on her head.

Officer Wells looks tired. Regretful. "Murder in the first degree."

"But why?!" Madison cries out, growling at the officers to get out of her fucking way. "What evidence have you got?"

Officer Wells looks back at the car before walking up to us, unaffected by Madison's murderous glare or my tense shoulders. "The evidence is damning."

"Damning how?" Kara asks, and he slides his haunted eyes to hers.

"We found a Halloween mask alongside her stepdad's remains. A devil's mask, to be precise. It had Keira's DNA on it."

"That's bullshit," Madison blurts. "Someone is setting her up."

I say nothing as I dig my nails into my palms to stop myself from pummeling Officer Wells to the ground for stealing Keira away from me. I want to ram my fist into his bearded face and listen to the crunch of his nose breaking. My teeth grind so hard that I worry my molars will pulverize.

"I'm sorry." He walks away, hopping into the car.

The sirens fade away into the distance and then it's just us, staring at the tire marks in the parking lot, our ears ringing from the loud sirens.

"I can't fucking believe this," Madison mumbles, swiping angrily at her wet cheeks.

"She killed Kit." Kara blinks at me, but Madison shoves her hard, causing her to stumble back.

"Shut up, you stupid bitch! Keira didn't kill Kit."

"The mask had her DNA," Hayley argues while I start to pace behind them.

"So? Someone is out to get her!" Madison all but shrieks.

I dig my phone out of my pocket and bring up my father's number. He answers on the first ring.

"What trouble did you get into now?"

"I need your help."

My family is good for nothing, but at least they have money. And money is a powerful thing. Luckily for me, my family has an endless amount.

My father says nothing, so I draw in a deep breath through my nose.

"They arrested Keira for the murders."

"Jimmy Hill's daughter?"

"Yes."

My father sighs, his beard rasping. "I told you to stay away from that girl. She's trouble."

"And I told you that's impossible, so don't try to make me."

"You get your stubborn streak from me. What do you need?"

"What strings can you pull?"

The girls are still bickering amongst themselves, their voices growing louder in the silence of the evening.

"Like in your case, I can make sure the news stays out of the media for as long as possible."

"Thank you."

"I'll see what else I can do, but there'll be a frenzy when the media finds out about this. Jimmy Hill's daughter gets arrested in connection with a murder spree, weeks before her dad is due to be executed... It's bad, King. Very fucking bad."

"Her mother threw her out."

"So she'll need the best representation money can buy."

"Take it out of my trust fund or whatever."

My father chuckles, the gravelly sound soothing the storm inside me. "Just keep yourself out of trouble for a while."

"You know I can't promise you that."

"I know. Do me a favor, son. You're no good to her or anyone if you go down a destructive path. Understood? You need to keep your wits about you. I'll try to help the best I can since you're hell-bent on being with this girl. But chances are, this won't end the way you want it to. I need you to prepare yourself for the fact that money can only take you so far. It can't make first-degree murder charges magically disappear. At best, it can shorten her sentence. *If* we're lucky."

My head hurts, and my stomach is in knots. I want to beat something up. To make my knuckles scream in pain. "Thanks, Dad."

"Don't thank me yet. Now is the time to pray for a miracle."

KEIRA

Death couldn't come quickly enough. Those are the destructive thoughts running through my head while I listen to the clock ticking on the wall. It's obnoxiously loud.

Tick. Tock. Tick. Tock.

They do this on purpose.

I know because I watch crime documentaries.

They leave you alone to let the anxiety build. First, they'll pretend to care. To want to listen. Then, they'll start putting pressure on you. Famous phrases such as *your story doesn't add up,* and *it's time to do the right thing and tell the truth.*

I'm in for a hellish night of grueling questions.

The room is small. One metal table, two chairs, and cream walls. The gray, ticking clock. A camera up in the corner.

I want Mom to come, but I know she won't.

No one will.

Because I have no one.

I'm alone.

Endlessly alone.

I'm sitting with my feet on the chair and my chin propped on my knees. My shackled wrists are tucked close to my body. I'm staring at nothing. I have been for hours. I know they're watching me. Waiting for me to do something.

I try to think of my dad, knowing he's been in this situation, too. He could sympathize with the state of mind I'm in.

I'm not scared or upset. I'm just numb. It's like I don't even exist. The clock keeps ticking, but time stands still. Maybe it's a good thing to be locked up before I can do even more damage.

The angel on my shoulder wants me to confess.

The devil cuts her neck.

We won't breathe a word, he whispers to me, slithering through my veins. *They deserved it.*

I listen. I let it soothe me.

They touched you. Used you. Defiled you.

My eyes sting from staring at one spot for too long, my limbs ache, and my heart slows.

Tick. Tock. Tick. Tock.

The door opens, and Officer Wells steps inside. Riveiro is notably absent, and I wonder if she will play the bad cop later.

This is the friendly phase. Officer Wells will set out to make me trust him. He'll have to try for a long time. Trust doesn't come easily to me.

He drops a folder on the desk and puts a plastic cup of water in front of me. "You must be thirsty?"

"I'm not." I am, but I won't accept anything from him.

Officer Wells sits down, dressed casually in jeans and a long-sleeved, maroon shirt. He wears a black tie with a pattern that I can't make out from here, and his beard is in that stage between stubble and too long.

"Do you know why you're here, Keira?"

"Murder charges."

He watches me, then sits forward, hunched with his elbows on his knees and his eyes on me. "They're serious charges."

I say nothing, and he stares at me some more. The clock keeps ticking. Officer Wells smells of coffee, cheap aftershave, and a hint of sweat. It's not unpleasant.

"Can you tell me a little bit about your relationship with your stepdad? What was it like? Were you close?"

"I know what you're doing."

"What's that?"

"You're looking for a motive. If I tell you we didn't get on, you'll want to know why and, from there, you can 'build a case.'" I make quotation marks. "Keira did what she did because of A and Z."

His lips lift in a barely-there smile. "You're intelligent."

I shrug.

"Look, I'll level with you. The world out there will compare you to your father. You know that. I know that. But that won't be the case here. I don't think you're a product of your father's evil nature."

"No?" I ask, looking at him directly. "You're accusing me of murdering people, and you're telling me you don't believe the tendency to kill runs in my veins?"

"You tell me, Keira. What do you think?"

I breathe a mocking laugh through my nose. "It doesn't matter what I think. Can we just cut to the fucking chase?"

"We can. After you talk to me for a bit."

My eyes roll. "Anything I say can and will be used against me in a court of law, remember?"

"What do you remember of your father?"

Frowning, I snap my gaze to him. "My father?"

"Jimmy Hill... I only know him as Jimmy Hill, the notorious serial killer who murdered sixteen women. The real number is probably much higher. I don't know Jimmy Hill the family man or Jimmy Hill the father. Why don't you tell me a little bit about him? Were you close?"

There's a thick lump in my throat now. I try to swallow past it, but it won't dislodge. "I was seven when they arrested him and broke into our home with drawn guns and barking dogs."

Officer Wells's eyes soften, but he stays silent.

"Mom was in the kitchen, preparing dinner. Dad was throwing me up in the air and catching me. I knew I was getting too big for the game, but he still made an effort because he said he loved it when my giggles lit the house up from the inside." I inhale shakily, staring down at an empty spot on the white table. My eyes blur as I think back on that day—the terror that ripped through me when the police kicked down the front door. "My father was playful. I remember that... He would read me bedtime stories and call me his princess. Adventure stories were my favorite. Peter Pan, especially. He said I was the only spot of light in his dark world."

"It sounds to me like you had a special connection."

I nod softly. "I thought we did, at least. After he was arrested, it all felt like a well-constructed lie. I was too young to understand when they arrested him, but I grew resentful as the years went by."

"It makes sense. How do you feel now?"

My gaze lifts to Officer Wells's face, and I take in the deep lines around his eyes. "I feel like I can understand him more."

Officer Wells straightens, his interest piqued. "Understand him how?"

I'm treading on very thin ice. Slightest misstep, and it'll crack beneath my feet. But a small part of me also wants it to crack so that I won't hurt more people. Is that what my father felt when he was finally caught? Relief somewhere deep inside of him?

At least now, locked up behind bars, I don't have to be a slave to the darkness anymore, but there's a bigger picture here.

A bigger monster.

Someone who's still out there, free to commit more murders because Officer Wells believes I killed all those people.

I wet my lips, glancing at the clock. It's almost midnight. Officer Wells could have kept me locked up until the morning and done his interrogation then, but here we are, burning the midnight oil. The rest of the staff, except for Wells and Riveiro, have gone home to their warm beds. I hope they get paid good overtime.

"I'm Jimmy Hill's daughter," I respond as if that explains

everything. Maybe it does. "People think one of two things when they think of me."

"What's that, Keira?"

I don't like it when strangers call me by my first name. My skin crawls. "They either feel sorry for me. 'Poor little girl. Her father was a monster.' Or they're afraid of me. They think I'm diseased and that it's a matter of time until I turn into my father."

They would be right.

I don't tell him that I understand my father's struggle with the darkness now. Or maybe that's presumptive of me? Maybe my father didn't struggle at all.

But no, that's not true. My father loved his family. Maybe he played a role—most serial killers lead successful double lives—but I don't doubt that I was the apple of his eye. His only spot of light in the darkness, like he would tell me before kissing me goodnight.

A monster isn't an emotionless robot. While driven by sinister urges and cravings that whisper cruelly in the mind, a monster is still capable of love.

In their own way.

I refuse to think my father never loved me and was incapable of human connection. I'm a monster, too. My father is probably the only person, besides King, who I feel connected with.

So I *know* my father struggled with his darkness. I know he was driven by a force beyond himself. Something that stole him from me. An evil, if you will, that whispered secrets in his ear.

The lights go out, descending the room into darkness.

"What the hell?" Officer Wells whispers. The scrape of his chair cuts through the silence as he rises to his feet. His phone screen comes on, lighting up his haunted face. He draws his gun, and I wonder briefly what good it will do when we can't see anything. But I don't ask questions. I stay silent while he puts the phone to his ear, his worried but determined eyes landing on me. Unlike him, I feel detached. I watch the scene unfold with mild disinterest. My heart hammers wildly in my chest, but I'm also strangely calm.

Wells hangs up the phone, grumbling something about voice-mail. He puts on the flashlight and darts it around the room.

"How does the third act end, Officer Wells?"

The beam lands on me and I squint, bringing my shackled hands up in front of my face to shield me from the too-bright light.

Officer Wells lowers the flashlight once more, sliding it toward the closed door behind him. "It doesn't end well."

"I know how it ended for the main detective in my father's case." There's a smile in my voice, and Wells hears it. The light slides away from the door and shines in my face.

Too damn bright.

"My father killed him."

"We caught you, Keira. It's a power outage."

I throw my head back and laugh, the cruel, cold sound bouncing off the walls. "You're so sure I killed all those people, huh?"

"A devil's mask with your DNA all over it was discovered with the remains of your stepfather. How do you explain that, Keira?"

"Circumstantial."

"Bullshit," he spits, jostling the light. "You killed him. *Butchered* him. You wore the mask."

"Fine, I wore the mask. So fucking what?" I'm annoyed now. "It's Halloween season. Every kid in the country has a mask. You can buy the same fucking one almost everywhere."

"That argument won't hold up in court, Keira," he bites out, unnerved by the sudden power outage.

"If it's just an outage, why are you pointing your gun? You look a little worried, Officer Wells."

Breathing harshly through his nose, he slides the light back toward the door.

The open door.

My heart jumps to my throat as a peal of laughter slips from my lips. Wells releases a string of expletives and takes a protective stance in front of me. His light darts across the room, chasing shadows.

"Welcome to the third act, Officer Wells, where no one is safe," I taunt him. "How about you remove my handcuffs, so I stand a fighting chance of defending myself."

"Not a fucking chance," he growls.

"The room is small. There are only so many places the killer can hide."

He whirls on me. "Will you shut up!"

"If you don't release my shackles, I'll die, too."

"We're not going to die." He pulls me up by my arm, guiding me behind him as we leave the small interrogation room.

The hallway is equally dark, void of windows. The only light source is an emergency exit light above the door up ahead. It's not much. The soft, muted glow does little to disperse the shadows crawling closer from every corner and reaching for me like taloned fingers.

A shiver rolls down my spine as a cold sweat beads on my neck. "Officer Wells?" I whisper, uncertainty sneaking into my voice for the first time tonight.

"Keep close."

Holding the gun with one hand, he extends his arm and pushes open the door to the reception area. We step through on light feet, careful not to make a sound. I can't help but feel eyes on me. Someone is watching us. Waiting for us to run like prey.

"Shit..." Officer Wells hurries up to Riveiro's broken body on the floor. That's when I see it. The drag marks of blood trailing through the reception area. The killer attacked her and stabbed her multiple times. Unable to run, she army crawled toward the exit door, hoping to escape.

"Fuck!" Wells rolls her over onto her back, his bloodied fingers sliding over her slick face as he brushes her black hair away from her cheeks.

The tangy scent of copper assaults my nostrils. I take a step back, only to meet a solid wall. *A breathing wall.* Before I can scream, a hand clamps over my mouth. The cold metal of a knife digs into my cheek as a distorted voice whispers in my ear, "We're down to the key players, Keira. Are you ready to run for your life? If I catch you, I will kill you."

The knife falls away from my cheek, and the robed killer walks around me, creeping up behind Officer Wells, ready to attack him from behind. He twists his head, and his devil's mask leers at me in the dim light, the sharp blade glinting in his hand.

I hold my breath, my heart thrashing so wildly in my chest that I struggle to think rationally. He's taking his time on purpose, seeing what I'll do.

I should scream.

Officer Wells is still hunched over Riveiro's lifeless body, his shoulders shaking with silent, choked sobs. He pleads with her to wake up.

Slowly, so fucking slowly, the killer turns back around before reaching out and gripping Officer Wells's hair. With a hard pull, he exposes his throat, and the haunting gurgling sound that follows turns my stomach.

Running forward to stop him, I soon stumble back when he turns around. Fresh blood drips from the curved blade, and my eyes travel down to the slumped body on top of Riveiro and back. *He killed him. He killed Wells.*

The masked man takes a step closer, and I inch away.

"The third act is the most exciting. Don't you think, Keira? This is when the plot twists happen, and the heroine wins against all odds. Only this is a story with a twist. That's why I chose you, Keira. You're a caged monster waiting to be released into the world. All you needed was a little push—a little *maturing.* And look at you now, so fucking perfect."

I slide my gaze past him to the entrance door. The door that he's blocking. I take off running the way we came, back through the hallway leading to the interrogation room, and through a second door. I can hear him behind me, dragging his feet, or at least I think it's his feet, until a pained whimper rings out.

I'm just about to ascend the steps to the second floor when his voice calls out, chillingly cold, "You don't want me to kill Officer Riveiro too, do you? She's still alive, but barely."

With my shackled hands on the metal rail, I look over my shoulder as the monster enters the narrow stairwell, tossing Riveiro to the floor. There's so much blood everywhere, a trail of it running the length of the hallway.

"You have two choices, Keira. You either come with me willingly, and I won't touch another hair on Riveiro's head, or we play a game of chase after I slice her throat like I did to Officer Wells."

Another pained groan fills the heavy silence while I stare at the devil's mask in front of me. The emergency exit light above the door offers only just enough illumination to make out the cold, soulless eyes visible through the holes. "What do you want with me? You're gonna kill me, so why don't you just get it over with? Why all of this?"

"Because the game isn't over. You'll soon see what I have planned for you."

I flit my gaze down to Riveiro, whose raven hair has escaped the ponytail. Dark, matted tendrils of her long strands stick to the blood smeared on her face, and her raspy, labored breaths are loud in the seconds that follow. I think of all the innocent people that have died because of this man's crazy obsession with my father and me, not to mention his obsession with awakening my killer instincts.

My hands fall away from the railing, and I take a step closer to the masked man. "You win. I'll come with you. No one else has to die."

A low, sinister chuckle fills the air as I carefully step over

Riveiro's broken, prone body on the floor, my shoes leaving footprints in the fresh blood.

"The game is over," I breathe, approaching him slowly. There's no way out of this. I have to play along, or more people die. This nightmare ends with my death, and that thought alone carries me forward.

His hand flies out and grabs me by the collar. He hauls me close, the bloodied knife digging into my throat as he taunts, "The game has only just begun."

KEIRA

Walking down the hallway, following the blood stains on the floor from when the killer dragged Riveiro, we enter the reception area, where Wells lies face down in a pool of his own blood.

So much blood.

My gaze dances across the dimly lit room, over the reception desk, to the camera up in the left corner.

Noticing, the masked man grasps the back of my neck, and his distorted voice slithers beneath my skin and crawls along each curvature of my spine. "They're disconnected. By the time we're done here, you'll be dead, and Blackwoods will think Jimmy Hill's daughter snapped and killed the officers."

"You have it all figured out, huh?" I sneer.

The cloying scent of blood and death mingles on the air. I try to get a look at the killer, but with the robe, the hood, and the mask, I can't see anything.

"There's only one problem," I point out, bringing my shackled wrists up to show him. "I can't flip and kill everyone if I'm shackled."

In a swift move, he slips his hand from my neck and grabs the chain, pulling it hard enough to send me flying to the blood-stained, grubby floor.

I fall on my side, and my temple bounces off the hard surface, rendering me defenseless as pain explodes behind my eyelids. Clutching my throbbing head in agony, I whimper into the dirty, cold floor. I'm nauseous with the pain. My brain feels like it's too big for my skull, each heavy throb beating loudly in my ears and gums.

Crouching down beside me, he slides my hair away from my damp cheek with the curved blade before grabbing a handful and hauling me to my feet.

I let out a pained cry, grabbing onto his forearm with cold and clammy hands. My scalp burns, the blonde hairs torn from their roots. Fear grips my throat. I claw and scratch, nails snagging on his robe as I fight him.

In the next second, he shoves me hard toward the reception desk. "Let's play a little game of chase. I know how much you like to be hunted like prey." He takes a step closer, and I push myself off the reception desk, my fingers curled around the edge. "Only this game ends in carnage."

I can hear the sickening smile in his voice—the bloodlust behind his intentions. Everything about this moment is designed to prolong and increase my fear. He feeds off it.

I don't think as I turn and run. The front doors are locked, and my trembling hands leave smears of blood on the metal handle and the icy-cold glass. Outside, the snow is falling, serving as a picturesque background to my torment.

"Don't let me catch you, Keira. I'll kill you slowly if I do," he calls out behind me when I sprint to my left into another hallway lined with office doors. I curse my choice when I realize it's a dead end. There's nowhere to run. If I enter one of the offices, I'm cornered. I can't run back the way I came, so I'm trapped either way.

Darting into the first room to my right—Wells's office—I quickly shut and lock the door. It's with great effort that I manage to push the heavy desk in front of it, causing the photographs on top to fall to the floor. By the time it's finally blocking the door,

I'm panting, and my head is throbbing with a deep ache. I step back, colliding with one of the desk chairs pushed to the side. Thick, heavy silence slithers out from the shadows to dance with my fear. It kisses the cold sweat on my forehead and grips my throat in a vice until I struggle to breathe.

I wait, listening to each heavy heartbeat in my head. Nothing happens. The silence screams. My heart slows before skyrocketing when the handle rattles violently.

I let out a startled scream, stumbling back.

The handle rattles again before something heavy crashes into the door.

Half bent at the waist and sobbing, I cover my ears and plead with him to stop.

He doesn't.

His foot connects with the door, and the loud bang is so deafening that I scream again.

"Please, stop! Please, just go away."

The handle rattles and the hinges threaten to give way the longer he continues kicking and punching the door. By the time silence descends, I'm sobbing almost uncontrollably.

I wait, but nothing more happens. My breathing soon begins to stabilize. I listen for any noise, any sign that he's still outside.

My feet move forward, but I stop myself. What if he's out there, waiting for me to feel brave enough to leave this office? Debating what to do, I scan the room. Except for a metal bookshelf to my left with a potted Devil's Ivy on top and a row of certificates on the wall behind me, there's not much in here. The room lacks personality.

As I step forward again, broken glass crunches beneath my shoe. I lean down to pick up the framed photograph, angling it toward the moonlight shining in through the window, careful not to cut myself on the jagged pieces of glass in the frame. It's a photograph of Officer Wells and his wife on their wedding day. He looks about twenty years younger, with a full head of dark hair and no sign of graying at the temples.

More importantly, he looks happy.

Not washed out, tired, and overworked like he did before he was brutally murdered by the killer.

As I drop the picture frame back to the floor, the window explodes to my right, and I release a blood-curdling scream. The devil's mask leers back at me through the now glassless window. My gaze flits down to the brick on the floor and to the desk barricading the door, then back.

I'm trapped.

Heavy feet land on the broken glass with a loud thud as he climbs in through the window, the crunching sound sending my heart into overdrive.

I'm desperately trying to shift the desk when he takes a taunting, slow step closer.

Then another.

"Oh, God, no," I whimper, pushing on the desk. The legs scrape on the floor, but I'm not fast enough.

Diving to my left, I grab a hardback from the bookshelf and throw it at him. He easily ducks, chuckling distortedly behind his mask as he takes another calculated step forward.

"It's over, Keira."

"Fuck you!" I hiss, tossing another book. "Fuck you and your stupid games!"

The mask tilts to the left, with jagged, pointed teeth and an evil smile. "That's not very nice, Keira. I *made* you. Without me, you wouldn't have discovered your full potential. Your beautiful, sinister legacy. The darkness that runs in your veins and spills with your blood."

My chest is heaving, and my arms ache from throwing book after book. Reaching up on my tiptoes, I grab hold of the Devil's Ivy and throw that, too.

The monster in front of me steps to the side as it goes flying, and I release a frustrated, defeated sob. I can't win.

"You're a vision when you're scared, Keira, with your glassy, wide eyes, tear-streaked cheeks, and parted lips."

"You're fucking sick!"

The devil's mask leers down at me when he kills the distance between us and drags the flat end of the knife over my cheek. "Says the girl who carved her stepdad to pieces. Oh, how I enjoyed watching the security footage. Seeing with my own two eyes how you took your time with him, reveling in your kill. You were a beautiful monster." He taps my parted lips with the curved blade, edging the sharp tip inside my mouth. "Don't you see? People like you, Keira, are superior humans. You're an apex predator. Not mediocre like all the other people here in Blackwoods. You're beautiful in your lethality. It's why people gravitate toward you. Why Liam harbored an obsession with you and now King. They all want to feel like they're part of the Hill legacy. Something that's bigger than themselves." Leaning in, he nuzzles me, the mask brushing the side of my face. "Prey is attracted to danger. It's the evilest, most sinister design by our creator. Religious people preach God is love." A soft, nefarious chuckle. "God is the designer of evil. Why else did he create the angler fish and parasitoids? Do you know what they are, Keira?"

Whimpering with fear, I shake my head.

"They're parasites, body snatchers that start their lives inside or on their hosts, usually in caterpillars. The parasite eats the caterpillar alive. Do you know what the fascinating thing about it is?" He breathes me in, easing the knife further into my mouth until I don't dare breathe. "It infects the caterpillar, causing it to protect its host while it eats it alive. The caterpillar ends up protecting its own killer. Isn't God so loving, Keira? That even a prey in the throes of death will vicariously attack anyone that tries to save it from its killer?" He hums, inching back. "Now, be a good girl and stick your tongue out."

Staring into the cold, dark eyes behind the devil's mask, I do as I'm told. The flat end of the cold blade drags down my tongue and back up, over and over, until he turns it, the sharp bite threatening to cut me.

"Do you like the taste of Officer Wells's blood? You should see it stain your tongue crimson red." He digs the blade in, making my heart rate triple. The burning sting is followed by a rush of warm blood dripping down my chin.

The knife slides away, and he grips my jaw with his leather-gloved fingers, staring down at the blood smeared over my mouth.

As I splutter a cough, more pours from my lips. I don't know if the cut was deep, but it is bleeding profusely. The coppery taste flows down my throat, making me retch.

"I want to play a little game," he says, pulling my lip away from my teeth with his thumb before grabbing me by the throat and ramming my head into the bookshelf behind me. "Have sweet dreams, Keira."

Darkness descends, sending me spiraling into an endless nightmare.

I startle awake with a gasp and scuttle back until my spine meets the cold, concrete wall. I'm in a small room, a basement by the looks of it. The thin mattress beneath me is damp, and the white, crumpled sheets are stained yellow.

I dart my gaze around the empty room, briefly blinking at the drain in the middle and the dried blood around it. The floor is dirty and gritty, and there are no windows.

In the upper left corner is a camera with a flashing red light. Someone is watching and waiting for me to wake up. Waiting for me to scream. To scour the room for a way out. *Anything* to escape this nightmare.

I do neither. I stare at the camera until I'm forced to blink. Until my heart rate is so slow, I wonder if it has ceased to beat.

Am I dead? Is this hell?

My tongue stings, my mouth tastes of iron, and I also have a dull ache in my head, an insistent throbbing from when he shoved my head into the bookshelf hard enough to cause me to blackout.

Eyes closed, I lean my head back against the cold, damp wall. The hairs on my arms stand on end from the chill in the air, and I pull my denim jacket closed around me, trying to preserve some heat. It doesn't work. I'm frozen to the bone in this damp cellar.

At least the single lightbulb hanging from the ceiling works. It could be worse. I could be submerged in complete darkness.

With my knees pulled up to my chest, I lean my cheek on them and let my eyes drift closed again. I'm tired.

Whatever shit the killer has planned, I want it over with. Even if it means I have to die. It wasn't that long ago that I wanted to put a bullet in my skull or slice my wrists open. Knowing I'll most likely die soon should comfort me, right? But it doesn't. Not when it's on someone else's terms and part of some twisted game. It will always come back to this. To my father. My legacy. I can't escape it, and I can't pretend it's not a part of me.

The lock sounds in the door to my left, the bolt sliding against the old wood. The rusty hinges creak loudly, and the door slowly inches open to reveal the robed killer and his red, metallic mask that shines beneath the fluorescent lightbulb.

He watches me for a moment, eerily silent as his chest rises and falls, his fingers tightening around the blade's handle. The curved knife has been replaced with a meat cleaver. I don't know what's worse—a thin, long blade or this fat one?

I lift my head and watch him while the seconds tick by. He doesn't speak as I wait him out. I refuse to let him see the effect he has on me. If he wants me to cry and plead, he'll need to make a move and not try to unnerve me with his silence alone.

His heavy boots finally shift, crossing the threshold. He walks up to me and grabs hold of my upper arm. I'm hauled to my feet and thrown against the wall behind me. Stepping onto the mattress, he digs the meat cleaver into my throat as his boots leave dirty footprints on the stained sheets.

"You removed my shackles," I comment. I'm not as calm as I portray, but he doesn't need to know how my heartbeat thrashes so wildly that I'm growing lightheaded. I will it to calm down.

"You need your hands untied for this next part." He digs his fingers into my tender wrist through the denim and drags me out of the room and down a narrow, dim hallway. I'm missing a shoe. My sock soon dampens as grit sticks to the fabric. I try to wrench free and run, but I'm shoved to the floor instead and kicked in the side.

Hot, blazing pain lashes across my ribs, and I roll over onto my front. Groaning pitifully, I dig my forehead into the ground. "Fuck, that hurt!"

"Get up!" Distorted, twisted, evil.

When I don't move fast enough, he pulls me up by my hair and shoves me forward while I clutch my burning ribs.

There's a door to our left, bolted just like the door to the room of horrors I was in. With a fierce grip on my arm, he slides the bolt aside, rams it open with his shoulder, and pulls me inside. It's dark in here. Dark and damp. The stench of blood prickles my nose. I crinkle it as the monster beside me pulls a string by the door, flooding the room with a harsh, silvery, fluorescent light. I blink, shielding my eyes with my hand while taking in the scene before me.

Two metal chairs.

Two tied-up people, each with a burlap sack over their heads and dressed in similar robes to the killer.

Stepping back, I collide with the devil behind me, who curls his fingers around my throat and points the meat cleaver at the people on the chairs. "Two people you care about. Only one of them gets to live. The choice is yours." The meat cleaver slides to the left, where a digital clock is mounted to the wall. "See how it ticks down? When it reaches zero, it's game over. If your friends are still alive, I'll kill you all. If one of them is dead by your hands," he points the meat cleaver to a camera in the corner to let me know he's watching, "I'll let the other one walk out of here alive, and you surrender yourself to be killed in their place. If I return and they're both dead, *you* get to walk out of here to see another sunrise."

"Why are you doing this?" I choke out around his tight grip on my throat.

"Why do you think? True monsters are psychopaths, remember? Soulless monsters, incapable of compassion. How deep does your illness run, Keira? How deeply rooted is it? Do you truly love the people you claim to care about, or is it all a nicely constructed lie, a facade you wear to hide the killer behind the mask?" His fingers ease up on my throat, stroking my pulse point. "Did your father ever love you, Keira? Was he capable of human connection? If you were tied to one of those chairs," he points the meat cleaver in the direction of the slumped figures, "would he have surrendered himself to let you live, or would he have slit your throat to save himself?" His mask presses into the crook of my neck as he whispers, "Would he have enjoyed it?"

"You forget one thing," I reply, gritting my teeth. "Psychopaths can love people in their own way."

"Well," there's a smile in his distorted voice, "that remains to be seen." He shoves me forward, then walks out of the room and bolts the door. I stand there for a moment, not daring to breathe or move as I stare at the tied-up figures in front of me. As soon as I remove the sacks, I'll know who they are, and this will all become a reality.

Right now, I can't guess. They're both dressed in the same black robes the killer wears to conceal his clothing, but I can hear their labored breathing and the rustling of their robes as they struggle against their binding.

Stepping forward, I pause. Duct-taped to their arm is a weapon each: a corkscrew and a small switchblade.

I stare at the corkscrew, wondering why the killer thought to include it. The message is clear: I have to kill the person with the chosen weapon.

My eyes skate to the clock on the wall. I've wasted five minutes already. Ten minutes left and counting.

Before I can let my nerves get the best of me, I walk forward and pull the burlap sack off the first person. It's Madison. I press my palms to my mouth, my head shaking violently back and forth. I can't do this. I can't fucking do this.

Her mouth is duct-taped, too. I peel it off, causing her to

wince. "Fuck, Keira, there's never a dull moment with you, is there?"

Choked laughter rumbles in my chest. Only Madison would joke in a situation like this.

She slides her eyes to the left, to the hunched figure beside her, who's wrestling against the restraints. I pull the sack off and stumble back when I see King staring up at me with his wild, dark eyes and unruly hair. His nostrils flare as his chest heaves.

Darting forward, I remove the duct tape over his mouth and fall to my knees in front of him. "Oh, God, I'm so sorry. Are you okay? Are you hurt?" Looking over at Madison, I ask her the same thing.

"I'm fine. We're both fine," King breathes out, clearly not fine as he grimaces in pain.

"Where does it hurt?" I ask, my voice edged with fear. I fall back onto my ass, pull my knees up, and clutch my head. Fingers braided in my matted hair, I pull sharply to distract myself from the mounting panic.

I can't do this.

I can't do this.

I have to do this.

Or we all die.

My gaze flicks up to the clock on the wall, only to slide back down to the dirty floor.

Seven minutes and counting.

Think, Keira. Think.

Jumping to my feet, I pull off both their weapons. The silvery duct tape is sticky beneath my fingers and a nightmare to discard. One of the strips sticks to my denim jacket as I crouch behind Madison, using the switchblade to cut through the ropes. I don't have a plan. All I know is that I can't possibly kill my friends. I can't pick one. I'm a monster, but I refuse to admit I'm incapable of love.

Madison throws off her robe and wrings her sore wrists,

while I free King. The moment he breaks free of the bindings, he stands from his chair, wraps me up in his arms, and whispers soothing words I can barely make out due to my roaring heartbeat.

Clutching him to me, I breathe in the scent of leather and peppermint. "He wants me to kill one of you."

"I heard," King replies, palming my head with his big hands and tangling his fingers in the blonde strands. "We'll figure it out."

Madison pulls me away from King and into her soothing embrace. "Are you okay?"

"No," I admit as I wrap my arms around her slim waist. Her puffer jacket is gone, and her red, wool sweater is damp and cold, just like the tickle of her dark hair against my cheek.

Cupping my cheeks, she scans her eyes over my face as if to reassure herself that I'm okay. I'm not, and her gaze soon snags on my bloodied chin and mouth, the crimson streak on my cheek. "What did he do?"

"It doesn't matter." I step back, scanning the room. Behind me, King removes the robe. The weapons lie discarded on the floor, so I pick them up. "What do we do?"

King looks away from the clock on the wall. *Five minutes.* "When he walks back in here, we run at him."

"Are you stupid?" Madison grits out, pointing to the camera. "He can hear us."

"Do you have a better plan?" A jagged tear in his black T-shirt reveals his tanned, tattooed skin and streaks of dried blood. Even now, beaten up and bruised, with his hair in disarray, King is beautiful.

So beautiful, in fact, I have to look away.

Madison trains her blue eyes on me. "Is there any way to beat him at his own game?"

"Yeah, rush him and kill him," King tells her.

"He'll see it coming from a fucking mile away. Besides, for all we know, he could walk in here with a gun."

"Screw you, Madison. How the hell do you suggest we get out of here otherwise?"

Four minutes.

My fingers tighten around the weapons while they continue bickering. I study them both, their haunted eyes that flash with anger as they get up in each other's faces. Madison has always been hot-headed. She pretends she doesn't care, but she does.

My thoughts circle to our childhood. Images of her kicking her bike when she didn't learn fast enough how to ride without training wheels flood my mind. How she turned to me, her long pigtails swinging with the movement, and said, "Stupid thing. I never wanted to learn anyway."

It's no surprise that King is hot-headed. I learned that early on, and I liked that side of him.

Three minutes.

Placing the weapons in the hem of my jeans, I slide between them, acting as a barrier. "Arguing won't get us anywhere." I look at Madison in front of me, then over my shoulder at King.

They glare at each other before deflating with defeated sighs. Stroking my hand over Madison's cheek, my gaze glides past her to the clock on the wall. I swallow thickly and force myself to look back at Madison. "We can't win against this killer. I've played his games before. He's always one step ahead."

"So what do you suggest we do?"

I palm her slender throat and press my forehead to hers while brushing my thumb over her sharp jawbone. Her breaths dance with mine in the small gap between us. We hover here, protected from the horrors that surround us. "I suggest we play the game."

"Wha—?" she chokes out with a sudden jerk, her eyes widening as she inhales a sharp breath. She looks down at her abdomen, where I still hold on to the switchblade protruding from her stomach.

"I'm sorry." I pull it out and stab her again. Her lips brush mine briefly as I jerk her forward. "It was you or him."

Releasing her, I watch her fall helplessly in a heap on the dirty floor. Her terrified, wide eyes find me as blood pours from between her fingers on her stomach. She looks down, releasing a weak, frightened sob before collapsing.

Behind me, King circles his arm around my waist and pulls me into his warm chest. "Babe," he breathes out, his breath tingling the side of my neck.

I let him turn me around and kiss me while the clock behind him ticks down the seconds to my own death. King will get to walk out of here a free man. He'll get to fall in love and be happy again. Free from monsters. Free from shadows. He'll get to live.

His sweet taste wraps around my aching heart, and I allow the pain of letting him go anchor me. I allow myself to set him free from the evil in the room. Evil that will forever taint his soul unless I release him from this prison.

In a quick move, I pull the corkscrew from my jeans and stab him in the side.

Releasing me with a pained grunt, he bends at the waist, clutching his midriff.

"It was you or me," I tell him, my voice empty and devoid of emotion. Looking up at the clock, I sigh through my nose. *Twenty-eight seconds.* "I'm sorry, but I can't let you walk out of here to fall in love with someone else. To *fuck* someone else," I emphasize. "You're mine, King. I would rather kill you than set you free."

His eyes slide away from the blood trickling between his fingers where he's clutching the slippery, maroon handle. "What the hell, Keira?"

So much blood.

I look up at the clock on the wall. *Ten seconds.*

Shoving King to the ground, we go tumbling on the floor, knocking a metal chair out of the way that collides with the wall. Wrenching the corkscrew out, I stab him again and again while he rolls in on himself, struggling to fight me off. The camera is at my back. The killer is watching and salivating over the kill. King finally manages to shove me off, then rolls over onto his front. He's too weak to push himself up and collapses to the gritty floor.

Climbing to my feet, I stagger back, breathing harshly. It's over. It's fucking over. I killed them, which means I get to live.

I played his fucking game and won.

I killed the only people I care about, proving to my own tormentor that I am a true psychopath.

Laughing loudly, I collapse against the concrete wall, barely feeling the cold, damp surface or noticing the stench of death in the air. Blood is everywhere—on my hands, my face, my hair, and my denim jacket.

It's caked beneath my nails.

"Hey, Dad," I shout like a crazed person. "I bet you would be fucking proud of me now!" When I look back at the clock again, a smile slowly lifts my lips.

Time is up.

"Let me out, you fucker!" I shout as the seconds tick by. "I played your stupid game."

I don't know how long I wait while the killer taunts me by keeping me locked away. He's doing it on purpose, watching me pace like a caged dog with rabies.

"Let me the fuck out!" I roar, shredding my lungs in the process. My sweaty chest heaves as I stare at the door, willing it to open. Another ten minutes pass before the lock finally sounds. I snap my eyes in the direction of the door as it slides open to reveal the devil's mask.

"You're such a fucking coward," I seethe when he enters, toeing the bodies on the floor with his boot. "Too afraid to show your face. It makes me wonder who the prey is? I don't fucking hide in the grass. I'm right here. Ready to kill you with my bare fucking hands." I toss the weapons to the ground, showing him I'm not scared. "We both know you won't let me walk out of here. You never let me win." Shaking my head, I laugh bitterly, but it dies just as abruptly, and I level him with a dead look. "Let's finish this."

Waving the meat cleaver in the air, he steps over the bodies and makes his way toward me, in no hurry to get started. Kicking the weapons behind him, out of reach for me, he tuts. "Stupid move, you silly girl. Now I'll hack your hands to pieces when you throw them up to defend yourself."

He comes for me then, and I duck as his meat cleaver sails through the air, smashing against the wall. I'm so fucking high on adrenaline that I'm laughing maniacally. I pop back up, rolling along the wall. We stare at each other, breathing heavily.

"I outwitted you this time," I breathe out with a chuckle. "You see, if you play the game long enough, you soon learn how to win."

"Oh, sweetheart," he replies, his distorted voice sending a trickle of shivers racing down my spine. "I always win."

My eyes slide past his shoulder. "Not this time."

Noticing my diverted attention, he begins to turn.

"You should have checked if they were truly dead. Oh well, too late now."

King and Madison fall upon him with the switchblade and corkscrew, and I watch them stab him repeatedly until he's in shreds. A dark-red pool of blood inches closer to my feet.

I step in it with my sock-covered foot, the fabric soaking up the blood as I stare down at the dead, broken body. King and Madison straighten up.

"I worried you would take it personally," I say to King.

"I kind of did when you first stabbed me with the corkscrew," he replies, dragging the back of his hand over his forehead and leaving behind a streak of blood, "but then I figured it out when you pretended to stab me in the stomach."

"The camera was at my back," I reply, crouching down. "He couldn't see what I was doing."

"You're fucking vicious," Madison says with a laugh as I inch my fingers underneath the mask. "You only stabbed him once, but I was stabbed twice. Not fair."

"I figured you're used to it by now after you were attacked in the bathroom," I jest. "The knife was shallow, and I didn't cut you near any vital organs. It'll sting for a while, but you'll be fine."

Inhaling a steadying breath, I slowly slide off the mask and discard it on the floor.

"What the hell?" Madison blurts behind me, her voice heavy with shock. I blink down at Kara's face, unable to grasp the truth in front of me. She killed Kit. Her own fucking boyfriend.

"The fuck..." King whispers.

Madison slides her fingers under my arm and drags me to my feet. "We need to leave."

Staring back at Kara's dead, empty eyes, I let King and Madison guide me out of the room, toward the staircase at the end of the hallway.

I'm still trying to figure out what happened. King's friend, Kara, was the killer all along.

But why?

Why would she do all of this? Why would she kill her own friends? Jasper? Kit?

The wooden steps creak beneath our weight. King is at the front, opening the door before stepping through and reaching for my hand. One look at the windows reveals it's still dark outside. We're in a cabin, somewhere remote by the looks of it. There are no streetlights outside, and the sky is void of the smog from the city center.

Moving away from the window, I search for a phone. We need to call for help. In the center of the room sits a red fabric couch with a tartan blanket. It's dusty, which tells me no one lives here.

"Where are we?" Madison asks, turning in a circle and staring up at the wooden beams that run the length of the ceiling.

"No fucking clue." King is looking out of the window now, holding the thick, red curtain out of place. "It's too dark to see anything, but it looks like we're in the woods."

Madison sits down on the couch, elbows on her knees, and scrubs her blood-smeared face. "How did the killer get you here, King?"

"I was ambushed on my way home."

"The killer, *Kara,* ran out at me from behind the kitchen door when I entered the room and shoved the burlap sack over my head. She held a knife to my throat."

"She had a gun when she ambushed me."

Madison lowers her hands. "I can't imagine she'd want to risk getting in a physical fight with you."

Leaving them to their conversation, I locate a phone in the kitchen and remove it from its holder. I'm not even surprised when silence greets me as I press it to my ear. Of course, there's no reception out here. No one lives here, so why would the phone work?

Placing it back in the holder, I grip the counter and let my chin rest against my chest. I'm exhausted now that the adrenaline is wearing off. I probably have a concussion, too. My head is throbbing incessantly to the point where my stomach clenches with nausea.

The door clicks shut with a soft creak behind me, causing me to stiffen. As I turn around, I pause. Photographs of me lie spread out on the floor like a sea of deception and lies.

Too many to count.

A sea of pictures documenting my life.

In the middle is a handwritten note.

After looking around the kitchen to ensure I'm alone, I bend at the waist to collect the note. I straighten up, reading the scrawled words.

> *Round two. Let's play another game. No one is who they seem. Call out King's name, and watch his face change when he enters the kitchen.*

Hands trembling almost violently, I breathe out a shaky sigh and blink down at the letter. '*Watch his face change when he enters the kitchen.'* I look up at the door and back. "King?" My voice is too weak. I call out again, louder this time. "King!"

His heavy footsteps thud on the floor, and then he opens the door and enters the room. His concerned eyes follow my gaze, sweeping across the floor, and he stiffens.

"What's this, King?" I watch him closely. The way his throat jumps. The look of terror on his face. Not surprise.

Guilt.

"What's this, King?" I all but shout, causing him to jerk his eyes to mine. I don't have to ask him if he took these pictures. Not when the truth is written all over his face.

In a quick move, I bend and pick up a picture of me in bed with Liam. I'm riding him cowgirl, head thrown back, my peaked nipples on full display, and Liam's cock between my legs. "You spied on me? Watched me fuck him?"

I toss the picture like I've been stung. Betrayal burns through my veins and coils around my heart like barbed wire. "Say something, for fuck's sake. How do you explain this?"

"He can't," Madison says as she enters behind King. "He's been obsessed with you for a very long time, and the dare was the catalyst that finally made him act on his urges."

"Shut up," King grinds out.

"Are you denying it?" Madison challenges him while I blink back tears at the fucking mess that's my life.

King says nothing, his dark, intense gaze sliding my way.

"What the fuck is real?" I ask, pleading with him to tell me he didn't spy on me for years. That he didn't photograph me fucking Liam.

He stays quiet, and it pisses me off enough to shout, "What the fuck did you do with the pictures, King? Did you jerk off to them?"

Looking away, he works his jaw.

My hand flies up to my mouth, and my eyes water. "You did." I stare at him as the seconds tick by, vaguely aware that Madison walks up to me and pulls me into her arms. I whisper, "But Liam... He's... We..."

"It's okay," Madison whispers, tucking my hair behind my ear with fingers that smell of tangy copper.

"You planned it all."

King's eyes darken and he takes a step closer, but I scream, surprising us all, "YOU PLANNED IT! EVERYTHING!" Then quieter, "Liam is dead, King. You planned it. YOU FUCKING PLANNED IT!"

"Shh." Madison tucks me into her embrace, and I let her hold me. "Calm down, Keira. We'll figure it out."

"And you're going to listen to her?" King growls. "A conniving bitch who's been after you this whole time, pretending to be your friend?"

"Fuck you!" Madison hisses over my head, her pulse fluttering against my lips at the crook of her neck. "Don't you think she's suffered enough?" Waving a hand at the sea of photographs between us, she continues, "Do you think she wants to be with you after you have stalked her for years? Do you think she wants to be with a sociopath?"

King's responding chuckle raises the hairs on my arms and neck. "You're good, Madison. I'll give you that. This is what you do; you play people against each other."

"Just leave," I whisper, unable to look at him.

Ignoring me, he directs his next question to Madison. "What are you gonna do? You haven't got a fucking clue what Keira needs. What she craves. She's complex. You know nothing about her darkness. But I do. Call it crazy. Call it whatever the fuck you want. But I know what she needs *because* I've watched her for so long. I never turned away. Never denied her. Instead, her darkness lured me in. How are you gonna wrangle it? You don't even have a fucking cock."

"I don't need a dick to pleasure a woman, you asshole!"

"If you think she's gonna fall for you, you're fucking naive."

I untangle myself from Madison's arms, fed up with their verbal sparring. "Leave me alone, both of you."

Neither of them says a word as I step over the sea of photographs, sidle past King, and leave the room.

No sooner have I exited the kitchen and slammed the door shut than a knife is pressed to my cheek. The sharp tip digs into my skin, and my hands fly up in a surrendering gesture. I peer to my side, careful not to cut myself on the knife.

Cocked to the side, the devil's mask glares back at me. "Don't you love a good surprise, Keira? I sure as fuck do."

My stomach plummets. Just when I thought this nightmare was over, it kicks back into gear, and we career down a hill. I don't know how much more of this I can take. How much more shit my battered heart and mind can handle.

"Make a single noise, and I'll gut you in front of your friends, understood?"

I nod, squeezing my eyes shut. "I understand."

"Good girl. Now walk."

MADISON

King continues glaring at me from across the sea of photographs, and I let my smile unfurl on my lips. His eyes narrow in response, seeing right through me.

"You know what I'm fucking capable of," he says darkly. "And the lengths I'll go to in order to protect what's mine. Threaten to steal it, and I'll bury you six feet under."

"You truly are a sociopath."

"Plaster whatever fucking title you want on me—sociopath, psychopath—it doesn't matter. The result is still the same. If you step in my path, I'll end you."

"You think she'll take you back after this?" I motion to the floor, sniggering. "Oh, King, stop fooling yourself."

His filthy, loosely tied Doc Martens crunch the photographs when he walks up to me. With his tattooed hands in his pockets, he tilts his head toward his shoulder and studies my face with a small smirk. "You really don't know what you're up against. The sheer fucking depths of Keira's darkness. She could hate me for the next century, but she'll let me chase her into the dark night if it drives away her own shadows. You see, she loves the respite I offer her, and she'll seek it in destruction, chaos, and pain. The only place where a true predator can find their damnation is beneath a much bigger and fiercer predator."

I let my gaze slide down his body; the breadth of his shoulders, the visible, tanned skin beneath his torn T-shirt, his leather belt and destroyed jeans, the thick bulge at his crotch, then back up. "You think you're the biggest predator in these woods?"

His eyebrow lifts, and the left side of his mouth quirks.

"You don't need muscle or strength to be at the top of the food chain." I dig my finger into my temple. "Even the seemingly weak can become the ruler of the jungle if they use this."

He huffs a condescending chuckle through his straight nose, his small smirk striking a match inside me.

King thinks he's all that.

King thinks he's so fucking special because he's good-looking, rich, and harbors an unhealthy amount of big dick energy. I'm not all that into boys, but even I can scent it in the air.

It fucking reeks.

I want to reach for a knife in the wooden block beside us and cut his damn face, if only to ruin his masculine perfection.

Before the thought can form fully, his hand shoots out, and he grips me in a chokehold. With his face so close to mine that we're breathing each other's air, he snarls, "There's only one king in this jungle, sweetheart, and that's me. *I* fuck the queen. Not you. Not Liam. No one else but me. You had a taste, but that's all you'll ever get, and I suggest you shut that pretty little mouth and stay away from my girl unless you want to join Liam in his cold grave." He shoves me away, then walks out.

"Asshole," I mutter, reaching for a knife in the block and sliding it out. The black plastic handle is solid in my hand. I smile, making a slashing motion in the air. King is fucking dead.

Stepping over the photographs, I take chase, exiting the kitchen. King is tall, over six foot three in height, and with enough muscle beneath his leather jacket to easily carve himself a spot on the football team if he so wishes. The only thing I'll carve tonight is his fucking dick from his groin. Let's see how well he can pleasure Keira without it. I bet he has never used his fucking brain to seduce a woman in his life.

No, a man like King has relied solely on his masculinity. But it takes a lot fucking more than pure testosterone to seduce a woman. It takes skill, patience, and mind games.

You don't seduce a woman through her pussy. You seduce her through her brain. If you play the game well, you can get even the straightest of girls to lift their skirts.

I learned that early on.

King comes to an abrupt halt outside the living room, and I raise my knife, ready to stab him in the back, when my gaze slides past him to the wooden banister on the second floor. Keira sits atop it with a fucking noose tied around her neck and a sharp knife pressed to her creamy throat. Behind her, the killer leers at us from beneath the metallic devil's mask.

"What the hell?" King whispers under his breath, entering the room. I follow, staring up at Keira, who is visibly shaking.

"Nuh uh, not too close now, lover boy, or I'll be forced to shove her over the edge. Do you think her neck will snap straight away, or do you think she'll choke to death? The drop is too high and you're not tall enough to reach her."

"What the fuck," King growls, his anger rising. "Let her the fuck go!"

"Ooh, I like it when you get angry. I bet Keira likes it, too. I bet it makes her tingle between her legs."

I slide past King, holding my hands up in defeat. "Let her go. There's no need for this."

"Are you seriously trying to talk me down with a knife in your hand?"

Inhaling a steadying breath, I slowly bend down and place the knife on the wooden floor. I keep my eyes locked on the devil's mask the entire time, never once letting them slide away. "Happy now?" Straightening up, I make a show of kicking it to the side. "I don't have a knife now. Please let her go."

A sinister chuckle rings out behind the mask. "So how does this end? I let her go and we all walk our separate ways? The sun rises in the morning, and we pretend that none of this happened?"

"Pretty much," I reply at the same time King blurts. "This ends with me snapping your fucking neck."

Rolling my eyes, I gesture in his direction. "Don't mind him. He's a sociopath, and they're known for their violent outbursts and inability to control their anger, unlike the psychopath in front of you." I motion in Keira's direction. "We use the words interchangeably, but they're not quite the same thing. Despite what King here likes to think, a psychopath is more dangerous than a sociopath as they're more calculated, unlike a sociopath who acts on impulse."

King sucks on his teeth, scoffing, then turns to me. "A sociopath is also unable to maintain a social life, unlike a psychopath who can successfully lead a double life right underneath everyone's noses, which is why most serial killers fall under that category. If we're going to bother with labels, I think it's a safer bet to call us all fucking psychopaths, wouldn't you say?"

"See?" I wave at him again. "Hot-tempered."

"Will you both shut the fuck up!" the masked killer growls, digging the knife into Keira's neck.

A trickle of blood trails down her pale skin, causing King to pace beside me like a chained beast. He's two seconds away from storming up the stairs.

I have to say, his protective instinct is impressive.

Alarming, but impressive.

"The third act is fun, right?"

King stops pacing, glaring up at the killer.

"Because I'm so partial to games, we'll play another one. If you lift the cushions on the couch, you'll each find a knife." The distorted voice sneers, "Not the one you kicked away, Madison. Don't cheat."

When we don't move, the distorted voice shouts, "Move!"

As one, we walk forward to the red couch. King is the first one to wrench the cushion away and dig out an eight-inch knife. I gulp, staring at the sharp blade and King's tattooed fingers wrapped around the handle.

"You too, Madison."

"Fuck it," I mumble, lifting the couch cushion and removing the knife. It's larger than the one I took from the kitchen. Longer and sharper.

"I'd give you both a gold star, but my hands are occupied." There's humor in the demented killer's voice. "You killed my friend in cold blood. I think it's only fair that you kill yourselves in cold blood, too. I want you to stab yourself in the gut, all the fucking way, until the handle is the only thing protruding. Do that, and I'll consider not killing your precious Keira."

"You're fucking insane," King snarls, and for once, we're on the same wavelength. This is fucking madness. I already have two stab wounds, shallow ones, sure, but it fucking stings. This knife will cause considerable damage.

"So you don't want to play?" To Keira, the monster says, "Do you hear that? They don't care about you enough to play my games. Unless they're willing to stab themselves in the fucking gut for you, are they really worthy of your time? Of a serial killer's daughter?" Aiming soulless eyes at us, the distorted voice adds, "Pathetic."

I hold my breath, watching King step up on the couch and jump over the back, landing with a heavy thud. His walk is cocky, his smirk even more so. "You think I wouldn't die to protect Keira? Do you think I wouldn't kill any fucker who threatens her safety? Even me?"

"Sometimes I do worry about you, King. You need sectioning," I mutter.

Throwing me a poisonous glare over his shoulder, he faces forward again. His masculine cockiness radiates off him in waves, and I wonder if this is how humanity survived in the first place—through sheer stupidity.

My thoughts shatter and my eyes widen when he lifts the knife and stabs himself in the gut.

"What the hell?" I run forward, rounding the couch as he doubles over, clutching his waist. Blood pours from between his fingers. This is not a joke. He really did stab himself. Keira is sobbing in the background.

"You really are stupid, King," I grumble, and with my hand clutching his shoulder, I look up at Keira as I stab my own knife in his stomach. It sinks through his flesh like butter.

The feeling is fucking euphoric, unlike anything I could have imagined. I've killed before, but there's something about killing the one person Keira cares about.

Probably the only one.

The girl in question releases a startled scream as King groans in agonizing pain. I slide the knife back out, inspecting the bloodied blade before stabbing him again.

"Oh, fuck," I moan, my lips brushing up against his ear while he bends over me. "See how easy it was to topple the king?"

I wrench the knife back out and reach up to catch the spare devil's mask Ava throws in my direction. "You were both so fucking easy to fool. You thought Kara was in on this? Fuck no..." I release a taunting, chilling laugh. "She had to play her part, or she would die."

Ava grins maniacally behind Keira. "Do you have any idea how fucking scared Kara was when she entered the cellar? I was so impressed by her. She played the role of a killer so well... And when King and Madison hacked her to pieces. It was fucking classic."

"You're sick!" Keira spits, her forehead beaded with perspiration. "You both are."

Sliding the devil's mask over my face, I stare up at her with a wide smile that she can't see. "Maybe... It's no fun hunting innocents. True predators need to be challenged. Do you think Mary, who works at the convenience store, is a challenge? Fuck, no. But you..." I point my bloodied knife at her, slowly inching closer to the stairs. "The daughter of Jimmy Hill. Born with the blood of a true monster in your veins. A sinister legacy to go with the famous name. Now that is a challenge."

"So, you did all this because you were bored?"

Lifting the mask and tapping my bottom lip with the bloody knife, I taste the copper on my tongue and hum. "Maybe a little bit. But you have to admit that it was fun. Brought a little bit of life back into this dead town." My lips spread into a smile. "Remember when I fucked you like a whore? How much you loved it when I pretended to fuck you like King? You got off on that, didn't you? Yeah, you did, with your pale little ass in the air, moaning into my pillow like a slut." I cackle with laughter, sliding my mask back down.

Behind me, King is on his knees, bleeding all over the wooden floor. He looks like a beautiful ghost.

"I'm not fucking happy about that, babe," Ava snarls, dangerously close to cutting Keira's neck. She always was possessive, my girl.

Keira's eyes widen, and I wink at her.

"Only just figured it out, huh? Are you disappointed that I'm not really in love with you or," I make quotation marks, "'obsessed' with you, like your dying lover boy here?" I fake pout beneath the mask while Ava laughs cruelly. "You were all part of a game, but don't worry. Ava chewed me out real fucking good when she found out I fucked you." I point my knife at Ava. "That was unfair, by the way, babe, since it was your idea in the first place that I should fuck Keira to piss off King."

"What did you expect? You should have learned by now not to take everything literally. Of course, I'm gonna be angry when you fuck other girls."

"See what I have to put up with?" I ask King behind me, who's stumbling into the couch. "The mixed signals she sends me. I can't keep up. 'Fuck her.' 'Don't fuck her.' It's a nightmare, that's what it is." I aim my sugary smile at Ava. "I think we're even, babe, considering that I let you fucking stab me in the school bathroom."

Ava snorts, tearing off her mask. Her angry eyes drill holes into my head. "You think me stabbing you is worse than you fucking another girl?"

"Uh, yeah!"

"It was part of the plan!"

"So was me fucking Keira," I point out.

Ava removes the knife from Keira's throat and points it at me. "Maybe I was testing your loyalty."

"Well, then it's your own fucking fault, isn't it? Don't order me to bang other girls if you don't actually fucking want me to."

Releasing a shriek, she's about to respond when Keira elbows her in the nose, busting it and sending her flying backward.

"Shit," I dart forward toward the stairs, but King throws himself at me, and we go flying to the floor in a flurry of limbs. He's weak from the blood loss but still strong enough to overpower me. His slippery hands secure my wrists over my head. I buck beneath him, attempting to shove him off. His maddening, demented smile flashes a hint of his sharp incisors. "Got you!"

I spit at him, causing his chest to rumble with amused laughter as I continue to struggle, my feet kicking out on the floor.

A shadow falls over his shoulder. Keira peers down at me with her slim hand fisted in Ava's blonde hair and the knife pressed to the underside of her jaw.

I swallow down the lump in my throat at seeing Ava so scared. If I get out of this in one piece, I'll kill them both so fucking slowly that they beg for death.

"I guess we'll see who the bigger predator is, after all," King muses, lifting my wrists and smashing them back on the floor. Pain blooms, shooting up my arms.

Rising to his unsteady feet, he hauls me up and throws me down on my back on top of the coffee table. In a swift move, he grabs the knife that Keira hands him and stabs it through my hand, nailing me in place. I release a hoarse scream, and my fingers flare out as blinding, hot-white pain surges through me. I pant through the agony, breathing so harshly that I think I might faint. Ava is crying behind me—the hunter, reduced to prey.

"Now," King snarls, grabbing me in a brutal chokehold. "Who wants to play a little game?"

KING

I 'm fucking in awe of Keira, dressed in Madison's devil's mask, when she walks back down the stairs holding the spare devil's mask that Ava tore off upstairs. She holds it out for me, and I accept it with a slight tilt of my lips and pull it on.

Ava is tied up in the armchair, and her pathetic, weak screams mix with her uncontrollable crying to create a symphony of horror in this small, remote, two-story house in the middle of fucking nowhere—a serial killer's dream.

Keira walks up to Madison, deliberately leaving Ava for last, wanting her to watch Madison beg for her life before my girl carves her up like a pig.

Applying pressure with the blood-soaked towel pressed to my stomach, I sit on the couch, studying Keira closely. She moves with the lethality of a panther, the sinister nature of the most notorious serial killers in the country, and the deadly grace of a woman who knows her worth.

Keira is finally coming to fruition, accepting her own destructive nature. It's a sight to behold. "Look what I found when I rooted through the storage cupboard in the hallway." She swings a rusty axe, biting down on her bottom lip. "Someone likes to chop wood."

My cock stirs at the slightly crazed quality of her voice. Keira is in her element, and I'm fucking lucky to get to call her mine.

"I bet that hand hurts. It looks sore," she taunts, pretending to swing at Madison's arm, who lets out a scream that hovers between a sob and a shriek.

"Please, no, I'm sorry."

"It's a little too late, don't you think?" Keira aims for her arm once more, laughing under her breath. "Besides, I should thank you. I'm like a fucking kid in a candy store."

With the axe clutched in her hand, she turns around, grips the back of the couch, and leans over me. She rips our masks off and slams her lips to mine. Her kiss is maddeningly possessive, driving me to the brink of hell and back. I want to burn in her wild flames. Feel them melt away my flesh. "You wanna take some photographs, babe?" she whispers into my mouth before sinking her teeth into my lip and licking away the blood rushing to the surface. She's so fucking sexual when she's in her element, and I'm in for a hell of a ride later if I don't die of blood loss first.

She disappears, much to my disappointment, only to return with a Polaroid camera.

I chuckle with surprise. "Where did you find this old thing?"

"It's an old house with lots of old things," she replies, directing her focus back to her helpless, terrified prey. "Now, where were we?" Dragging a line with the axe's rusty blade between the swell of Madison's tits, all the way down to the apex of her thighs, she drawls, "You know, in this country—one of the very few with the death penalty in the western world—we like to say, 'An eye for an eye.' It sounds so fucking poetic when we dole out justice, but in reality, it's just an excuse for monsters like me to rectify our actions. A good one, I might add. Especially since I had to wake up to a fucking decapitated head on my pillow. That wasn't nice, Madison."

I snap a photograph while she points the axe at a terrified Ava. "Jasper was your friend. He was King's friend, too. While I am the devil's daughter, I do happen to like King a lot. And when you hurt the king, his queen retaliates. I'm sure you're familiar with the rules of chess. The queen is the most important player. I think I'm going off on a tangent. Where was I? Chess? Crazy killers? Blah, blah, blah. Let's just fucking chop the arm off." She swings, and I press the button on the camera just as the axe embeds itself in the coffee table.

"Oh, shit," Keira blurts, jumping back when Madison's arm severs, the hand still nailed to the worn wood. "Holy fuck," she exclaims with a crazed laugh, unbothered by the screaming in the room. "Did you see that, babe?" she asks me. "Oh, please, fuck, tell me you got that."

The photograph slides out of the camera, and I wave it in the air. "I've got you, babe."

Keira's eyes glitter with excitement. Slipping past me, she returns with a torn bed sheet and sets to work tying a tourniquet. "We don't want you to die just yet, Madison. The night is young. Well..." She peers at me over her shoulder. "My boyfriend is bleeding out so maybe we do need to hurry this up."

Groaning a laugh, my head lolls on the couch. "Wouldn't want to deny you of your kill."

"I forgive you," she says, dropping the bloodied axe on the couch and kneeling between my legs.

Raising the camera, I snap a picture of her beautifully haunted face.

"We're both insane, and maybe we belong in an asylum somewhere. I don't care about the pictures or the stalking. What matters is that you found me. You *chased* me. You helped me discover my full potential."

My throat bobs, and I stare down at her as she rests her cheek on my thigh and lets her eyes flutter closed, her dark lashes fanning her pale skin.

"Finish this," I whisper, brushing her blonde, blood-streaked hair off her brow. "And once I'm stitched up, I'll chase you through the woods until your lungs burn and your legs threaten to give out."

Propping her chin on my thigh, her sky-blue eyes slay me. "I need you to hurt me for being a bad girl. I shouldn't give in to my darkest desires like this."

"I'll hurt you," I promise as she leans in, snatching up my index finger with her teeth before sucking it clean of my blood.

Looking up at me and releasing it with a pop, she rises to her feet and grabs the axe before whispering in my ear, "I love you, King Knight."

My eyes flutter open, instantly landing on Keira by my hospital bedside. She has changed into clean clothing and sits wrapped in a gray blanket. The beep of machines fades out when her lips spread into a blinding smile that sets my soul alight. She's my downfall. My demon masquerading as a beautiful angel.

"You're awake."

My head rolls on the pillow, and I offer her a smile of my own. The stitched wounds on my stomach throb with a dull ache as I reach for her hand. She immediately grabs it, placing a kiss on the back.

"Miss me, baby?" I tease, stroking my thumb over her knuckles.

Keira doesn't miss a beat. "So much, King."

Smiling, I wince at the pain. I've lost a lot of blood and had a transfusion.

Her apple scent invades my nostrils as she leans in and whispers, "I have good news."

"Yeah?" I wet my lips, adjusting my head on the soft pillow. "Tell me, baby."

The scrape of her chair rings out in the small room as she scoots closer. Placing her forearm on the mattress, she strokes my unruly, black hair away from my brow and trails a line between my eyebrows and lips. "Riveiro survived."

I hum in agreement, enjoying her burning gaze and how it stirs my cock, despite the dull pain in my body.

"The cameras were all off. She's testifying that someone else attacked her while I was in the room with Wells." She lowers her voice, eyes sparkling with excitement. "Her story fits with ours. Everyone thinks Ava is responsible for the killings."

After Keira hacked Madison to pieces, she stabbed Ava with a knife to make it look like self-defense, not wishing to explain to the police why she took an axe to all her limbs. We needed a scapegoat, and Ava was it. Let's just say they'll never find Madison's remains, and Ava is dead, so she can't tell the truth about what happened.

"That's great," I reply, palming the back of her neck and pulling her down to my lips. I need to taste her. Need to reassure myself that it's all over.

She hums against my possessive, hungry lips before breaking away to kiss my jaw and neck. Her wet lips graze my ear as she whispers, "It's over."

"Can you please climb onto this hospital bed and ride my dick. I'm hard as a fucking rock, and it's torture to be this close to you and not be allowed to touch you."

Her sweet giggles fill the air but then she climbs on, shocking the daylight out of me.

"You're wearing a skirt."

"I had a feeling you'd need looking after." She settles beneath the thin blanket, lifts my hospital gown, and guides me to her sweet cunt. The heart monitor gives away my excitement as I grip her hips while she sinks down on my dick.

"You're not wearing any panties," I choke out, digging my fingers into her pale skin.

Her dirty, black Chucks stain the white sheet. She begins to move, riding me like she's longed for my cock as much as I've longed for her, careful not to hurt my dressing.

"I fucking love your dick!" Keira grips my chin, pressing her damp lips to mine. Then she bites me and rolls her hips. "Fucking love how good it hurts when I'm not ready."

"Fuck," I grunt, arching my neck as the heart monitor goes wild beside me. "You fuck so fucking dirty, baby."

It's true.

Keira fucks me like she owns me.

And she does.

"This fucking pussy," I grind out, bruising her hips with my tattooed fingers.

"Smile, baby."

The Polaroid camera is in my face. It clicks, then whirs. Tossing it down beside me, she grabs my hand and wraps my fingers around her pale, slender neck. "Choke me."

I slap her soft ass with my free hand, the sound muffled beneath the thin blanket. "When I'm let out of here, I'm gonna fuck your ass so good you won't be able to sit for a week."

Her teeth sink into her bottom lip until a bead of blood rushes to the surface. She makes no move to remove it, and my balls draw up tight when it slides down the curve of her pale chin.

"Come inside me, King. I want to your cum to trickle down my legs when I stand up."

"Your dirty fucking mouth is going to get you into trouble," I reply with a grunt, my breaths growing choppy. Keira is doing it on purpose. It's there, in that damn sparkle in her eyes when she smiles and rides me harder.

Throwing my head back, I grit my teeth, fighting her as much as I can, but it's a lost battle. Her slim hips move beneath my hands with expertise. Harder and faster. Rolling and grinding. I come, spilling my cum deep inside her tight cunt as it strangles my dick. She looks so fucking pleased when I finally manage to stop shuddering. I'm sure she stole my fucking soul just now.

Climbing off me, she lowers her skirt, and I watch a trickle of cum seep down her thigh. There's something so primal about knowing I've marked her as mine.

That's my cum smeared on her thighs. Not any other fucker's. I want to finger it back inside her. "If I weren't attached to all these wires, I would lick you clean."

Sitting down and crossing her legs, she peers over her shoulder at the closed door before twisting around and pushing her ass up in the air, one knee propped on the chair.

Like a fucking tease, she lifts her skirt and bares her round ass to me. Spreading her cheeks apart, she drags a finger through our mixed juices, drawing a line from her pussy to her puckered hole. I push up on my elbows when she inserts it knuckle deep.

"Fuck, baby," I whisper while she fingers her ass, her pussy glistening with need. More of my cum trickles out, and she removes her digit to swipe it up before working two fingers inside her sweet ass.

Leaning on one elbow, I bite my knuckles as she continues to torture me. "You're fucking evil."

"You wanna fuck me here, baby? Want to fill my ass with your dick?"

"I want to eat your ass," I admit.

Rocking back against her fingers, she moans deep in her throat, the way she does when I fuck her.

Just when I'm about to beg her to climb onto the bed and stick her ass in my face, she slides her fingers back out and sits down with a dangerous smile on her lips.

My chuckle is laced with shock, disbelief, and so much humor. "You little tease."

Her shoulders lift and fall unapologetically. "Consider it an incentive to get better."

"Oh, trust me. I'll be out of here before you know it."

"I see you're awake," a voice says from the doorway, causing Keira's eyes to widen. She slaps a hand to her mouth to stifle a giggle when a middle-aged nurse with a beaming smile and a clipboard walks in.

Winking at Keira, I smile back at the nurse. Keira snatches the Polaroid camera and the printed picture from the bed.

"When can I get out of here?"

"Oh, not so fast, young man. You're lucky to be alive. After the ordeal that you've been through, we need to ensure you're healing well before we can release you back into the wild."

Keira flips me off playfully, and I narrow my eyes at her. The little shit is stirring trouble for me already.

While the middle-aged nurse takes my blood pressure, I imagine a million ways to fuck my girl, all of them ending with her coming around my dick, on my mouth, and on my fingers.

Spreading her legs slightly, not far enough to raise suspicion but far enough to entrap my gaze, Keira bites her lip seductively. This girl will be the death of me.

Then she lifts the camera and snaps another picture, making up for all the years I stalked her.

KEIRA

As I exit King's hospital room, I pause. Cassie is here, seated across the hall with her amber hair tucked behind her ears. She looks strangely vulnerable, staring off into the distance, wrapped up in her long winter coat. Meanwhile, I'm freezing my tits off in a leather skirt, a black, wool turtleneck, and Chucks.

I don't usually wear skirts so when Cassie finally turns her head, her eyes immediately land on my bare legs. She looks back up at me, then stands. I still haven't moved, unsure what to say. We've drifted apart recently. It's partly my fault, too. I could have reached out to her, but I didn't.

"Are you not cold?" she asks carefully, making me smile as she nears.

Chewing my lip, I shrug. "I wanted to give King an incentive to get better so we can get the hell out of here."

That makes her laugh softly, a tendril of her amber hair sliding forward from behind her ear. "Did it work?"

"Yes, I'd say so."

Cassie nods, smiling. Then, with a jerk of her head to the coffee vending machine behind us, she asks, "Can I get you a hot drink or anything?"

"Sure."

We walk over to it in silence while the soft hum of conversation from passing nurses and doctors surrounds us. The tension between us is strained but comfortable at the same time. I realize that while Cassie and I can fall out, we'll always fall back together eventually.

She pays for the drinks, and we exchange glances while the machine whirrs. Cassie ordered a hot chocolate, and the rich cocoa scent mingles with that of antiseptic. She hands me my latte before walking over to the seats.

Following her, I take a small sip but wince when it scalds my tongue.

Chuckling, Cassie blows on her chocolate. "It'll be a while before you can drink it."

"You don't say." I sit down beside her.

Seconds tick by while we let our drinks warm our hands.

Cassie clears her throat and turns her body halfway to face me. With her eyes downcast, she says softly, "I've been a terrible friend."

I look at the freckles on her nose that are visible even in winter, the amber hair falling into her eyes, and the way she worries her chapped lip.

"I can't believe Ava killed all those people."

"Me, neither."

"You must have been so scared when you were kidnapped."

Wetting my lips, I lie, "Yes, I was."

Cassie looks up at me from beneath her long, wispy lashes before training her eyes back on the steaming drink clutched in her hands. "I'm glad you're here, Keira. That she didn't..."

Kill me.

The unspoken words hang in the air, heavy and intrusive.

Deciding to offer an olive branch, I reach out and grab her hand. We're both broken and terrible friends, but we have each other in this messed up, ugly world.

"I'm sorry I didn't believe you."

What she doesn't admit out loud is that she believed I killed Liam. Her instincts are more attuned than she'll ever know.

I squeeze her hand, silently telling her it's okay.

We sit in silence, taking hesitant sips of our still too-hot drinks. It's comfortable to hold her hand like this, watching nurses and doctors go about their day. Knowing King is in the room across from me.

"I'm in love with King," I admit. I've never said it before. Never admitted it out loud. It feels good to tell my friend.

"I know," is Cassie's simple response. Squeezing my hand, she takes a sip of her chocolate, then shrugs. "You've been in love with him for some time."

"Emotions scare me."

"They scare us all," she whispers, sounding haunted. Then she shrugs again, offering me a small smile. "Are you heading home now?"

"I don't have a home anymore."

A crease forms between her brows. "What?"

"Mom threw me out."

"She did what?" Her eyes bug out as she lowers the cup from her lips.

I fucked her husband. "Family drama," I reply instead with a shrug, removing the lid and swirling my coffee. I take a sip, grateful that it's not scalding hot anymore.

"Your life belongs in a soap opera," she blurts, a disbelieving laugh slipping from her lips, and I join in.

Our shoulders shake, tears streaming from our eyes.

I swipe at my cheeks with my sleeve. "It's true, though. What a fucked-up mess."

Humming in agreement, she drinks the last of her hot chocolate. "Your father is a notorious serial killer, your quarterback boyfriend vanishes, you're cheating on him behind his back with one of the richest, most sinister boys at school, your mother throws you out, and you get kidnapped by a crazy, murderous schoolgirl. You can't make this shit up."

My stomach is in stitches as I laugh, covering my mouth with the back of my hand. "You make my life sound so bad."

"Not bad, just wild." Nudging her shoulder with mine, she wraps me up in a hug. "I'm sorry I've been such a shit friend."

"I've been one, too. We're both shit friends."

My words make us both laugh.

"The shittiest friends," she replies, sniffling.

I hug her tighter, fucking grateful that she's here. "It's over now. The killer is dead."

"Thank fuck, I don't think I could handle any more deaths."

Breathing her in, I let her sweet smell soothe the ache in my heart.

"I fucked Liam," she whispers quietly. So quietly I almost don't hear it. "It's why I resented you so much. You didn't want him, but he pined after you like you were the ultimate prize. I was a pawn to boost his ego in the midst of your fucked-up relationship."

Staring at the vending machine and the choices of drinks, I don't blink. I don't do anything as her words sink to my core, settling like a missing drop in a calm ocean. When I finally reply, she's clutching me so hard that I can hardly breathe. "I get it now. Why you retreated."

"I told you, I'm a shit friend. I've done some shit things."

"We're both shit friends."

Her heartbeat thuds against my chest, beating in time with mine. "I don't want any more lies between us."

"Me neither," I lie, flicking my gaze to King's hospital room. There are truths I can never tell her.

Truths that only belong to King and me.

Truths that bind us.

"If you ever fuck King, I'll carve your heart out from your chest. You know that, right?" It's the most honest statement I've ever made.

Laughing softly, she leans in and palms the back of my neck

with both hands, her brow pressed to mine. "You don't ever have to worry about that. King is obsessed with you. If any girl tried it on with him, he'd chop off their hands. That man sees no one but you. It's alarming, but also hot—if you're into that kind of possessive, alpha, stalker vibe."

"He's the Bonnie to my Clyde," I admit, inhaling her breaths. "Some boys are just so toxic, so *consuming*, that you can't stop yourself from burning in their flames."

"You can sleep at my house," she whispers, sliding her hands from behind my neck to squeeze my upper arms. "Let's stay up late, watch crap movies, and eat too much popcorn."

"I fucking love that idea," I reply with a smile. "And let's make a promise."

"Anything..."

"Let's not allow boys to come between us again."

Unless you make a move on King.

"Never." She holds up her pinky between us and waits for me to interlink mine with hers. Her emerald orbs twinkle with something fierce as she looks me in the eye. "And let's not allow girlfriends to come between us either. We're best friends until the end."

"Deal."

We share a smile, studying each other while whispered secrets float like feathers in the wind. Secrets that will forever remain buried.

ENDINGS AND NEW BEGINNINGS

With his hand hanging over the steering wheel, King peers through the windshield at the gloomy, red-brick building in front of us.

The Death House, as it's called.

"I wish you would let me come in with you," he murmurs before directing his brown eyes at me. "Let me be there for you."

"I need to do this on my own," I whisper through the lump in my throat. The day is here. My father is due to be executed in less than an hour. I'm not sure how I feel. Hurt, if the ache in my chest is anything to go by. I'm mostly numb, though, as if my mind has shut down to protect me.

Looking up through my lashes at the snowflakes melting on the windshield, I whisper, "Do you think that will be me one day? Strapped to a gurney?"

The leather seat creaks beneath his weight as he shifts his body to face me, his hand still hanging over the steering wheel. "You think I'd let anyone entrap you and cut your wings? Strap you to a gurney and pump your veins full of poison?" Sliding his hand from the wheel, he cups my chin and strokes his thumb over the swell of my bottom lip. "Never in a million fucking years."

"They hunt monsters like me."

"I won't let anyone hurt you."

Breathing a soft, grateful sigh through my nose, I look back at the Death House. My father is in there. I wonder what he's thinking, what he's feeling. Is he scared or simply resigned to his fate?

Tears prick the backs of my eyes as I admit a truth of mine. "I'll feel so lonely after this." Looking back at King and the tic in his jaw, I continue, "I haven't had a relationship with my dad for years, but at least I knew he was alive. After this... I'll battle with my darkness alone."

"You're not alone. Never alone."

Blinking rapidly, I wipe beneath my eyes. "I know that. I do. But my father... Whatever I am, whatever illness runs through my veins runs through his, too. We're the same flesh and blood. After today, I'll never be able to think to myself again, 'At least my dad understands.' He won't be here. I don't want to turn into him." My voice breaks, and I choke back a sob. "But I already *am* him."

"Babe, no. You're you—a beautiful, dangerous masterpiece. Don't ever tell yourself that you're not perfect. We all struggle with our own darkness. Sure, yours is a destructive force, but you're still fucking perfect. You're strong. Not weak. Instead of thinking of yourself like a soulless monster and a product of your father's twisted legacy, remember that your dad fathered an apex predator."

When I give him an incredulous look, he hurries to add, "Okay, that came out wrong. What I mean is that you're stronger, more dangerous than anyone else in this town. It's the survival of the fittest. Forget about humanity's invented moral constructs for a second, and let's look to science. You're at the top of the food chain. Every once in a while, an animal is born with something different. Something that will carry that species forward. Maybe psychopaths or sociopaths, or whatever title you want to plaster on people like us, are evolving humanity. Maybe in the grander scheme of things, in the eyes of evolution, emotions and empathy are weaknesses. Maybe we're evolving to become less emotional."

"I thought it was the other way around."

"Does it matter?" he whispers, capturing my chin with his hand and bringing my eyes to his. "Does it matter, Keira? Are other people's opinions of you so important that you're willing to suppress yourself and your happiness to please others?"

"I don't want to end up like my father."

"And you won't. Do you know why?" Leaning in, he captures my lip between his teeth before releasing it and whispering, "Because you're not him. You're something so much more powerful. You bring me to my fucking knees every day."

I slide my fingers into the dark hair at the nape of his neck and crush my lips to his, sucking his tongue into my mouth. His blood rushes to the surface as I bite down and moan. I want to straddle his lap and lose myself in him. I want him to make the horror in front of us disappear.

Instead, I break the kiss and reach for the door handle. "Wait for me, King."

His hand is back on the steering wheel while his other hand readjusts his hardening dick inside his jeans. "Are you sure you don't want me to come in?"

I want nothing more, but I need to face my own demons and do this alone. With a shake of my head, I open the door and step out into the chilly evening air. My boots sink into the snow as I push the door shut and look up at the imposing building. I'm sure the misery can be felt in the air. There's something sinister lurking in the shadows, masquerading as justice.

While I'm driven by urges that can't be leashed, urges that drive me to do unspeakable things, these righteous people commit murder in the name of the law. How they sleep at night is a mystery to me. I suppose it's easy to reduce a human to a monster when you judge them by their sinful actions alone. Once you strip them of their humanity, it's easy to justify your own heinous actions by telling yourself that you're doling out justice.

But justice to whom? The victim's families? What about *his* family? What about the people who love and care for him? Are they not humans? Or are we reduced to monstrous animals, too?

I'm the one who'll have to spend the rest of my life punished by my father's actions. Besides, who will dole out *my* justice?

Oh, right. That would be me.

The vengeful daughter.

The orphaned killer.

These are the toxic thoughts swirling in my head as I pull my new blue-and-white plaid teddy jacket tighter around me and walk through the crunchy snow toward the entrance with my head ducked to hide my face from the paparazzi. They're frothing at the mouth to get the money shot. It's not every day the country executes one of its most hated serial killers.

I can feel how tense King is even from here as the cameras flash and reporters shout questions at me from behind the barrier. I hurry past, my eyes burning with tears. This all feels so fucking wrong. My father is about to die, and these people care about their payout. They don't care that I'm about to witness my father die or about all of my regrets for not reaching out sooner. For letting my own sense of pride and hurt keep me from seeing the man behind the heinous crimes.

I have never felt more conflicted in my life. I couldn't have reached out sooner—I was too hurt, too traumatized from witnessing the FBI kick down my door and haul my father out of there—but I also know I'll always regret pushing him away. I'll carry that regret deep in my heart until the day I inhale my last breath. Especially now that I can sympathize with him in the most twisted, sickening way. Now that his struggles are my struggles. Now that I need his wisdom the most to stop me from following in his footsteps.

The fight between good and evil.

The angel and devil on my shoulder.

I'm ushered inside and led down a narrow, white-painted hallway toward a room next to the one housing the victims' families. The soft hum of their muted conversations drifts through the paper-thin wall as the door clicks shut behind me.

There's only me here.

I'm the only person who showed up for my father tonight.

I pause mid-step and slide my gaze over the countless metal chairs that should be filled with family members. Chairs that echo loudly.

My bottom lip trembles, and I quickly wipe at my cheeks with my sleeve, inhaling a steadying, much-needed breath before walking up to the center chair at the front. I sit down and lift my gaze. The ugly, green curtains behind the large window are drawn. My reflection reveals the haunted eyes of a scared little girl behind the brave mask.

That's what I am.

Fucking scared.

Suddenly, I'm that seven-year-old girl again who watched her father get dragged out of the house by force as the room swarmed with barking dogs and tall men dressed in black. My thoughts swirl back to the shouting. Deep, scary voices yelling at my dad while I stood cowering by the sofa with my hands pressed over my ears. I peed myself then, dressed in my little pink nightgown. My mom stumbled out of the kitchen, pale as a ghost.

No one noticed me standing in a puddle of my own piss that was slowly turning cold.

And then my father was gone.

And it was so fucking silent.

My breath trembles. I shake myself out of the memory, digging my nails into my palms.

"I can do this," I whisper. "I can do this."

The curtains slide open, and I inhale a sharp, ragged gasp when I see my father staring straight at me. Strapped to the gurney, the veins in his arms bulging, he looks so helpless. Nothing like the indestructible man I remember from my childhood. Nothing like my hero and the country's most infamous monster.

My tears fall. I can't hold them back. Neither can I hold back the sob that follows. I bite down hard on my violently trembling lip and slowly rise to my feet, but I'm too weak.

Too shaky.

I slump back down and allow myself to break. If only for a second. I truly hope the hurting families on the other side of the wall get some sense of closure from this moment.

For me, it's a void opening up. An endless nightmare from which I will never awaken. All I've ever known is loss. Maybe my illness isn't a result of the man in front of me. Maybe the world created what I am. And now it wants to plaster a title on me to categorize me, when the truth is that I was taught from childhood that it's too dangerous to love. Too dangerous to feel.

Everyone hurts you.

Disappoints you.

Your own fucking parents.

Your own hero.

Society.

My father never once looks away from me as though I'm his only anchor in this moment. I wish desperately that King was here. I was wrong to ask him to stay outside. I need his hand in mine. I need his steady presence. I need someone to run to that little girl and scoop her up. Tell her everything will be okay, even if it's a lie.

"Do you have any final words?" The warden's voice cuts through my emotional upheaval. I want to choke some fucking sense into him.

That's my broken, monstrous father you're stealing from me.

But I keep my lips shut. Somewhere deep inside me, no matter how much I'm hurting or how resentful I feel about our broken society that lets people like me down, I know my father caused so much hurt and destruction. I know the families on the other side of that wall will never kiss their loved ones again. I know they were never offered the chance to say goodbye.

I know we live in an imperfect world where all sides have two stories. They will always know him by his heinous crimes. Never the sides of him that I saw.

"Let me start by saying sorry to the families. I know nothing I say tonight will ever remove their pain, and I don't expect forgiveness. Nor do I ask for it. My actions caused unimaginable suffering, but they also ruined my own family. And for that, I'm endlessly sorry."

His words are meant for me. His eyes drill into mine, glassy with tears as if he wants to imprint his final words on this planet into my heart.

"To my sweet, beautiful daughter, who I lost because of my actions, I am sorry. I'm sorry you've had to live with my tainted surname. I know it hasn't been easy on you, but I need you to know..." He strains his neck as far as his strapped limbs will allow him. "I *need* you to know that you're not me. Whatever the world may throw at you, whatever darkness you encounter, you're not me. Do you hear me, sweetheart? Don't let the burden of my legacy break you down. I don't want you to feel guilty about *anything.* You can always talk to me. Even when I'm no longer here. You hear me? Because I get it. I *get* it!" His intense eyes send shivers down my back. He's talking about my darkness, the monster that's growing stronger inside me. The urges threatening to rule me. "I get it, okay? But you're strong. You're my little girl, and I will always love you. Always root for you. But today, I have to pay for my actions. You must promise me you will be strong. Promise me."

I nod softly through my cascading tears, and he sighs contentedly as if he's reassured.

"Good. And remember that I love you. I will *always* love you."

With that, he nods to the warden, and I clamp a hand over my mouth, shaking my head almost violently. "No, Dad..."

Seconds tick by as he stares up at the ceiling while I fight desperately not to break down. King was wrong all along. I'm not the biggest apex predator. The criminal justice system is.

My father inhales a ragged breath. I jump off my seat, watching him roll his head, his eyes finding mine.

And then he simply stops.

His eyes flutter shut, and that's it.

The poison is slowly killing him, immobilizing every muscle in his body, fooling us into believing he has simply fallen asleep.

I stand with my hands pressed to the glass as the minutes tick by, praying for a miracle that won't come.

The warden eventually walks back in, pressing his fingers to his wrist before announcing his death. The curtains slide closed, and I wait.

I wait for some sense of justice to be felt.

Can they feel it on the other end? Is their anger, hurt, and thirst for revenge quenched? Is this it? Are they happy a supposed chapter has been closed by another death?

I'm fatherless.

And motherless.

An orphan.

Rubbing my fingers on the window as my breath steams up the surface, I close my eyes and press my temple to the glass. I don't want to go back out, broken and ruined, only to be photographed by cold, soulless reporters and paparazzi.

The last couple of months have been an endless nightmare, with so many people dead. And now it's all over.

I dreaded this day for so long. I feared losing my only connection to the happy memories of my past. The only light of my childhood, no matter how tainted it was. Now I have to maneuver this maze alone. To come to terms with the decisions I made along the way. Now I need to learn to wrangle the monster inside me, or it'll be me strapped to that gurney one day. I have to adapt, blend in, outsmart. Stay one step ahead.

The door creaks open to reveal King in all his handsome glory. He watches me carefully as if he's unsure if his presence is welcome or not. "They let me come see you."

"He's dead," I whisper, steaming up the glass with my shaky breath. "He's really dead."

Striding up to me, King lifts me by my hips and guides my thighs around his trim waist. He holds me to him like he's worried I might break. He's so strong and solid and everything I need at this moment. He's my hero now. The only person who knows what I need, who's attuned to me.

"You should have let me be here," he whispers into my hair as he rocks us. "I hated being so far away when I knew you were hurting."

"He looked at me the entire time."

"Shh, don't cry. I'm here. I'll always be here for you."

"When we graduate," I whisper, breathing in his smell at the crook of his neck, "I want to move somewhere. Change my name."

"Start over," he finishes for me. "How do you feel about being a Knight?"

My lips spread into a smile, despite my sniffles. "Too soon, King. Too soon."

KING

TEN MONTHS LATER

The air is scented with popcorn, hotdogs, and cotton candy. Shrieks to my left from one of the rides cut through the tinny music.

Concealed behind the shadows of a nearby tent at the town's local carnival, I watch Keira laugh with Cassie near the concession stands. My girl is mouthwateringly beautiful in a red-and-black-gingham, zip-up, flannel jacket, boyfriend jeans, and red Vans. I love that her style is so effortless. Keira doesn't go out of her way to be attractive; she just is.

Bringing the Polaroid camera up to my face, I take a picture. It whirs as I lower it and follow Keira with my eyes, watching her bite into a hotdog while Cassie laughs around a mouthful of fries.

The element of surprise is something I keep alive with Keira. She loves the chase, but the chase can easily become predictable.

She thinks I'm away with my family for an important dinner tonight—a dinner she whined that I didn't invite her to.

What she doesn't know is that I planned it, so I could catch her unaware. My little devil.

She's not at all who she portrays to the world. I find it fascinating to watch her blend in, like the color green in an army print. But she's not green. Instead, she's every shade that makes it up. Hiding in plain sight.

She's become more comfortable with herself in the last few

months and is finally able to let go of some of her guilt over her legacy and the conflicting emotions inside of her. Of her own urges that are growing stronger. That's why I'm here tonight. To offer her a safe outlet for her darkness.

Stalking her has become one of my favorite pastimes. If I thought the urge to watch her from afar would dwindle now that she's mine, I was mistaken.

I like the anticipation and the hunt.

I like knowing I'll soon be hurting her in the best way possible, just waiting for her to sing the safe word.

To this day, she never has.

No matter how deep we dive into her complex, twisted, and downright dirty desires, she never puts a stop to it.

I slink out from the shadows when they walk closer to the edge of the carnival, near the tree line. I was hoping she would walk this way. My opportunity to strike finally comes when Cassie turns away to discard their garbage. Finding no trash can, she excuses herself.

Keira doesn't follow. Instead, she fishes her phone out of her jacket pocket. Soon after, my phone vibrates in my jeans. She's so fucking pretty when she's unsuspecting. I thought that maybe she would figure it out, but she never did.

Sneaking up behind her, I clamp a hand over her mouth and drag her away from potential witnesses, deeper into the shadows. Her survival instinct kicks in straight away, and she begins to fight me. I'm sure she knows it's me and can smell my cologne, but it's instinct to fight and lash out when ambushed.

Concealed by the trees, I haul her deeper into the cold night, until the sounds of the carnival are far away.

Until I'm sure she can scream, and no one will hear her.

Tossing her to the cold, hard ground, I plant my feet and adjust my skeleton mask. She rolls over, and her hair sticks to the tears on her cheeks as she stares up at me through those wide, blue eyes that cause my dick to jump in its denim confines.

Sliding my hand out from my pocket, I flip the blade up with a twist of my wrist and drag my tongue over my bottom lip beneath the mask. "What's the safe word?"

I ask her this every time. No matter what, I need her to know the power is in her hands.

"Reaper," she breathes out, keeping her eyes locked on the sharp blade in my hand beneath the silvery moonlight.

Tossing the camera to the ground, I pull out the second item from my pocket. "See this, baby? It's a dog leash. Now run like a little pet. If I catch you, I'll leash and strangle you with it while fucking your ass."

In the next second, she's up on her feet and running blindly into the woods. She didn't even have to think about it.

She knows I'll hurt her and make her bleed.

My breaths are visible in the cool autumn air as I set off jogging. I can hear her up ahead, zigzagging in her panic.

Imagining her thrumming heartbeat, I inhale the stirrings of her unbridled panic deep into my lungs.

"I can taste your fear, baby," I call out, stopping to listen. As a twig snaps to my left, I set off in that direction. She's close; I can sense it.

"You like it when the big bad wolf chases you, don't you, my little slut? One of these days I'll make you dress up like a little bunny rabbit, with the white ears and everything. Just imagine how fucking delicious you'll look when I make you bleed." Chuckling to myself, I pause to adjust my aching cock. Fucking hell, she turns me into a monster every time we play this game.

Movement behind me has me spinning around as she darts past. I sprint after her, ducking beneath branches and jumping over logs. "You'll grow tired soon, baby. You can't outrun me. You know that."

"I'm at least gonna try," she shouts somewhere in front of me before jumping out from behind a large rock and running through a thick cluster of trees. I decide to wait her out, knowing she'll want to hide somewhere to catch her breath.

Breathing in the pine and soft earth, I take slow steps forward, careful not to crush sticks beneath my feet or do anything to give away my location. Cassie will be looking for her now. It's only a matter of time before she calls my girl. When she does, I'll know exactly where Keira is hiding.

She never learns. Silence your phone, crouch down low, and don't make a single noise.

I almost laugh out loud when her phone starts to ring. Keira curses loudly, hidden behind a tall fir tree. Silencing her phone, she jumps up and runs out, straight into my hard chest.

I clamp my hands down on her bony shoulders before twisting her and shoving her down on the ground. In a swift move, I fall to my knees, grab hold of the hem of her jeans and yank them down her thighs, baring her pale, round ass.

Keira screams, rolling onto her back and bringing her knees up to her chest before kicking me hard in the chest.

Falling back on my ass, I laugh loudly. "So fucking feisty, baby." I throw myself on top of her, pressing the switchblade to her creamy throat. She immediately grows still, and her struggles cease. She knows I'll cut her if she makes a single move.

Knows this is predator versus predator.

The only way out is to submit.

"There's a good girl," I taunt, reaching down between our bodies to cup her cunt. "Now be quiet for me."

Baring her teeth, she seethes while I strip her of her jeans before snapping her panties straight off. "Fuck you."

I'm laughing loudly, fucking loving her attitude.

Knife pressed to her throat, I one-handedly slide the leash around her neck, admiring how the brown contrasts beautifully with her translucent, pale skin and blue veins.

I jump to my feet, Doc Martens planted on each side of her

knees. She stares up at me as I make a show of rolling the dog leash around my hand. "Should I call you my dog now?"

Grinding her teeth, she says nothing, but I don't miss how she clenches her bare thighs. She hates me a little bit. Or maybe she hates being submissive as much as she loves it.

"What do you prefer, baby? To be called a dog or a dirty little whore?" Unbuckling my belt with the hand holding the knife, I slide it through the hoops. "Pick one."

Defiant to the end, she clamps her mouth shut. If not for the leash around her neck, she would try to run.

"Is that how it's going to be?" With a careless shrug, I wet my lips. "Fine by me." I strike her with the belt, right across her pretty thighs.

When she screams, my balls ache.

Fuck, how they ache.

Stepping to the side, I strike her again.

Keira has always been partial to whipping. Imagine my pleasant surprise when I found out.

Crouching down in front of her while she sobs, I make my intention clear as I drag the flat end of the knife over her cheeks. "Look at your pretty face. So fucking beautiful. I think I'm gonna fuck it up tonight. What do you say, baby?"

Her fiery, sky-blue eyes land on mine, and then she spits at me before lashing out with clenched fists and open palms.

"You little fucking..." I grunt, overpowering her with my hands, not wanting to cut her just yet. I need her to feel my brute strength. To know that she stands no fucking chance against me. I slap her once, stunning her. "That's enough."

A soft moan slips from her sweet mouth, and I smirk as I rise to my feet. "See this, baby?" I hold the belt up, dangling the end over her face. "It's gonna hurt."

"No, no, no," she pleads, squirming on the ground, her blonde hair tangled with pine and dirt. "Please, no."

Sweet melody.

"Say the safe word, baby. Say it, and I'll stop."

"Please don't hurt me." Crocodile tears of the manipulative kind cascade down her cheeks. I'm hard as a fucking rock, deciphering the truth behind those pleas for me to stop.

Please, don't.

Please, hurt me.

I strike her face with the belt. Nowhere near as hard as her thighs, but hard enough for a red welt to blossom.

Rolling over on her side, she sobs.

"What's worse? That sweet ache between your legs or the sting on your cheek?"

Jumping to her feet, forgetting about the leash around her neck, she runs. It pulls taut, and I haul her back into me. She's a feral, wild animal, scratching and clawing at anything she can reach. The leash. Me.

I let her tire herself out as I hold onto the leash, pulling it taut enough to cut off her airflow. When she finally calms, I lean down to her ear and whisper, "Drop to your knees, baby. I want to see that ass in the air."

Breathing harshly, sweat coating her forehead and neck, she tries one last time to free herself from the belt.

My thumb slides along the blade, tempted to use it on her. But I don't. Not yet, anyway.

"Do it." My voice is final, brokering no argument.

Her knees slowly hit the ground in defeat, and I round her.

"Dirty little girls like you deserve to be punished." I cup her chin. "Is that what you want? To be humiliated?"

"Yes," she admits quietly as her bottom lip quivers enticingly. I love the scent of her arousal and fear as it mixes with the earthy smell of the forest. It's a heady concoction of seduction.

"Lick my shoes."

Her eyes widen fractionally, but I grip her chin hard and dig my fingers into her smooth skin.

"Lick my fucking shoes!"

This is what she needs, what she craves. I see the truth in her eyes when they mist over with that darkness inside her that can so easily be turned on someone else.

"Did I fucking stutter?"

"No, you didn't."

My fingers release her chin to slide into her blonde, dirty hair. I pull the strands, cock throbbing when she winces. I love her pain. How it sparks in her eyes.

Releasing her, I flip the blade back up threateningly.

Keira lowers herself down on all fours and peers up at me as she darts her little pink tongue out.

"Ass up in the air. Finger your cunt while you lick my shoes."

Balancing on one hand, she slides her other one between her legs and licks a hot path up my shoe. The silence is soon broken by the sounds of her wet cunt while I patiently watch her drag her tongue over my shoes so fucking obediently.

"Such a good girl," I praise, tugging on the dog lead to gain her attention. "Such a good little slut."

Unzipping my jeans, I push down the front and let my dick bob free. "You did such a good job licking my shoes clean that I think you're deserving of this now. Don't you?"

Opening her mouth, she eagerly leans in, but I press the knife to her cheek. "Not yet. Not until you tell me what I want to hear."

A red line forms where the knife digs in. Her seductive eyes gaze up at me, pleading for more depraved acts.

More.

More.

Keira is never satisfied.

"Please, King, can I suck your cock."

"No, you can't."

Confusion flickers in her eyes.

"But you can fight me while I tear through your cunt." In a quick move, I shove her down onto her stomach, forcing her screaming face into the dirt, and nail her to the damp ground with my cock.

Oh, the fucking fight she puts up, spluttering while she wriggles and screams under me as snot and saliva strings form between her nose, lips, and the ground.

My balls slap against her clit, and my fingers wring her hair in such a tight grip that I'm sure I'm tearing it from the roots while she pleads with me to stop.

I fucking love the word *no* on her lips.

Her racking sobs and clenching pussy.

"You're strangling my dick, baby," I growl with a grunt. "You can pretend all you want that you don't like this."

Keira arches her round ass against me and claws at the ground, the dirt clogging beneath her nails. "Please, stop, King. Please, please, please."

Sliding out from her cunt, I palm her neck, forcing her face further into the dirt as I work my dick inside her ass. "Own the pain, baby. No one can hurt you as good as I can."

Her screaming intensifies, interspersed with heaving sobs.

"You love it, don't you? My cock in your tight ass."

"Stop..."

"Use the safe word." I start to move, releasing the back of her neck before sliding my hand beneath her and pressing the knife to her throat, ensuring she stays still while I pound her ass. "If you want me to stop, just say the magic word." My damp lips press up against her ear as I smile tauntingly.

A moan bubbles up from her throat. A beautiful, haunted sound that drives me fucking wild.

"I love taking you like this," I whisper, pressing the knife to her throat and bruising her hip with my fingers as I fuck her into the damp moss. "Like a dirty little slut. *My* slut."

"King," she sobs, her face smeared with mascara, dirt, snot, and tears.

"Yes, baby?" I ask, tearing off my skeleton mask and tossing it beside us on the ground, even though I already know what she wants.

"I need more."

Biting her earlobe hard enough to draw blood, I lift my chest off her back and settle on my knees with my dick still buried deep in her ass.

Shoving her jacket and jumper up to her shoulders, I run my fingers down each vertebra while fucking her nice and slow. I press the blade to the top of her spine, smack her ass hard, and slowly drag the blade down, all the way to the dip of her ass.

Keira hisses through her teeth at the sharp sting, but it soon morphs into a dark sound of pleasure when I slip out from her ass and drag my tongue up the length of her spine, lapping up the coppery blood.

"So fucking good," I murmur, sliding my tongue all the way back down until I'm *there,* at the dip of her ass. With my hands on each creamy cheek, I spread her apart and lean in to circle her puckered hole with my tongue.

Relinquishing any pretense of a fight, Keira moans. She loves it when I eat her ass—the depravity of the act.

Especially when we're out in public.

Chest rumbling with a masculine moan, I dig my fingers into her ass cheek. Call me selfish, but I get a kick out of reducing a dangerous creature like Keira, a deadly killer, to a greedy whore for my tongue, cock, and fingers. Anything I'm willing to give her.

I crawl back up her body, flip her onto her back, and bend her in half with my hands on the backs of her knees. "Look at your puffy, wet cunt."

Craning her neck, she looks down at herself, seeing how aroused she is.

"Finger yourself while I fuck your ass," I order, pressing my cock against her tight exit and sinking inside her slowly.

Everything about her is perfection.

Seeing her covered in dirt, blood, and welts does dangerous things to me. I want my marks everywhere.

"You know I'm fucking crazy about you, right?" I ask when she dips two fingers inside her pussy while biting down on her lip.

"Yes, King." Her voice is breathy.

"So fucking crazy about you that I will kill anyone who so much as looks at you with lust in their eyes."

"You can't go around killing everyone who eyes me up."

Releasing one leg to press the sharp tip of the knife to her throat, I warn, "I'm just as much of a monster as you. Territorial as fuck and crazy about my girl."

Her heavy eyes gaze up at me. She's close.

"And that goes for you, too," I grit out when the pleasure becomes too much. "If you cheat on me again or get some stupid idea into your head about leaving, I'll end you."

Sinking her teeth into her lip in an entirely sexual way, she pushes up on her elbow, forcing me to remove the knife or cut her. She lets me see the dark truth in her blue, now almost black, eyes. "I love it when you sweet-talk me. Trust me, babe, you've seen what I'm capable of. If you so much as look at another woman, I will take my axe to you."

"*Fuck,*" I groan, my dick pulsing. "You talk so damn dirty."

Keira keeps her heavy eyes locked on mine while working her fingers faster and harder, pussy juices dripping down to her ass. "You should have had an obsession with a sweet girl, King. This thing between us can only end in death."

Dropping the knife to the grass, I grab the leash and yank her up to me, kissing her until we're both breathless. She guides me to sit, then turns around. With her back pressed to me, she lowers her ass back down on my cock and rides me cowgirl.

"I'll face death any day if it means I get to be buried deep inside you like this." My hands slide up beneath her sweater and jacket to palm her heavy breasts. I kiss her sweaty neck, biting the sensitive skin.

"I love feeling you in my ass," she whimpers, her head falling back on my shoulder. "I love that it hurts so fucking good."

"I love *you*," I admit, rolling her hard nipples. "I love you so much. I'll burn in hell for you."

"Don't go sweet on me now." She rolls her hips, grinding against me.

Grabbing the small of her waist, I take over, bouncing her up and down on my throbbing cock to the soundtrack of her sweet moans and my choked grunts.

I come with a roar at the same time she whimpers through her orgasm, rubbing her swollen clit with her small fingers covered in mud and wet pieces of crushed leaves.

We stay like that—her back crushed to my chest through the layers of our clothes and her boyfriend jeans in a heap on the forest floor.

She breaks the silence first when she begins to laugh. "What the hell am I going to tell, Cassie?"

I chuckle too, kissing her damp neck, the spot where her pulse flutters wildly. "Tell her Little Red Riding Hood veered off the path to grandma's house."

"She'll ask about my cheek. I can't believe you whipped my face." Her laughs grow louder and deeper before settling into giggles. "You're fucking crazy."

"Are you trying to tell me you didn't like it?"

"Oh, I loved it. But I don't know how to explain it away."

"Maybe a tree branch slapped you in the face."

"Plausible. But why did I venture into the forest in the first place?"

"Curiosity?"

Laughing, she slaps me gently. "She'll never fall for that."

"You know what the solution is, right?"

Sliding off me, she collects her jeans. "Moving away?"

"You read my mind."

Her affectionate smile is soft. Changing the subject, she slides on her jeans while I buckle my belt. "I'm so glad we're going to the same university."

"Did you expect anything else?" Digging in my pocket, I toss her the crumpled Polaroid pictures I took earlier. "You know how deep my obsession with you runs."

If it were anyone else, they would run for the damn hills. But Keira's darkness matches mine. She's unfazed by how dangerous I am now that she's mine. Before Hayley's silly dare, Keira was a secret obsession of mine, sure, but I never took it further. Never tried to steal her from Liam. I was content to watch her from afar, but there's no going back now that I've had a taste. Her own darkness runs just as deep, if not deeper. She gets me like no one else. That's why we're perfect together and drawn to each other in this imperfect, messed-up world. I saw her when no one else did.

She offered me a safe space to unleash my monster while she let hers out to play. As long as we get to howl beneath the full moon, the world is safe from us.

"Come here," I order, gesturing with my arms.

Keira climbs onto my lap and wraps her arms around my neck as she peppers kisses over my face. I fucking love her like this: sexually satisfied and glowing with happiness.

"You know you're my queen, don't you?"

She hums, dragging her tongue over my stubble, along my jaw, all the way to my ear. "And you're my king."

KEIRA

TEN YEARS LATER.

"What is this?" I giggle, inhaling the distinct scent of fresh rain, fir trees, and the late evening air.

King drops his hands from my eyes. He places them on my shoulder and leans down to smile against my ear. "This is me helping you slay your final demons."

Staring up at the derelict, old-as-fuck cottage in front of us, I release an uncertain soft laugh. The paint is peeling, there's a large crack in the broken window by the front door, and the rotten, wooden steps look like they might collapse any minute. "By taking me to a shithole for the weekend instead of a five-star hotel with a fancy restaurant? I think you need to work on your romancing skills, King. You're slacking in your old age."

He smiles against my ear and slides his hands down my arms, over the fabric of my green wrap coat. Interlacing our fingers and kissing the crook of my neck, he whispers, "I bought it."

Choking on my own spit, I try to turn in his arms, but he won't let me. "You bought this place?" I all but splutter. "Why?"

"Because in order to slay the last of your demons, you needed somewhere where no one would think to look. This derelict place in the middle of nowhere officially belongs to Mr. Norman. Of course, Mr. Norman doesn't exist."

"King," I say as my eyes widen. "You faked the paperwork?"

"Don't worry yourself about the details, baby. My point is that this place can't be traced back to us if anyone ever tries for some strange reason."

"I can't see why anyone would even know this place exists."

"Lots of hunting," he teases, his breath hot on my ear. "We can come out here and play all we want. No one will ever hear you scream."

The cold is seeping in through my coat, and I shiver in King's arms. "Is that why you bought it? So we would have somewhere for you to chase me?"

"Maybe. But maybe there's also a surprise for you waiting inside."

I frown skeptically while studying the house. It really is a shithole.

"Go on," he coaxes. "Take a look inside."

"Have you brought me here to kill me? Is that what this is? My final resting place?"

Sliding his arms from around me, he shoves his hands into his pockets and peers down the straight line of his nose at me. King looks too good for words in his denim, fur-lined jacket and black jeans. His dark hair falls over his brow, curling enticingly at the end, and his brown eyes glitter beneath the silvery moonlight.

He lifts his chin toward the house and says in a voice laced with something nefarious, "Take a look, baby."

Casting a glance at the house, goosebumps raise the hairs on my arms when I shiver. There's something in the air tonight. "What have you done, King?"

As I look back at him, he cups my cheek and strokes his thumb over my reddened skin in a ghostly touch. "I told you, I will always look out for you. I fucking hate seeing the demons in your eyes and the way you try to hide that jagged crack in your mask. Everyone deserves justice, Keira. Even you. Society won't give it to you, but I will."

My body gravitates closer to King the way it always does, and he leans down to cup the back of my neck, his warm palm engulfing my shivering skin. He presses his soft, damp lips to mine and nips me with his teeth. A playful, quick nip that shoots tingles straight to my core, and a delicious promise of what's to come later.

Untangling myself from his gravitational orbit, I walk up to the house with hesitant steps. The ground is soft from all the rain we've had this unusually mild winter. Not snowy like that day ten years ago when I stared up at the Death House. I never set foot near that town again after we left Blackwoods and went to university. But whenever I encounter an article about their infamous death chamber, my heart twinges. Even to this day, ten years later, it's working through inmates.

King came with me to my father's funeral, and Cassie was there, too. It was the moment I decided that she was worth our imperfect friendship. No matter how much we dislike each other at times, she was there for me when others shunned me. I had no one besides her and King. Not even my mom. That's how you weed out the bad eggs from the good ones.

The few people who crawl out from the woodwork to actually support you. She was that friend to me when I had to bury my father and lay the past to rest. Unlike the world, she didn't tell me my father was a monster who didn't deserve a funeral or to be mourned. King's father took care of the costs. He even let me stay with King when I had nowhere else to go.

King and I have been inseparable since then. We went to university together, then moved far-fucking-away from our past and bought our first house. King followed in his father's footsteps, working remotely for his father's company while I stayed out of the limelight as much as possible, turning down countless book offers and tell-all interviews. Even now, my father's legacy is a stain on my record. But I never changed my surname. Even when I wanted to. It's the last thing I have of my father, and I stubbornly cling to it as an honor of the small little light in his otherwise dark soul. The light only I saw through my innocent young eyes.

In order to move on, I've had to embrace my inner child, that young girl who had her entire world thrown upside down. King paid for therapy for a while, but I spent most of it staring through the window while the therapist tried to prod me with questions.

I don't like talking about my father or my inner struggle with my own urges that won't stop whispering in my head. I only open up late at night, wrapped up in King's arms as the moonlight shines through the half-closed blinds. Only then do I dare whisper aloud about my desire to do unspeakable things...

King never judges.

Never tells me I'm sick.

Demented.

Evil.

All the things my mind screams at me.

I stop in front of the rotten steps, looking back at King, who watches me from beneath his dark lashes with a sinful smirk. A vagrant breeze moves his hair across his forehead, and he looks back out at the forest when a wolf howls at the moon.

I turn too, gripping the railing as more wolves joins in with the haunted sound that somehow speaks to the ache in my soul.

When King looks back at me, there are glittering tears in my eyes. "I'll be right behind you."

Bypassing the rotten steps, I jump up on the porch and slowly make my way inside the derelict shed. Much to my surprise, it has electricity. And when I press the switch, the living room floods with light.

I gasp at what I see: a chair in the middle of the room, and a tied-up, naked, struggling man with a burlap sack over his head.

As I step back, the plastic sheet on the worn, wooden floor crinkles beneath my boots. I've been here before. The same unwelcome excitement I felt then floods me now. It terrifies me. Staring unblinkingly, I startle when King puts his hands on my shoulders.

"Aren't you going to see who it is?"

"This is wrong," I whisper.

"Depending on who you ask. But in our fucked-up world, this is justice. No one fucks with my girl and lives to tell the tale."

My heart gallops wildly in my chest as I step forward, inching closer to the naked man. His hairy beer gut is bruised, and it's evident by the marks on his arms and torso that King had fun with him before tying him up and offering him to me like a sacrificial lamb.

Looking back at King, I hesitate.

With a quirk of his sinful lips that reveals a hint of sharp incisors, he slides his dark gaze past me to the struggling, sweaty man in front of me. "Ten years ago, this sorry excuse of a man added to your trauma. Forcing more skeletons to crowd in your closet. I've waited patiently, letting sufficient time pass to stop suspicion falling on us, but even the most *righteous* have to face the reaper sooner or later. And this man will pay for his sins tonight. I would have liked to bring you the governor on a platter too, but unfortunately, that pig died of a heart attack two years back. Unluckily or maybe luckily for him, depending on how you look at it and how vengeful you feel."

"King," I whisper, swallowing around the thick lump in my throat. "It won't bring my father back. It won't erase the past."

"True, but it will give you closure. An eye for an eye. Isn't that what we teach our kids? This is no different. One man's justice is another man's crime."

Inhaling a shaky breath, I reach out to pull the burlap sack from his head. I know I must face this part of me sooner or later. Repressing it won't work much longer.

I pause, my fingers curling in toward my palm. Something stops me from removing the sack.

"I know you're scared," King says behind me. He's closer now, his presence heating my back. "I won't let you fall to the darkness. I'll never let you get lost."

"Do you promise?"

His soft lips brush up against my ear as he reaches around me and grips the brown fabric. "Have I ever lied to you?"

"No," I admit, placing my hand over his big one. "Never."

We lift the burlap sack together, and King discards it on the floor. I inhale a sharp breath, staring into the eyes of the gagged man in front of me.

The same man who asked in an emotionless tone if my father had any last words, while my world crumbled around me for the second time.

Recognition instantly flickers in his gray, round eyes that are too big for his perspiring face.

King's steady presence behind me prevents my knees from quaking as I stare my own nightmare in the eye. He places the cold metal in my palm, and I cut myself on the blade when I close my hand around the knife. His lips return to my ear, his tongue darting out to taste my earlobe. He sucks it between his teeth before whispering, "After you have slayed your final demon, I'm gonna go down on my knees, while you're covered head-to-toe in blood, and propose. And you're going to say yes. You're going to make me the happiest fucking man on earth. And no one, *absolutely no one,* will ever hurt you again. Not in the past. And certainly not in the future. Do you hear me, baby?"

"Yes," I whisper, feeling the stirrings of evil inside me as a smile slowly lifts the left side of my lips. "I hear you."

To the man in front of me, he echoes the words that tore my heart to shreds ten years ago. "Any last words you would like to say?" He shifts behind me, and then I hear the click and whir of his Polaroid camera. Removing the picture, he waves it in the air before reaching out to remove the gag.

The man in front of me splutters and coughs. Fiery, fearful, and defiant eyes glare up at me. "You're nothing but a disgusting fucking monster, just like your father! You won't get away with this. You'll get the needle just like he—"

"That's enough of that bullshit," King says, sounding bored as he forces the gag back inside the ex-warden's mouth. "Mr. Righteous. How many killings have you overseen as part of your job throughout your career? I think it's safe to say you have overseen more killings than my girl here has carried out in her entire life. Unlike you, she represses her killing urges. So who is the biggest monster?" His voice rises until he screams, "So who deserves the fucking needle, huh?! You! You fucking twisted dick!" Snatching the knife from me, he rams the blade into the warden's thigh, inches away from his femoral artery. Blood rushes to the surface, pooling around the protruding black handle. "I don't give a shit what you do. Right or wrong. But you don't fuck with my girl and steal her fucking father away from her—monster or no monster— and live to become an old man. The day you forced me to hold my future wife while she cried herself to sleep for weeks was the day you signed your own fucking death warrant, so stop crying like a fucking baby."

Pressing my lips together to stop myself from laughing, I place my palm over his racing heart. "Babe, calm down. I'll take it from here. Just... I don't know... Do what you do best." I gesture to the camera in his hand while his eyes spit fire at the wailing man in front of us. "Take some pictures or something."

King finally tears his stormy eyes away from the warden and pins me to the spot with his dark, intense gaze.

"I'll be fine," I reassure him, stroking his stubbly cheek as he breathes like a provoked bull. "He can't hurt me anymore."

With a snort, he walks toward a nearby couch, pointing an accusing finger at the warden. "Spit the gag out and shout bullshit at my woman one more time, and I'll cut out your tongue and shove it up your ass."

This time I do laugh, clamping my hand over my mouth.

"What?" he barks, flopping down onto the moth-eaten couch, his booted foot resting on the edge of the dusty coffee table.

I lower my hand, clearing my throat. "You're just kind of cute when you get worked up, is all."

He levels me with a glare and sweeps his arm over to the screaming warden, who's about to make his chair tumble over with all of his squirming. "He insulted you! I'm not gonna let that shit fly."

"Do you want to kill him instead of me? Purge some of that anger?"

"If this is where you start discussing the difference between a psychopath and a sociopath, I swear I will throw shit." He looks around the barren room as if he'll find something except for the coffee table to toss.

"Well, sociopaths struggle to control their impulses."

He levels his glare at me again, and I have to admit that it arouses me when he gets hot-headed.

"Do you want to kill him?" I offer again, my tone laced with sugar and all things sweet.

Kicking up his other foot on the table and crossing them at the ankles, he spreads his arms out over the back of the couch. "This is your show, baby. I'll just watch."

"Feeling calmer?" I tease, bending forward and curling my fingers around the handle embedded in the warden's thigh.

"Not in a million fucking years. Not until he's in pieces and you're over here, covered in blood and riding my dick. Or better yet, I'll fuck you face down in it over there." Lifting his chin, he indicates the sheet-covered floor by my feet, which will soon be swimming with blood.

"I love your filthy mouth. Now be a good boy and shut it while I play." I look the man in front of me in the eye and let my smile unfurl. "It's nice to meet you again under such interesting circumstances. If you didn't know, I'm Jimmy Hill's daughter. Tonight, I'm your prison's warden, and I'll be overseeing your execution." Walking my fingers up the blade of the knife, I let the darkness inside me seep through my pores and shadow my soul. The angel on my shoulder is nowhere to be seen now. Not when the devil is coming out to play.

"I want to play a little game that I like to call...." In a swift move, I pull the knife out and stab him in the arm, relishing in his bulging eyes and the sweat that breaks out across his forehead. "... scream for me."

The End

Also by Harleigh Beck

Sins of the Fallen

Touched by sin

Touched by Darkness

The Rivals Duet

The Rivals' Touch

Fadeaway

Counter Bet Series

Counter Bet

Devil's Bargain

Standalones

The King of Sherwood Forest

Kitty Hamilton

Novellas

Sweet Taste of Betrayal

Entangled

ACKNOWLEDGMENTS

Let's keep this short and sweet for once. I'd like to start off by thanking my readers. Thank you for giving my book a chance. Your support means the world to me!

Thank you to my ARC readers. The sheer interest in this book blew me away.

I'd also like to extend a special thanks to the following lovely people:

Paula, thank you for being my best friend and putting up with my crazy nonsense. Here's to book eleven. Where's it going to fit on your bookshelf?

My hubby, thank you for reading this book and refraining from drowning me in the bathtub. Not that we have one, yet. But keep those thoughts out of your head and remember that I'm terrified of water.

K.L Steele, for being such a genuine and wonderful human being. I'm cheering you on always!

Courtney, thank you for always being there and for bolstering me when I need it the most. As I always say, authoring is lonely work, and you make it less so.

Cindy, you're a gem and you need an acknowledgment! Thank you for being so genuine and lovely.

Nat, Anna, Gill, and Jen, you bring a smile to my face every day with your crazy antics. Thank you for all the support and for the laughs.

Emily, I can't thank you enough for your professionalism and knowledge. You always go over and beyond.

Hannah (HC Graphics), thank you for making this cover. No words can express how much I love it!

Hannah (Green proofreads), thank you for editing this baby.

Kimberley, thank you for proofreading my manuscript with such a keen eye for detail.

Nisha, as always, thank you for helping me out with the promotion. Also, thanks for listening to me on my bad days.

Kaitlyn, thank you for your support as my PA. I'm not the most organized author in the world, and you have made it a heap easier for me.

About the Author

Harleigh Beck lives in a small town in the northeast of England with her hubby and their three children. When she's not writing, you'll find her head down in a book. She mainly reads dark romance, but she also likes the occasional horror. She has more books planned, so be sure to connect with her on her social media for updates.

Printed in Great Britain
by Amazon

36735456R00234